Twelve-Foot Circle

A mystery based on everyone's true story

by

Richard Schuette

Richard Schuette is a professional writer in the Twin Cities. His interest in curling began when he served as unofficial coach and chaperone for his son's junior rink from 2002 to 2007, playing out of the St. Paul Curling Club.

This is a work of fiction. For historical accuracy, the author has used the actual names of players who participated in the 2008 U.S. national curling championship playdowns. All descriptions and accounts involving the names of living players are purely fictional.

ISBN-13: 978-1505776881

Acknowledgements

I have set this fictional story in towns and counties throughout the Upper Midwest. In many instances, I have used the actual names of the local curling clubs and tried to include recognizable features that make these clubs unique. In some instances, however, I invented clubs where they do not yet exist.

I wish to thank my editors Aaron Rolloff for helping me get the story going in the right direction and KD Krueger for helping me make the grammar, style and syntax readable. I would also like to thank the many curlers, young and old, who offered their time and advice to help me understand the nuances of the sport and how curling has changed over the years. I also wish to thank Steve's Curling Supplies in Madison, Wisconsin, for allowing the use of the company's name.

I especially wish to thank former Hibbing Curling Club president Paul Vendetti for supplying valuable information regarding the rinks (teams), draws and facility preparation for the 2008 national championship playdowns. For the sake of historical accuracy and out of respect, I have used the real names of players on the ten rinks that participated in the event. All descriptions of living players or their curling styles, skills or strategic approaches to the game are purely my invention. (I received approval from the USCA for the fictional 11-rink format necessary for the story.)

I have made every attempt to remain true to the traditions, rules and spirit of the ancient game of curling. In order to show the greatest respect for the USCA, I invented the American Curling Union (ACU) as the governing body sponsoring the fictional 1969 national championship playdowns described in the story. This book has been endorsed by neither the USCA nor any actual curlers named throughout.

Richard Schuette
Author

How to read a curling scoreboard

Blue		1	3		7								
Blank 6 Points	1	2	3	4	5	6	7	8	9	10	11	12	13
Yellow	2	4		5		8							

Both rinks' (teams') accumulated points are posted across the center of the scoreboard. (This scoreboard allows for up to 13 points to be scored by either or both rinks in the game.) To track the running score, keep tabs of the 'end' number hung above or below the running point tally down the center. The rink in the lead will have the 'end' number posted furthest down the scoreboard.

In this example, the blue rink scored two points in 1st end. The yellow rink scored one point in the second end. The blue rink raised their total to three in the third. The yellow countered with one more in the fourth, to trail the blue rink 3-2. In this eight-end match, the yellow rink won in the last end by scoring two points to leapfrog ahead of the blue rink, 6-5.

The blank posted at the bottom of the scoreboard signifies that neither rink scored in the sixth end.

Locations of towns and curling clubs included throughout the story

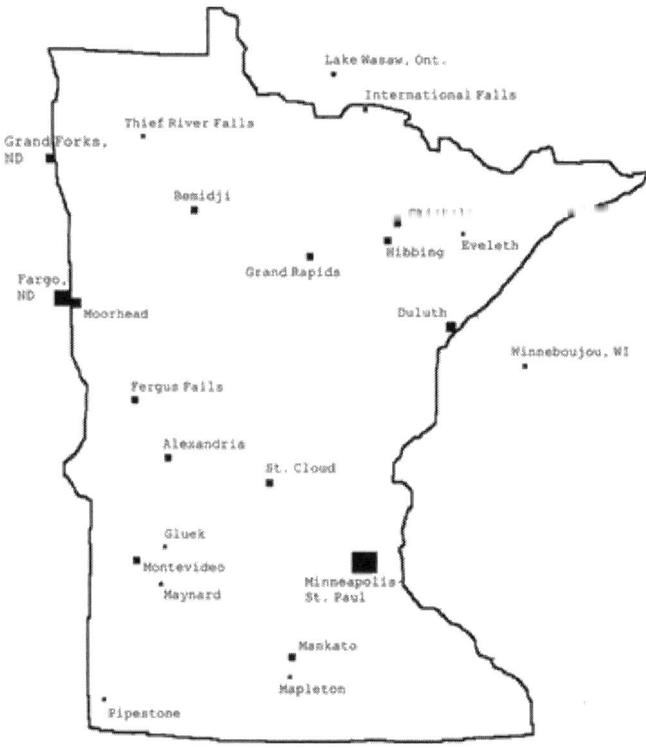

Prologue

Michigan Rink - Gold	**Minnesota Rink - Silver**
Lead: Jim Coventry	Lead: Paul Stenner
Second: Dale Harder	Second: John Mistovich
Third: Steve Talbert	Third: Mickey Bellows
Skip: Norm Thunger	**Skip: Freddy Schade**

First Rock

As much for luck as for good practice, Minnesota Lead Paul Stenner tipped the gray granite rock onto its rounded edge and rubbed the exposed running surface with his bare palm. Even the smallest fleck of debris adhering to the bottom could cause the best curling shot to dig into the ice and veer abruptly off target. Satisfied that it was clean, he rolled the heavy rock onto its base and stood erect to gain sight of his target, one hundred and twenty-some feet down the ice. Squinting and cupping one hand over his eyes to cut down the glare of the overhead lights, Stenner could see his Skip, Freddie Schade, standing a few feet inside the twelve-foot circle, tapping the ice with his broom head. As he tapped, he held his right arm parallel to the ground, palm open so his men at the far end of the sheet could see it clearly. When he was certain he had his player's attention, he moved a small step to his left, let his broom head come to a rest softly on the ice and stood stock-still. Stenner nodded from the hack and waved in recognition. The directions were clear. Place the shot on the broom. Easy on the handle. Center-front of the house.

With his ritual complete, Stenner carefully set his right foot against the hack and squatted to realign his bearings, low to the ice. With the broom handle tucked firmly beneath his left armpit for added balance, he fitted the fingertips of his right hand around the silver handle of rock #1. Standing eight feet apart and some fifteen feet in front, his two sweepers waited for him to explode from the hack, on a straight line between them. Anxiously bent over at the waist, with brooms at the ready, John Mistovich and Mickey Bellows took a final second to glance toward the far end. The success or failure of the shot would ultimately lie in whatever magic they could coax out of their brooms. The men would exhaust the next several seconds shuffling quickly ahead of the rock, with their broom heads moving like parallel pistons in coordinated, machine-like precision; responding to their Skip's furious yells to **sweeeeeep!** vigorously, or the gentle call to **cleeeeeean** slowly.

This first rock would be, at once, critically important and

monumentally futile. The shot called for Stenner to bring his rock to rest at the front edge of the house, expecting a very slight right-to-left curl. If it drifted a little too far right or left, it could be inconsequential; or worse, serve some unforeseen benefit to the opposing team. If the shot was too light, it would stay well short of the house.

Stenner was nervous. He stood again to align himself one final time. He re-fit his right foot, reset his broom handle and squared his shoulders directly at his target. This would be the first of sixteen rocks thrown on this first end, in a match scheduled for ten ends. Everyone in the Grand Forks Ice Arena knew that in a very real sense, there was nothing significant about the opening shot. In a butterfly-effect sort of way, though, it could affect the decisions made by every other player throughout the match. It was exactly this paradox that Stenner liked most about being rated among the best Leads in the country. First rocks rarely settled things in any curling match but he liked to think that, in some microscopic way, his shots could also make all the difference in the world.

"What do you think about the ice speed?" he asked.

"Depends on how hard you throw it," came the predictable response from Second, John Mistovich. "No groove worn down along the center track. It'll be a little slow...or keen. Could run fast to start. But the crowd is building up in here. It's ten degrees colder than it was for yesterday's match. People need to stop breathing. That's always the problem with these major playdowns —they let people watch. The humidity in here might be frosting it up and change things even more."

"Yeah," added Vice Skip Mickey Bellows. "It's freezing outside, and we're pretty close to a wall. That might make it drag a little, or fall off. Freddy must know something, though. What's he asking you to do? Lay it up a little short?"

"What's Shady asking for? Lay it up a little short in the house?"

Stenner ignored the question, steadied his feet and sank himself low into his final delivery position.

"Well, gentlemen," he said. "We may be in this match for all the wrong reasons but here we are, so let's win it. First rock. We'll know a lot more in about thirty seconds."

Part I

Rescue

Saturday, August 23rd, 2002

Novelist Alan Moore wrote that life has no pattern, except what we imagine after staring at it for too long; no meaning except whatever we impose.

My mother called to tell me she would be flying directly into the San Carlos Airport in San Mateo, rather than the Norman Y. Mineta International in San José. She intended to stay with me for a week. She was quick to assure me that her visit would cause me no inconvenience.

She would eat all her meals at restaurants.

"Yes, you will," I said, "I scrape together a free meal at the restaurant at the end of my shift."

She would rent a car.

"You will have to," I insisted. "I will need mine to get to work all week."

She would sleep on the couch.

"That will be appreciated," I answered. "I work long shifts on my feet. I need sleep."

None of it dissuaded her.

From my years living with her through high school and college, I knew that her visit would be everything she promised it would not be. I considered my slim options to avoid spending a long week with her. If it came down to it, I had enough seniority at work to get myself scheduled for some double shifts. I could even plan my hours throughout the week so I wouldn't return to my apartment until after two a.m. closing time.

True, I didn't want to spend time with her, but that wasn't the real reason I didn't want her visiting. The truth was, she would be a face full of reminder of everything I left back home in Minneapolis, and I didn't want to be confronted by it.

I had moved out to the Bay Area about a year after graduating from DeVry University, after finally admitting to myself that my computer programming skills weren't part of the economic development plan in the Twin Cities. An acquaintance convinced me there was enough work in Silicon Valley for independent contractors looking to work for the *big Internet guns* — whoever they might be. The morning I left home, my mother hardly spoke a word as she helped me pack. She offered a few comments of disingenuous support and encouragement but I knew she had her doubts. With twenty-seven hundred dollars remaining from my student loans in my pocket,

I packed the back seat of my old Honda Civic and drove west. A week later, I found myself illegally parked behind a boarded-up strip mall near the Golden Gate Bridge late one night, shivering myself to sleep. I could only wonder exactly what little sliver of the entire adventure seemed like a good idea at the time.

I didn't stay in San Francisco very long. In fact, I didn't stay in San Francisco at all. The *Affordable Apartments for a Unique Bay Area Lifestyle* I had researched on the Internet, turned out to require a first month's deposit plus rent, along with a one-year lease. I had that covered, but the small studio flat rented for three hundred fifty dollars more per month than the out-of-date website had advertised. My dreams of living the bachelor life in a *spacious balcony unit overlooking the beautiful central courtyard pool, just blocks from shopping, nightlife and regional attractions* never materialized. I drove around the city the entire first day, occasionally checking out a rundown apartment complex that was always three or four hundred dollars more expensive than my meager resources would allow.

After accepting defeat, I backtracked several miles into the California desert hill country of the San Joaquin Valley, to the little village of Volta. Of the two apartment complexes in town, one had a sunken-level studio unit available for an affordable month-to-month lease and a low deposit. It wasn't the bachelor pad of my dreams, but I could stretch out enough to get myself dressed and fed in the morning. From the lower-level window, I could look upward and see a nondescript fast food joint immediately across the road. It wasn't all bad. By craning my neck forward and to the left four or five inches, I could also make out the corner of the town's only gas station.

During my first few weeks in California, I began every day by driving in the direction of San José through Morgan City, where I discovered a public library that would allow me to surf the web for local job openings. By late autumn of 2001, I was slumping door-to-door through office parks, filling out job applications at every business with an unlocked door. It didn't take long to realize that I had as much chance of landing a tech job in California as I did back in the Twin Cities. Eventually, I bit the bullet and ordered new résumés and fifty business cards, which included a bullet-point list of my meager qualifications. When I picked them up from the print shop, I stood for a moment staring at the sum total of my life, organized neatly onto a three and a half inch card. In order to give the impression that I was a local resident, I signed up for a post office box at a UPS store in Santa Clara and used their street address on my cover letters. It wasn't long before every *big Internet gun* in town had filed away my résumé with assurances they would get back to me when a job came open. With every rejection, my memory replayed an old tape of my father, *"A person is only a person through other people, Jack. It's not always what you know. It's not even always who you know. But it's always* ***when*** *you know them that matters."*

I soon found myself driving an hour each way to and from a night job that I landed at a small gyros grill in Sunnyvale. It wasn't a good career move, but I was out of options. I didn't know anybody in California and the contacts I was making at *PitaPit* would only keep me tied to one of the millions of fast food joints that dot the California suburban landscape. It wasn't long before my Visa credit card statement and student loan bills began catching up to me, conveniently forwarded by my loving mother.

Incredibly, I was soon able to parlay my only real job skill — native English — into a better job as a table server at *Kanuba's Greek Bistro and Bar* in Fremont. I stayed a half-step ahead of total destitution by tacking on additional shift hours on Saturday evenings, when tips were likely to be higher. With the little extra money coming in, I started looking for better living arrangements. When a one-bedroom unit became available on the third floor of an apartment complex a mile from the bistro, I found just enough wiggle room in my budget and signed a year lease. For the next eight months, I lived hand-to-mouth, wondering how in the hell I was ever going to break even, or just catch an even break.

My 1992 Honda Civic hatchback had once belonged to a high school friend before his parents bought him a new car as a payoff for getting into an Ivy League college. Before he took off for Dartmouth, I argued for two weeks with my mother to offer him five hundred dollars to buy it for me. It would be just what I needed for cheap transportation to my college classes. In the five years I drove it around the Twin Cities, I added less than two thousand miles to the odometer. In less than one year in California, I tacked on twelve thousand more. The engine had more than one hundred seventy thousand miles on it and I knew that the next major breakdown would be its last. I convinced myself that when the car died or when my apartment lease was up — whichever came first — it would be my excuse for moving back home.

It's true that my shit stunk in California and I knew it. And talking to my mother that day on the phone, it became clear that she knew it, too. So with deep resignation, I caved in to her request to visit. She wouldn't have to sleep on the sofa; I would. And yes, she could use my kitchen for meals. To save at least one scrap of dignity, though, I lied and told her my shift manager screwed me over at the restaurant and put me on late nights all week. That meant she would need to rent a car if she expected to get around. I congratulated myself when I suddenly remembered that my Honda was a manual transmission and she wouldn't be able to handle the clutch and stick shift, anyway.

So on a hot Saturday afternoon in late August of 2002, I found myself standing on my third floor apartment balcony in Fremont, watching for her rental car to pull into the parking lot below me. Despite my e-mail giving her very specific written directions from the airport directly to my door, I wasn't surprised when I saw her on the far side of the parking lot, standing outside of her rented navy blue Chevy Malibu, squinting in the opposite direction. I quickly set my Coke on the railing and ran down to meet her with a hug that was certainly as uncomfortable for her as it was for me.

To my surprise, her suitcase was only half-full and very light.

"Is this your only bag?" I asked.

"Well, I have another little travel pouch in the back seat. Oh, and my purse. But I can carry them," she replied.

She tugged the items from the rear seat and set them on the car roof six inches in front of my face as she locked the doors. I snatched them quickly and pointed us toward my apartment stairwell about forty yards ahead of us.

"So, exactly when is this birthday party you intend to go to?" I finally asked, as we reached the first landing. "And I still can't believe that's why you're really here."

She was quiet for a moment as she stopped on the second landing to catch her breath.

"I'm fat and out of shape," she said, ignoring my question.

"You need to quit smoking," I said over my shoulder. "And for Pete's sake, you look fine. In fact, it looks as if you've lost about ten pounds since I left home last summer. You never told me you were on a diet."

"I did quit smoking," she replied, shouting up the stairwell toward me. "It's been two months now. And I'm not on a diet. Well, at least not until recently. I've lost twelve pounds. I expect there to be some old friends at the party, so I've been starving myself to get back into a size ten."

"So, when is the party?"

"This evening," she said, brushing past as I pushed open my apartment door.

She looked around for a brief second and then slumped onto my old sofa. It was the only worthwhile piece of furniture that came included in the furnished apartment.

"In fact, it's already nearly five o'clock. I'd like to freshen up and take off right away if you don't mind. Didn't you say it could take an hour to get to San Mateo?"

She carried her suitcase into my bedroom, closed the door and came out a few minutes later in a different white blouse but the same knee-length, green and silver paisley print skirt. As she stepped in front of a mirror in my bathroom, I peeked into the bedroom and saw the meager contents of her suitcase emptied out across the bed. After ten more minutes, she emerged sporting a new face that I hardly recognized.

"You look great," I said. "Do you know how to get to where you're going? You won't be coming back here until late after dark."

"I have a printout of directions. Oh, and the man at the auto rental said the car has one of those new GPS devices."

I offered my doubts that she even knew what the acronym stood for.

"I'm a real estate agent," she reassured me. "I can find any address down any back alley or side street in the smallest neighborhoods. I'll be fine."

I accompanied her down to her car and held her oversized purse as she crawled behind the wheel. She set the keychain in her lap and pulled out the small printout directions to the Flanders Banquet Hall in San Mateo. I watched her fumble with the GPS buttons on the dash and heard her mumble an epithet to Lucifer before giving up.

"You need to turn the car key in the ignition to power up the unit," I said.

"Too advanced for me already," she answered through the open door, "I'll just drive to the general area and ask a gas station attendant."

"This is California," I said. "Even if the guy speaks English, he won't know the directions to his own house."

While reaching over her shoulder for the seat belt, she hadn't noticed that the QuickRent key ring had slipped off her lap and dropped onto the edge of the doorframe alongside her seat. It hung there dangling, half out of the car. Just as it was about to drop to the pavement, I quickly leaned forward to snatch it.

"Oops, let me get..."

But it was too late. In the instant I was bending down, she gave the car door a heavy jerk to slam it shut. The edge of the door swished past my left ear, lightly tossing my collar-length hair with a rush of air. I flew with an instinctive backward leap, rolling painfully onto the rough, pebbly pavement several feet from the car; my elbows and hands were badly scraped and stinging with pain. That was inconsequential compared to nearly having my head sheared off at the neck. From my viewpoint near ground level, I became an unwitting witness to what was to become one of the most significant and defining random moments of my life.

I could see through the car window that my mother had somehow remained blissfully unaware of my near-death experience, as she sat deciphering her little pocket map. Not only was she unfazed and unimpressed by my aerial acrobatics, it never dawned on her to ask why on earth I was suddenly sitting on my ass ten feet from the car, with blood flowing down my forearms.

I slowly realized that things had not turned out okay, after all. Although my body suffered only minor injuries, I had no way of knowing just how much those few seconds frozen in time would impact my life so many years later.

"Where is my car key?" she asked, while rummaging through her purse. I was too angry and too dizzy to answer. I jumped to the side of the car, horrified and speechless as I realized what had just happened. The key was caught between the bottom of the door and the doorframe. The shiny red plastic key tag hung harmlessly outside of the car, unscratched. I stood for a minute to regain my full faculties. I watched as the tag spun in slow motion, revealing the large white QuickRent logo on one side, slowly rotating; as if I needed a reminder of the toll free phone number printed on the reverse.

After a brief moment, my mother also realized the magnitude of the moment. She opened the car door slowly. We watched the gnarled, twisted key drop limply onto the pavement. It lay fractured, useless and really quite dead. I tried to say something. The words formed between my clenched teeth, but I could not force them to come out. I could only hear myself expelling the impulsive breath of air I had subconsciously gulped while hurling myself clear of the car door. There, lying at my feet on the hot pavement in front of me was a perfect metaphor for what my life had become: a bent, useless mess that no amount of straightening, grinding or polishing was ever going to make straight.

"Oh, God!" she said. "What do I do now?"

"Oh, I'm sure they gave you an extra key," I said, hopefully. "Check the glove compartment."

Empty, except for the folder containing the rental contract.

"Check in the arm rest compartment and ashtrays," I added, sounding just slightly more panicked.

Empty, except for an old gum wrapper.

"Check behind the sun visor mirrors," I said, with a tone of clear anxiety in my voice.

Empty, except for the reflection of dismay in my mother's haunting blue eyes.

My head was racing. I quickly grabbed at any attempt to save my evening.

"I'm supposed to be at work in an hour, Mom. Or I'd let you take my car."

"As you were so quick to point out, Jack," she reminded me. "I don't drive a stick shift."

"Well, we have to call the rental car place and see what they do when something like this happens," I said.

"Do you think they'll send someone out here to bring us another key right away?" she asked.

Only my mother could ask that question without a hint of irony in her voice. In her world of successful real estate, if a potential customer wanted to tour a house at any time of day or night, they were likely to find an agent willing to show up with the entry code to the lock box. Naturally — in her world — car rental companies did the same thing all the time.

"I doubt it," I said, as I visualized seventy-five dollars in Saturday evening tips disappearing into the air. "But if they have a spare key at their airport office, I can get out there in less than an hour to pick it up. You won't get to the party any time soon and I won't get to work on time. That's no big deal. I think we can make it work if I get going right away."

With faint hope, I added, "This can't be the first time something this stupid has happened."

But as things turned out, it actually *was* the first time something that stupid had happened. It was already past five-thirty when somebody at the rental desk finally answered the phone on the fifteenth ring. Despite my whining protests, *"Sorry, there really isn't anything we can do until morning"* was the best I could cajole out of the teenage girl with a Los Angeles dialect.

For the sake of putting on a show for my mother, I resorted to a hopeless argument.

"But your contract paperwork says you're open 24/7."

"Well yeah, like, we are open 24/7, but only for, like, picking up and dropping off cars."

It was Saturday. I would have to call back Monday morning. The manager had already left for the day.

"Huh? You're telling me they left a nineteen year old Valley Girl in charge of a million dollars worth of cars...with no manager on duty? How did you score a gig like that?"

The young woman's argument was obviously concocted, but I didn't push her any further. In fact, I didn't blame her for wanting to get off the phone and get on with her weekend. I could hear her saying to herself, *"Cripes, not another one of these morons. I'm ready to walk out the door with my paycheck on a Saturday evening and I make the mistake of answering a call from an idiot with a silly-ass problem like this. No way"*

I had seen it happen a hundred times at the restaurant. Some drunken jerk and his date would walk in and take a booth five minutes before closing time, only to order a small plate of cheap appetizers. I generally made up some lie about the kitchen closing a few minutes early because the chef got sick or the health department shut us down. Sometimes it worked. Now rental-girl was giving me the same treatment.

I hung up and relayed everything to my mom sitting at the kitchen table. Her hands began to tremble as she tried to straighten the hopelessly-mangled key with her long pink fingernails. When she finally spoke, her voice broke and her eyes were glistening.

"Do you have a pair of pliers we could use to straighten this?" she asked.

"No. I've never needed any tools here at the apartment so I've never bought any," I replied quietly. "Besides, it's not just bent. Look, the teeth have been mashed down and some are broken off. Your car door must have hit them just right."

I examined the key more closely to see if there was anything salvageable. There wasn't.

"Maybe a locksmith or a hardware store could cut another one," she suggested.

"No, not this late on a Saturday," I sighed. "Besides, these types of car keys have computer chips in them now. There's undoubtedly a code inside that won't allow it to be duplicated by just anybody. We would have to find some guy named Guido."

After a few seconds, I set the key onto the table and looked up to see my mother hanging her head.

"Jack," she said. "Will you drive me?"

I lowered my head seven or eight inches to her level. I had never seen her like this — not even when she and my father were working through their toughest problems before the divorce. Not even when things periodically slowed to a crawl in the Twin Cities real estate market. Now, here she was in my kitchen, crying over missing a party that seemed completely damned senseless in the first place. None of it made any sense, and I wasn't equipped to respond.

As I sat there wondering what to do next, I realized that her tears must certainly have been about more than simply missing out on an evening with some long-lost friend or two at a party. The party was nothing more than a front. That much I realized. But a front for what? Something else was on her agenda, but I sure couldn't figure it out.

"Sure, Mom," I sighed. "I'll take you. I just need to call my manager to let him know I'll be late. It's Saturday night and he'll be upset, but I'm scheduled for a bunch of hours this week, anyway. Let me clean up, then I'll get you to the dance hall."

After another pregnant pause, she looked up.

"Will you stay at the party with me? There are some things we need to talk about."

I sighed as I thought about the night I had in front of me.

"Yeah, Mom, your birthday just passed. We can celebrate it together."

We drove through the heavy Saturday evening traffic to San Mateo mostly in silence. Once or twice, she tried to begin a conversation but abruptly bit off her words after a brief phrase or two. Something wasn't right, but I didn't want to pursue it. All I knew was that I was staring at a long, meaningless evening.

It was already past seven o'clock when we pulled into the parking lot of the Flanders Banquet Center. There were more cars than I expected for an old retired elementary school teacher's birthday party. Even my mother commented that she was surprised so many people would come all the way to California for the party. I pretended to care and even suggested that it would be fun for her to visit with so many of her old childhood chums from back in Iowa.

As a young girl, her family had moved briefly to Sacramento when her father landed an employment contract as a farm bill lobbyist at the California State Capitol. It was the early 1960s, but somehow the corn growers in the Midwest breadbasket were already linking arms with orange growers in central California. The Singletons only stayed for one legislative session and Mom never quite figured out exactly how things all fit together about the move and the job. She often said she never liked the people and never wanted to return. Subliminally, it may have been one of the reasons I chose to move there as my escape from my suburban childhood in the Minneapolis suburbs. And now, here she was, expressing surprise at the number of people that would *come all the way to California* — as if coming to visit her.

As I circled the parking lot, I began to feel good at the prospect of losing myself in a large crowd. Although I still doubted whether there would be a single guest my mother might vaguely remember, there wasn't much sense complaining about it. If my best arguments couldn't keep her from flying nearly sixteen hundred miles from the Twin Cities, it sure wasn't going to stop her from walking another one hundred feet into the banquet hall.

Upon entering the building, I realized immediately why the parking lot was so full. The Flanders had been built sometime during the late 1970s and was actually two individual large party rooms on either side of a wide central corridor. Guests were greeted immediately inside the door by a pedestal sign of white plastic letters; an arrow pointing left showed the way to *Hall A* for Harold VanDerKant's birthday party. An arrow pointing right directed people to the Eltorno-Havens wedding reception in *Hall B*. A triangular bar stood at the distant end of the wide sixty-foot corridor, serving guests spilling out from their respective parties on either side. Metal coat racks with hat shelves ran down the full length of the corridor on both sides. The bar was clearly the moneymaker, and probably subsidized the rental costs for the individual banquet rooms.

Judging by the dress and age of the people meandering in and out of Hall B, it was probably not a first marriage for either Eltorno or Havens. Most of the group appeared to be middle-aged or older. As I peeked in, the American Legion bandleader was getting the joint jumpin' to Chubby Checker. Toward the far corner of the room, above the guests seated at their tables, I could see a lot of gray heads bobbing and swirling around the dance floor. A forty-ish woman in a silky gold cocktail dress and a man in a dark suit were circulating among the tables. I decided they must be the famous Eltorno and Havens, immortalized in plastic letters on the sign at the entrance.

"I'll be over at the wedding reception on side B, if things dry up on our side of the house," I quipped, as I found an open coat hook for my mom's light sweater and my tattered Minnesota Twins baseball cap.

From the corridor, we took a quick look into Hall A, to get the lay of the land before entering our party. I was pleasantly surprised when I saw a significant number of people already seated or milling around the oversized room. Even if nobody else showed up, the ninety or so guests already gathered in the room would be adequate to get lost in the crowd for the evening.

"Can I get you a drink from the bar before we find a place to sit, Mom?"

"Vodka on ice," came her quick reply, as she squeezed herself through a small conversation clogging the doorway.

When I returned with our drinks, I found her hovering near the punch bowl, scanning the tables for a face she might recognize and a place we could park ourselves for the evening. The hall was about sixty feet square and included a forty-foot length of buffet tables set up against a wall nearest the entry doors. There was an empty DJ platform covered by a makeshift canopy, with a twenty-foot square portable dance floor occupying the entire center of the room. Twenty or more six-foot diameter tables were scattered indiscriminately throughout the room to the right, left and front. In some places, there were only inches to squeeze between the chairs. The table of honor, including a gilded throne for the old man, was set against the distant wall, with the tables nearest by already filled to capacity.

I took my mother by the elbow and led her toward the guest book lying on a small pedestal podium. She scanned the book from the beginning, searching desperately for a name — any name — that would justify her coming this far to wish happy birthday to someone who couldn't possibly remember her.

"Do you see any names you recognize?" I asked softly, but received no response.

"What about your old friend from Burlington? Is she signed in?"

Again, no response.

Occasionally, she read a name, just loud enough for me to hear above the chatter in the room. For emphasis, she would tap her finger on an address line, which in most cases included only the city and an occasional e-mail address. Based on the number of finger taps and mouthed words, I determined there were possibly four or five names she may have vaguely recognized. But I had my doubts. She finally came to an available blank line, picked up the pen and added *Melinda D.*, leaving the address box blank. As I began writing my own name on the following line, she snatched the pen and handed it to the man exhaling whiskey vapors behind me.

"Nobody will know you," she scoffed.

With her vodka in her hand and a rum and Coke in mine, we made our way further into the room. I was relieved to find an empty table near a side wall toward the rear kitchen door, where I could sit invisibly, waiting for an opportunity to slip out to the bar.

My mother quietly mixed a half-cup of fruit punch into her drink and set the cocktail on our table, planning to return to it early and often. In usual style, she began greeting anyone who walked nearby, as if thanking them for flying all the way from Paris, Hong Kong or New

York to attend the party. As the guests exchanged polite greetings among themselves, I would hear her make occasional references to my name. When I looked up, I would invariably find an outstretched hand reaching across the table toward me. With a polite nod and a handshake, the embarrassing formality would end and I would retreat beneath my cone of silence and cloak of invisibility.

We sat alone for several minutes, until our table eventually filled with late-arriving guests, who all turned their chairs toward the dance floor. Sitting with my back pressed against the wall, I was safe from joining any unwelcome conversation, completely anonymous and hidden from view behind an uneven row of heads. After a few minutes of polite table talk, my mother once again set down her glass, excused herself and squeezed her way through chairs and tables, where she melded once again into the gathering cluster near the center of the room. I followed her with my eyes as long as I could, but the DJ was beginning his act and I quickly lost her in the small crowd jumping onto the dance floor.

"Cripes, look at that fool," I suddenly heard a young woman's voice moan from the next table, several feet to my right. "The jackass thinks that hopping up and down is some kind of jitterbug. What the hell is that? A mating dance?"

With my eyes remaining fixed on the crowd, I said loudly enough to be heard, "Yeah, I've seen *grande mal* seizures with more rhythm."

I heard a throaty chortle, but I didn't dare look up — yet.

"And look at the food piled on that guy's plate," came the young woman's voice again. "I'll bet the old fart's family didn't count on paying the bill for all that."

"Nope," I said, this time daring a slight sideways glance. "They probably budgeted for about ten or twelve bucks a plate, so I guess three or four people won't be eating tonight."

The game was on and it was going to be fun. When I finally embraced the moment by looking up, I found a slightly round-faced young woman in her early twenties, sporting a fresh, blond Princess Di haircut that barely touched the top of her ears. She wore a fire engine red dress and black dangly earrings, matched by an uncomfortable-looking black choker necklace that made a harsh line across her throat. The entire look was either three years out-of-style or two seasons ahead of its time. I thought it was a perfect look for her smallish, five and a half foot slender body and bitchy attitude.

I leaned over toward her but didn't embarrass either of us by extending a stiff, insincere handshake.

"Hi, I'm Jack DuMot. I drove my mother here tonight from Frisco,"

I lied. "She flew in for this party this afternoon. She screwed up with the rental car, so here I am."

"Yeah, except nobody who's actually really *from* San Francisco ever calls it Frisco," she said with a faint smile. "Hi. I'm LaVon Bever. You could call me Vonnie, but don't. I'm visiting from Minnesota. My friend is the daughter of the bride at the wedding over in Hall B. We graduated from college in May and this is a last fling for us before starting our working lives. I got bored picking through all the guests over there, so I got another drink and thought it might be fun to take on a new challenge with your crowd."

I started to say something, but she had already returned her attention to the matter at hand.

"Christ, is that old guy up there for real?" she scoffed. "What's his name, VanDerKant? They should have set him up in a bed."

"Maybe we can slip out to the bar later," I dared.

To my horror, she burst out with a loud laugh.

"Oh, my gawd!"

I was relieved when I realized she had ignored my awkward pickup and was pointing at someone in the room.

"Check out the big hair on that social lush. I'll lay you ten-to-one odds that she's from Iowa."

I tried to follow her finger in the direction of the dance floor but my eyes stopped at the end of her bare, unpainted fingernails, chewed short and rough. After a second, I saw that she was aiming her abuse directly at a small group of people that included my mother, who stood staring at us from no more than fifteen feet away. Mom squinted at our table for a moment and scowled at me. She abruptly stopped her conversation and walked over to fill a fresh cup of punch, throwing us a look that was cold enough to refreeze my ice cubes. There was no denying it; she had heard every word and she was mad as hell.

"Yup, that's my mom," I said, taking the last few sips of my drink. "But she's not really such a social lush. And you are right about her. She was born in Mason City. Then she lived down near Iowa City for several years during high school. Old VanDerKant was one of her teachers somewhere along the line, I guess."

LaVon and I wasted away the next part of the evening hurling unfair insults at the people throughout the room. In fact, my entire first encounter with her proved to be a grand sniping contest, with both of us vying for the most malicious remark. As the evening wore on, I grew increasingly intrigued by her analytical, critical mind. When I learned she would be returning to Minnesota to start her first year teaching at a Minneapolis middle school, it settled a debate that had been raging within me for months. I would ask my mother whether she had an extra room in her new house in South Minneapolis. I was ready to come home.

Sitting at the bar in the corridor an hour later, sparks really began to fly — not romantically — literally. It began with a muffled scream above the noise escaping from wedding party. The din temporarily became a hushed buzz and then grew into a crescendo that spilled across the corridor and filled the building. In a few seconds, we could clearly identify why people were yelling, as smoke began to fill the rooms and corridor. It was only then that the fire alarm sounded and the automatic sprinkler system began pouring down torrents of water from the maze of pipes running overhead.

"**Run! Fire!**" someone from inside one of the large banquet rooms was yelling to make himself heard above the growing din of the crowd and the onslaught of water. The central corridor was already jamming with people pushing toward the main doors and out into the parking lot. Another scream went up when somebody shrieked that the main exit wouldn't open. Within seconds, people were clambering over each other like goats at the feed trough. Every direction quickly became stuck shut with people pouring out from every direction. I jumped onto the bar to survey the scene and look for options.

"We'll never get to those front doors!" I yelled down to LaVon. "We'll have to head back through the kitchen or through a side exit in a banquet room — if we can get to either one."

I jumped down and poked my head through a swinging door behind the bar, leading into the kitchen. A thick, heavy cloud of dark gray smoke billowed toward me, knocking me backward. I let the kitchen door swing shut and gave it a light push, as if to physically block the smoke back into hell. I jumped onto the bar again and grabbed LaVon's arm as if we had known each other all of our lives.

"Even if we tried to go through the kitchen," I yelled, "we'd be overcome by the smoke. It would be impossible to get through there."

I ran to the other end of the bar and looked around, but could see no chance of escape.

"Your mother!" I heard LaVon cry. "She's still in the banquet room. Can we get in there?"

I surveyed the lines of coat racks and hat shelves running the length of the corridor.

"We'll have to hope she got out through a side exit," I yelled. "We'll crawl along the shelves above the crowd and try to get in there to get to an exit. We might find her. I don't know what to do if we don't. Hopefully, she's already outside."

I stretched an arm and a leg over to the flimsy metal shelf, testing it for weight as I pulled myself over the narrow gap. No guarantees, but it would have to do. As I squirmed around to pull up LaVon's one hundred and fifteen pound frame behind me, I felt the shelf bend a little under our combined weight. We immediately stopped moving and stretched on our stomachs to give gravity a chance to catch its breath. On the other side of the corridor, several other people were already following our lead with disastrous results, as the racks collapsed beneath them.

We quickly crawled above the edge of the crowd until we got as far as the entry doors into Hall A. One side of the double doors remained jammed shut against the crush of people trying to force their way through. The crowd was thick and I realized that jumping into the middle of it would get someone hurt — probably me. It also would have put us right in the middle of a mob, with no way to move or nowhere to move to. I yelled to LaVon to slide back about fifteen feet, toward a large vent panel we had crawled past. I easily lifted the grating off the hooks on our side of the wall, but had to shove and punch at the inner grate, where it fell onto the floor below with a loud thud. I squeezed my way through and dropped about six feet onto the punch table and then quickly to the floor. An instant later, I heard LaVon crash hard; the table and punch bowl giving way beneath her as she hit the floor with a curse.

Surveying the room, we found that the sprinkler system hadn't operated fully on our side of the building, with only a few small sections toward the rear spraying water. The front part of the room was packed with party guests; half trying to get out the double doors into the corridor and the other half pushing toward the single side exit leading directly outside.

"Crap," I yelled, "we're trapped in here LaVon. God, I'm sorry."

I looked up to see the ceiling rafters and upper regions of the high room filling with smoke. More people were already trying to slide through the vent opening above us, dropping to the floor and tumbling at our feet. I knew there was no escape the way we came. We were hemmed in by masses of panicking animals.

An instant later, a hissing sound erupted from a pipe near the ceiling and a wall of water plunged down onto the center of the room.

"We have to get under that water," I yelled to everyone within earshot. "We won't be able to breathe out here in the open! We can't fight our way through those people crowding around the doors! Let's work our way along the wall and get to safety under one of the tables under the sprinkler. Then let's hope we can make a run to the exit when the jam clears!"

I pulled LaVon against the sidewall and we huddled near the floor, just out of reach of the cascade of water. The smoke began pressing downward, descending like a blanket and creeping toward us as we cowered on our hands and knees. Within a few seconds, our small group was crawling with our heads only inches from the floor. By the time we reached safety beneath some tables near the dance floor, we could see less than a few feet in any direction.

I yanked down a drenched tablecloth with a loud crash of centerpieces, silverware and plates full of soggy cake. I pushed one side of it into LaVon's hand and yelled for her to use it as a filter from the smoke. The last thing I remember seeing before pulling the other end over my own head was a large tongue of dark orange flame shooting through an air vent above the rear door to the kitchen.

As I held LaVon close, I realized that she was either unconscious or already dead. My lungs and throat were burning unmercifully and I felt my head begin to spin. I couldn't hang on, and I realized that I could be dead in another few seconds, as well. Suddenly — or maybe an eternity later — through the rush of water, screaming and breaking glass, I heard some shuffling and the loud but muffled voice of a man.

"Move toward the windows. If there is anyone in here, stay down and yell out! "

I dared to pull back my covering and opened my eyes for a split second. They instantly burned and watered as my nose scorched with pain. I tried to yell, but my vocal cords couldn't respond. About two feet beyond my reach I could make out the hazy outline of what appeared to be something large and blocky. I squeezed some water from the tablecloth into my eyes. Pain. I rubbed my eyes hard with the palms of my hands. More pain. I gambled on opening them again. Scorching pain. But this time I could see the shapes shift a little. There, an arm-length in front of me, was our only hope — but it was beginning to move away!

I dropped the cloth, closed my eyes, and lunged forward desperately, barely gripping the object with my fingertips. Whatever it was, I felt it turn in my hand. I heard the muffled voice again and a hand reached down and snatched me roughly by the elbow. Only then did I recognize that I was holding onto a fireman's boot. Without knowing what was happening, I found myself being dragged through water and debris toward a door, pulling LaVon's limp body behind me.

"My mother!" I cried out as we were carried through the exit door to the parking lot. "My mother is in there somewhere."

"We'll check it out!" came the reply from one of the gurney attendants. "We hope we have everyone out."

"What about the other people that followed us under the tables?" I yelled at him.

"Oh, Christ, there are more of you?"

"Yeah, I think seven or eight of us. Some people are still hiding under the tables."

"We'll get somebody back in there quick, but right now we need to get you two to an ambulance."

"You mean she's still alive?"

"Just barely. But not for long if she doesn't get some oxygen."

We were taken to a first aid area at the far end of the parking lot, where paramedics administered medical treatment and quickly prepared us for the ambulance ride to the hospital. LaVon regained enough consciousness to lift the oxygen mask an inch, as she turned toward my gurney.

"Did they say anything about your mom?" she choked out.

"I haven't heard. I hope she's somewhere in the crowd that got out…or maybe at the hospital already."

The ambulance attendant began to reset our masks, but not before I heard LaVon's hoarse whisper, "You are one hell of a great first date, Jack DuMot."

Sunday, August 24th, 2002

Altogether, there were twenty-six of us admitted to nearby St. Therese Hospital in San Mateo for treatment and overnight observation. Most suffered serious contusions and broken bones resulting from the panic to get outside. Surprisingly, there were no serious burn injuries, as the flames were contained in the kitchen and the cooks and wait staff got out safely. The local fire station was less than two blocks away and the rescue team and ambulances were on the scene within minutes. About the time LaVon and I were huddling beneath the tables expecting to die, people were already pouring out to safety through broken down doors and smashed windows.

My heroic decision to lead us toward the furthest point from any viable exit meant we were the last two to get out of the building alive. The other four who had followed us through the vent, across the dance floor and under the tables, were all found dead of smoke inhalation. They were the only resulting deaths and I felt responsible.

I immediately began asking the staff about my mother. It took a few hours to sort out the details but I eventually learned that she had been among the most seriously injured. She was brought in for treatment, but not to St. Therese — and not because of injuries. Apparently, during the initial rush to the exit doors, she was pushed to the ground and trampled. A large man finally reached down to pull her off the floor, probably as much to save his own life as hers. Once outside, she made it to the parking lot, where she collapsed from cardiac arrest. A cop found her lying between cars and she was rushed in critical condition to the intensive care unit across town at San Mateo Regional Medical Center. When I asked about calling her room, I was told that she was still unconscious.

Late the following afternoon, LaVon and I were released from St. Therese Hospital. My left hand was held fast in a cast but I couldn't recall exactly how I suffered the injury. Apparently, I broke a knuckle or two when I punched through the air vent. LaVon's ankle was wrapped tightly in an ace bandage for a high ankle sprain, sustained when she crashed down onto the table behind me. Both of us felt damned lucky we lived to tell about it.

We hired a cab for the drive to San Mateo Medical Center and quickly hobbled past the front desk and down the institutional-green hallway to the intensive care ward. When we found my mother's room, a nurse quickly pulled me aside before we could enter.

"She suffered a serious stroke during the night and is still in very critical condition. I don't know what to tell you. She hasn't regained consciousness and the doctor's don't know if she will. She may be able to hear you, but we're not sure."

We found her in a deep sleep, hooked to a full array of monitor cables, I.V. drips and other assorted tubes. Her mouth appeared oddly twisted into a downward turn. An orderly told us that she had apparently awakened briefly during the night and talked for several minutes with her shift nurse, who was now off duty.

"Mom," I said, gently nudging her shoulder.

Nothing.

"Mom, it's me, Jack," I said again with another light shake.

Again, nothing.

"Mom, this is the girl I met at the party last night. This is LaVon Bever. We were sent over to St. Therese Hospital across town for treatment last night."

My mother's eyes opened a thin slit and fluttered several times before falling shut again. Her lips began to quiver as her mouth tried to form some words.

"Firpo?" she whispered.

It came as a shock to hear her use the old nickname my father pinned on me when I was a young boy. I hadn't heard it in years and, in fact, it may have been the first time I ever heard my mother call me by it. She flicked an eye open and looked first at me and then LaVon.

"Rude," she said, grimacing, while reaching a fist toward us over the bed rail.

"Rude," she said again, with a little more emphasis. "I...I...find...rude."

Then silence.

"Well, I'm sorry you find her rude, Mom," I said gently. "We were just poking some fun at the party guests. LaVon didn't know who you were out there by the dance floor. Neither of us wanted to be at that party. We didn't mean to be hurtful. Not to you, anyway."

I didn't know what to say next and was grateful when LaVon stepped in.

"I didn't mean to be rude to you, Mrs. DuMot . When the fire broke out, we tried to find you to get you out safely. But the smoke was too thick and everyone was in a panic. We couldn't see. We couldn't find you. We nearly died ourselves."

There were several seconds of silence. I took LaVon's hand, retreated a few feet and leaned down to whisper in her ear.

"Typical of her," I said quietly. "We all go through hell but she can't get over being called an old drunk."

"**No! You...Ruuuude!**" My mother suddenly yelled again, straining the words through a twisted crack on one side of her mouth, while stretching and shaking her clenched fist violently toward me. We jumped back, as the nurse called out to a nearby technician for help. I had never seen anything like this and I was appalled. LaVon took another step back, as Mom's upper body unexpectedly arched upward and her arms flailed over the bedrail, as if to gather full steam for another outburst. But it never came. I caught her fist between my hands and squeezed it tightly as her eyes darted around the room in an unspeakable fear.

And that was all. The person who had always been the spirit of my family, even when unintentional or uninvited, closed her eyes, relaxed her taut back and dropped limp onto the mattress. The heart monitor above her bed stopped beeping and released a steady drone. I dropped her tight fist down by her side and stepped back to give the medical team room to scurry around the room. But there were no dramatic attempts to revive her. Everyone already knew it was hopeless. The doctor called the death of Melinda Anne DuMot at exactly 3:20 p.m., Sunday, August 24th, 2002. Perfect, I thought, as they pulled a sheet over her face and ushered us out of the room. She died with anger in her voice, fire in her eyes and hatred in her heart — while shaking a clenched fist at the world.

Before I knew what happened, LaVon and the nurse were down on one knee beside me, each with a hand held firmly under my arms, helping me to my feet. A station assistant pulled a chair out of thin air and helped me into it. With the smoke charring my lungs, the tearful lump forming in my throat and the last remaining remnant of my family lying dead on the other side of the door, I began gulping and rasping loudly for air. I couldn't breathe.

Part II

Resuscitation

10:00 a.m. Saturday, December 29th, 2007

More than five years later

By ten o'clock on most Saturday mornings, my wife was typically descending our stairs in her oversized surgical scrubs she wore as pajamas. From my customary chair at the kitchen dinette table, I would peer over my open Mac laptop and watch her slip across the kitchen linoleum, grab a Coke from the fridge and then deftly light a cigarette as she twisted her small body past me into the living room During the warmer months in Minneapolis, she headed immediately toward our screened front porch, where she would begin each morning with eight ounces of Coca Cola in one hand, a Marlboro light in the other and the newspaper spread out across the wicker table. As fall turned to winter, however, the numbing outdoor temperatures made her usual routine unbearable. Sometime during mid-October, she typically slipped imperceptibly into plan B; cracking open a living room window an inch to exhale her cigarette impotently against the incoming autumn chill.

LaVon was a light smoker. I had never lit up cigarette in my life. It was something she deeply distrusted about me. As a condition of marriage, though, I conceded that allowing her a few quick drags every morning wouldn't do too much harm to my lungs.

Nevertheless, vices have a way of evening themselves out in relationships. I was addicted to several cups of strong coffee a day. She had never tasted a sip in her life, and that was something I deeply distrusted about her. A daily habit of draining a fresh-brewed pot every morning was one of the few positives by-products I had packed along with me when I returned from the Bay Area, immediately after my mother's death in 2002.

People stand high on their ceremonies, traditions and bad habits. Daily rites are powerful things, and LaVon and I allowed each other our indulgences. That December morning in 2007 should have been no different, but there was one surprising exception. Rather than ritually cracking open a cola and lighting up, LaVon pulled down a stained mug, sniffed at the coffee pot, wrinkled her nose and poured herself half a cup. Hoping I hadn't noticed, she promptly disappeared behind the refrigerator door to top it off with skim milk. I watched as she took a sip.

"How can you drink this sewage?" she spit, adding some cold water to thin it down even more.

"When a horseshoe floats in it, the coffee's ready," I said.

She moved to her usual living room window, opened it her customary crack and took six or seven deep drags of her cigarette before pushing the remaining two inches through a hole in the screen. She gave the filter a flip with her fingertip and the smoldering butt sprung out into the fresh snow to join dozens of others scattered about. She slammed the window shut and moved further into the living room. It was a winter-morning ritual that hadn't changed since the first year of our marriage. I had learned quickly that it was not something to be trifled with.

Good, I thought. The events of the weekend were already arranging themselves into neat little rows and columns. There would be nothing too out of the ordinary and nothing that didn't fit into the right category. *There is a place for everything and everything in its place*. And as Martha Stewart would add, *that's a good thing.*

But I was already learning in my young adult life that arranging our lives in tidy categories is no shelter against the arbitrary and unforeseen. Randomness creeps in from every quarter. Probably all day. Probably every day. We erect our own versions of mosquito nets, doing what we can to protect ourselves from the irritating little incidents and nuisances that bite, sting and otherwise cause us to itch. All the while, though, those random irritations are constantly whining in our ears as they bang chaotically against our protective walls, trying persistently to get at us.

On that particular Saturday morning, a few days after Christmas in 2007, events and expectations appeared to be lined up neatly and in their proper order. From the longitude and latitude of my dining room table, I couldn't possibly have charted the randomness which was about to infest my world over the following six short weeks. For if there is such a thing as a *Grand Plan,* it is that the universe is expanding and we must expand with it. Life cannot be put into boxes and labeled for safe-keeping forever. The unforeseen, the haphazard and the unpredictable eventually eat their way through, squeezing in and driving us to distraction, as we slap and swat in vain. We grow anxious about having our faces and ears tickled in the dark. We search frantically to find the little cracks and holes, so we can push them out again. But we never can.

Like every other millennial I knew, I had lived my entire twenty-nine years of life wrapped securely in the calculated spontaneity that somehow leads a suburban male from adolescence, through his teenage years, and into early adulthood. It is claimed that Woody Allen once said, *"Eighty percent of success is just showing up."* So that's what I did. I just showed up. After all, when you're a kid growing up in a suburban rambler home in New Brighton, attending the local public schools and living off the fat of the middle-class land, little else is necessary.

But I wasn't like so many of our neighbors who were born on third base and thought they hit a triple. No, I was born on second base and rather enjoyed the view from the middle of the infield. Life was just a matter of keeping the confines of my world safe and within reach. It meant placing one foot before the other, rolling out of bed every morning and taking one day at a time. After all, isn't that what our great grandparents worked so hard for? To tame the wild man inherent in all of us.

I placed myself — and most other people — squarely within the zoological category of the risen ape, with little interest in evolving to the higher order of the fallen angel. I spent years carefully nurturing a *persona non-persona*. Throughout my middle teenage years, I restricted my social life to handful of acquaintances, only one or two of which I would call friends. I was proud that I didn't need people and prouder still that people didn't need me. While others seemed always to be searching for an unknown something or other over the next horizon, I never felt that I ever lost anything worth finding. I shrugged when schoolteachers forgot my name or classmates brushed past me without a nod. I found myself most comfortable balancing at the highest point on a bell curve, from where I could survey the distant horizons of success and failure in either direction; wondering which side I would eventually tumble toward. By my late teens and early adulthood, my presence became as imperceptible as hydrogen but as noxious as methane.

My one episode of monumental failure in the Bay Area was enough for me and taught me all I thought I needed to know. After all, I had tried to follow Oprah's guide to success. I took life by the horns. I kept my eyes open. I woke up and smelled the coffee — then drank most of it. I quit waiting for someone else to make things happen for me. I followed through on every tired old cliché that Dr. Phil and every other self-righteous talk show host ever preached. For a young man who had no ambitions beyond just showing up, however, grabbing life by the horns was too much like catching a tiger by the tail.

Everything seemed too big, too hard and too hard to calculate. So I returned to the measurable and the comfortable, where I intended to remain. When I returned to Minneapolis, I was confident that I had successfully escaped safely back into my metaphorical mosquito net. It came in the shape of a small red brick house on a quiet city neighborhood street, which I had inherited as one of my mother's few remaining worldly possessions. She had earned her real estate license when I was in kindergarten, and she worked her way up to become one of Milltown Realty's top agents in the Twin Cities' northwest suburbs.

Shortly after my move to the Bay Area, she called to say she had purchased a small house in the Crotawood area of Southeast Minneapolis. The news seemed peculiar. After hawking thousands of properties for nearly twenty years, one old house on one old city street was suddenly the house of her dreams. She argued that suburban living simply wasn't convenient anymore, so she sold the only home I ever knew and moved to 127 James Avenue. When she died without a will, the probate court awarded it to me, along with a handful of her old furnishings, an untold number of boxes of her personal belongings, some fading photographs and her late model white VW Passat coupe. When LaVon and I were married several months after the funeral, that inheritance was virtually the only thing we could claim to our names.

It felt as if the little house was a perfect fit for the two of us, with a screened front porch and a brick fireplace, which some previous homeowner had cemented shut to keep out the squirrels. We shaped the floor space on the lower level by strategically dividing the large front room with various pieces of furniture. We used an old sofa and chair to carve out ten-foot living room. My family's old avocado-green Formica dinette table delineated the eating area from the wide-open kitchen at the rear. The first floor also had just enough room to squeeze in a bathroom, a small linen closet and an eight-by-ten foot windowless space my mother used as a bedroom. The bath and closet we used regularly. The small bedroom, however, immediately became our walk-in storage space for boxes, bags and drawers full of Mom's former life, which LaVon and I never quite got around to sorting through. The upstairs included only a half-bath, walled off in a corner of a single large open attic space, which we facetiously referred to as our master bedroom suite.

For me, that old house, on that old street, in that old city neighborhood became more than just a home. It was my center for disease control, where I felt inoculated from the viral distractions that make life too difficult to manage. Looking back over that time and over those events, though, I have come to learn that we can never be fully immunized from the randomness that infests our lives. I wasn't immune then, and I now know that I will never be again.

When I heard LaVon set her cup down on a coffee table and flop onto the overstuffed beige armchair in front of the television, I knew it was safe to breach the silence.

"G'morning," I said, without looking up from an essay posted on a website someone had set up for frustrated philosophers.

During my second semester of community college, my advisor convinced me to register for a twentieth century philosophy class. While other students valued the subjective reasoning and unfounded opinions of some of the modern philosophers we studied, I was attracted to the precise logic required to win a good argument. I realized that I could sink my teeth into the topics without ever having to work at it. Every semester thereafter, I wove a philosophy, social history or humanities class into my general load of computer science courses. If I had cared enough, I could have added a double major to my transcript. But I discovered early on that there is a vast expanse between learning how to win an argument and passing the required coursework. Although I read every textbook and added a cynic's perspective to every class discussion, I found the writing assignments tedious and out of reach. I loved the mathematics of a tidy *if-then-therefore* formula, but I couldn't be bothered with arranging annoying evidence and rational thoughts neatly on a printed page. My earliest attempts resulted in Cs and Ds, accompanied by many heated conferences with my teachers. So, I did what video games teach you to do if you can't get to the next level: I gave up and hit the reset button. I continued to register to audit the classes but then would simply ignore the coursework and withdraw from class before the finals. *I just showed up.*

My wife took another sip of her coffee and pulled the remote out from under the cushion.

"Chelsea and Liverpool are tied at zero-zero. About twenty minutes into the first half," she mumbled before clicking the mute button.

Before shutting down my laptop, I checked my desktop calendar. A note popped up reminding me of LaVon's annual Kappa Kappa Iota sorority party at Minnesota State University in Mankato later that afternoon and evening. We would be staying with one of her college friends until Sunday evening and then return to home late Monday, New Year's Eve. We would have all of New Years Day Tuesday to ourselves before LaVon returned to her teaching job on Wednesday. I was looking forward to the second half of the long weekend.

Strange, I thought. She hadn't said anything about it all week. I remembered the details of the invitation when it arrived in late October. On years when the stars aligned on the calendar, party organizers planned the event for the Saturday evening between Christmas and New Years. To be politically correct, they called it a *Holiday Extravaganza* rather than a Christmas party. The timing also meant that MSU students would be conveniently out of town on winter break, which left ample parking on campus. The event typically started with an early dinner at a local restaurant at six o'clock, before moving to a dance at one of the campus gyms later in the evening. LaVon knew instinctively that I had put it out of my mind within minutes after entering the date on my calendar. She hadn't said a word about it since, so it was possible she had forgotten all about it or no longer wanted to bother with it...I hoped.

"I think we should leave here around three o'clock to get down to Mankato in good time," I gambled.

"Why the hell are we going to Mankato?" she shot back reflexively. "Oh, yeah, the sorority party. No, let's leave before two. I want to spend some time with Bussy and get to know her husband before heading to the restaurant. I'll call her this morning and let her know when she should expect us."

As I closed my laptop, I glanced out of the side kitchen window to check the weather. We had received our first snowfall of the interminable Minnesota winter the previous week, unusually late for the Twin Cities. Blanketing the ground and shrubbery were nine full inches of what the weatherman assured us would be only widely scattered flurries. Everyone in the Midwest pretends to love a white Christmas. Now that Christmas was over, though, it could start melting and get on with spring. Too often, a beautiful white Christmas turns into a tiresome white Easter.

As always, the side of the neighbor's house a few feet to the south blocked any hope of knowing what the day would be like. One of the problems with older city neighborhoods is that builders in the early decades of development got greedy. To maximize interior space, they sacrificed the size of yards. The space between the houses was relegated to a narrow strip, typically just wide enough for a sidewalk lined by a few hostas. Whenever I shoveled or mowed the narrow strip, I wondered whether I could be suspected of voyeurism, as my head bobbed back and forth just a few feet outside the neighbors' windows.

My wife opened our front door and tiptoed in her bare feet across the cold wooden floor of our screened porch to retrieve the daily newspaper. On rare occasions, the Star Tribune lay on the front steps, near enough to scratch it closer with a foot before picking it up from the ice and snow. Within a frozen few seconds, I would hear the screen door slam shut as she retreated quickly into the warm house. But like most winter days, the STrib hadn't landed within reach of LaVon's left foot that morning. In fact, like most winter days, it lay out at the street curb, more than twenty-five feet from our front porch door. Until spring arrived, the sight of the frozen, stale news lying out on the tundra forced most daily subscribers to do exactly what LaVon did that morning — leave it in the gutter. It would be easier to tune in the smiling faces on *Good Morning America Weekend Edition*. At some point during the day or week we might venture out to retrieve it, but just as often not. And it wasn't as if we could do anything about it. Despite filling the circulation department's automated message system with complaints, we rarely got the paper delivered all the way to our front doorstep after the first snowfall of the winter.

With a slam of the front door, I heard LaVon scream an oath to Satan as she ducked back into the warmth of our living room entry.

"Crap. He left it out by the curb again. You'll have to get it later," she said, moving past me toward the toaster for her usual breakfast. "Christ, I've got a headache from last night."

A headache? Is that what she was calling it? We both knew what it really was. Several of her young and single co-workers had popped in unexpectedly the previous evening. One glass of wine became two. Two turned into a bottle of merlot. A bottle of merlot turned into whiskey sours. I had grown accustomed to watching her enjoy those evenings but they always resulted in consequences we would both regret the following morning.

"Yeah, I'll pick it up when I step out to get the mail. The mail guy should be here in a few minutes. Can you wait that long?"

"Yes, I can wait!" she shot back. "Cripes, Jack, I was just asking."

"No, LaVon, you didn't just *ask*," I returned the volley. "You said that I'd *have to get it* when I went out for the mail."

I looked up after a few seconds and caught her staring a hole through the back of my head.

"You know, Jack," she said. "You're a lot like a stale fart. Do you know what I mean? You just linger in space and make everyone in the room miserable. Just about the time people can't stand the smell, you just kind of blow away...like a fart in the wind."

"Jeez. Sorry. Yeah, yeah, I'll get it," I said, half to myself. "Then I'm going to work on that little contract programming job I picked up from American Sign last week. They want it finished by the first of the year. I'd like to work on it until about one o'clock. Then we can head down to Mankato."

Wait for it, I thought. Here it comes.

"So today you're finally going to work on that project?" she sneered. "You haven't worked on that damned thing since last Tuesday. How many more unemployment checks do you get? Did you send out any résumés or follow up on any from last week?"

I knew she didn't expect an answer, so I didn't give her one.

"Here's the Saturday mailman now," she said. "It looks like he's not freezing his ass off, so maybe it'll be a little warmer for the trip down to Bussy's."

I waited a few minutes for the mail carrier to pass before stepping out onto the cold porch. For some unfathomable reason, the original homeowner had attached the mailbox on the hinge-side of the doorjamb, opposite the opening. My mother never bothered to move it during the months she lived in the house and, of course, neither had I. Retrieving the mail meant holding the door open with my right arm and stepping across the top step to capture the precious deliveries in my fingertips. Occasionally, I would lose my footing and spill down onto the sidewalk, sending bills and loose advertising fliers across our small front lawn. On a windy day, it often meant watching a piece of useless junk mail or perhaps a Publisher's Clearing House winning ticket blow half a block down James Avenue, where I left it to become someone else's problem.

That particular morning proved successful, however, and I quickly looked through the pile before stepping back into the house. A quick flip through the envelopes revealed the usual Saturday fare, including my weekly unemployment check from the Minnesota Department of Economic Security. Only two more months, I thought, and I would go off the public dole. I continued to look through the random assortment, including a late Christmas card from our plumber, a handful of bills we wouldn't pay on time, and an assortment of department store coupons for products we would never buy. I had been waiting for documents to arrive from American Sign so I could bill them as an independent contractor, but still nothing. As I began to imagine the argument I intended to have with them, my mother's words suddenly came back to me, "*You enjoy being angry, don't you, Jack*?" I realized that she was probably right.

As I opened my unemployment check, I heard a sharp yell from somewhere near the kitchen sink. "Don't forget the newspaper."

Back out on the porch, I looked down the sidewalk and then down at my bare feet. In front of me lay twenty-two feet of cold cement, lined on either side with a pile of snow from the previous snowfall. We rarely used our front walk in the winter months. City ordinances forced property owners to shovel the boulevard walkway running parallel with the street, but the Powers-That-Be said nothing about finishing the job up to the homeowner's front steps. Between Thanksgiving and April Fool's Day, if the snowfall accumulated to more than ten extra minutes of work, I rarely bothered.

I looked down the walkway and tried to calculate the time it would take to get down to the curb and back. With the wind at my back, about nine seconds, I figured. I took another second to weigh my options. Do I just make a run for it? Or do I take the time to run upstairs for my sneakers?

"Take my advice — I'm not using it," I grumbled to myself as I dropped the stack of mail onto the porch wicker table and stepped out into the cold. For dramatic effect, I inhaled a lungful of arctic air and took a giant leap down onto the flat sidewalk. The bare soles of my feet burned on impact, but I found myself only a few long strides away from my target. If I moved quickly, I figured I could shave two or three seconds off my calculated time.

As I danced down the frozen sidewalk, I suddenly thought of my dead father and his quote I hated hearing most, *"Our lives are so controlled by twists of fate, Jack, that we must always be prepared to improvise."* Just as I was about to give up and retreat to the relative safety of our porch floor, I realized that I had already come more than half way. Just three more steps. Two more hops. One last leap and the newspaper lay in my hand.

More than two thousand years ago, the historian Herodotus said that very few things happen at the right time or in the right order. I had lived my life trying to prove him wrong; but those next few seconds standing barefoot and shivering on that ice-covered concrete sidewalk would become one of those rare snapshots in my life which I would one day look back on with amusement.

Not for the first time, I saw the rectangular white business-size envelope caught up in the lowest branches of a shrub on the border of our property line. Our neighbor, Eric Crampton, had planted the bush a few summers earlier, along with about thirty other bushes, small trees and perennials. It was part of his summer-long pretentious landscaping plan designed to improve his property value by making adjacent lots look pathetic. The envelope might easily have been a piece of discarded junk mail blown there from any trash can from any house on any local neighborhood street. I had first noticed it several months earlier but decided to leave well-enough alone. There was no way of really knowing how long it might have been lying there, trapped and hidden by leaves, weeds and snow. After all, bits of wind-blown trash littered every winter every before the Minneapolis Public

Utilities Department swept the roads clean in early May.

But still, there it rested, rustling gently among a score of wrinkled red berries, a dozen dried orange leaves and a single plastic yellow price tag. It was calling to me, as if ripped from the lines of a poem, *"Life loves to be taken by the lapel and told: I am with you, kid, let's go."* True, I could have continued to ignore it until the wind eventually blew it into another yard, in a different neighborhood on another gray winter day. Would it really have mattered?

As I turned to retrace my steps to the house, my eyes remained turned inexplicably toward the shrub. I felt the echo in the stiff wind, *I am with you, kid, let's go*. From my distance of about fifteen feet, I could see that the envelope had become unglued at the seams. The open flap had wrapped itself around a small branch, pasting it in place just above the snowline. Time and the elements had taken their toll, as dampness caused the ink on the address line to bleed into dark streaks across the front. The entire bottom edge melted into the snow in blurred shades of gray and black. Clearly, this was no longer the piece of junk mail I once thought it to be. Whatever it was, wherever it had come from and however it may have found itself part of the landscaping, it had earned my respect and deserved a quick look.

I ran quickly over to snatch the tattered envelope from its snare. My bare feet were stinging with cold and I thought again about my slippers. *"Take my advice, I'm not using it"* I repeated to myself, as I beat a diagonal retreat back across our lawn back to the house, stubbing my big toe on our Brinks home security sign buried beneath the snow.

Sitting down again at the dinette table, I heard LaVon's muffled voice descending the stairs. I suspected she was talking to Bussy on her cell phone, making final arrangements for the weekend trip.

"The mail and the newspaper are here," I yelled, vaguely raising my voice in her direction. She replied with a nondescript holler but I had already become distracted by the headlines.

"Sun's out, too." I added vacantly. "And it's not too cold yet. Paper says it should be a decent day for the ride down to Mankato."

As usual, I sorted through the mail by separating the junk pieces into a recycling pile on one corner of the table. Like every day since being laid off from my job, my mind went immediately to my unemployment check. I read the net dollar amount on the voucher sheet — two cents less than the previous check, I noticed.

I checked my laptop calendar and quickly re-counted the number of weeks remaining for state unemployment benefits. It had been more than three months since I lost my job and my financial world was set to collapse in late March. *Wasn't anyone out there hiring?* I folded the check secretly into my wallet and promised myself to deposit *most* of it into our joint checking account when the bank reopened Wednesday following the New Year's holiday. I knew the deposit would show up online when LaVon balanced the checkbook. Until then, though, I was safe from the inevitable arguments that came stuffed along with every check.

ProtoCommand

Losing my job on that Thursday afternoon in early September came as a complete shock to me, although there was no reason it should have. I had been working at the company for five years and the signs of failure were everywhere, if I had only taken the time to look.

Looking back on things, the fact I was employed at all was one of those quirks that can neither be fully explained nor completely understood. I was never quite sure exactly why I moved out to California after college, but I managed to convince myself it was to find a job. During one of my mom's frequent telemarketing calls to persuade me to move back home, she told me about a job opening as a programmer for ProtoCommand, a private software development and prototype technology company in St. Paul. As usual, I told her I had no intention of giving up on my California dream. Intuitively, though, I knew that my independence out there was only a façade. I knew I would always have her to fall back on. When she died while visiting me in the late summer of 2002, everything changed.

After moving back to Minneapolis and handling the details of her death, I phone-interviewed with a handful of managers at the company, and was asked to start work as soon as possible. I reported to the department manager's office the third week of September and was immediately assigned to a project team working on a subcontract for Boeing. For the first time in my life, I felt like I belonged to something bigger than my own little world.

Although my teammates and I typically worked more than fifty hours each week trying to get things right, the entire scope of the job remained beyond our reach. We didn't think anybody on the management ladder really understood the scale of the project, either. We were left in the dark. From what I could gather from the spec sheets sent down to us every Tuesday morning, the project was apparently part of the next generation of lightning strike detection equipment for Boeing's 7-series passenger jets. Unofficially,

ProtoCommand executives code-named the project LighTect. I suspect the managers at Boeing quickly dubbed it, *"Those damned idiots in St. Paul."*

Specifically, my job was to write C++ subroutine code to determine the reaction time between a lightning detected in the vicinity of the aircraft and the navigator's response. Although I never heard exactly how my part of the program would be used, I concocted the idea that it was a critical component of their flight-training simulator. My work, I imagined, would save thousands of lives someday.

The project had its difficulties, to say the least. Most of my time was spent debugging glitches, followed by writing additional code to patch the patch. Not surprisingly, LighTect was soon nicknamed LieDetector by other employees throughout the company. Some days, our mistakes had to be corrected within hours. Other days, Boeing would change the specifications on a dime, only to tell us to hold off for a day or two before proceeding. We were always behind schedule and it nearly always meant working late or playing catch-up on weekends.

After a time, the entire project began to seem rather pointless, but it didn't matter to us. My team was young and eager and we each took some pride of ownership in the futility. We were all new to the corporate world and we were doing a job we had spent our young lives dreaming about. We were living large and we turned a blind eye to the inevitable. The way we had it figured, if Boeing was willing to pay the salaries of six cocksure, pimply-faced programmers to develop one small subroutine, who were we to question it?

My teammates and I were stuffed into individual beige five-by-five foot cubicles that were shoved ignominiously against a wall in a room originally constructed to house the company's large mainframe computers. To ensure we would never forget where we were to sit every morning, the head janitor even wrote our names in grease pencil onto the brick wall directly over our respective cubicles. The entire set-up never seemed very permanent, but there we were: Nary Sonli, Josh MacInerny, Jacob Margot, Aaron Franklin, Cory Abbott, and my cube, Jack DuMot, 1-198.

During the computer explosion days of the 1970s and '80s, the room had housed eight over-sized Crays, which relied on early-model parallel vector processors. When the computers ran for hours at a time, overheating was a constant problem. A low platform served as a false floor, installed to allow air conditioning to flow beneath the large machines filling the room. It was more than two years before I learned not to stumble on the low step whenever I entered the room. By the mid-1990s, the mainframes were obsolete and had been removed, but a grid array of bolt holes still punctuated the length and breadth of the floor panels throughout the room.

The door entering from the hallway was at the center of a large glass-paneled wall, which ran the entire thirty-foot length across the front. The back wall included six large floor-to-ceiling windows, giving us a view of the back alley leading to the loading docks. The transparent room inevitably earned the nickname *the fish bowl.* In short order, of course, my small group became referred to throughout the company as the guppies.

Although the thermostat on the back wall was set at a perpetual seventy-four degrees, the room felt interminably cold. We could never decide whether the display registered several degrees higher than the actual room temperature, or the glass simply made the room *feel* like an ice castle. Adding to the subterranean chill, the room echoed like a cavern. Winters were especially hard, but even during the muggy Minnesota summers, I typically ended up pulling on one of my dad's old hand-me-down gray Mr. Rogers cardigan sweaters, which I left draped over my office chair every night.

Perhaps my strongest memory, though, is that the platform floor never saw the bottom side of a janitor's broom. The room was so dusty that *snow globe* would have been a more apt nickname. Turn it upside down, shake it and watch through the glass as the dust bunnies floated about the room before eventually resettling on every surface. Shortly after my first month on the job, I caught the custodian by the elbow one day and asked about having the room cleaned. He handed me an old broom from a nearby janitor's closet and said, *"Oh, I never go in there."* To avoid wearing paper dust masks, we kept the broom and a smelly damp mop in the corner. When we could no longer handle the filth, one of us would agree to give the floor a lick and a promise — typically about every three weeks.

Fortunately, our jobs were virtually paperless. On many Friday afternoons we circled our chairs for a brief strategy meeting about emptying the trash can. About once a month we would set it out in the hallway with slim hope that the cleaning crew would empty it. Most Monday mornings, we found it exactly where we had placed it, still full of our odd bits of sticky candy wrappers and other trash that was permanently glued to the bottom. When the bin inevitably overflowed, we emptied it into the large wastebasket in the men's room — under penalty of death, if caught.

Despite its storied past, the company used the large quirky room as extra space for just six PC server towers and a small assortment of out-of-date furniture and equipment. Oh, and the six of us. It was impossible to know whether management eventually intended to fill the room with additional employees, or we were merely tucked out of the way until the Boeing contract came to a merciful end.

No, the job wasn't much, but it was a paycheck and it put some meaning into my meaningless life. I could measure it and count on it. At that time, it was all I needed. After all, when you pour a single drop of water into an empty bucket, the pail is no longer empty.

There was nothing unusual about that particular Tuesday afternoon on the particular early-September day I was fired. We had all returned to work-as-usual the morning after our three-day Labor Day weekend; each with our own creative lie about the number of hours we had worked from home. Throughout the day, we were slowly getting back into the swing of producing programming gibberish, which we privately knew would never save the world.

It was never in the corporate budget to wire each of our cubicle spaces with an individual phone, so the six of us shared a single line with a single extension number for the room. Installing it within arm's reach of our desks never seemed to be a top priority, either. The line terminated at an early-model black receptionist console set on the printer table at the far corner of the room. The few times it rang, it was usually of no consequence who answered it. After a ring or two, one of us would inevitably give our chair the mighty heave necessary to roll our way across the expanse of linoleum floor panels. We quickly dubbed it Mr. Toad's Wild Ride as we challenged ourselves to pick up the receiver before the required third ring. On that Tuesday afternoon, on that particular September day, though, nobody was in a hurry to answer.

As the phone began its prohibited fourth ring, I finally volunteered, and then pushed off hard against the front edge of my desk. My chair made its three practiced revolutions before rolling to a stop within arm's reach of the receiver. I picked up the handset and pushed the blinking button.

"Hello, LighTect room, Jack Du..."

Before I could finish my greeting, department manager Bill Ordway's voice interrupted, barking at me to get up to his office at my earliest convenience. *At my earliest convenience*, my ass, I thought. We both knew that his earliest convenience meant dropping everything and running at a fast trot to catch the next elevator up to the third floor. He might as well have added, *"I'll see you in thirty seconds"* before slamming down his handset.

There was nothing so unusual about getting the phone call, or the request to report to Ordway's office on the double. In fact, any one of us who answered that phone on any given day might have been asked to come upstairs for any reason. Usually, it was to get a new set of commandments from Boeing in Seattle. Near the end of the month, it was usually to retrieve the new encryption code for exchanging project information with each other by e-mail. But this time, I knew things were different. It wasn't the end of the month and we were still working on program changes from the previous week. But there was something else that made me feel uneasy.

Ordinarily, the voice on the other end of the phone would have been that of our department secretary, Tina Bucholz. *"Hi, Jack,"* she would say, somehow knowing each of our voices immediately. *"Can you come up to Bill's office to pick up the new specs?"* Whenever it was the big guy who made the call, though, it was a crapshoot whether he would eventually guess who he was speaking to.

"Hello, Josh, no Jake, no Aaron, no John, yeah, John DuMot, right?" he would guess. I would finally end his misery, *"Hi, Bill, this is Jack DuMot."*

But this call was different. No Tina. No Ten Commandments from Boeing. No litany of names. The entire conversation consisted of nothing but a simple order to come up to his office ASAP. As I hung up, I had a strange recollection of something my father frequently said, *"In business, nothing good ever comes out from behind a closed office door."* I rolled slowly back to my computer keyboard and clicked the mouse to save my project notes. Without a word spoken, I suddenly felt all ten other eyes in the room staring. All I could do was shrug.

"I'll be right back," I said. But as I walked from the room, I heard my own dry voice croak, "*I think*."

Bill Ordway was discreetly and rudely referred to among the lower castes of ProtoCommand as *Gimp* because of a slightly disjointed leg that caused him to shuffle his right foot slightly when he walked. Backroom legend at the company had it that a junior manager once worked up enough blood alcohol count at a Christmas party to ask him about the injury. Bill would only say that it was either a birth defect or an injury that occurred at a very young age. He had carried the limp and accompanying offset wrist from his earliest memory.

When ProtoCommand hired him directly off the University of Chicago campus in the late-1970s, he was in his late-twenties with a wife and infant son in tow. He had caught the attention of the founding partners during his senior year, when he was part of a small group of geeks who developed a software program that revolutionized the university's billing process. He was fond of telling people that he was one of the few people in America who still knew that the acronym **COBOL** stands for **CO**mmon **B**usiness-**O**riented **L**anguage.

As the software world changed, he found ways to change with it. Scattered around his office, he had haphazardly hung an untold number of framed programming certifications. Psychologically, Bill knew exactly what he was doing as he hammered each one of those awards to his walls. By God, nobody was going to tell him *anything* about computer programming. After a brief meeting in his office on my first day, I came away thinking that either the man was a bona fide genius, or the company paid him to pass certification exams.

Bill was a roundish man, with thinning black hair and a broad face punctuated by a wide nose and bushy gray eyebrows. Despite a Scandinavian surname, his dark complexion betrayed a Mediterranean heritage. He had been managing director of subcontracts at ProtoCommand for at least seven years, appointed to the position after working his way through every other department at one time or another. He was in his mid-fifties and I always suspected that he wanted everyone to be afraid of him. In truth, though, nobody really was.

Bill's pride was his late son, Jason, who apparently had played minor league pro baseball for the Charlotte Knights AAA team. Rumor around the company had it that he was always just one hitting streak away from a call-up to the White Sox. According to Tina Bucholz's version of the story, Jason was killed in a shooting accident while hunting with some teammates in western North Carolina, when his gun accidentally fired as he climbed through a fence. His hunting partners immediately ran toward the sound of the shot but found him tangled in the barbed wire, already dead from a twelve-gauge hole through his chest. As far as any of us could tell, Bill never talked about sports except when talking about Jason. As winter turned to spring, his conversation inevitably turned to Jason and the anticipation of a new baseball season. As he was fond of saying, *"No poetry ever written has fired the imagination more than those two words, Opening Day."*

Jason was in his early thirties and engaged to his pregnant girlfriend when the accident happened. With a single phone call from the Watauga County sheriff's office, Bill Ordway lost his treasured son, a future daughter-in-law and a grandchild that he so badly needed in his lonely life. He was never the same following Jason's death. After years of managing people by growling, gnarling and scowling, everyone quickly discovered how vulnerable the old guy really was. Despite his best efforts at being a jerk, he could never separate himself completely from the loss. New employees were quick to complain about his ragged edges but anyone who really knew Bill would quickly set the record straight. Everyone has a story, but Bill's story — nobody envied.

He was the go-to guy for anybody with any kind of software question or problem. My team must certainly have been a constant pain in his ass, as one problem after the next eventually landed on his desk. If he was frustrated by our ineptitude, however, he never showed it. He was within a few years of early retirement and he must have considered us his job security, at least until his pension and social security benefits kicked in, anyway. As we struggled to complete the simplest projects, he always managed to handle us with an even hand. Despite working for him for five years, I never came to know the man very well, but I held him in awe. As I got off the elevator that afternoon, though, I knew that nothing good could possibly come from behind his closed office door.

Tina was standing near her desk in the outer office, directly under a florescent ceiling fixture, which cast a pale yellow patina across the top of her rich, smooth black hair. As I walked past, I gave her a polite smile and nodded hello, expecting her usual smile in return. Without looking up, she waved me through with the soft flick of her hand. Coming from someone who always made it a point to glow at us through the glass fishbowl wall, her posture didn't bode well.

As I stepped into Bill's office, he looked up from nibbling on a cinnamon cracker. He tossed the manila file folder onto his desk and I could read my name and employee number labeled across the front. He quickly brushed aside a few crumbs and took a sip of water to clear his throat. I stood nervously for a brief moment while he took another few agonizing seconds to push the box of Keeblers into a lower desk drawer. It was clear that he was damned-near as uncomfortable as I was. I decided it may have been the first time in his life he didn't know exactly how to express himself.

As he started to speak, he choked on a crumb and called for Tina to bring him another cup of water. In a few seconds, she stepped in with an insulated brown plastic pitcher along with two Styrofoam cups. He filled one cup, drank it quickly and offered me the other only half-full. I took a sip out of politeness, but never lowered my eyes from his face. He appeared beaten and resigned. For the first time in my years working for the man, I felt as if I had somehow gained an advantage, or at least stood on even footing.

"John, we're going to offer you a severance package you better not refuse."

It took another few seconds before my thoughts cleared.

"It's Jack, I've never gone by John," I said. "What did you just say? What did you mean?"

He cleared his throat and tried to take another sip from his empty cup before starting again.

"We're going to offer you a severance package you better not refuse," he repeated without changing a word.

As I tried to figure out exactly what he meant, the room spun and my head went vertigo. Then I knew exactly what he was trying to say. I was in the process of losing my job and the son-of-a-bitch was in the process of joking about it. I regained my bearings and sat down in a chair. He poked his reading glasses higher up his nose and looked at me as if to say, *"I didn't tell you to sit down."* His face softened when he realized that I didn't intend to ask his permission.

"Why me?" my voice squeaked.

"Because you're the one who answered the phone," he said, with no hint of irony.

"A severance package that I better not refuse." I repeated aloud.

After hearing it put that way, I didn't see any choice except to sign the agreement he shoved across the desk toward me. The package that I better not refuse, it turned out, included nothing more than paid health care benefits for three months. Bill was proud to point out, though, that I could extend the benefits by paying three hundred dollars a month for the COBRA plan at the end of ninety days.

"Oh and here's your check for your unused vacation days," he added.

"Big deal," I said loudly, surprising myself with an angry tone. "Four days of pay and health insurance I don't need and can't afford."

He looked crushed that I accepted his generous gesture with such an air of ingratitude. The next moment, as if summoned by a secret button beneath the desk, the janitor walked in and escorted me from the inner office and out past Tina, where I saw her glance up to catch my eye.

"I'm sorry, Jack," she whispered as I walked by. "I knew last month. I wanted to tell you guys but I was under strict orders not to. Did he tell you why you were cut?"

"Just bad luck that I answered the phone," I answered. "It's just my appointed hour. He said it could have been any one of us. I guess he's practicing one of those random acts of kindness that you read about on bumper stickers."

"Random act of kindness? What? No. That's not true," Tina said. "He knows there's nothing kind about what's going to happen."

It wasn't supposed to work out this way. Two years of community college, followed by two more years in the Computer Science program at the University of Minnesota, followed by eighteen months getting C++ programming certification at DeVry University had all come to nothing. Nearly six years of higher education and forty-two thousand dollars in student loans and it didn't matter a tinker's damn to anybody. Not to Bill Ordway. Not to my co-workers. Not even to the janitor. None of me mattered to none of them. My twenty-nine years of life, education, and experience had been sucked into a black hole. Everything which I had come to identify as part-and-parcel of my manhood was suddenly scribbled over by a signature on the bottom line of a severance agreement that I better not refuse.

The janitor hovered as I scooped a handful of personal items into a box that had mysteriously appeared on my cubicle chair while I was in Ordway's office. In my confused state, I absent-mindedly started to explain to my teammates how far I had progressed with my programming code. When Cory Abbott gave me a *what-the-hell* look, I quietly reached down and flipped off the computer. As the janitor snarled at me to hurry, it occurred to me that it might have been one of the few times he had ever stepped foot in the room.

On my desk was a form requiring me to write out the usernames and passwords required to access my computer. I filled in my employee number as my username and added "Firpo79" as my common password. My father had given me the nickname *Firpo* when I was no more than six or seven years old, when he and I shared our Saturday evenings watching local All Star Wrestling reruns on a Minneapolis television station. One of the wrestlers claimed to hail from Argentina and called himself Pampero Firpo. He quickly became one of the most notorious villains in the local wrestling market. He was a freak with raging black eyes and unforgettable wild and matted hair. My dad knew that he scared the crap out of me. He loved it, though, when I imitated the wild-eyed glare and convulsive shrieking that was part of the wrestler's trademark. I developed a love-hate relationship with the character, which my dad considered charming.

The nickname *Firpo* became one of those secret intimacies shared between a father and son; somehow strangely out-of-bounds for anyone else, including my mother. As payback for Firpo, I nicknamed him *Crusher*, as we bounced around our living room practicing step-over-toe-holds, figure-four leg locks and full-nelsons, usually in sync with Mom's hollering something about losing an eye. When WTCN television stopped broadcasting AWA wrestling from the beautiful Calhoun Beach Club in Minneapolis, I ceased my fearless roar and our nicknames for each other sadly slipped into a cave. At some latent level, though, the name Firpo stuck to my ribs. Over the years, I continued to use it as my password, as a way to log on to my father.

As the janitor ushered me through the glass door and out into the world of unemployment, I nodded toward my former co-workers. They each sat silently at their desks, exhibiting the telltale slump of survivor's syndrome. Before stepping off the raised floor and out into the hall for the final time, I reached back into the room and emptied my personal items into the trash and then jammed the collapsed cardboard box tightly into the very bottom of the can. Now the no-account jackass would *have* to empty it, I thought.

I pulled my elbow out of his grasp and turned to leave the room, leave the building, and leave my steady paychecks behind. For the past few years, I had spent most of my waking hours in a thirty-by-twenty-foot room with these young men. Now, the last thing I would remember about any of them would be the *am-I-next* expression on their faces. As the glass door began to close behind me, I quickly poked my head back into the room and yelled cynically, "If the phone rings, don't answer it."

I drove around the local area for several hours, worried about how I was going to explain everything to LaVon. She knew all about my trouble finding a job right out of school. In fact, she knew I was a failure-in-training when we first met at that banquet hall out in San Mateo that night. Now she would know that I wasn't even competent enough to keep an entry level programming job for an aging buggy-whip factory on its last legs. When I finally walked through our back door into our kitchen that evening, I was more than three hours past my usual arrival time. Without a word exchanged between us, an unholy emptiness crept across her face. Like a migration of green algae across the surface of a pond, the loathing started at the lowest point of her chin, moved up across her mouth to her cheeks and nose, then spread east and west to fill her eyes before moving northward over her forehead to the crown of her head. In the end, nothing remained but a few contours on an expansive, stone-cold open prairie of hate that I recalled had once been a smiling face.

I had been in the presence of *the look* before, but only at a glancing blow. She typically held it in reserve as her final salvo in a battle with an inept store clerk or rude customer service representative. But this was different. Now the revulsion was aimed at me and I had never experienced it point-blank before. It was an empty, dark place that could not be penetrated by any mortal words of explanation or apology. I simply walked out the rear door to the back alley, got into the car, and drove around the city until I was sure she was in bed asleep.

So, with the third ring of a telephone and a slice of Bill Ordway's gallows humor, my attempt to create something of myself in the corporate world came to an end on that particular afternoon in early-September of 2007. I wish I could say something dramatic like, *"My life changed forever."* But to be more truthful, my life changed *back* to exactly what it had always been. Before I met LaVon. Before the fire. Before my mother died. Before ProtoCommand. Indeed, despite everything, my life had come full circle. I chalked it up as a dismal flop in a world that was increasingly proving to be too large, too heavy and too difficult to manage. Over the few short years of my adult life, I had managed to pull off a feat that most people are unable to accomplish in a lifetime: I had completely circumnavigated the world of failure.

When you are between jobs, time moves at two speeds simultaneously. Living hour-to-hour, your days become a constant drag of scanning job sites and classified ads, checking job postings and re-creating yourself on every résumé and for every interview. In a parallel dimension, though, the kitchen calendar is also a constant reminder that large chunks of time disappear as if sucked down the disposal. *What happened to October? How did it get to be the week after Thanksgiving? No, it can't be nearly Christmas already.*

I was beginning to panic, but I didn't dare show that side of the calendar to my wife. She was being dragged along for this ride and she didn't like it. Our marriage was a mile wide and an inch deep, with each of us occupying the unstable muddy ground on opposite banks. *Lonely* wasn't exactly the word for it. Nor was *boring*. In fact, it defied description by any simple word or phrase. Never a Cinderella romance to begin with, our relationship became a place to park our frustrations with our work, with our neighbors, with our lives and finally with each other. It was life, but it wasn't living.

From what I could tell, neither of us needed to individually accept the blame for what we had become as a couple, but neither of us accepted the responsibility to fix things, either. After all, our relationship wasn't really broken. It was just never tuned right to begin with. What was born of fire had cooled over time to gray ashes; lit only by the glow of an occasional hot cinder. We both recognized it and we both silently agreed to the other's expectations and terms. Not working. Not broken. Not worth it. It didn't seem to make a difference.

So much of what we had become over the years hinged on our frustration with our jobs. LaVon had been hired by Minneapolis School

District #1 as a full-time seventh grade teacher immediately after graduating from MSU. Despite her initial excitement about the job, dissatisfaction began filtering into our evening conversation within months after the start of her first year. Each year, as summer vacation drew to a close and Labor Day approached, she grew increasingly distressed, often to the point of physical illness. Heading into her fifth year, she was quite clearly fed up. One day it would be the politics in the teachers' lounge. The next day it would be dealing with an irrational parent. She began ranting about immigrant students who couldn't read and American kids who couldn't write. By the end of September, she had marked our calendar with every holiday. On any given Monday she could recite the exact number of days remaining until the end of the school year.

It's not that teaching was a bad job. As her friends reminded her, she was lucky to be working in a large city school district. In truth, she didn't have the temperament to be an effective educator, and she knew it. The textbooks at MSU didn't teach survival techniques for being locked in a room with twenty-four unruly young teens for six-hour days. She began seriously talking about working part time as a substitute. Could we make ends meet with our bills and student loans? Would ProtoCommand give me a raise? Could I get a promotion? Did I have enough job security? No, no, no and ultimately, no.

The unemployment check folded into my wallet that late December morning brought it all rushing back to me. For the first time since losing my job, I began to feel a sense of despondency. It must have been exactly what LaVon felt every day as she headed off to another schoolroom full of unappreciative kids with raging adolescent hormones.

I knew from experience: The longer I remained unemployed, the less employable I became. *"If we can be nothing else, let us at least be honest with ourselves"* my father would say whenever he caught me trying to rationalize the irrational. But who was I kidding? Despite all of my education, I had been less than successful at ProtoCommand. Truth be told, my entire team of misfit programmers had been misplaced into that world. I consoled myself by saying that in a matter of months the rest of those guys would be fired, too. Six hapless young men, dropped into a glass cage. We slumped around aimlessly, consuming, digesting and pooping out whatever scraps we were handed. All, it seemed, for the twisted entertainment of spectators.

10:30 a.m. Saturday, December 29th, 2007

As I stood in the kitchen that morning, fumbling through that small stack of mail, I came to some honest conclusions. It wasn't just the loss of my job that lay at the root of my problem. It was the loss of any sense of direction. I was wandering aimlessly with no direction to turn to get myself on track. As small as I tried to make my world, it was still too large.

"What did you yell to me up the stairs a few minutes ago?" LaVon came down asking. "You know I can't hear you when I'm up there."

"Oh, I just said the mail is here, and I have the newspaper, too. It wasn't worth repeating."

She picked up the jumble of envelopes and fliers on my recycle pile and began flipping through the papers.

"What's this old thing? A Christmas card?" she asked, handing me the tattered letter I had retrieved from under the neighbor's shrub.

"I don't know. It's empty. It's been lying under a bush over at Crampton's since last summer," I said. "I noticed it again today and thought it might be something, but it's just junk mail. Toss it in with the recycling."

"Well, it sure looks like it was addressed to somebody named DuMot" she said.

I felt my eyebrows shoot up in surprise as I looked closely at the wrinkled and stained envelope in her hand.

"Let me see that."

There was no return address on the upper left-hand corner, nor anything written across the back flap. Trying to make out what remained of the smeared ink bleeding down the front was nearly impossible. But she was right. Beneath the smears, streaks and smudges, I could clearly read the last name, DuMot. Whatever the first name had been, however, it was impossible to tell. It was completely obliterated beneath a smudge of black. At the end of the second line I could read what remained of 127 James Avenue. The city and state were completely illegible, but that didn't matter.

"What do you think was written at the beginning of the second line?" she asked. "It looks like LKA."

"LKA, Last Known Address," I said absently, trying to get a glimpse over her shoulder.

LaVon pulled back the flap and used her blunt index fingernail to scrape something adhering to the inside of the envelope.

"Look, it's not empty," she said, holding up a two inch strip of white typing paper. It was damp and the blue ink had run and smeared, but the handwriting was still clear enough.

"*Arv — February 23 — Ø*. Hmm," she said, handing me the paper. "Were you supposed to have a rendezvous with a girl named Arvis on February 23rd, at Club Zero in St. Paul?"

"Arv. That's my dad," I said, looking closely at the handwriting.

"Your dad?" LaVon questioned. "You always claimed that he's been dead since '01 or '02, I think."

"Yeah, he died in February of '02," I repeated blankly. "It's hard to believe it's coming up on six years already. His real name was Arvil, but I never knew him to go by anything except Tommy. I heard one of his close friends call him Motty once, but it never stuck. He was always just Tommy to everyone. I didn't think anybody even knew his real first name."

I turned the paper over in my fingertips a few times and held the envelope near the window for added light. No, I still couldn't make out the first name on the address line. I should have tossed it on the recycle pile, but I was struggling with something that I couldn't take the full measure of. The postmark was barely legible but I could see that it had been mailed from Grand Forks, North Dakota, the previous February. It looked like either the 21st or 22nd. I realized immediately that it might have blown out of our mailbox on the 23rd, the date written on the small slip of paper it carried.

"What the hell do you suppose this is all about, LaVon?" I asked.

"Who knows," she said without looking up from the newspaper sections she had spread across the table. "But the damned thing has been out there since last winter. Whatever it was, it doesn't matter anymore."

I threw the empty envelope onto the table but tucked the little slip into my wallet. I pushed a section of newspaper off to one side and sat down again at my laptop with my coffee mug near my right elbow, as usual.

"I need to work on my project for a few hours," I said. "Then let's head down to Mankato."

3:00 p.m. Saturday, December 29th, 2007

It drove me nuts that we were leaving for the sorority party more than an hour later than first intended. It meant we would be searching for an unfamiliar address just as the afternoon light was disappearing. I tossed our small suitcases into the back of our Passat and slammed down the trunk in frustration.

As always on longer road trips, my wife drove. State Highway 169 south out of the cities was unfamiliar territory to me. LaVon, on the other hand, knew the route between Minneapolis and Minnesota State with her eyes closed...because that's how she usually made the return trip after a late night in the cities during her college years.

As we sped through the small third-tier suburban towns of Shakopee, Chaska and Jordan, the urban landscape began to open up on either side of us. A double set of railroad tracks flanked the north side of the highway, connecting the Twin Cities southwestward toward the Dakotas and beyond. A few abandoned BNSF boxcars were pulled off on sporadic sidings along the track. I wondered if they could have been the same boxcars I had seen parked there nearly five years earlier, on my first trip to Mankato for our wedding.

"BNSF," LaVon said, interrupting my thoughts. "My mother used to work for Burlington."

"Really? When?"

"When I was a little girl, back home in Missouri," she continued. "The railroad still maintained a small office in Burlington, Iowa. My mom made the trip across the border three days a week for a job in their finance department. Things sucked on farms during the mid-eighties, and most farmers or their wives ended up taking whatever job they could find in a nearby town. Burlington was the nearest thing that passed as a city within seventy-five miles. I guess it's something I wanted you to know about me."

I looked over in surprise. This was new information about her past — a topic that was typically off limits for discussion. Whenever anybody asked her where she grew up, her standard response was, "Northeast Hell."

Northeast Hell was actually a farm near Unionville, Missouri. As she described it, the place was as far from real life as you can get. Knowing that nobody has ever heard of Unionville, Missouri, she always added quickly, *"Oh, it's just six miles across the border from the bright lights of Cincinnati...Iowa."* If the person gave another puzzled look, she would simply say, *"Exactly. Now you know about my hometown of Northeast Hell."*

Several minutes passed before either of us spoke again.

"You seem awfully quiet," I broke the silence between us.

"Bussy and Jeb have somebody else staying at their house," she answered quietly. "I think she said his name is Tony. He's Jeb's brother or something."

"I suppose he'll be staying all the way through New Years?"

"Yeah, he's an older guy. I think I met him once during my senior year at MSU. Bussy knew him and introduced me. If I remember right, he's married with two kids. I think they live up on the Iron Range."

"Does it bother you that he'll be there?" I asked.

"I'm not sure. I was really hoping hoped to spend time with Bussy. We'll see."

Mid-winter days in Minnesota are mercilessly short and the dim December sunlight was already beginning to bury itself into the hills in front of us. My recollection of the scenery along the Minnesota River Valley came back to me vividly as it sped past our car windows. During the summer months, this stretch would be green with oaks and silver maples stretching up the sides of the bluffs. The rows of fruit trees would be heavy with green apples peeping between branches and leaves.

In winter, though, the sense of driving through a primeval river valley was even more pronounced. The gray trunks of bare orchard trees emerged in parallel lines out of snow covered fields, fenced neatly into square packages. The tops of the bluffs were set against the bright blue Minnesota winter sky, with grazing pastures and hayfields creating a white patchwork rising to the top. Tufts of hay and dried alfalfa poked through the snow everywhere in the fields. With the low afternoon sun beginning to lengthen the shadows, it was impossible to judge distances. We might have been two hundred yards from the bottom of a bluff; we might have been a mile from the top.

The railroad tracks moved further off the highway but remained intermittently visible along our entire route, on their way to the Green Giant processing plant in Le Sueur. Eventually, they would connect to larger communities settled by Northern European immigrants throughout southwestern Minnesota. Cities like New Ulm still bear the social imprints of the modern Hun invasion between 1880 and 1910. German restaurants, blue collar manufacturing jobs, breweries and dairy farms continued to comprise the local flavor and economy.

These farming lands of central Minnesota were the real world of Laura Ingalls Wilder and her pioneer counterparts. Here could be found remnants of the real Little House on the Prairie. This was the landscape of Walnut Grove, not those mountainous California backdrops Hollywood producers set up behind Michael Landon and Melissa Gilbert. One hundred and fifty years ago, this was Dakota Indian prairie land, just beginning to be settled into trading towns named Le Sueur, St. Peter, Blue Earth and Sleepy Eye. The Minnesota River Valley was originally part of a Sea of Grass that stretched between the badlands of the Dakotas and the woodlands along the banks of the Mississippi River, rolling lazily through the bustling Twin

Cities. Quite accurately, it has been said that St. Paul is the end of the East and Minneapolis is the beginning of the West.

The scenery jostled something else in my memory, as well. Checking where we were on my road atlas, I recognized the names of a few towns about sixty miles to the north. This was the world my father knew and talked about from his childhood — at least on the few occasions he bothered to talk about his childhood at all. Like LaVon, he also came from farmer stock and, like LaVon, he left home when he was barely eighteen. After a six-year stretch in the Navy, he moved to Minneapolis and attended Dunwoody Vocational School to become a pipe fitter, never to return to his childhood home.

After one of his frequent arguments with my mother, he dragged me along for a drive out into farm country, somewhere west of the cities. Beautiful landscape to be sure, but I didn't want to be there. I didn't know where we were going and I didn't listen to anything he was saying along the route. It was likely that we drove toward his old stomping grounds but I was only thirteen or fourteen and didn't pay attention. Cows and gently-rolling farm fields were not adequate compensation for missing my Sunday afternoon television shows. He never made his past a part of our family life, and I didn't care why.

I pulled by wallet from my hip pocket and found myself looking again at the little slip of paper. It had dried somewhat and I rubbed it gently between my fingertips as I read the smeared, single line of handwriting over and over again: *Arv — February 23 — Ø*. Nope. Nothing had changed about it, yet something seemed somewhat more vexing. What was it? What was I trying to compute? *Arv — February 23 —Ø*. February 23rd? The smeared ink on the paper blurred as my eyes began to well-up. February 23rd ...it was sinking in. February 23rd....it sunk in a little deeper. February 23rd...it sunk into my bones and it hurt. February 23rd...my father's birthday.

Michigan Rink - Gold	**Minnesota Rink - Silver**
Lead: Jim Coventry	Lead: Paul Stenner
Second: Dale Harder	Second: John Mistovich
Third: Steve Talbert	Third: Mickey Bellows
Skip: Norm Thunger	**Skip: Freddy Schade**

First End

"That's the way to work those brooms, boys," Michigan Skip Norm Thunger hollered down the ice. "We'll take points anyway we can get them."

At the conclusion of each end, only the rink with a rock — or rocks — sitting nearer the center than any opponent's shots are awarded a score. By the time Thunger crouched in the hack with the final shot for the end, the tightly-packed Minnesota silver-handled rocks all lay as counters for potential points. Unless Thunger and his sweepers could coax a perfect shot to the center of the house, Minnesota would take a deflating early three-point lead that would change the remainder of the game. But sliding his shot on target without clipping another rock was only part of the equation. In order to score, his shot also had to stop its forward momentum at the right place, and at the right time.

A combination of a perfect release, the right delivery speed and aggressive sweeping resulted in Thunger's rock coming to rest within three inches of the dead center of the house. As the players removed the rocks to prepare for the second end, the entire Michigan rink was aware of the magnitude of what had just occurred. Yes, they were relieved to avert a disastrous start, but it was more than just a single point hung on the scoreboard. With one final perfect throw and sweep, Thunger had chiseled three shoulda-been points from the heart of Minnesota's repugnant Skip, Freddy Schade.

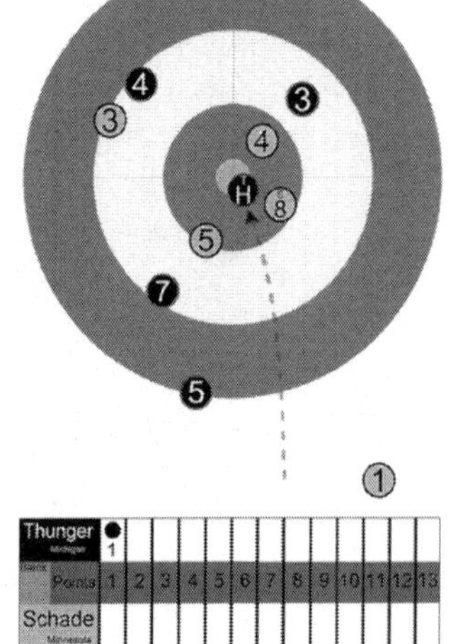

For the people gathered in the arena, the score meant little. It might as well have been 100–0. The winner would be advancing to the championship game later that afternoon, but throughout the arena, the stench of injustice hung in the air like gathering storm clouds.

4:00 p.m. Saturday, December 29th, 2007

By the time I was in my early teens, I realized that my parents were destined to pull the plug on their marriage. It was just a matter of who would finally cave in. To my surprise, it was Dad who finally broke the stalemate. While he and I were painting our main hall one Sunday afternoon, he suddenly stopped, carefully set his sage green paint roller into the paint pan and pulled off his favorite Minnesota Golden Gopher sweatshirt.

"Firpo," he said quietly, "You just shouldn't have to be part of this anymore."

When I quickly agreed that I was tired of painting, too, he shook his head silently. His eyes were glistening with tears and I realized that he wasn't talking about finishing the paint job. He was talking about our family. Until that moment, I had never seen him cry. In fact, I wondered whether he ever had. But why had he finally decided to throw in the towel after more than twenty years of marriage?

"You and Mom don't fight that much," I said.

"No, it's not the fighting," he answered. "In fact, the arguments are the only things that still breathe some signs of life."

Neither of us ever said another word about it. I could only assume there was one big final blowup, perhaps late at night or some other time when I wasn't around to witness it. For the previous three or four years, my parents hadn't spoken much with each other. Yes, they discussed paying bills and the occasional wedding or funeral of a friend or neighbor. Often, though, it was as if they were just tossing words into the air for the other to catch. They talked *at* each other and *toward* each other, but never actually seemed to speak *with* each other.

Even their fights seemed one-sided. Mom typically started yelling about one thing or another. Dad's universal response was to get into the car and drive away for several hours, without ever saying where he was heading off to or when he would return. Occasionally, he slipped out to our back steps to sit quietly smoking one of his infrequent cigars. In a fit of rage late one summer evening, my mother locked him outside. He spent most of the night curled up under an old yellow tarp, hopelessly trying to fight off mosquitoes. I first learned about it a week later when I asked him about the dozens of red welts covering his legs and arms. Before he could answer, Mom interrupted, *"Because your father is too stupid to carry his house keys."* Later, she broke into tears as she confessed that her anger and frustration had gotten the best of her. Dad never talked about it and I never told him I knew. Whenever I saw him out on the back steps by himself, I left him alone. Besides, what was I going to say?

My father certainly wasn't blameless. I recall that many of their arguments began when he came home from his Local Union #539 pipefitter job complaining about a tough plumbing project. Often, he claimed his lower back ached. At other times, it was his hands or knees. Sometimes, he said he could hardly hold his tools because his wrists hurt too much, *"Those damned pipe wrenches were made for gorillas."* My mother insisted he see a specialist but a series of X-rays and MRIs revealed nothing. As he entered his mid-40s, he began taking advantage of his generous union sick days. Some days he would call in with an upset stomach, other days it was a migraine headache. I began to suspect that maybe Mom was right. Maybe he just really hated his job. *"You should have thought about a college education, so you could get out of that line of work. Now it's too late."*

After he told me about his decision to leave home, he spent the next month quietly moving out — one car-load at a time. Without me realizing it, he was disappearing before my eyes. His presence in my life had never been an extravagant light show in the first place, but now he just dimmed and faded away. One afternoon I noticed that he didn't come home from work. For all I knew, he might have been gone for two or three days already. I didn't ask my mother about it; I was afraid she hadn't noticed, either.

I had no idea where he moved to after he left the house. I was already seventeen, so weekly visitations weren't part of our routine. I would receive occasional telephone calls, *"just checking in"* and we would make periodic arrangements to meet at a local restaurant to try to catch up with each other's lives. Over a Chinese buffet, he might say a word or two about a current building contract. Mostly, though, we just sat quietly in each other's company. Apparently, he must have figured out that his work-a-day-world stories weren't on the top of my personal interests. Our planned get-togethers tapered off to an uneventful end and we settled into periodic phone conversations.

I eventually graduated from high school with a whopping 2.40 GPA, high enough to get accepted into any one of the community colleges that dot the Twin Cities metro area. To save money, I decided to continue living with my mother while pecking away at classes at Normandale Community College. After a year, my dad stopped calling the house altogether. That was okay with me. Our conversations were becoming one-sided and contrived. I had made a handful of acquaintances in my classes; homework and video games filled up the rest of my life. To occupy her time, my mother had her real estate business, as well as what was left of raising me through my school years. It took several months before I realized that Dad was no longer part of our lives. All Mom could muster was, *"I know, Jack, and I'm sorry. We tried to make the pieces fit, but we just can't find a better way."*

The final divorce settlement dragged out for nearly a year. She insisted on keeping the house, while he would keep his union pension for himself. Mom's lawyer insisted that the settlement should include monthly alimony. Somehow, the court didn't see it that way.

The year I started kindergarten, she had passed the Minnesota real estate exam and signed on with a small broker in a Minneapolis northern suburb. A big-ticket sales career proved to be a perfect fit for her outgoing personality and fiery temperament. Within three years, she became a regular member of the Twin Cities Top Realtors Club. The distinction allowed her to move to more prestigious agencies, where she eventually became one of the north metro's top agents. I never knew her annual income, but the judge obviously did.

Throughout the divorce, Dad never really fought against paying support money or any other part of the property settlement. He was less than ten years away from early retirement, so the pension pie was open to equitable distribution. By the time the lawyers finished arguing, she settled on keeping the house. The five years remaining on the mortgage and thirty thousand dollars in unnecessary attorney's fees and court costs left a bitter taste in her mouth. Dad walked away with his union job, his full pension annuity and, presumably, a strong pair of bootstraps.

It took a couple of years for the dust to settle from the divorce but we eventually moved on from it. She admitted to me once that she had no idea whatever happened to him after we lost touch, nor did she care. For the first seventeen years of my life, he was just quietly here, there, and somewhere in my world. Then, we all just moved on. His last words when dropping me off after an evening together were always, *"You know how to get hold of me."* But that was no longer true. In 2002, when my mother called me at my California apartment to read the news article about his death in a single-car rollover accident, I felt indifferent. Despite her soft tears, I could not muster any sense of loss. He was already too far gone for far too long.

LaVon and I passed another half hour in general silence before reaching the outskirts of North Mankato.

"How far have we driven?" I heard myself asking.

"About an hour and a half," came her quiet reply.

"I asked how far, not how long," I said. "I mean, how many miles have we driven?"

I had awakened a sleeping giant.

"Jeeze, what the hell does that matter?" she snapped back. "Why is the exact distance, time and weight always so damned important to you, Jack? It's like a freakin' obsession with you. You measure and calculate everything down to the thirteenth decimal point. There will always be 5280-some feet in a mile, and there will always be about eighty miles between our house and Mankato.

"Just asking," I said quietly.

"What the hell does it matter how far we've come? All that should matter is that we're not there yet," she added with disgust.

"I don't know why it matters to me," I said defensively. "I guess somehow I just breathe easier knowing. I don't know why."

"Breathe easier?" she snorted. "Hell, Jack, sometimes I don't think you breathe at all."

She tightened her grip on the steering wheel and glared through the windshield in silence.

"No," I finally added. "You're right, LaVon. Sometimes I can't breathe at all."

She glanced sideways at me for a brief second or two, as if ready to demand what the hell I meant by that and then let it drop. She glanced down at the odometer.

"About seventy miles, I guess," she finally sighed. "I hope we get there soon or we'll have to head out to the restaurant right away. I wanted to visit with Bussy and Jeb a little first."

"Do you know exactly where their house is?" I asked, more sheepishly this time.

"No, but Jeb took the phone and gave me the address and general directions when I talked to Bussy this morning. We go to Highway 14 and then head a little south. He says we'll see it from the main road."

"You know where the highway is, though, right?"

"Nope. I just know how to get directly to campus and my old apartment. I couldn't even tell you where my old family home is from here."

"The road atlas is a little confusing." I said. "There's a Holiday station up ahead. Pull in and I'll ask someone. I have to pee, anyway."

Inside the store, I carried a six pack of cola and bags of potato chips to the red laminate checkout counter. I opened the atlas and asked the teenage clerk if he could show me the exit onto Highway 14.

The blank look on his face told me more than I needed to know.

"You see, dear, this is why men don't ask for directions," came a voice from immediately behind me in line. "Whenever we bother to ask, nobody ever knows, anyway."

"Oh, shush," said his wife, standing next to him.

I turned to follow up on the opportunity.

"Do you know where the exit to Highway 14 is?" I asked, showing him the map page.

"Yeah, it's Minnesota State Highway 14, but it's also marked as County Road 23. It's about ten miles further south yet. I couldn't guess what exit number it is. We don't use exit numbers very much around here. Just the road names and highway numbers. Are you from the local area?"

"I'm from cities," I answered. "It's the same up there. Exit numbers don't seem to be a Midwest thing, I guess."

As the pimply-faced clerk handed me the receipt, my wallet slipped out of my hand, spilling out a slew of loose cards and scraps of paper. The old gentleman bent over to help pick up the contents, handing me one item at a time. I nervously re-stuffed everything into various slots and compartments where credit cards, driver's license, photos and an occasional dollar bill should have lived. He stopped for a second and scanned the back of one card, which included my computer username and password. Before handing it back, he read it aloud.

"Firpo? Odd name. I recall there used to be a wrestler up in the Twin Cities went by the name of Firpo back a long time ago. Is that the guy this refers to?"

"Nope...well, sort of, I guess." I said. "That's the nickname my father gave me when I was a kid. We used to watch old wrestling reruns together. It's just a password I use now."

"Firpo," he said. "Funny name and now I see it twice in one day."

"Twice, really? Why? Was the old guy in town making a public appearance for some reason?" I asked, searching for something to say as I re-organized my wallet. "I thought he was dead."

"No, I mean, yeah," he replied, "The wrestler probably died years ago. But there's a story in the local newspaper this morning about a curler named Firpo. He won a regional playoff match this past week. He curled out of Mankato quite a few years ago. It's a funny name that stands out, that's all."

"Yeah, it is unusual," his wife added, scowling at the way I was haphazardly shoving everything into my wallet with no sense of organization.

"It's just an old nickname," I said.

I picked up my purchases, tossed everyone an insincere thank you and headed out to the car.

4:50 p.m. Saturday, December 29th, 2007

We pulled into the driveway just as the last of the evening light was surrendering to nightfall. Jeb and his brother looked on from the front doorstep as Bussy, LaVon and I gave each other an awkward group hug, accompanied by my insincere assurance that it was great to see her again. I broke away and began emptying our travel bags from the rear of the car, while sizing-up the surroundings.

The red brick farmhouse came right out of the early 1920s, with a few renovations affecting its original architecture or outward appearance. No doubt, the entire farm was originally carved out of free government land, tilled out of prairie and woods sometime during the homesteading years of the late nineteenth century. Likely, when the farm became prosperous enough, some previous owner replaced the original wooden structure with brick. The spirit of a working farm could still be felt in the layout of the surrounding yard. The barn and the main outbuildings had long-ago disappeared but a detached tar papered tractor shed still stood at the end of the long gravel driveway running well past the back of the house.

In all likelihood, the farm once sat in blissful isolation, a wind-swept quarter mile or more from its nearest neighbor. Several very old poplar trees lined the border of the yard, thirty or so feet from the house. It was common for Midwest farmers to plant a row of these fast-growing tall trees along the northern side of their yard as a feeble defense against the Canadian snow and subzero wind chills charging out of the open plains of Alberta. The handful that lined the edge of Bussy and Jeb's yard would have been the fourth or fifth generation of the originals.

The Currier & Ives scene was quaint, to be sure, in part because it looked so completely out-of-place in its modern milieu. Depending upon your point of view, it was either an eyesore that had been allowed to deteriorate in the middle of a planned community, or the last remaining vestige of all that was once good and wholesome about the agricultural Midwest. To me, it seemed a travesty that the beautiful open space that once stretched outward in all directions had been criminally transformed into a tightly-packed maze of cul-du-sacs, crowded with late-model beige and gray split-entry houses occupied by well-intentioned young families.

In the warmth of the living room, Bussy formally introduced us to her husband, Jeb, who immediately offered me a Red Stripe beer.

"I started drinking these when *The Bus* and I went down to Jamaica for our honeymoon last year," he said.

Jeb's brother Tony, it turned out, was actually Tony Perkovich, an old high school friend who had apparently moved in for the long-haul. He insisted that we refer to him as *T*, as if making people pronounce two syllables was too much of an unnecessary effort. He was visiting from Grand Rapids on Northern Minnesota's Iron Range, caught between infrequent job openings at the taconite mines and saw mills.

"Well, at least you and I will have something in common for the weekend," I joked as I shook his hand uncomfortably.

When he shot me a confused look, I clarified, "Both of us living off Bussy and Jeb's generosity for a few days, I mean."

LaVon looked him up and down as if she didn't know quite what to make of him. A simple nod was all the approval she could muster.

I looked at my watch. We had taken off from Minneapolis later than planned and the trip down State Highway 169 took a full thirty minutes longer than I had calculated. We had less than a half-hour to settle in before taking off for the dinner portion of the evening. LaVon accompanied Bussy upstairs for a quick tour and I slipped into the downstairs bathroom to change out of my sweatpants and t-shirt. Jeb offered me another beer but Tony intercepted it deftly and plopped himself down on the sofa.

"While you guys are bored to tears with that crowd, I'll be sitting on my ass watching the MSU hockey game against St. Cloud State."

As I shifted quietly in my chair, I fully realized that none of us felt very comfortable with each other's company. When the girls finally came downstairs, Jeb and I relieved the tension by bantering back and forth about whose car to take to the restaurant. With the sun already set, the outside temperature had sunk below zero. Even the windchill of -15° didn't faze Jeb, though, and I somehow lost my argument to drive our Passat, still relatively warm from the trip. Irrationally, the four of us crawled into his ice-cold 1992 Ford Bronco. The exterior of the vehicle was covered with a gray film of road salt and the interior reeked of cigarette smoke and spilled beer. LaVon and I had to kick aside more than a few empty bottles before squeezing into the cramped rear seats. Jeb managed to grind the frozen engine to a start, but it was obvious the old heater and defrost unit weren't up to the challenge of a late-December Minnesota evening.

What could have been a cozy, warm trip with quiet conversation in our warm car, turned into a miserable, teeth-chattering arctic expedition. Our moist 98.6 ° breath hitting the subzero surface of auto glass quickly formed a thick frost on the inside of every window. We stopped talking as Bussy vainly used a credit card to clear a small space immediately in front of Jeb's face. It was lost on both of them that leaning over the dash and exhaling hot, steamy curses directly onto the windshield only caused the problem to grow worse. I prayed that either of them could see even ten feet in front of our headlights. From the rear seats, we could see nothing.

When we came to an intersection that required making a left turn across double-lane of highway, I sweated nervously. Jeb scraped a tiny peephole through his side window and asked Bussy to do the same on her passenger side. Through the frost on the rear windows, I could see the auroras of several headlights approaching us at highway speed.

"Well, I can't hardly see a damned thing," Jeb said as he pushed on the accelerator, "but I'll try to make it."

"You've got to do better than try!" I hollered, as our rear end barely made it to the safety of the center median just as an oncoming car swerved past our taillights; its horn blaring.

In previous years, the dinner portion of the evening had always taken place at the Bracket Family Diner, owned and operated by the parents of a sorority sister. This particular year, however, the venue was changed to accommodate the increasing number of spouses on the RSVP list. The change inevitably resulted in hard feelings when the Brackets realized they would be losing several thousands of dollars in annual revenue during the holiday season. Not surprisingly, word spread quickly that 2001 Homecoming Queen Kari Bracket would be unable to attend for undisclosed health reasons.

As we pulled into the parking lot, Jeb triumphantly announced that we had arrived. Apparently, he reasoned that arriving twenty minutes late meant there would still be several parking spots available near the front door. As we circled for a third time, Bussy instructed him in her most colorful grammar to, *"Find one of the spaces along the outside row and park this damned thing, for Christ's sake."*

LaVon and I squeezed ourselves out of the rear doors and stepped into the full brunt of the arctic wind. LaVon suddenly froze and caught my arm, stopping me from taking another step. We stood silently immobilized; not believing what we were seeing before us. Bussy popped out from between the cars and found us standing motionless.

"Oh, Gawd, Vonny, keep walking!" she yelled. "I'm freezing my ass off. Let's get inside."

"Look, Jack," LaVon whispered. "It's the Flanders Ball Room."

6:20 p.m. Saturday, December 29th, 2007

We stood in that parking lot on a subzero evening in south-central Minnesota staring at what was nearly a blueprint replica of the Flanders Banquet Hall in San Mateo. Sure, there were minor differences, but not many. The same large front windows hemmed-in the same double set of entryway doors at the center of the building. The same large black shutters neatly framed the rows of windows along the front and sides. The same canopy sheltered the final twenty feet of sidewalk leading up to the entrance. In nearly every respect, the exterior resemblance to the Flanders was unmistakable.

From where we stood, we didn't need to go further. We knew exactly what we would find if we stepped inside. The same pedestal sign with cheap white plastic letters would stand immediately inside the door, instructing guests to proceed to either Hall A on the left or to Hall B to the right. Coat racks would be running along the same wide central corridor, leading to the same tri-sided bar at the back. It even dawned on me that it was Saturday evening; there would likely be a wedding reception in one of the halls. No, it wasn't a perfect replica, but enough resemblance to refresh terrible memories for us.

"My God, Jack, it can't be."

"No, LaVon, it can't be. But there it is."

"I can't go in there, Jack"

"No, I can't either. Do you want to skip the meal and just head to the dance later?"

"Yeah, can we do that?"

I turned to Bussy and tried to form an explanation. She knew the story about the fire and understood our feelings. Jeb complained about being hungry but Bussy made it clear he didn't have a say in the final decision. He looked resentful but what the hell did I care? He didn't figure to be my idea of good company for the evening, anyway.

On the way back to the farmhouse, we briefly recounted the story of the San Mateo fire and how it resulted in my mother's death. Jeb admitted that he understood completely why we didn't want to relive it all. As a group, we decided to put together a few sandwiches and enjoy a nice evening of conversation in front of the farmhouse fireplace before heading to the dance on campus at eight o'clock.

As we pulled into the driveway, however, my visions of some

warm, quiet hours sharing a bottle of wine were dashed when Bussy suddenly had a profound idea that sunk my heart. She recommended that Jeb, Tony and I should all head out to a local bar for a few drinks, while she and LaVon remained back at the farmhouse to catch up on their lives. It would be a great opportunity for me to get to know the two men in Bussy's life. After a beer or two, we could swing back to the house to drop off T and pick up the girls for the dance. Despite my protests, LaVon clearly thought it was a perfect idea. There was nothing I could do or say; I was destined to play nursemaid to two half-drunken idiots for the evening.

As we stepped into the warm living room, we found Tony slumping down the stairs toward us, wiping his mouth with a hand towel.

"I'm sick as a dog," he said. "It must have been something I ate. I'm going right back up to bed."

The five empty beer bottles near the kitchen sink betrayed that he wasn't suffering from bad oysters.

"It's your loss, T," Jeb chuckled.

It turned out that Jeb's favorite bar was in Mapleton, a small farming community twelve miles south of Mankato. I complained that it seemed a little too far to drive for a couple of beers but he brushed me off. He won on the choice of bar, but I won the consolation prize by convincing him to allow me to drive my car.

As we pulled onto County Road 22 heading south, Jeb explained to me just how and why a beer joint so far out of town became his favorite bar. Like Tony, he was originally from Grand Rapids and moved to Mankato to attend college. After four semesters, he dropped out, in part because of academic disinterest but primarily because he had run out of drinking money. After several weeks of living hand-to-mouth, he found a job as an unlicensed hack for an under-the-radar taxi company in town. He typically took weekend shifts in order to score some extra tips from generous drunks. On Saturday nights throughout the late fall and winter, he would frequently get called to The Haymaker Bar and Grill in Mapleton to pick up one or two customers who couldn't find their cars. After the bowling or curling league games ended, the guys often took their parties down the road to the Haymaker. Typically, it would be the last fare of the night so it became a habit to turn off the meter, pull up a chair and join the group for a cozy hour or so until the bartender kicked them out at closing time.

"They even allowed me to run a bar tab for a couple of months," he beamed. "I finally got one gentleman to pay it off, though, in exchange for a free cab ride home and a collaborating lie to his wife."

As we approached Mapleton, something began feeling familiar, but I couldn't understand what or why. Pulling off the highway toward the remnants of the town's main street, we passed alongside a low cinderblock building with a steel roof. As I looked at the mural painted along its entire side facing the road, I remembered that I had seen the building somewhere in my past. When I saw that the unpaved parking lot shared space with an adjacent apartment building, I knew it wasn't just déjà vu.

"Was that the curling club we just passed?" I asked.

"Yup. Only a short way to the bar," Jeb responded with a smile. "That club is the main reason for the cab fares out of town this time of year."

Suddenly, the memories rushed back to me in a stream.

Over one long Thanksgiving weekend, when I was ten or eleven, my father and I were watching a television show featuring a compilation of unusual sporting events from around the world, including curling from Scotland. I was fascinated, as rocks and sweepers slowly rumbled down a narrow lane of ice at a pace I could respect; aiming toward a target that looked like, well — a target. No amount of play-by-play commentary could help make sense of the rules during the ten-minute segment of the show but that didn't matter. From what I could see, nobody was getting hurt and only the rocks were getting pushed around. When the show went to a commercial break, I turned to my father, *"I don't understand what's going on but I'd sure like to try that."*

His eyes flashed and he jumped from his chair. *"You bet!"* he yelled, but then made the mistake of rushing to my mother with the news. Throughout my childhood, my father tried everything to get me involved in a sports league. The number of activities I quit was exceeded only by the number of activities I refused to try. Swimming lessons — two weeks. Tennis — three lessons. Soccer — two practices, one game, one kicked knee. Even tee- ball was a dismal failure and the league returned my parents' money after the first game. I could only imagine what my dad — a farmer's son who once climbed into pens with ornery sows and rutting bulls — thought of having a kid who wouldn't climb as high as the third rung of the monkey bars. At the conclusion of every school year he would come home with another marketing pamphlet about a local youth sport program. And every year, Mom helped me escape with my body and self-esteem intact.

As I listened to my parents argue about registering me for yet another youth league, I had every reason to suspect that this latest episode would end the same way. But I was wrong. The following Saturday, I was on the ice playing with other kids in the junior program at the St. Paul Curling Club. When I started actually showing some skill and interest over the weeks that followed, Dad became insufferable. On many weekends that winter, he put together a team — called a rink — of other local kids and entered us in junior events at curling clubs, always in the coldest towns he could find throughout the Upper Midwest. The final junior *bonspiel* of the season took place at the small club in Mapleton. I didn't remember much from those whirlwind weekends, except that we hardly ever won a game. Most of those towns and clubs were very much alike. The parents were typically curlers themselves, who enjoyed watching their kids get into the game. The highlights for the kids, though, were card games between matches and playing the earliest versions of some video games in our hotel rooms until three a.m.

I could never imagine why those cold weekends meant so much to him, except that it put us in the same car and hotel together for three days at a time. They typically cost him a Friday afternoon of vacation and he always paid for an extra hotel room for himself. During the two or three hours between our matches, he was always off somewhere in the nearby town and never hung around to talk with the other parents. As far as I could tell, though, he never missed a single shot of a single game. It all became quite routine, really. My rink would come off the ice after another loss and he would take a few minutes to point out a few things we did well, as well as few things we could have done differently. Then he would slip me a few bucks for snacks and leave me to be supervised by other parents until our next game was scheduled to begin.

While packing for a junior 'spiel in Grand Forks one Friday afternoon, I complained, *"If you like this so much, Dad, why don't you learn to curl, so I can quit?"* He mumbled a cryptic promise about *"never stealing anyone else's destiny"* and we headed off for another cold, bleak club in another cold, bleak town. After the final junior bonspiel in Mapleton in early April, I never stepped onto a curling sheet again. It was only one wintry season but it was the most extended sports experience of my life. I had managed to forget about it over the years.

Jeb and I walked into The Haymaker to the typical Saturday evening bar scene of soft chatter and the drone of Fox News on the big screen. It was shortly after six and a few local families were finishing their burger baskets as the town regulars slowly started to drift in to watch a game on one of the corner TVs. As she took our order for beers, the waitress nodded a familiar hello to Jeb and asked about T. During his brief time in Mankato, Tony Perkovich had apparently already been making a name for himself, I thought.

We sat at a corner table near the bar and tried to strike up a meaningful conversation. Hell, who was I kidding? I didn't care whether it was meaningful or not. Any conversation would do. We both knew that it was going to be a long hour and a half of nursing beers and running through our repertoire of bar jokes. In less than ten minutes, we had completely discussed the personal details of our life stories and fully recapped the familiar episode of When-Bussy-Met-LaVon. We soon discovered that our only real talking point was the small curling club we had passed on the way through town. I adjusted my sails and moved with the prevailing wind.

"I've been to that curling club," I started. "When I was a kid...I curled one year on the junior league at the St. Paul club. I didn't remember it until we drove past the building on the way here tonight."

"Really?" Jeb responded. "You curled? I'm on a league with Bussy at the Caledonia Club in Mankato. Our club claims to be the oldest curling club in Minnesota. I'm not sure if it really is but since nobody ever checks, they run with the story. Ever been there?"

"I don't know. Probably. It was a long time ago," I returned. "My dad used to haul me all over Minnesota, Wisconsin and North Dakota for junior bonspiels. He loved it. I hated it. Well, I acted like I hated it — the curling part, anyway."

"So, when was the last time you were down this way?" he continued. "Why don't you finish your beer and drive back over to the club and check things out. You can swing back here at seven-thirty and we'll head back to pick up the girls for the dance."

I was impressed. It was a damned clever way to get rid of me and I was grateful for it. I slipped on my coat, handed him a fiver to pay for my beer and quickly headed for my car.

Walking through the front entrance of the curling club, I was immediately struck by the unmistakable bouquet of hotdogs and nachos drifting out from behind the snack bar. After a minute or two, the scent of the chemicals used for making artificial ice began taking over. The building droned with the sound of curling rocks rumbling down the ice, as several club members were already warming up for the start of their evening league matches. Most of the tables out front of the food grill were filled with people catching up with each other's lives over the previous week. Out on the ice, players were stretching and practicing their deliveries and sweeping skills. I soaked up the sights and sounds, which I hadn't realized had sunk so deeply into my bones during that single winter, nearly twenty years earlier. On sheet number six, along the far wall, a game was already underway. I slid myself into the row of old theater seats the club had installed for spectators to watch through the plexiglass.

In an instant, a thousand memories came rushing back. I remembered this club. I remembered the clicks of the brooms sweeping and the sound of the rocks rumbling as they glided and spun slowly down the ice. It had been so long ago but I turned into that child again as I recalled that little corner of my life. I remembered the faces and sounds and voices, and then even the names of a few of the kids who were regulars on the junior circuit. I even recalled that it was at this club that we won our final game against a rink from Eveleth. When our final shot landed for the winning point, I looked through the glass to see my father jumping up and down, high-fiving everyone within his reach. To my horror, he even hugged the mother of an opposing player who was lying on the ice crying.

"By God!" I heard his muffled yell carry over the top of the glass wall. ***"We just beat a rink from the Iron Range! The Iron Range!"*** Improbable as it was, a rag-tag group of prepubescent boys from the Twin Cities suburbs beat a mighty rink from northern Minnesota, where ice was invented. Perhaps it happened quite frequently. We didn't know that. We were awarded a small trophy for winning a single game during the tournament. For my dad that weekend, though, even my mediocrity was something he could finally be proud of. It turned out to be the only trophy I would ever win. I was embarrassed by it so I stuck it into the bottom of my sock drawer, where it eventually dissolved into the emptiness of time.

I sat with my Coke and watched the game, shaking my head whenever a shot drifted off target; or flailing my arms in frustration when the sweepers gave up too soon. Parents attending the junior bonspiels tried to convince us that curling is the world's greatest spectator sport. During my games, I would glance through the glass to see my dad reveling in discussions about strategy and technique; his hands and arms articulating every point. But as a bunch of bored, hungry kids stuck in an ice-cold curling club all weekend, most of us just didn't get it. There was none of the physical attraction of football; no fast action like hockey; no spectacular diving catches like baseball. To most of us, we were simply sliding a rock that was too heavy, down a sheet of ice that was too cold, toward a target that was too far away. Our best hope was that it would come to a stop anywhere in the vicinity of where we intended. As I sat watching that game in front of me, though, I began to understand why it means so much to people who understand the game at its deepest levels.

The full size of the playing surface is roughly one hundred forty feet long and a little more than fifteen feet wide, with a twelve-foot target of concentric rings — called the *house* — on each end. At the dead center of the rings is the *button*, approximately twice the diameter of the curling stone, itself. A full curling rink includes four players; *Lead*, *Second*, *Third* and *Skip* — who is typically the best curler and serves as the captain and strategist. Every player has a unique role and is generally called on to make a specific type of shot.

Curling rocks are approximately eleven inches in diameter and weigh forty-two pounds each. Nearly every curling stone used at clubs around the world were hewn from blue hone granite quarried from Ailsa Craig, a small island off the west coast of Scotland. The curling world should panic that the quarry might one day run dry.

A colored handle is attached atop each rock, with the numbers #1 through #8 assigned to each rock of both colors. One rink will play handles of one color, blue for example; the opposing rink will play the other color, yellow for example. The players on each rink alternate two shots each with the corresponding opposing player. The blue *Lead* throws the #1 rock, followed by the yellow *Lead* throwing the #1. The blue Lead then follows with the #2 rock, followed by the yellow Lead throwing #2. Then it is each rink's *Second*'s turn to alternate rocks #3 and #4; then the *Third*'s #5 and #6; and finally the *Skips*' turn to finish with #7 and #8. Altogether, sixteen rocks complete what is appropriately called an *end*.

The scoring is much like bocce ball and horseshoes. Only the rink ending up with a rock, or rocks, closest to the center button receives a score for the end. To be counted for scoring, though, any portion of the rock must lie inside the twelve-foot diameter circle. It is possible — but rarely happens — that one rink records all eight of its rocks closer to the center button than any rocks from the other rink. The feat is referred to as an *eight-ender* and is said to be as rare in competitive curling as pitching a no hitter in baseball. If neither rink ends up with a rock in the house, it is referred to as an *open end* and a *blank* score is hung on the scoreboard.

The players then gather the rocks, do an about-face, and return play down the ice toward the house at the other end. At the junior bonspiel level, the youngest children often play six-end matches. Older kids and adult league matches are typically eight ends. Major championship games consist of ten ends. In the event of a tie score after the final regulation end, sides play an extra end or more to determine the winner. At any point during the match, the trailing rink may forfeit with a handshake. Curling is recognized around the world for its unique spirit of camaraderie both on and off the ice. Players are expected to police their actions and behavior during games. Like golf, protecting the sport's integrity and tradition of fair play is paramount when making decisions about rules and scoring during the match.

In a sense, every end of a curling match is a mini-game of its own. Some rocks will remain in play throughout the end, while others will be brushed to the side for being too short, too long, or bumped out of play. Frequently, one rink may have several rocks lying nearest the center — referred to as *counters* — late in the end, only to have the opposing Skip throw the final shot and land it *right on the button* to win the end. Having the last shot — referred to as the *hammer* — is a decisive advantage, and it plays a significant role in the strategy throughout the match.

Having the hammer, however, does not alternate democratically between the two rinks from end to end. The rink that scores points on an end must relinquish the hammer to the opposing rink for the ensuing end. Generally, the side with the hammer has the best chance of winning the end, but if the Skip doesn't use it effectively the other rink can *steal* points. Strategically, the Skips for both rinks play the largest scoring role with their final shots, but it is critical that the position players do their parts with their own rocks, setting up the final scoring opportunities.

I spent several minutes watching the game before turning my attention toward the critical commentary spewing forth from nearby spectators. It's no wonder nearly every curling club installs a half-inch pane of plexiglass to separate the players on the ice from the critics in the crowd, I thought. Curling is a difficult game and it takes years to get good at it. Is this what my father loved about it? The strategy? The second-guessing? The woulda, coulda, shoulda? I touched the glass and strangely recalled a handwritten curler's prayer I had read posted in a curling club somewhere in northern Minnesota: *Lord, give me skill and plenty of class, to match the wizards watching through the glass.*

I watched the match for several more minutes until one rink pulled away with three points in the sixth end and two more in the seventh. As I buttoned my coat for the cold drive to retrieve Jeb and head back to Mankato for the girls, I read a few of the advertising posters and banners hung throughout the building. Typical of most clubs, a few accolades to local players who had won rink honors at a state or national level hung from the rafters above the ice. Hanging twenty-five or so feet above sheet number four were a handful of large hand-stitched maroon banners listing state and national men's champions. Not bad for this small club, I thought, but not at all like Bemidji.

Arguably for curlers worldwide, the Bemidji Curling Club can be revered as a pilgrimage site on par with St. Peter's Basilica, the Temple Mount, the Bodhi Tree and Mecca. Despite its international prominence, however, the club's humble steel-frame building barely casts a shadow onto the adjacent softball fields. Like many clubs, the site includes an upstairs bar and shares its main entrance with a hockey arena. First-time visitors to northern Minnesota can be forgiven for thinking that all public buildings come complete with an attached bar and a hockey rink. City planners know where the money flows, after all. As local planning commissioners will tell you, "There's no sense being a damned fool about these things."

Inside the Bemidji club, the rafters and walls drip with championship history, with dozens of banners dating back decades hanging from the ceiling and walls. Every state and national champion, every Olympian, every world class American curler — *ever* — must have stepped onto the ice at the Bemidji Curling Club at some point in their lives. Men, women, seniors, juniors, and probably blind and paraplegic curlers, too. I recalled that my dad dragged my team up there for one junior bonspiel just so we could know what it meant to play on the same ice and use the same stones as some of the greatest curlers who ever lived. But with a deck of cards in one hand and a hot dog in the other, the experience was lost on us.

But there at the Mapleton Curling Club just a handful of championship banners hung above my head, pushed around feebly by the warm air flowing through the overhead blowers. I chuckled to myself as I counted and read the various accolades stitched onto banners:

Men's Minnesota State Champions – 2003
Third Place Men's U.S. National Championships – 2003
Men's Minnesota State Champions — 2004
Senior Men's Minnesota State Champions — 2004
Second Place, Men's U.S. National Championships — 2004

No, the Mapleton club wasn't oozing tradition like Bemidji, St. Paul or most clubs across the Midwest. Nonetheless, I realized that someone had strung together some very impressive years while curling out of that small southwestern Minnesota prairie town.

I turned my attention to the individual names on the first banner. *Lead Sam Thames*; *Second Bud Leach*; *Third Harry Simms*; *Skip...* Suddenly the room wobbled beneath my feet. My jaw dropped as I drew a deep breath. I stared upward, confirming and then reconfirming one of the names. I read the next banner. There it was again. And again on the next. And the next. My eyes darted between the banners several times. Screaming down to me was one name that wouldn't let go of its grip. It couldn't be. But it must be. *Skip Arv Firpo.* The coincidence was too mind-boggling and improbable. The combination of the names *Arv* and *Firpo* could only be a nickname used by my father. But how could it be? He had been dead since early 2002 — more than a year before any of the championships listed on the banners hung overhead.

Michigan Rink - Gold	**Minnesota Rink - Silver**
Lead: Jim Coventry	Lead: Paul Stenner
Second: Dale Harder	Second: John Mistovich
Third: Steve Talbert	Third: Mickey Bellows
Skip: Norm Thunger	**Skip: Freddy Schade**

Second End

The second end proved to be a reversal of fortune for Michigan. Minnesota's Skip Freddy Schade hit a beautiful double take-out with the hammer after Michigan players failed to protect the middle. Freddy let out a loud whoop from center ice as he watched his shot clear two of Michigan's wanna-be's off the four-foot circle. When the mixed assortment of caroms, ricochets and spin-offs came to their final rest, three of Minnesota's silver-handled rocks found themselves frozen securely nearest the center, leapfrogging the team to a 3-1 lead.

"That'll teach you sons-of-bitches," Freddy yelled, while pointing at Michigan Skip Norm Thunger, with an index finger protruding from a heavily bandaged left hand. Mike Bellows quickly leaned forward with his room and pushed Schade's arm downward with a rough jerk.

"Come on, Freddy," Bellows said quietly, "Keep your comments to yourself. They're here to win, too."

Schade pointed toward the scoreboard, with a number one hung next to Thunger's name.

"You can have your god-damned single," Schade continued yelling. "We just hung a triple on ya." Boos and catcalls began pouring down from the stands the second they hung the points on the scoreboard. Freddy Schade was stirring up the crowd. Officials from the American Curling Union overseeing the championships didn't like his antics anymore than the crowd did. But they also knew that getting people to pay attention to the game on the ice would take people's minds off the events of the previous evening.

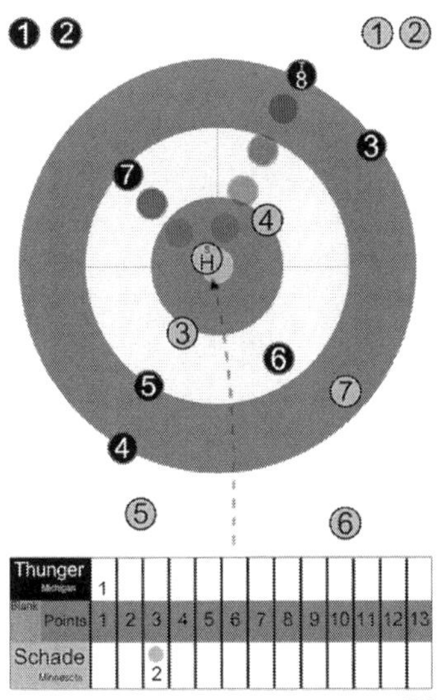

Saturday Evening, December 29th, 2007

When I regained awareness of my surroundings, I realized it was well-after seven o'clock, so I rushed back to the bar to collect Jeb. I was not surprised to find him nursing his fourth longneck. I paid the bill and ushered him to my car.

On the return trip to the farmhouse, a thousand questions and doubts raced through my head. Get a grip, I thought. *Arv* wasn't necessarily short for *Arvil*, and there could be a million people with that name in America. *Firpo*, however, was more problematic. The Mankato area was a part of Minnesota that had been settled by a large northern European immigrant population with names like Nordskog, Jensen, Schmidt and Schneider. Southern Minnesota even had a large group of Irish settlers. Okay, so a transplant moved in from another part of the country. It might be *possible* to find a sir-name like Firpo, but highly unlikely. But it was the *combination* of the first and last name that my skeptical mind just wasn't ready to accept.

"Say, Jeb," I started cautiously, "Do you get the local newspaper? I heard there's an article in today's edition that I'd like to read. I think the story is something about a curler named Firpo."

"Firpo?" he repeated. "Yeah, we get the daily paper, Monday through Saturday. I've got the paper at the house. I'll dig it out for you."

Jeb suddenly wrapped his stomach in his arms and doubled over, as if trying to stifle a puke. The subzero wind chill made the thought of rolling down the window unbearable but I saw no other choice. I pushed the passenger window button on my door handle and the immediate blast of cold air shook him upright. His cramps apparently let up a bit and he continued.

"Some guy named Firpo used to curl at the local clubs around here. He made the news a lot and then disappeared several years ago. Why?"

"Well, it's just that I heard about him earlier today." I said, "Then I saw his name on some banners hung in the curling club."

"He's got his name hung up at the Mankato club, too," Jeb said. "That was before my time. Hell, I think he's a national champion or something."

I suddenly found myself fully intrigued.

"With a name like Arv Firpo?" I asked, watching Jeb search his door grip for a way to roll up his window.

I pushed the auto button on my control panel and turned up the heat another notch.

"Hell, I don't know. Is that his first name? Arv? I'll check next time I'm at the club."

"The banners dated back a few years, to '03 and '04, I think. Does he still curl in Mapleton?" I asked.

"Could be. He just kind of disappeared. Like I said, it was before Bussy and I started curling. So you saw his name on some banners? What's the big deal about him? Is he a relative?"

"Na. But I guess I'm still a little interested in curling," I lied. "On our way down here this afternoon, a man at a gas station said something about a news article in today's local paper. I'd like to read it, that's all."

"Ok, but I feel like crap. Help me remember to pull it out of the trash tomorrow morning," he said, as he quickly cupped both hands over his mouth. I had the feeling he wasn't going to make it seven more miles back to the house. I dropped the conversation and pushed hard on the accelerator.

As we swung into the driveway, I could see LaVon and Bussy's silhouettes engaged in conversation on an upstairs bedroom window shade. The lights on the lower level of the house were all turned off, including the Christmas decorations out front. Toward the backyard, though, I could see a dim glow spread across the snow behind the garage shed. Jeb caught me looking toward it, wondering.

"T parks his new SUV back there." he said. "He probably wasn't too sick to run out to buy another pack of smokes. The dome lights in those newer models stay on for a few minutes after you park."

Jeb quickly jumped out of the car, ran a few feet out into the snow and heaved the contents of his stomach several feet into the yard. "I'll be fine now," he added.

Inside the warm living room, we found our wives descending the staircase, wearing their party dresses and bejeweled finery. Bussy was in red; LaVon in a shiny slate grey, with three crystal buttons the size of quarters fastening the front of her jacket. I couldn't recall her ever wearing it and certainly didn't remember when she bought it. The two women wore similar strappy black open-toed shoes with glistening rhinestones running the vertical length of their impractical high heels. When I explained that the trip would be several miles across town to the MSU campus, everyone agreed to ride in our warm car, if for no other reason than to keep the girls' feet warm.

To start a conversation, I relayed what I had seen in the Mapleton Curling Club, including the coincidence about my father's name and Arv Firpo. I was disappointed that nobody mustered more sincere astonishment. My story only led to the inevitable college anecdotes about bowling alleys, pool halls and bar rooms.

LaVon glanced at me from the passenger seat and said dryly, "What is it you always say, Jack? The first liar doesn't stand a chance."

Throughout the dance, LaVon and I sat quietly, distracted by our own thoughts. She wandered off on several occasions to talk with a familiar classmate, but just as quickly returned to our table to hunker down behind her scotch and soda. Occasionally, I found myself alone with Jeb as our wives jumped up to catch up with an old friend who happened by. We made a game of reading their lips as they used us as visual aids to explain what had become of their lives.

It was obvious to everyone that I was not interested in being there, but my distraction had nothing to do with unfamiliar surroundings. I couldn't escape thinking about the events of the day. When my mother died, I was the last man standing from either side of my extended family. It had been several years since I had last given my father a second thought. I once had a brief interest in searching for his gravesite but had only a vague idea of where to start. An afternoon on the Internet came up with nothing. I recalled that his car accident occurred somewhere near his hometown in western Minnesota. Even if my mother had still been alive to point me in one direction or another, I doubted whether she could have been much help. It was anybody's guess who might have made final arrangements to bury him. I finally speculated that he had probably met another woman who took care of everything, then disappeared back into her private world.

So many years had already passed since his death and I had rarely thought of him across that wide span of time. Suddenly, walking into that cinder block curling club in that little farm town was bringing back a rush of memories. Not complete, vivid memories; more like a dim mist hovering gently above a room. It was annoying that I could neither reconstruct him nor erase him from my mind. It was impossible to touch what I was trying to understand. It was impossible to understand what I was trying to touch.

I pulled the slip of paper from my wallet and stared at it again. *Arv — February 23 — Ø.* It seemed strange reading his name, *Arv.* It was certainly one of the rare times I had ever seen it in print. Our family mail was always addressed to Tommy. But there it was — Arv, along with his date of birth. It still made no sense. Was there some connection between that envelope and his birthday? There had to be. But LKA? Last Known Address? The envelope was addressed to DuMot. Was it intended for me, my mother or for Dad? If it was meant for him, why had it been addressed to a house he never lived in? And nearly six years after his death? And what did the — *zero* refer to at the tail end? I let my mind zip through the logic. I couldn't measure or calculate any of it, but I intended to. Because I needed to.

I was caught off guard when LaVon whispered that she wanted to leave the dance early and head back to Bussy's. I was happy to oblige. I chalked up her discomfort to the rush of bad memories from the banquet hall earlier in the evening. We spoke to Bussy and Jeb about leaving but neither seemed inclined to end their evening so early. By then, Bussy was having too much fun dancing with old friends. Jeb was having too much hair-of-the-dog. He seemed to have warmed to me somewhat, though, and even urged me to drop '*the old lady*' back at their house, then return to the dance. After a few brief objections, he finally tossed me his house key and told us to leave the front door unlocked. He and *The Bus* would catch a free ride home from one of his cabbie friends.

The drive back to the farm house was spent in silence until LaVon finally dropped a bombshell.

"Jack, instead of driving back home tomorrow afternoon, like we planned, would you mind if I stayed down here with Bussy over the long weekend?"

"No. I don't see why not," I answered. "I can come back down here early Monday afternoon to pick you up, so we're back in time for New Year's Eve."

"No, not Monday," she said. "Plan for sometime on Tuesday, New Years Day. I'd like to spend New Year's Eve with Bussy again, like we used to in college. You and I never go out to party, anyway. Buss and Jeb don't have any family in the area, either. I think it would be nice to spend the whole long weekend with them. I'm sure they wouldn't object to you staying, too — if you want — but I think you'd probably rather have some quiet days to yourself, to work on your job-hunt."

"Well," I countered, "You're right. I really don't want to stay down here with them. No, I don't mind if you stay. I'd like to come back down around noon on Tuesday and spend a couple of hours, though. I don't want to turn right around to head back home."

"We'll see," she said. "I'll call you sometime on Tuesday and let you know how things look. If it gets too late in the afternoon, I'm sure she'll be willing to drive me back up to the cities."

From our guest bedroom upstairs, I heard Bussy and Jeb return from the dance sometime around one a.m. I finally drifted off to sleep about thirty minutes later, but arose before anyone else was awake.

Sunday Morning, December 30th, 2007

I was surprised when Jeb came down at eight-thirty, followed by Tony a few minutes later. Over a pot of weak coffee, the three of us sat awkwardly at the table, mumbling occasional half-sentences and monosyllabic noises about the previous evening. Tony still appeared to be a bit pale, only occasionally glancing upward toward the light. Jeb complained that the dance lacked the energy he was expecting. It was his first sorority dance, and he was anticipating great things, from what he had heard. First, he got too bored with the music; then too drunk to notice.

The Sunday paper suddenly thumped against the side door and startled the three of us into activity.

"If that's the newspaper, I want the sports section," Tony said. "I ended up staying in bed all evening. I want to see how the hockey game finished up."

I reminded Jeb about digging out the previous day's edition of the local Mankato Herald, admitting that my curiosity about Arv Firpo had kept me awake a good deal of the night. He handed me a stack of paper from an old corrugated box under their kitchen sink and added, "Knock yourself out."

I flipped through the sections until I found what I was searching for.

Area Curlers Headed for Nationals

Duluth. The Arvil Firpo rink, including two members with ties to Mankato's Caledonia Curling Club, will once again be heading to the National Championships, February 16th - 23rd in Hibbing.

The Minnesota regional championship game was one for the ages. The Chris Johnston rink out of Grand Rapids, playing blue handles, had taken the lead by one point after the ninth end, leaving the Firpo rink with the critical last shot for the final end. The two rinks played well throughout the tenth end, trading exceptional shots. Johnston appeared to have the match wrapped up when his final shot raised one of his rink's rocks onto the back edge of the button, leaving the front of the house well-guarded. Playing the yellow handles, Firpo slipped his final #8 rock (*the hammer*) between two guards and successfully bumped Johnston's counter off the button and over the end line, out of play. Firpo's shot stopped almost dead center, giving his rink a point and an apparently tying the game, requiring an extra end.

As Johnston's players started clearing their rocks, however, Firpo's Vice Skip Gusty Steinham (Mankato's Caledonia Curling Club) suddenly called for a measurement between two opposing rocks, each touching the edge of the four-foot ring. After a lengthy tense delay to measure, judges determined that the Firpo rink's yellow rock #5 was, indeed, closer than the blue rock by less than a quarter inch. The Firpo rink was awarded the additional point, making it two points for the tenth end and giving them the game and the regional championship.

The Johnston rink initially protested, arguing that players had already begun moving the rocks, which would have invalidated the request for measurement. After a lengthy video review, it was determined that only players from the Johnston rink actually moved one or two of their own rocks, none of which were involved in the measurement.

Afterward, Johnston was disappointed, as it would have been his third trip to Nationals. "When I realized that we gave them an inch to slide the rock through the front guards, I knew he wouldn't miss," Johnston said. "I've been curling against Tommy for the past eight or nine years. He's the only player I've ever seen who could have made exactly that shot, exactly when he needed to make it. I wish him all the best up at Hibbing in mid-February."

'Tommy' has long been Arv Firpo's nickname among his closest friends. He curled for three years out of the Caledonia Club in Mankato before moving to the Mapleton Curling Club for several seasons between 2003 and 2005. Although he typically curls in several bonspiels throughout Minnesota and the Midwest every season, he no longer registers for national events under any club affiliation.

This will be Firpo's third trip leading a Minnesota rink to the Nationals. Other members of the Minnesota rink include Lead Kent Marquis (Bemidji), Second John Paulheim (Bemidji), and Third Gusty Steinham, from Mankato's Caledonia Club.

I read the individual lines in the article more carefully. *I've been curling against Tommy for the past eight or nine years...'Tommy' has long been Arv Firpo's nickname among his closest friends*? Impossible, I thought. It couldn't be. But there it was.

When everyone was awake and downstairs for breakfast, I read the article excitedly and tried to sell them on the colossal coincidence between Arv Firpo and my father, Tommy. Bussy, Jeb and Tony laughed it off. LaVon considered it more judiciously and took a moment to re-read the news article for herself.

"I see your point, Jack," she said, "but your father is dead. What you're suggesting just doesn't happen in the real world."

"No, you're right," I had to agree. "It doesn't....but still."

"When ten people tell you you're drunk, lie down," Jeb added.

I knew I wouldn't be able to sit still all day with so many questions rattling around inside my head. The thought of drinking beer and watching meaningless football games all afternoon wasn't something I could tolerate. My first thought was to immediately jump on Bussy's computer and search for Arv Firpo or Tommy Firpo or every other possible variation. My request drew a hearty chuckle from the group. *"Yeah, right, as if we spend perfectly good beer money on something as useless as a home computer and the Internet."* I then scoured the StarTribune sports section to see whether there might be some expanded articles about the regional curling finals, but found nothing. My last option was to ask about using the Internet service at the public library. I was quickly reminded that it was early Sunday morning. After another half-hour of watching me pace and fidget, Jeb suggested that one of the local cyber cafés near campus might be open. From there, I might as well drive back to Minneapolis for the remainder of the weekend.

"You certainly ain't going to be any fun staying here with us."

I threw my few extra clothes into a paper sack and insincerely thanked everyone for a great time. After a quick peck on the cheek, I told LaVon I would drive back down to pick her up mid-afternoon on New Year's Day. With a half-hearted wave, I ground my ice-cold car to a start and headed down the road to find the coffee shop Bussy found listed in the local yellow pages. I had no idea where I was heading, except that Tony said it was *"on the northeast corner of the campus — near the BP station."*

"For someone who's new in town, you certainly know your way around," I joked nervously, as we shook hands goodbye.

As I pulled into a parking spot, I was relieved to find the manager unlocking the doors of the CyberCup Café. Inside, I immediately fired up one of the public PCs lining a low shelf against the back wall. Despite a slow connection speed, I survived the interminable wait for the Windows screen to surface and the Netscape icon to appear. A quick click and a handful of keystrokes later and I was transported to my personalized Google home page, where I started with specific searches for articles and images.

Arv and Arvil Firpo brought up several old articles and references to curling playdowns, including the online version of the Herald news article. The name *Tommy Firpo* returned additional entries from the league tables at various curling clubs throughout Minnesota, but most were several years old.

After several long-tail searches chasing down links buried deep within other sites, I found a few additional references to championship teams and individual awards dating back nearly ten years. I found interviews and some video of curling shots, as well as a handful of photos taken from behind the glass or the upper reaches of an arena, but no close-ups that would prove that Arv Firpo was, in fact, Tommy DuMot. Although I hadn't seen him for a dozen years, I had a good idea of what I was looking for. The few photos I found were long-distance shots of a stocky, muscular man with a narrow face and thinning gray hair, which might have been him, but nothing conclusive.

I spent the next two hours reading all the content I could find. I also jotted down the names and addresses of the various printed publications containing relevant articles. Many of the sites included nothing more than the registered rink name for a particular bonspiel. Typically, the registration listed only **Firpo Rink** and seldom listed the other players. This was typical of the sport. All members of the team play an important role, but the curling world only recognizes the Skip.

It was past one o'clock when I flipped my fingers through my thin stack of printouts and handwritten notes. Altogether, I had just six names to check out, along with a few addresses to follow up on and two full-length articles to read. It wasn't much to go on for my efforts, but it was enough to start digging deeper. What I couldn't make sense of, though, was why any of this suddenly mattered so much. I took one last look at a photo posted on one of the sites. Something was animating me in a way I had never experienced. What was I setting myself up to discover?

I considered driving straight back to Minneapolis but realized I would never be closer to my father's home town of Gluek — a speck on the map about seventy miles further to the northwest. I could spend the night in the area and visit the Chippewa County Courthouse on Monday, where Dad's death certificate would settle everything.

Sunday Afternoon, December 30th, 2007

The little town of Gluek turned out to be a few miles further north along bumpy, icy country roads than it appeared on my road atlas. The trip took on an added dimension when I stopped for a quick lunch at a New Ulm Burger King, then drove around town for an extra twenty minutes. This was where LaVon and I had spent our honeymoon weekend following our outdoor wedding in Mankato.

New Ulm is a nice Midwestern river town, surrounded by hills and farm fields. Its skyline is dominated by old-world church spires and brick buildings with neoclassical architectural details. Originally, German immigrants settled the town and it quickly became famous for two Midwestern hallmarks: Schell's Beer and an amateur town baseball club that has produced a handful of major league players. Along with the brewery, the town's most visited landmark is an odd memorial known locally as Hermann the German, a thirty-two foot statue of Arminius, a first century Germanic chieftain. Exactly why city fathers considered old Hermann's feats against the Romans particularly relevant to a city on the Minnesota prairie isn't explained in the visitor guides. Nonetheless, he now stands as the official symbol of stoicism and steadfastness for all German-Americans.

As a honeymoon destination, New Ulm isn't Niagara Falls or a Caribbean resort, but it turned out to be a great little getaway for us. I found myself most excited about the sex and the town's remnants of northern European culture. Despite being somewhat of a busman's holiday for LaVon, she honestly seemed to enjoy our three-day stay and found several hours every day to shop and sightsee on her own, while I slept off our late nights.

It was nearly three o'clock when I finally passed through Granite Falls and read the sign entering Chippewa County. By the time I found Gluek, the early evening darkness was already beginning to win its battle with the short Minnesota winter day. The single main street was already deserted; whether because it was late Sunday afternoon or forever, I couldn't tell. I was in luck to find a small gas station diner still open for the evening. I ordered a cola and asked the lady behind the counter a few questions.

"No, I'm afraid I'm kind of new around here. I've never heard of the family name DuMot. Check the records at the courthouse in Montevideo. It's New Year's Eve Day tomorrow but they'll be open. My husband works in the water department. He has to go in."

As I headed back to the highway, I took another look around the deserted little town. From the looks of what remained of it, I doubted whether I would learn anything more by returning the next morning. It appeared the area hadn't been part of James J. Hill's ambitions as he grew his railroad empire westward out of St. Paul. Early prairie communities like Gluek either thrived or died depending upon the lay of the political landscape determining the route of the new railroad tracks. Barons often owned entire towns along the rail lines, but Gluek clearly wasn't one of them. The grain elevator silhouetted against the dusk sky was the only thing still keeping the town alive. I gave the main street a life-expectancy of perhaps twenty more years. It was no wonder my father left at eighteen years old and never looked back.

Monday Morning, December 31st, 2007

The quiet pace at the Chippewa County Court House reminded me that it was New Year's Eve day. It wasn't an official holiday but it was close enough. Only a skeleton staff was on hand to go through the municipal affairs of state. When I tried to explain myself to a secretary temporarily assigned from the water department, I received little more than a blank look. Eventually, the young lady called another clerk, who proffered only vague hope. When I persisted by explaining how far I had driven, she escorted me to a computer near some file cabinets marked *birth and death certificates*. After a few false starts she pulled up everything in the alphabet range of A—E and we looked through the Ds together for *DuMot, Arvil*.

When we came across a handful of birth certificates for DuMot, she stopped scrolling the file names. At the bottom of the group she clicked on a name and magnified the screen. *DuMot, Arvil, Peter, Granite Falls Municipal Hospital*, born to father Peter and mother Medora. Attending physician: Dr. Philip Osterhuis.

"That's him," I said, with noticeable excitement in my voice.

"OK, so much for proving he was alive," I said. "Now, where do we look to learn more about his *death*?"

We searched the e-file of death certificates and quickly found the list of DuMot names again. The pdf of my dad's certificate came up with a large **COPY** stamped across the top margin.

"It was a long-shot that his fatal accident occurred in Chippewa County, too" she said. "Otherwise, we wouldn't have it on file here."

There on the screen in front of me was proof-positive that whatever wild fantasy I may have been entertaining in my heart had all come to nothing in my head. LaVon was right. People just don't resurrect themselves after half a dozen years in the tomb. *"Three days, maybe,"* she had laughed. *"but not six years."* I had to accept it. My dad was morally, ethically, spiritually, physically, absolutely, positively, undeniably and most reliably dead.

I squinted to read what I could of the small, scribbled handwriting on the screen.

Cause of Death: *Severe subdural hematoma resulting from blunt force trauma in a single-car rollover accident. Pronounced dead at scene.*

Date of Death: *February 10, 2002*

Place of Death: *Montevideo, Chippewa County, MN*

The last line of the certificate included space for the county coroner's signature and printed name: *Dr. Mark O'Brian.*

The name, the date, the car accident — everything I had never known about him was right there in black and white. Well, nearly everything. I recalled my mother reading the original news article over the phone. We discussed the coincidence that the accident occurred on my birthday but the story didn't list specific details about how the rollover happened. She guessed that his neck may have been broken as his car rolled over. Now at least, I knew. Based on the coroner's brief description, I speculated that he had cracked his head against the interior of the car with sufficient force to kill him instantly. At least, I wanted to believe it killed him instantly.

I pushed my luck and asked whether the county kept burial or cremation records. She escorted me to another room and pulled out an old microfiche. The language was a bit cryptic but I eventually learned that his gravesite could be found at Holy Savior Lutheran Church in Maynard, only fifteen miles further southeast. I was in luck. I could pop into Maynard to check out the church cemetery and get back on the road toward home in a matter of an hour or so.

Maynard turned out to be a town only slightly larger than Gluek, but hanging on tenuously by a railroad spur line that still serviced the community's grain elevator and lumber yard. Holy Savior, sitting on the southern edge of the town, was one of three churches still serving the dwindling population. Its cemetery spilled out a side door and ran about forty yards down a hillside toward a broad sweep of open pastureland. A quick visual census of the headstones told me there were more dead people in town, than alive.

The main road fronted the church property with open farm fields and pastures neatly framing the entire three-acre package. The peeled, gray rectory on the north side of the church had been long-since abandoned by generations of preachers' families. A poorly plowed parking lot replaced the front lawn and only a few trees still remained from the original apple orchard; planted to supplement the preacher's pay in the early days of the congregation. It was clear that some old homesteader had donated this narrow patch of unneeded land to the Missouri Synod, in trade for eternal salvation. Even in the bleakness of winter, the scene was idyllic.

There were, perhaps, two hundred headstones in the yard; a few dating nearly as far back as the 1894 date carved into a church's large cornerstone. I began picking through the grave markers, which began beneath the low branches of a tall, undisciplined spruce tree growing too close to one corner of the building. By the time I reached the end of the first row of twenty markers, my toes ached with cold and my leg muscles burned from lifting them through the deep snow.

As I continued down the rows, the German, Swedish, Slovakian or Norwegian names rolled silently through my head one after another. I wondered how schoolteachers could have possibly kept peace among the mixture of cultures thrown together in their wooden, one-room schoolhouses and out in the playground at the end of the day. On many of the stones I found the German phrase *Ruhig im Frieden* and searched my memory for German vocabulary as I tried to translate the accompanying Bible verse. Every one of these names had a story to tell, I realized, but the people lived their lives in obscurity and anonymity. Only a handful of their neighbors and close family members could possibly relate to sharing their frustrations, fears and dreams. Welcome to my world, I thought.

Too often, I paused over the marker of a baby or toddler and surprised myself by wondering about the indescribable anguish the parents and grandparents must have felt as they buried their child that day. I thought of my own brush with being a parent in 2005, when LaVon casually looked up from her TV dinner and announced, *"I was pregnant."* I tried to respond, but found myself at a complete loss. I stammered helplessly for a second before realizing that she had spoken in the past tense. I *was* pregnant, not I *am* pregnant. She quietly took her plate to the kitchen sink, poured herself a glass of wine and went up to bed. I never even lifted my head from my pizza to look into her eyes that evening. No further discussion of it ever seemed necessary.

"Who are you looking for?" I suddenly heard a loud voice from the top of the hill, startling me with a jump and quick jerk of my head.

"Oh, um, DuMot," I yelled back toward the voice. "Last name DuMot."

"Oh, Yeah?" he said, drawing near. "After all this time? I'm Ed Knoblechner, head of the elders and the only active member of the building and grounds committee."

"Are you working today?" I asked. "Is the pastor around?"

"Yes and no. I fix the roof in the spring, mow the lawn in the summer, rake leaves in the fall and shovel snow in the winter. The pastor lives in Granite Falls and rides the circuit between a few churches around here most Sundays. About all that's left for him to do in this town is to marry 'em and bury 'em, though. You'll find a few DuMot markers a little further down the hill."

"A few markers? Were some of my dad's relatives buried here, too?" I thought to myself. I suddenly wished I had insisted on reading the files for the various DuMot names that popped up on the courthouse computer, but the clerk clearly hadn't been interested in allowing me to linger.

Down the hill, in the furthest corner of the yard, Knoblechner pointed out what I was looking for. Partially hidden by three overgrown scruffy pine bushes, I found two large marble stones standing about ten feet apart. Between them was a low horizontal granite block, clearly of a more recent date, topped by about six inches of fresh snow. The larger stones displayed the names of my grandparents, Peter and Medora, including the dates of their deaths, 1969 and 1971, respectively. Even this little chiseled bit of information was more than I had ever known about them. My dad rarely talked about his family and I had always figured it was because they died several years before I was born, so it just didn't matter.

I immediately assumed that the smaller gravestone between my grandparents' plots was that of my father. As I cleared off the snow, though, I found that it had no inscription; only a shallow empty recess designed to hold a missing metal plaque. It was possible the nameplate had become detached but it seemed more likely that it had never been attached in the first place. Whoever handled the details of his death probably didn't think it mattered much. I could understand that. He's gone now, so move on. It scared and saddened me a little to think that some stranger watched as his casket was lowered into the ground, then simply turned to walk back up the hill, got into a car and drove away forever. We all deserve more than that, I thought.

I scratched around in the snow in dim hopes of finding some remnant of dead flowers or other memento of a recent gravesite visit. I knew I was really hoping to find evidence that my mother had learned of the cemetery and had long-ago paid a visit; but nothing turned up.

"Trying to find out more about some ancestors?" old Knoblechner's voice suddenly broke the silence. "I remember the

DuMots' funerals. Lots of people around here do."

"Well, I'm only interested in one gravestone," I said. "I never knew about this cemetery. What was so special about the funerals that people still remember them after all these years?"

"Look at their stones again," he said. "What do you notice?"

I read each of my grandparents' names on the large stones again, checking for spelling mistakes or some grammatical error in a pithy Bible quote. Nothing unusual jumped out at me. The names were certainly spelled correctly. Even if they had been misspelled, I thought, it wouldn't have been enough to become the stuff of local legend, even in a small town like Maynard. Only after I looked more closely at the dates of their births and deaths did I understand what Knoblechner wanted me to see. I'm not sure how I missed it on my first read-through.

"They each died exactly on their birthdays!" I said incredulously. "Both of them?"

"There's more," he said. "Look again and do the math."

I studied the dates for a few seconds more.

"My God! They both died exactly on their fifty-sixth birthday, but two years apart. Was it some kind of weird suicide pact?" I asked.

"Could have been, I suppose," he said. "But not likely. They both died in accidents." Knoblechner went on to explain that somehow the farm tractor rolled over Peter. He got himself pretty mangled up. The police and coroner determined that the tractor must have jerked forward on him as he was checking the engine. But many people doubted that it was an accident.

"And you, Mr. Knoblechner?" I asked. "What do you think?"

"If you ask me, a mistake like that just doesn't happen to a man who had been farming all his life."

"And my grandmother?" I continued, nodding at her stone.

"Medora tried to hold onto the farm for a little while but couldn't afford the help she needed to keep it going. She sold it and moved into town to run a little dress alterations business for farmers' wives and local clothing stores throughout the area. There were still some of those main street shops around in the early seventies. One day, one of the storeowners swung by to drop off some dresses that needed hemming. When Medora didn't answer her door, he went around back and found her dead with a broken neck and a garden pitchfork through her chest. There was a broom up on the porch roof, so it appeared she fell off when she got too close to the edge while sweeping out the gutters."

"It appeared she fell? But you don't think so?"

"An accident? Landing on a hay fork? Who sets a pitchfork on the ground with its tines facing upward like that?"

"Suicide?"

"From ten feet off the ground? People who commit suicide tend to want their bodies discovered right away. The coroner said she had been dead about two days before the man discovered her. If it was suicide, it seems she would have jumped off the roof in the front yard, not out back where she knew her body would be eaten by coyotes, foxes and crows. There was no way of telling whether she died of the broken neck or the fork through her heart."

"But this is an impossible coincidence," I said.

"Yep," the old guy said. "That's precisely what a lot of people said — an impossible coincidence. In fact, a lot of people still say it. That's why so many locals still talk about those funerals nearly forty years later."

'And my dad's funeral?" I asked. "Anything special about his?"

"Couldn't say, young man," he said, turning to lead me back up the hill. "I wasn't around for it. Seems like nobody was. The fresh grave and headstone just showed up there one day."

There is no place on earth colder than a windswept Minnesota graveyard in the dead of winter. Knoblechner and I were both shivering as we picked our way through the grave markers, taking the most direct route possible back toward the top of the hill. Along the way, we discussed a few more details about my grandparents' deaths. He recalled that a neighboring businessman ended up purchasing my grandmother's house in town sometime during the late '70s, but tore it down to expand a commercial building. There wasn't anything left of the house or lot.

In the parking lot, I thanked him and affirmed that I would return in the spring to check out the DuMot farm. I would also bring along a new nameplate to attach to my dad's grave.

"He always went by the name Tommy, so that's what I'll put on the marker," I said casually. "Then all the locals will remember him."

Squinting and shading his eyes from the bright sun reflecting off the bright snow, Knoblechner turned and looked once again down the hill toward my family's plots. He turned back to face me and paused for a few seconds before speaking again.

"Who did you say your father was again?" he asked.

"Tommy. Tommy DuMot," I said. "I just think it will be more appropriate to use his familiar nickname on his headstone — so everyone around here will recognize it."

"So Tommy was your old man?" he repeated. "Go figure."

Michigan Rink - Gold	**Minnesota Rink - Silver**
Lead: Jim Coventry	Lead: Paul Stenner
Second: Dale Harder	Second: John Mistovich
Third: Steve Talbert	Third: Mickey Bellows
Skip: Norm Thunger	**Skip: Freddy Schade**

Third End

Ordinarily, getting the hammer back for the third end should have given Michigan a big advantage, but that's why there are four players on each rink. Every player and every rock makes a difference. Occasionally, even at the highest levels of curling, the rocks simply don't stay where you want to put them. The Skip with the final shot isn't always left with an opportunity to make it count.

As Michigan Skip, Norm Thunger, knew all too well, using the last rock to minimize damage — rather than score a point — is sometimes the best you can do. As he squared his shoulders in the hack and stared at the opposite end of the ice, he knew he had virtually no chance of breaking through with a clear shot to the center.

After two misses trying to clear out the middle by Third Steve Talbert, Thunger was left staring at lost opportunity. There was simply no safe way to get past the logjam of rocks clogging the front of the house. His only real chance to salvage anything, he thought, was to raise a teammate's rock forward. He had two choices: risk a long raise of his rink's #3 rock parked eight or more feet in front of the house; or play a safer forty-five degree clip of Michigan's #5 on the left outer edge of the eight-foot circle, hoping to push it lightly to a stop near the button. Tough, yes, but certainly possible. The correct angle, sweeping, speed and curl must all conspire to complete a perfect shot.

As he followed the rock out of the hack, his line of trajectory felt true, as did his body's form and speed. As the right-handed Thunger released the handle with an in-turn a decimal point before crossing the blue foul line, he urged it forward with a gentle turn in a counter-clockwise direction, pressing gently with his fingertips, as if stroking a baby's cheek. As the rock moved forward, Thunger continued his slide, remaining in his familiar low-tuck position, tracking his shot like a bloodhound on a fresh scent. As he hovered low over the ice, he could sense the cold, icy air reaching up to tickle his chin and nose just inches above the surface. As his momentum carried him forward, he barked and howled directions to his teammates out front. By the time sweepers Jim Coventry and Dale Harder had reached the distant hog line ahead of the rock, the Michigan rink knew that the critical fourth calculation — the curl — was failing them.

They had started sweeping too early, keeping the rock's momentum ahead of its curl bite. Now, as it began its deceleration, the shot wasn't turning as much as calculated. There wasn't anything anyone could do except watch it slide harmlessly past the target rock, missing to the left by a full two inches; finishing out of the money. Minnesota won two points with their #3 and #5 rocks; heading into the fourth end with a large 5-1 lead.

"Well, I got angle and speed right," he said quietly, "but that shot should have moved another two or three inches to the right to catch our #5. The ice is changing too quickly. We learned something from it, now let's not give away what we know. Schade may not have noticed and he's not the type to listen to any of his players. We get the hammer back for the fourth end, so we'll probably pull a point or two out of it. We'll try to use what we know to steal something back later in the game."

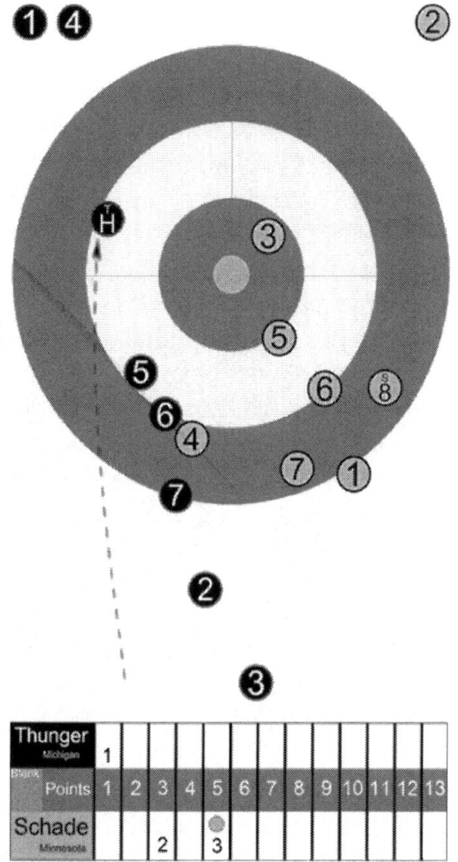

Monday Evening, December 31st, 2007

With delays for blinding wind, icy roads and a quick truck stop meal, my one hundred twenty-five mile drive from my father's gravesite to Minneapolis took nearly five hours. I was over-tired as I plowed my car through the fresh-fallen snow in my back alley driveway. When my wheels began to spin uselessly, I shoved the gear lever into park and left the engine running for another minute. I had long-ago given up bothering to pull into the undersized garage stall.

Sitting slumped against the steering wheel, with the fan lightly blowing warm air into my face, I took the opportunity to make a mental checklist. First, I would spend more time on the Internet, checking and crosschecking the small bits of information I had gathered at the coffee shop. Then, I would make some contacts from the names and addresses I uncovered. I also wanted to learn more about the curler, Arv Firpo. One of my first calls would have to be to the United States Curling Association. I reasoned that it just couldn't be possible for a man to gain such notoriety among curling fans while remaining invisible to the rest of the world.

My questions had the nagging persistence of a horsefly. At some level, I knew I wouldn't settle this within myself until I met the man and talked to him in person. Somewhere, somehow, I would find his phone number, his hometown, or even his e-mail address. I would contact him to arrange a personal meeting. After more than a decade of never giving my father a second thought, he was suddenly lighting up some unidentified dark corner of my life; like a dying ember stirred to life from beneath the cold coals.

After shaking myself awake ten minutes later, I switched off the ignition, locked my car and stumbled across the back walkway toward my kitchen door. As I kicked off my shoes in the warmth of our rear entryway, I realized how dead-tired I really was. Saturday's pile of mail remained sitting on the table, including the old blurred envelope I had recovered from beneath Cranston's shrub. We had forgotten to turn off the coffee pot, so I poured the last half-inch of the burnt sludge down the drain. On the corner of the kitchen counter, there were three new messages blinking on the answering machine; they could wait until morning. I flicked off the kitchen light and felt my way through the dark and dragged my bones upstairs to bed.

Tuesday, January 1st, 2008

By six o'clock the following morning I was in my usual place at our dinette table, coffee cup at my right elbow and my laptop fired up to see whether 2008 would start out better than 2007 ended.

After a quick peek at the BBC and Reuters news pages, I started the real work of looking further into the information in my thin stack of notes. For the remainder of the morning and into early afternoon I tracked down every possible search about Arv and/or Tommy Firpo. Unfortunately, I discovered that my research at the Mankato café proved to be more exhaustive than I initially hoped. There was very little new information to be found. Despite cross-referencing every word of my notes and following some interesting but unfruitful tangents, I ended up gathering only a handful of additional names and news clippings. I didn't hold out much hope that any of it would lead me anywhere. I came to the conclusion that the Internet was coming up www.useless.com.

Altogether, I uncovered the names of eleven of Firpo's current or former players, but little else. A quick search revealed their club affiliations but not their cities of residence. It wasn't necessarily a given that the men lived in the same town as the curling club, either. Maybe. But not necessarily. The Mankato Herald newspaper article was still my hottest lead. It included the names of the current rink members and their affiliated curling clubs. I hoped I could at least make some intelligent assumptions from that.

I checked every online directory source and even resorted to calling directory assistance to request the phone numbers of the people named in the article. It took more than an hour of dialing, waiting on hold and arguing with some operators, but I finally got the phone number for one of the men listed in the article. Get hold of him, I reasoned, and he'll help me find the others. Locating the men named on Firpo's prior teams dating back more than six or seven years, however, proved to be more of a challenge. Of the names of former players I had on my list, directory assistance was only able to help me locate the phone numbers for three. Not great, but not bad, either. In all, I had the names and last known phone numbers of four curlers who currently or formerly shared the national curling spotlight with Arv Firpo. It was a good bet that at least one of them maintained some kind of contact.

I argued with myself about whether to bother making the phone calls on New Year's Day. *"Nobody would be home,"* I thought to myself. *"Even if I reached someone, he certainly wouldn't want to be bothered by a complete stranger during a college football bowl game*." I put the phone down, then picked it up again; repeating the action several times before I got up the nerve. This didn't have to be tough, I thought. Keep it simple. I would introduce myself then tell the guy that I read the article in the Mankato Herald and that I'm interested in talking to him about his championship rink. If he pressed me, I would tell him I was doing research for an article about curling. If push came to shove, I could even promise to include his name in the article. All I wanted was information about Arv Firpo, damn it. It should never have to come to a discussion about my father. It should have been simple enough to get up the courage to make the phone calls; but it wasn't and I didn't know why. Was I afraid of not finding any answers? Or worse, getting answers I really didn't want to hear?

I finally stepped away from the phone and paced my living room floor to think things through. The entire episode was irrational and absurd to begin with. If I cared that much about it, all I really needed to do was to wait until mid-February and then drive four hours north to Hibbing to attend the national championship playdowns. The Arv Firpo on the ice would either be a total stranger — or my father.

Call it procrastination, but I settled my internal debate by googling the United States Curling Association and writing down the contact number of their headquarters in Stevens Point, Wisconsin. From the list of names on the page, I decided I would start with Director of National Playdown Events, Daniel Graber. But as I started punching my cell phone buttons, I remembered it was New Year's Day. It would have to wait until the next morning when their staff would be back in the office.

I stood and stretched my arms. With few breaks to empty my bladder and refill my coffee cup, I had been hunched over my keyboard for more than seven hours. In another hour, our living room would start losing the daylight that still filtered through the blinds. I checked my watch and began to wonder about LaVon's phone call. I had expected to hear from her by one or two o'clock. It was already past three. She would know I wouldn't love the idea of making the long trip down to Mankato only to turn right around to drive back home in the dark. I considered calling her cell phone or Bussy's house, but I knew that rushing her would only make for a longer, colder return trip. As I reached for the phone on our kitchen counter, I noticed the blinking red light on the base unit, reminding me that I had not yet checked the messages from the weekend.

The first two recorded calls were from LaVon's co-workers at the middle school. Both wished her a happy New Year. The second woman wanted to discuss *how things went down*. The third message was from LaVon, time stamped just a few minutes after I had left her at Bussy's on Sunday morning.

> **Jack, don't come down to Mankato to pick me up on New Year's. And don't call to ask why. Just go into the basement and look through your mother's boxes, in the pile by the furnace. You'll find everything down there that I want you to know. Over the past year, I've tried to talk to you, but we just aren't in a place where we listen to each other, anymore. Or I'm just not in a place where I'm ready to talk, maybe. So look in the basement. I guess we both need to get down to digging through our foundations.**

My heart pounded in my throat. What the hell did she mean, *"Jack, don't come down to pick me up?"* How was she going to get home? A ride from Bussy, maybe? LaVon was supposed to be back in the classroom teaching the next day. I replayed her message and quickly pressed the speed dial to call her cell phone. No answer, so I left a voice message. I called Bussy's home phone number but after a dozen rings, I knew she didn't intend to answer, either. I reverted to trying LaVon's phone again but didn't bother leaving a second message.

Our basement was an old storm cellar in the truest sense of the word. I doubted whether my mother had ever descended into that pit and LaVon and I dared to go down there only rarely. The narrow wooden steps inspired no confidence they could bear the weight of an adult. Some prior owner had replaced the original handrail with a rough two-by-two board; more apt to give the user slivers than support. The neglected concrete floor was cracked and uneven after years of standing water from rainstorms and snowmelt. The walls were rough sandstone blocks that retained large patches of their original whitewash from the 1920s. In the hot summer months, the smell of mildew pervaded everything. In the chill of winter, the air temperature rarely reached above sixty degrees, even with the converted oil furnace blazing.

Some years before, the light switch at the top of the stairs had been disconnected. A long piece of twine served as a pull cord, strung loosely to a ceiling fixture attached to the joists. Pulling on the cord was always a crapshoot. As I gave it a tug, I was relieved to see the dim light of a single sixty-watt bulb penetrating the space below me. At the bottom of the stairs, I saw that the shadows of the furnace and water heater fell across the pile of my mother's old belongings, making it difficult to search for whatever it was LaVon wanted me to find.

I was never sure what my mother had planned when she announced that she had purchased the old house. When I moved in, I found her furnishings and thirty-five years of accumulated junk piled and crowded everywhere throughout the first level. To make room for LaVon, I immediately moved most of the boxes and unused furnishings into the basement. After a few weeks of rising damp, though, I spent an additional Saturday afternoon laboriously hauling a large amount of it back up the narrow steps and packing it into my mother's small first-floor bedroom or out to the garage. What remained down in the basement was either too heavy to carry back up, or dismissed as useless. The various piles were all meant to be very temporary, of course, but we somehow never found the time to sort things out. More than five years later, old china, Tupperware and an odd assortment of boxes and small furnishings remained stacked against the wall near the water heater; covered with dust, spider webs and mouse turds. Nothing is as permanent as a temporary arrangement.

Standing near the warmth of the burning furnace, I surveyed the dimness surrounding me. An old electric washer and drier were pushed against a far wall, installed beneath two windows which had forever been covered with thick burlap sacks. Their gold color betrayed them to be relics from the 1970s, left there to die a lonely death by some previous owner. Soon after moving in, I tried using them once but the washer leaked and the dryer made a loud whining sound, as if screaming in pain and begging for mercy. From then on, LaVon and I used the laundromat just a few blocks down the street.

Several copper water pipes ran away from the central water heater, twisting in all directions and fixed strategically to bare joists just a foot above my head. In the corners, the pipes either pierced upward through the floorboards to reach the faucets upstairs, or they took right-angle turns and continued until they terminated somewhere among the jungle of tubing and conduits running everywhere overhead. Spider webs clung to every surface and filled every gap between the joists. The window ledges were covered with cobwebs crowded with dead spiders and egg balls, filtering the dim light sifting through the weeds filling the window wells outside.

I cleared off a thick layer of dust from the top of the pile of old belongings, causing two or three Teflon pans to drop onto the floor with a loud clang. The next stratum included an old green shower curtain covering a stack of five or six picture frames set on top of an old end table. I picked up the frames and rubbed the edges, recalling childhood years when they once stood neatly on various shelves throughout my family's New Brighton home. I held each one closer to the bare light bulb, to see the photos more clearly. Most were empty frames but one familiar picture was of a trio of teenage boys that included my father, taken on a road trip to Milwaukee. The three friends stood against the rear trunk of an old Ford Fairlane, parked near the entrance to the Miller Brewing Company. I suddenly realized that it was the only photo I had of Dad and I regretted that the boys each had their baseball caps pulled too low to reveal any details of their faces. I recalled that my parents displayed the photo for years on a shelf above our Motorola TV-stereo cabinet in our family room.

I set the picture frames carefully aside and shifted the pile to get at the next layer of DuMot civilization. As I shoved aside one of the tables, a grey metal box slid onto the floor and the lid sprang open with a dull thud. When handful of unfamiliar notes, cards and photographs spilled out across the floor, I sensed immediately that this was what LaVon wanted me to find. I gathered up the scattered paper and stuffed the stack back into the box, then pulled an old broken office chair directly under the light. I retracted a thin handful of papers, not knowing what to make of it all. By the layer of dust smothering the lid top and sides of the box I guessed it had been several months since it had been last opened. Whatever it was that I held in my hand, it wasn't anything LaVon had hidden away during the recent few days or weeks.

Within a few flips through my fingertips, though, her intentions for me finding the box started to come into focus. Not crystal clear focus yet — that would take another confused minute — but clear enough. In my hands was an assortment of birthday cards, Christmas cards and general *thinking of you cards* with all the syrupy Hallmark poetry you would expect.

"From me?" I said aloud, startling myself.

Not hardly. They were all signed with a several *X*s, a few *O*s and a few more *X*s on top of *O*s. Most had no signature but more than a few included the moniker *Tea Time* hand-scribbled across the bottom. There were no postmarked envelopes accompanying the cards, so it was impossible to determine how long ago LaVon had received them, or from whom. I wanted to believe they were from an old high school or college relationship but as I dug deeper, the evidence wasn't in my favor. It didn't take long to figure out that these cards were all fairly recent, certainly within the previous year or two. She was in the middle of an affair and this was her way of finally admitting it. But an affair with whom? A teacher at her school? A friend of a friend? Someone she met during her periodic memberships at health clubs?

Beneath the cards were several three-by-five inch color photos of various landscapes and landmarks, including one of her sitting on a Vespa scooter, wearing an oversized helmet and laughing like I had never seen her laugh. My heart sank as I flipped through the pictures. LaVon at a shopping center, smiling. LaVon sitting at a picnic table, giggling. LaVon gleefully toasting the camera with a beer and cigarette. There was no doubt she was never happier...and I wasn't anywhere to be found.

My heartbreak turned to anger, though, as I searched the pictures for clues. The evidence I finally found brought a lump to my throat. There, behind the Vespa, at the distant end of the picnic grounds was the unmistakable base of Hermann the German in New Ulm. When the hell was she in New Ulm other than with me? It had to have been taken while we were on our honeymoon. I looked at the other photos again. Suddenly the evidence was everywhere. Whoever *Tea Time* was, he was involved with her before our marriage and he had the balls to remain involved through our honeymoon and beyond.

I could find no dates on any of the correspondence. Our wedding was five years ago, I thought. Could she have been carrying on this affair right under my nose for that long? I opened up a few more of the e-mail printouts and handwritten letters. Most were pointless little reminders of how much he loved and missed her. Several conveyed enough information that I could begin piecing together some of the details between the lines. After dropping out of college at MSU, the man had returned to Grand Rapids, got his old high school girl friend pregnant and got married. He then apparently had a second kid two or three years later. He lost his job at the paper mill and couldn't find work, which added to the misery of being married to a woman he had grown to hate. If he could ever get through the divorce, though, LaVon would love being his kids' step-mother. It was an agonizing decision but he had to do it. He would leave his kids behind and only see them on weekends. He could move in with some friends and find work *"down near you."* The next year wouldn't be easy but being a little closer to her would be worth it.

I reread some of the letters as the jigsaw pieces began to fit together in my head. I looked at some of the cards again and read the name scribbled across the bottom: Tea Time. He was from the Iron Range. He has kids but he doesn't see them very often. Tea Time — T — Tony Perkovich. Suddenly my hands began to tremble with rage.

Tony — T —wasn't just visiting with old-friends Jeb and Bussy in

Mankato for the weekend. He had been living at their farmhouse. For how long? Nine or ten months? With Jeb and Bussy's help, the entire weekend had been an elaborate ruse to set me up. I wondered what perverse pleasure they all got out of watching me fall for it. I wondered, too, whether I would have listened and understood if LaVon had simply come out and admitted everything to me. No, I thought. Not likely.

I sat for a long time running through the entire setup. LaVon pretending not to know Tony when they were introduced. Had the restaurant location really been changed to a new banquet hall that just *happened* to look like the Flanders? Or was it all pre-planned in order to give her an excuse for going back to the house? Oh, and wasn't it clever of Jeb to take me out to a bar while she and Tony slipped out someplace — or upstairs to a bedroom. Yes everything fit, right down to the waitress at the Haymaker Bar asking about Tony, as if he was a regular customer — because he was. And, LaVon — what was up with that phone message from a friend, asking *"how things went down over the weekend?"*

I started sifting through my memory to find moments of reasonable doubt about her fidelity. But I was too tired. My entire marriage had been a circus act of Ringling Brothers proportions. She had pulled off the trapeze and high wire acts right under my nose. I didn't know why she would work so hard to keep up the farce for so many years, but I would work on figuring out that part later.

There was a great deal more evidence spread across my lap and scattered on the floor but I really didn't need to read it. I scrunched everything into the box and walked over to the rear of the furnace. I removed the burner panel and an eerie flickering burst of flame hopped out, penetrating the dark corner. Over the next hour, one piece at a time, I touched each one of her lies and deceptions to the row of flame; watching as each one floated down onto the smoldering pile at my feet.

With the warmth of the open furnace brushing my face, I became aware for the first time how cold and tired I was. I leaned back against the wall and slid down to the floor; watching the last few folded scraps of my marriage burn themselves into ashes. I buried my head in my arms across my knees and broke into tears until I fell asleep.

12:50 a.m. Wednesday, January 2nd, 2008

I woke with a jolt when the house suddenly creaked from the frigid winter air outside. Despite the general coolness of the basement, my face was sweating from leaning only feet away from the open furnace panel. I shook myself fully awake and checked my watch to find that it was after midnight. My throat was searing after hours of inhaling the smoke from the burning papers still lingering in the air.

As I replaced the furnace panel, I noticed that the date of installation for the updated regulator had been stamped in April, 2001, during the brief period my mother lived in the house. Odd that she never told me about it. I grew accustomed to her weekly phone calls detailing every facet of her life, always culminating with, *"When are you going to move back home?"* Something as major as a broken furnace certainly would have made it into the subject line of an e-mail or the headline of a phone message.

I walked aimlessly around the basement for a moment, thinking of how much LaVon's betrayal hurt. Periodically, I slapped the walls angrily with my open hand or pulled violently at a pipe along the overhead joists. When I found one of the copper hot water tubes to be unusually warm, I traced my hand along it, walking the length of the cellar wall and turning ninety degrees to follow the bend at the corner. As I paused to scrape a wad of dust from my fingertips, I looked back and scanned the maze of organized confusion running above my head.

Plumbing pipes and sewer lines. This was the world my father had known his entire adult life. On any given workday he might have been freezing ten feet below ground in a basement or fighting the wind on the twentieth floor of an unfinished high rise. *"No matter what the weather conditions,"* he would say, *"heavy pipes and tubes don't connect themselves. Computers can't program a machine to handle the infinite number of valves, spigots and joints required to move water from point A to point B."* I realized for the first time he must have spent his entire day working on his knees or lying on his back, stretching sore arms over his head or squeezing his large hands into a cramped space to solder a stubborn fitting. There in that cellar, I was surrounded by his world. Cold, dark places in the winter; hot, damp places in the summer. Except for his frequent complaints about back pain during his later years, our family never talked very much about his job. His life was made up of unyielding steel pipes, sharp copper edges, red-hot soldering irons and toxic PVC adhesives. My mother would sell a house and we would rehash the details for a week. I would write a mediocre paper for English on a Tuesday and we discussed it at the dinner table until Friday. Even the comings and goings of our neighbors merited more attention than his job. He must have known instinctively that his world of pressure fittings and connector joints didn't stand a chance in our home. For the first time in my life, standing there feeling sorry for myself in that cold, dark, miserable crypt, I began to come to grips with what he meant to our family and what our family must have meant to him.

Like plumbing, he did his job beneath the surface, under the floorboards and between the walls — moving the sewage of our family life from point A to point B. Like a water main, he was functional and mundane — and invisible. *"The arguments are the only things that still breathe some signs of life"* he had said on that long-ago Sunday afternoon. He didn't elaborate then, but standing there with cold hands and spider webs smattered across my face, I was beginning to understand. He didn't walk away from our family because of irreconcilable differences with my mother; he walked away because he felt he made no difference at all.

Until that moment, I never understood what Friedrich Nietzsche meant when he said, *"When you stare into an abyss...the abyss also stares into you."* Unexpectedly, I was beginning to recognize and understand the deep hole in my father's existence. In the end, the chasm must have looked unbridgeable. So he backed away from the edge and tried to fill the abyss with...what...curling? But what difference was there between his life and mine? I was spending my life staring into a deep, empty canyon, too. But I chose to fill it with the silt of mediocrity, indifference and cynicism; too weak-in-the-knees to back away from the edge.

I stood shivering for another moment. Why did it suddenly take sifting through a pile of knick-knacks to create this inner commotion I was feeling? When Dad left home, I never felt a minute of remorse or anger. It was simply a reality. Except for the coincidence that he died on my birthday, even the matter-of-fact way my mother relayed the news was, well — matter-of-fact. Everything I ever thought of him was matter-of-fact. When my mother died, the excitement of LaVon at my side filled the immediate void. But there I was, standing in the dankness of a cold basement, thinking about my own irrelevance.

When I reached the far wall near the washer and dryer, my stockinged toe brushed up against a short length of one-inch copper pipe. I picked it up and hopped onto the washing machine to get a closer look at the overhead pipes at eye-level.

"I'll bet this froze one winter and needed to be replaced," I whispered to myself as I ran my fingers along the repaired length of pipe. "That must be when Mom had the furnace regulator fixed, too."

I looked at the short piece in my left hand and discovered a split running three-quarters the length along one side. The leaking section had been cut out and a new one neatly soldered into place. It was another anomaly so alien to my mother's nature. Why wouldn't she have told me about this when it happened? For God's sake, she often left phone messages with no more pressing information than to tell me she was vacuuming the floor or doing the dishes. But something as major as the furnace dying and a pipe bursting — nada?

Mom only lived here a year, I reasoned. It must have been replaced before she moved in. In fact, she probably insisted that it needed replacing before she signed off on the home inspection. That must have been the case with the furnace, too. The prior homeowner took care of the problems but didn't bother to clean up after himself.

I had myself convinced until my knuckles bumped the pipe cutter resting across a parallel row of pipes near the repair. When I brushed off the dust and shifted it in the light, a lump formed in my throat. Etched onto one side of the handle were the large words: *DuMot Property of LU539. Minneapolis Local Pipefitter Union # 539*. It had belonged to my father.

I ran my fingers along the length of its red plastic handle, scraping my fingernail over the rough etched letters. It somehow meant the world to me that I was holding an implement my father had once held in his hands and may have used every day on his job. I smiled as I recalled times I tried working with him to repair something under the car or in the basement of our New Brighton home. Out of frustration, he would toss a ratchet handle across the floor with an invective to heaven. After rummaging through the bottom of his old tool box, he would pull out a heavy mallet and declare, *"It always comes down to needing the hammer!"*

I absent-mindedly spun the round cutting blades with my fingertip a few times. The gap between what I knew to be true and what wasn't making sense was beginning to grow too wide. My trip to the Chippewa County Courthouse and gravesite was quantifiable, black-and-white objective proof that my father was dead. But it was growing impossible to dismiss the connection between those banners in the curling club, the newspaper article in Mankato and the tool I was flipping back and forth in my hands.

Things weren't making sense to me. My mother would have called a professional handyman for any necessary jobs and repairs. Even if she had kept a few tools with her, a pipe cutter was hardly a recommended household item. And she would never have been able to fix the pipe herself. A neighbor, maybe? Again no. Not Mom. After living in New Brighton for more than twenty years, she knew only a handful of our old neighbors on the cul-du-sac. After such a short time in South Minneapolis, she certainly wouldn't have known anyone well-enough to ask for help. I again craned my neck upward to examine the pipe joints more closely. That was a professional fitting and soldering job. Did she loan the cutter to a plumber who had forgotten his own tool? No, a professional contractor would have everything he needed, either on his belt or out in the truck. There could have been a dozen reasons that pipe cutter was lying down there beneath our floorboards all those years. For most people, any one reason could have made perfect sense. Regarding my mother, though, none made any sense at all.

Think, damn it, I thought. What was the timeline? Was she already living in this house when Dad died in the accident? Or was she still living in New Brighton? Could he have helped her fix the pipe shortly after she moved here, just before he died? *NO!* I distinctly remembered something she wrote me in an e-mail after she decided she would put our old house on the market. *"Your father's ghost will always ramble around this house,"* she said. *"Now that he's dead, we all need to move on. You moved on to California and I'll be moving on to a cute little house I found in South Minneapolis."* He was already dead and buried when she sold the house in New Brighton.

I allowed myself to follow the fantasy as if he had not died. The pipe burst. She called him and he came to fix it. Likely, he might have installed the new furnace regulator when it went out, too. If so, it meant that she knew how to contact him and it probably also meant that he was still living relatively close by. She still relied on him and that meant that, at some level, he still cared enough about her to help out when she needed it. But try as I might, I couldn't tie up the loose ends. If he was really still alive, why wouldn't he have tried to remain in contact with me, too?

I pulled myself back up onto the dryer and sat staring at the far wall for several minutes, allowing an indescribable sadness, fear and loneliness to descend. I took stock of everything that had happened that day and the fact that I was only a short step away from total despair. I had no job, no money, no friends, no family and now, no marriage. My only connection to the world I knew was a thimbleful of possibility that my father might still be alive.

I came to the gripping realization that I was dragging the razor-sharp edge of the cutter wheel across my left wrist. Whether for five seconds or twenty minutes, I couldn't know. I stopped with a jerk and hurled the tool across the empty cellar floor, watching as it crashed and ricocheted into a far corner. As if on cue, a centipede suddenly dropped onto my head from the joist above me, tickled down my ear and came to rest on my shoulder. I quickly brushed it off with a shudder and watched as it scurried into the black, damp space beneath the furnace. I sighed at the realization that I was just as unwanted and repulsive as that bug. But damn it, if that ugly little worm could find some comfort in a dark and unwelcoming corner of the world, so could I.

Part III

Revitalization

Michigan Rink - Gold	**Minnesota Rink - Silver**
Lead: Jim Coventry	Lead: Paul Stenner
Second: Dale Harder	Second: John Mistovich
Third: Steve Talbert	Third: Mickey Bellows
Skip: Norm Thunger	**Skip: Freddy Schade**

Fourth End

“**Hurry!**” echoed the long, loud yell from Michigan’s Skip Norm Thunger, already down flat on his stomach at the center of the house to get a better view of the rock rumbling slowly toward his nose. “**Hard! Hurry!**” he yelled again, now on one knee as the gold-handled #4 rock began to curl unexpectedly early, threatening to clip the edge of a long guard. “**Hurry Hard!**” came his frantic cry again, this time accompanied by an urgent plea, “**Keep sweepin’ her straight. We need her to get past ’em. She’s crashin’ left, boys. Lean on ’em!**”

With three ends complete, the Minnesota rink had taken a 5 - 1 lead into the fourth end but wasn’t comfortable with the way the game was playing itself out. Players on both rinks knew the ice could just as quickly tilt the other way. The surface was already changing and strategies were changing, too. What had been swingy and slow over the early ends was beginning to turn keen and straight, as tracks along the center of the sheet began wearing smooth. Throwing the rock with T-line weight in the first end was now likely to result in a shot drifting deep into the back of the house, or beyond the end line. Over the remainder of the game, keeping a rock in play would become more difficult with each shot. At the midway point of the match, the team that could adjust to the changing strategies and conditions would have the clear advantage.

To start the fourth end, Minnesota’s Lead Paul Stenner and Michigan’s Jim Coventry traded shots at the front edge of the house, congesting the middle for the later rocks. Seconds John Mistovich for Minnesota and Dale Harder for Michigan had little choice but to use their two shots to clear some space for the shooters that followed.

Strategy for the Thirds is unique to each end, depending upon the lay of the rocks left in play from earlier shots. If the house is clogged, Thirds may use their shots to take out guards and keep the center open for their Skips. If one rink has several rocks already lying for counters, posting additional guards out front may be the best way to force the opposing Third to waste shots clearing them out. The fact that Michigan held the hammer for the end would be the critical factor in the shot selections for both sides.

When Minnesota's Third Mickey Bellows stepped into the hack with his #5, there was only a small smattering of rocks resting toward the sides and rear of the house, but the path was clear to the wide-open center. Minnesota had two rocks sitting on the edge as counters, but without the last shot, it was doubtful they would remain relevant. It made sense to fill up the center and hope that Michigan would miss a shot. You never knew whether an outlying rock at the edge of the house might stick around until the end to add to the points.

Bellows dropped his #5 rock onto the front edge and Michigan's Talbert followed with a heavy take-out that rolled both rocks out of play. Bellows then placed his #6 rock onto the button but knew immediately that it wouldn't last long. It didn't. Talbert took it out with a light roll, leaving his own #6 as shot-rock, the single rock in the house lying closest to the center. But it rested several feet behind the button and of no real consequence. As the two Skips surveyed the house, ready to step up for their shots, the path to the center remained wide open.

Minnesota's Schade knew he had to use his shots defensively to clog up the path to the middle. He needed both of his rocks to land toward the front center and count for possible points, but serve double-duty to guard the button at the dead center. Knowing he had the final shot, Thunger had the advantage of being on offense. He could use the first of his two shots to clear out any rock that Schade used as a block. He would then use the hammer to go for the button and take a point — maybe two points if the rocks rolled in his favor. There were still enough ends remaining in the game. Michigan didn't need to catch up all at once. One point at a time would work out fine.

But with his first rock, Schade woke up the crowd with an unconventional strategy. Rather than placing his shot to the front center of the house with a cold draw, as the Michigan rink expected, he struck one of his side guards, raising it into position about five feet into the center of the house. It was a reckless, aggressive decision that was designed to create some possible confusion and throw his opponent off guard. In a usual game, Freddy would never have considered it. But this wasn't a usual game. It was only by a twist of fate that these rinks had been given a second chance to replay a semi-final match to advance to the championship game. Both had lost their matches the previous day. Thunger's Michigan rink was edged out after a rink from Wisconsin scored two points in the tenth end. Later that evening, the great North Dakota rink had spanked Freddy

Schade's Minnesota rink handily, 9-2.

But this was one of those second chances that come along only rarely in life. The curling gods had made a mockery of everything by smiting the clear favorite North Dakota. Schade figured he must certainly be part of the punch line. Over his teammates' objections, he tossed years of experience aside and considered a comedic alternative to rational strategy. Freddy figured there would be no better time to throw an opponent off guard. Holding a four-point lead this early in the match made the decision a little less reckless. In the end, he concluded, what would it matter if it didn't work? At most, Michigan would probably end up winning the end with only a single point, anyway, handing the hammer back to Schade coming back the other way for the fifth.

The gods regaled as Schade's rock clicked into Minnesota's #3 and bumped it fifteen feet forward into the front of the house. But the helter-skelter scattering Freddy had hoped for was of no consequence, as the rocks apparently didn't want to play along. No matter, Freddy thought. There was now one of Minnesota's silver handles sitting as the new shot-rock. Thunger was left with the choice of either clearing it out and opening up the middle again, or ignoring it to go directly for the center. Either way, it would cost Michigan a precious rock.

Unlike Schade, Norm Thunger decided that discretion was the better part of nonsense. He didn't have the luxury of a big lead. He was chasing the game and needed to chip away with every remaining rock. He typically didn't gamble with his shots and this certainly wasn't the time to start. Not yet, anyway. Taking out Schade's rock and keeping the center clear for his second shot was his only real option if he wanted to retain any chance to score a single point for the end.

As Thunger released his shot at the line, however, the crowd groaned. The frosty gold metal handle stuck slightly on the moist fingertips of his leather glove and required an extra little push of energy. It didn't seem like much, but in a world where mechanics must work hand-in-hand with physics, it was too much. Rather than the slow, steady two-and-a-half rotations perfected after years of practice, Thunger released the handle with too much rotation. The speed was right but the excessive spin could cause the rock to curl unpredictably, possibly crashing uselessly a foot or more to the right of the target.

Missing this shot would give Minnesota a decisive edge. Schade could use his second shot to protect his rock near the center, rendering Thunger virtually impotent with the hammer. His rink couldn't afford to fall another point behind. In order to clear out the center for the last shot, his rock needed to stay on target.

Sweepers Jim Coventry and Dale Harder recognized immediately what needed to be done. Thunger sprung up out of his slide and ran down the ice behind the rock yelling loudly, '**Sweeeeep!** I gave 'er too much handle. Sweep 'er straight. We need this one to clear out Schade's guard.'

The broom heads became a blur of long straw bristles moving like machine cams just inches out front of the rock. As the rock drew over the hog line, Third Steve Talbert, holding Thunger's broom as Vice Skip, left the house and jumped into the fray, ready to do whatever was necessary but staying well out in front of the main sweepers to avoid a pile up. Thunger dropped to one knee and then down to his belly to get an ice-level view of whether his shot would stay on course, all-the-while yelling directives.

"Careful, Jim. Rock coming!" he yelled.

Coventry gave a practiced hop to avoid tripping over a stone lying in his walking path.

"Keep your brooms far enough out front boys, don't burn our rock. Don't trip. We need this shot to count."

Because of the efforts of the sweepers, the shot swung less than a foot off line and carried far enough to click Schade's #7 several inches to the right. Not much, but enough. Thunger's rock continued forward another three feet and came to rest touching the back edge of the center button. It became shot-rock, with Freddy Schade down to his last opportunity for the end. Power sweeping by Coventry and Harder had salvaged the errant shot and forced Schade's hand to minimize the damage.

Freddy looked down the ice toward the sparse muddle of silver and gold handles strewn uselessly at the outer edges of the house. What would he give to have one of his teammates' shots back? A rock — any rock — sitting just six inches further to the right or left, or perhaps two feet deeper into the front of the house could give him options he would kill for. He thought again about something his junior coach told him as a young boy, "Curling is the most democratic of all games, Freddy. Every rock gets a vote and every vote counts. Don't waste your vote"

Schade squinted down the ice as he stood behind the hack, ignoring his Vice Skip at the far end. Taking out Thunger's shot-rock was Schade's only real option. This time, though, there would be nothing cute. To reach it, he would need to come out of the hack slightly right of center and rotate his rock to get a minimum curl to the left. He knew how important it would be to ensure that his shot struck — then stuck — as close to the center as possible. He needed Thunger to aim at it, and hit it. Sure, he was sacrificing a single point to lose the fourth end, but he'd get the hammer back for the fifth with a three-point lead.

When Freddy released his #8 rock, he knew it wasn't perfect but it would do its job.

"It always comes down to needing the hammer," Freddy said, as his shot slowly tracked tracked toward the house.

The Minnesota sweepers didn't have to work too hard to keep the shot on its intended path. It lightly bumped Thunger's #7 rock forward three feet, then rolled itself only a few inches left. With no guards plugging up the paths to the left or right, though, there remained a wide alley to the center.

With the hammer in hand, Norm Thunger calmly squared himself in the hack and slid out with confidence. His shot was nearly perfect as it knocked out Schade's #8 and welded to the ice near the button to gain the single point for the end. Michigan was now trailing only 5 – 2 as the men prepared for the fifth end.

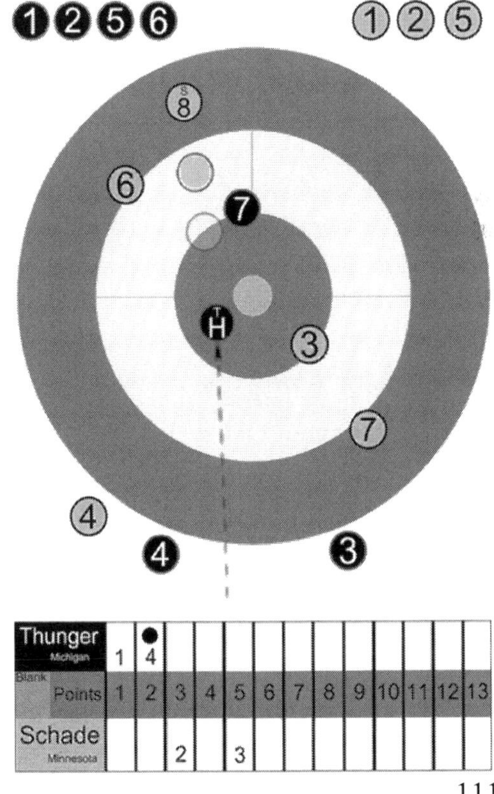

Wednesday, January 2nd through Friday, January 18th, 2008

The following morning, I ran throughout the house in a blind rage, looking to trash everything that reminded me of LaVon. Within a few minutes, though, I realized there were no memories left to destroy. Well, at least none she would care about, anyway. I discovered her dresser drawers empty and only a few of her oldest tattered sweatshirts hanging in her bedroom wardrobe. Everything else in the house was either my few meager belongings or things left over from my mother. I realized for the first time that we had started our marriage with nothing and I had most of it left.

From right under my nose over a period of weeks, months or even years, LaVon had slowly removed her few articles of clothes and personal belongings from the house. Even her bathroom toiletries were gone from under the sink. I found only a few nearly-empty tubes of lotions remaining on her side of the medicine cabinet. She and Bussy would probably replenish her supply on a single trip to Walgreens. My God, I thought, the girl is good.

After five years, she was out of my life as if she had never been in it in the first place. There was nothing I could do about it even if I had wanted to. I still didn't understand why she went ahead with a total sham of a marriage for so long but I would get more answers as the divorce progressed. We both got what we needed out of the arrangement.

I decided the best catharsis would be to focus on finding everything I could about my father. I placed my first phone call to Dan Graber at the Unites States Curling Association, explaining that I was Arv Firpo's nephew and trying to locate him. Frankly, I was expecting more information. Dan was as helpful as he could be but he really didn't have anything I could use. I asked him about club affiliations for playdowns.

"Well, Firpo's what you might call a freelancer," he said. "He suddenly appeared on the national stage a few years ago. At first, he registered out of Mankato and Mapleton. Then I heard he was a member at a couple of northern clubs."

"So what club do you think he may be a member of now?"

"Like I said," he continued, "maybe none. He doesn't affiliate anymore. We don't force people to register from a specific club. We encourage it because the clubs like the publicity. But it's not required."

"Damn," I said. "How can a guy hide so well?"

"He's a real mystery to all of us," Graber continued. "He's been the talk of the curling scene for quite a few years. Up until a year or so ago, he would show up at bonspiels and cashspiels all over the area, always using an alias nickname. But after the 2007 national championships ended last February, he almost completely dropped out of sight. I've heard rumors that he typically heads to Canada after most of the clubs close in the Midwest. Those Canucks never stop curling."

"Does he play at the worlds or try out for the Olympics?" I asked.

"We've asked him about that but he shrugs it off. It's as if he's trying to bury himself even deeper in a hole somewhere. But then suddenly, his rink resurfaced early in December to qualify for this year's national playdowns up in Hibbing in mid-February."

"You said he used to register for cashspiels? What's that?"

"A cashspiel is a very competitive bonspiel with an emphasis on winning some pretty good prize money. The biggest of them will draw teams from across the country. Good teams use them as warm-ups championship playdowns. The winning rink splits the cash from the pot of entry fees. Usually, it's no-questions-asked. You can usually find cashspiels going on at some club or another nearly every winter weekend."

Graber took a few minutes to explain the seasonal curling scene in the Midwest and talked about Arv Firpo's rinks.

"You said he entered pretty frequently, up until a year or so ago," I said. "Not anymore, though?"

"Well, it's like I said, Jack, he completely disappeared from the curling scene right after his rink lost in the finals at the 2007 nationals out in Utica. Nobody heard anything from him again until the regional qualifiers last month. Now he's back. But back from where and for how long, nobody knows. His players don't even understand it and most of them think it's awkward. But he's a great guy and it's everyone's dream to sweep for him. He can pick a snow flea off the edge of a guard rock and stop his shot dead on the button. We just take him as he comes."

"It sounds like I'm out of luck," I said.

"Maybe not. Worst case, he'll be in Hibbing for the championships next month. You can catch him then. Or he might also be part of a Hot Shots traveling exhibition out of Manitoba. They're on a local tour throughout the Midwest this month. You might find him with that group. If you're good enough — and Firpo is — you can make a small little living at curling if you're willing to live like a gypsy."

"Okay, I'll keep calling around. Somebody will know where to look."

"Look, I'll tell you what, son," he said. "You say you want to interview him for an article. He — or someone on his rink — will have to contact us during the next month to get official information for the championships. We expect all registrations to be submitted at least two weeks before the playdowns start. We have to run background checks on every player. I'll tell everyone on staff here to let him know you called. I'll even post your phone number on the bulletin board in the office. If you talk to him, send your article to us. I'll see if we can post it on our website."

"Yeah, maybe," I said. "I'd sure like to find him."

"If you find him," he said. "Don't press him so hard that you scare him off. Curling needs him."

Over the next two weeks, I did everything I could to keep my mind occupied and my frustration from boiling over. I finished the project for AmericanSign and mailed it to them with a letter demanding payment. I also took some time to send out a handful of résumés with a deepening worry. I was nearly out of savings. Without LaVon's paycheck, I wouldn't be able to make ends meet on my few remaining unemployment checks. The jobless rate throughout Minnesota had been slowly ticking upward throughout late 2007. The newspaper headlines were beginning to sound increasingly ominous about an impending deep recession heading into 2008, using opaque phrases like credit crunch, housing bubble and market correction. It all portended trouble for those of us already caught on the outside, looking in.

I wasn't always very good at keeping my emotions in check, though. During one interview, I knew it was time to pull myself off the job market when one HR director admitted the company wasn't actually hiring. They thought it was a good idea to build up a database of good candidates...*"for later in the year when the economy turns around."* I casually stood up, yanked my résumé out of her hands and turned to leave.

"Yeah," I said, "and I don't suppose it hurts you to look busy so the axe doesn't fall on your department, too."

My search for Arv Firpo took me to unexpected corners of a world I knew very little about. I looked up the organizers of the Hot Shots tour in Winnipeg and called the agent responsible for putting the exhibition together. Much as they would have loved it, Arv Firpo never traveled with their group.

I called the old phone numbers Graber gave me from his records. I wasn't surprised to find that each one was disconnected. I then turned my attention to following up every possible lead and vague connection from my Internet research, but that, too, got me nowhere.

Everyone on my list knew Arv Firpo, but that's as far as it went. As best anyone knew, his sudden appearance on the national scene dated back only as far as the 2002 playdowns season. "If you're a good curler," one former teammate chuckled, "you don't call him, he calls you. He's a little like God, that way. He'll use the good ones. The bad ones will want to use him."

I learned that curling at the national level is different from *bonspiels*. Very rarely will all the players on a rink come from the same club. In fact, it is often the case that all four players come from different clubs scattered across the four corners of the state or region. *"If you agree to play on his rink,"* one man said, *"he'll show up at your club about a week before the event. You spend a few days talking about strategy but you really don't throw too many rocks. He expects you to already know how to throw. When you practice, you always have the ice to yourself, either very late at night or very early mornings when the club is closed."*

When I asked questions about his personality, I got the same general response from everyone. *"He's a nice guy, but being on his rink gets pretty intense. After playing with him once, a lot of guys won't agree to join him again."* It seemed that everyone liked him and they all knew they would win with him, but many also admitted they just couldn't compete at his level. I heard it more than once, *"He never misses a shot."*

"But he must live somewhere, or have some way to contact him"' I pleaded. *"He can't just materialize out of thin air."*

"You're right," one man said, *"he can't, but that's exactly what he does. He emerges out of the ice just minutes before a match and freezes back into it within seconds after the final handshake. He appoints the Third — the Vice Skip — to handle every detail. Except winning...he takes care of that himself."*

I eventually reached everyone on my list, with the exception of one man whose wife broke down as she explained her recent divorce.

"If Arv Firpo ever curled with my ex-husband I don't give a damn if you ever find the sorry son-of-a-bitch." To which she added after a brief pause, *"Nothing personal against Arv, you understand."*

From everyone I talked to, I got the same modus operandi: The wind blows him in. He wins. The wind blows him out again.

I turned my attention to contacting his current teammates listed in the Herald newspaper article. I got generally the same story but with one minor twist. The week prior to the regional championship playdowns in December, he asked his players to come to a little burg of Winneboujou in western Wisconsin, about an hour and a half east of Duluth. Somehow, he got keys to the town's three-sheet curling club. The group would talk strategy all day and then practice in the vacated club until late into the night. They holed-up in a little rundown motel in the middle of a nearby cornfield, with no outside contact allowed. The only focus was on winning. On the Friday morning of the start of the playdowns, he rode with Gusty Steinham over to the Duluth Entertainment Complex for the matches.

"He rode with another player?' I jumped in to clarify. "So, he didn't have a car?"

"It puzzled us, too. We weren't sure how he got to that small town. We joked that there was nothing there but a grain elevator, four bars and a few sheets of bad curling ice. My God! What did those poor townspeople do in the summer?"

"So you guys practiced together for the entire week? He never did that before?"

"Not that I know of," he replied. "He was pretty intense that week. Not much fun to be around. For the championship round up in Hibbing, though, he expects us to practice on our own. He says we won't be able to get together as a rink until a day or two before the matches. Yeah, right. Like we can just show up at the club, walk out on the ice and win."

"From what I hear," I said. "It sounds like it's possible."

"Yeah, maybe," he laughed. "You know, Jack, we wonder if he might be in some kind of trouble. You know, getting out of competitive curling. A medical problem, maybe. He acted as if Hibbing will be his last chance to win the big one. Nobody deserves it more. It's a tough life, traveling the circuit the way he does."

"So you have no idea where he is or how to get hold of him?"

"If he calls, I'll tell him you're looking for him."

I chased down every obscure lead I could uncover buried inside a wide assortment of articles and news clippings. I went back to the Internet to check out the listings of clubs throughout the Midwest and southern Manitoba and Ontario. After calls to every club on the charts, I learned that Arvil Firpo wasn't a registered member at any of them. Everyone I talked to knew him, though. Although his name was larger than life, the man could hide right in front of your face.

Saturday Morning, January 19th, 2008

After weeks of trying, I finally had to admit that my only option was plan B: I would simply drive to Hibbing in mid-February and see for myself whether champion curler Arv Firpo was a pseudonym for my father, Tommy DuMot. My plans changed one Saturday morning, however, when I walked into my kitchen one afternoon discovered my answering machine message light blinking.

> **"Hello, is this the Jack DuMot residence? This is Tina Bucholz, from ProtoCommand. Jack, could you call me back here at my office extension. I have something you may want. Thanks, bye."**

Tina Bucholz? Bill Ordway's secretary? What could she have for me? An old coffee mug I left in the bottom of a desk drawer? My old gray cardigan I left draped over the back of my chair? No, I thought. Someone would have thrown that junk away months ago.

Tina Bucholz was about twenty-seven years old and attractive in a small town way, without being intimidating. During her final semester at Hamline University in St. Paul, she landed an internship in the ProtoCommand marketing department, where she was immediately hired full time upon graduation. For about a year and a half, most of her co-workers treated her like a piece of crap. The company got virtually free labor out of her, paying just one step above minimum wage.

Eventually, her competence and cheerful disposition were too much for her office mates to bear and she found herself transferred to Human Resources. She was bright, young and friendly. Not a good mix for JoAnne Cuthright, the HR director since the Taft administration. The few times I had any dealings with JoAnne, I came away with the certain knowledge that she considered people to be evil, clearly stupid and an outright pestilence upon the earth. I never quite understood how anyone with her piss-poor temperament could make a career out of helping people solve their problems in the workplace.

Tina was transferred to HR by unlucky happenstance. The vice president who initially hired her for marketing had hoped to assign her to the sales department as quickly as possible. When funding fell through, Tina was left in a holding pattern until the money ran out. To keep from losing her obvious talent, the VP created a filing job in HR. Unfortunately, he forgot to ask for JoAnne's approval. The oversight was clearly a slap in her face and she immediately set her mind on two objectives: 1) Getting the vice president fired; and 2) getting Tina's irresistible smile and infectious attitude out of her department. Upper management eventually broke under the weight. After a year of listening to incessant bitching, the VP was fired and the poor sap apparently never worked in the tech industry again. Trying to get Tina transferred, on the other hand, eventually backfired. After another six months of Cuthright's bellyaching, the company experienced a financial hiccup. The CEO was suddenly *"sorry-as-hell to have to lose your experience, JoAnne."* Tina stepped in for several months to clean up the department before Bill Ordway brought her on as his personal assistant.

I vividly recalled my last brief glimpse of her face at ProtoCommand, as the janitor escorted me into the elevator. Tina didn't owe anything to anyone, yet she honestly seemed to care about what was going to happen to me — and everyone else on my team. I figured that it was just the way she was wired. I didn't want to feel good about anything at that moment, but there she was, offering words of encouragement as if to say *"chin up, old chum."*

I listened to her voicemail message again. She forgot to leave her extension number, so I began looking up ProtoCommand's website to find the staff directory. Before I could get very far, though, my phone rang. It was Tina. Hearing her voice again brought back a rush of memories. I immediately pictured her in the way I wanted to remember her; smiling from a round face with shoulder-length straight, dark hair that gently whisked side to side with her every movement.

"Jack? Hi, this is Tina," came her soft voice. "Sorry to bother you on a Saturday."

We took a minute to catch up. I explained that I was still out of work and lied about some promising prospects. She explained that our former boss, Bill Ordway, had died a few days before Christmas. In other news, nearly everyone in my old software development department either was already out of work or soon would be. In fact, the company fired the rest of my old team just before the long Thanksgiving weekend. Somehow or another, the conversation swung around to our personal lives but I was too embarrassed to delve into the problems in my marriage. To keep the conversation moving ahead, I found myself mentioning the scant evidence that my father might possibly still be alive.

"Well, I hope you discover that it's true," she said. Then added, "Funny, but your dad is the reason I'm calling. Next Friday will be my last day on the payroll here and I'm cleaning out my desk. They left me to handle Bill's office, too. I'm here boxing up his personal items right now. You remember all the stuff he had on his walls?"

My mind drifted back to the handful of times I stood in that office. There were dozens of framed certificates, letters of appreciation and photographs covering nearly every inch.

"Yeah, I remember. He was a certified genius and he never allowed us to forget it. Maybe you should honor him by hanging his death certificate on his wall, too. How did Old Gimp die, anyway?"

There was an awkward silence on the phone. I knew I had stepped over the line with my comments. After a few seconds, she spoke again.

"You don't know everything about Bill's story, Jack. He was actually a great person once you took the time to know him. But I don't blame you guys for not liking him. I'm not sure exactly how he died. I was on a short vacation over Christmas week. I was down visiting my aunt when it happened. The company never even tried to notify me. I learned about it the morning I returned to work. Later that same day, they gave us notice that our department would be eliminated by the end of January. We can talk more about it later. As I started to say, Jack, there's something here I think you should see. Can you make arrangements to come down to ProtoCommand?"

"You mean right now?" I asked, surprised.

"No, too many people are working in the office this afternoon. How about early tomorrow morning, Sunday. We'll be alone."

"Sure, no problem," I answered. "Will I get past the guards?"

"The company cut security a few weeks ago. They said I could keep my key until Monday. I'll meet you at the side door about seven o'clock. I'm sure nobody else will be around."

Eary Sunday Morning, January 20th, 2008

The following morning, I pulled my Passat into ProtoCommand's empty parking lot and found Tina already standing huddled against the building, bundled against the icy wind in a white ski jacket and scarf. She still looked every bit as delicious as I remembered her, but her hair was an inch or two cuter. Just as I remembered, too, she still suffered from a case of terminal enthusiasm. She stepped toward my car with a friendly wave and directed me toward a parking spot near the entrance.

"These security cameras haven't worked in over a year," she said, pointing upward as she unlocked the heavy metal door. "Whenever Bill put in a requisition to repair them, some bean-counter always found a reason to nix it. Management figures that as long as the cameras appear real, it should be enough of a deterrent. There's nothing left of the company worth stealing, anyway."

"Like people who steal a Brinks Home Security sign to stick in their yard but never actually pay for the monitoring service," I said. "It only protects them from the honest people."

She looked at me, cocked her head and asked innocently, "Do some people really steal security signs and do that?"

"You'd be surprised," I answered sheepishly.

Inside the building, Tina led me down the dark hall and past the fishbowl. I stopped for a moment to reminisce. Our old row of cubicles lay disassembled and stacked against a wall. The phone console on the opposite end of the room had been removed, with the terminal jack left to dangle impotently from a ceiling panel. Only the dust on the floor looked the same. I noticed that my name was the only one still written in grease pencil above the spot where my cubicle once stood.

"The guys left your name up there as a memorial. We lost the Boeing contract in early November and they had this room cleared out a few weeks later. It was like you guys never even existed. By early December, the entire first floor was nearly vacant. It was just a matter of time before the whole software development department would be shut down, too. The company is just a consulting service now. Didn't anyone on the team call you?"

As we stepped off the elevator into the dark third-floor hallway, I reached for the overhead light switch but Tina stopped my hand. Inside Bill's dark interior office she flipped on a small table lamp in the corner. It provided just enough light to see that she had already packed half-dozen boxes. Only a small clutter of his personal items filled one corner of the large desk, which had been pushed awkwardly toward the center of the room. It was clear that someone from the executive suite had wasted no time cannibalizing the black leather desk chair and an antique oak filing cabinet.

"You don't know how he died?" I asked, as I absent-mindedly flipped open a large box pushed against a wall.

Tina admitted that the details were still a bit sketchy but she relayed everything she knew. A few managers from other departments had invited him to lunch to celebrate his birthday on Friday, December 21st. Everyone swore he acted fine all afternoon. When he didn't come in to work the following Monday, people were worried. Somebody called his house but he didn't answer. When they needed some important information later that afternoon, a junior manager drove out to his place. His apartment door was unlocked, so the guy stepped inside and found him dead on his sofa."

She interrupted herself, reached into a wastebasket and tossed me an empty prescription bottle.

"They found a full ninety-day supply of this medication on his kitchen table. Well, it was nearly full, anyway. Only a few pills were gone, but certainly not enough to kill him. It wasn't like he poured a fistful down his throat."

She finished the story with few additional details. The medical examiner ruled it an accidental overdose, but nobody knew for sure. As she finished, I noticed her lower lip quivering and a streak of mascara running down her left cheek.

"Who took care of the funeral arrangements?" I asked.

"Twenty-five years with the company and they left him to rot on a slab at the St. Paul police morgue for nearly a week, while they looked for a surviving family member," she said bitterly. "When I got back into town after the New Year, they just turned everything over to me and washed their hands of him."

"Did you finally find someone in his family?"

"It was tough. I didn't know where to begin. Then HR discovered that his pension benefits and insurance policy listed a cousin in Omaha as sole beneficiary. A probate lawyer named Joe Nehmer. The guy hadn't talked to Bill in more than twenty years but he suddenly found himself with more than four hundred and fifty thousand dollars dropped into his lap. I hope he needed the money."

"Cripes, really?" I asked incredulously.

"Yeah," she continued. "He took some time to fly up here to handle the probate details with me. Closing out credit cards, that kind of thing. We worked together and did what we could but Bill didn't leave a last will. At least not one we could dig up anyway. After a quick memorial service here in town, a local funeral home handled the details to fly the body down to North Carolina, where he's buried near his son. The probate courts will keep everything tied up for awhile. We left all of his household belongings untouched in his apartment. Mr. Nehmer said he would come back in late March to inventory everything and arrange an estate sale. I will get reimbursed for any expenses. The money doesn't matter to me, as long as this company doesn't try to claim a dime for storing his car in their parking lot."

"This Nehmer guy is a lawyer," I said in a disgusted tone. "He's probably already at the top of the food chain. Then Bill turns around and gives him even more money. And you get diddly-squat for your years working with him. And to top everything, you get stuck taking care of his final affairs, too. Where's the justice?"

"It's not always about justice," she answered. "To those who have much, more will be given. Bill entrusted me with more important things in his life than money."

"And to those whom much has been given, much will be expected," I retorted. "So, you're sure Nehmer will bother coming up here to help you finish up the final details? After he has all the money in the bank, I mean. Maybe he'll at least let you keep Bill's car for all your efforts."

"Maybe, but it's not a liquid asset, so it may have to be sold in the estate sale. I suspect Mr. Nehmer will try to claim that money, too. So, yeah, he still has enough skin in the game to help me finish this. That's all that really matters."

By the tone in her voice, though, I could tell that it really *wasn't* all that really mattered. I changed the subject.

"You don't think it was suicide," I said. "But you also don't sound convinced it was accidental. We all knew that he was never the same after his son's death a couple of years ago. Maybe one more lonesome Christmas season finally got to him."

"Are you asking whether he was depressed?" she responded. "I've asked myself the same question. The pills are prescribed as antidepressants so, yeah, he might have been addicted and lost track of how many he was taking. I never saw the final medical report. Bill was acting very strangely during December. He wasn't depressed, really. But it wasn't the satisfied, resigned feelings they say people get when they've finally decide to commit suicide. He was quiet, but upbeat and nice enough. I noticed that he was spending more time here in his office with the door closed. I just thought he was thinking about retiring and handling personal details. His job was likely to be eliminated after we lost the Boeing contract, too."

"So what did you want to show me?" I asked, as I tossed the empty prescription bottle into the trash can. "If it's my old coffee mug or sweater, you could have thrown them away."

"I did a long time ago," she chuckled, handing me a framed black and white photograph from the coffee table. "First, I want to show you this. Look at it closely."

I held it directly under the lamp and looked carefully. It was an old group picture of Navy shipmates; the men in dress uniform lined up in multiple rows on deck. A banner displaying ***U.S.S. Harbough*** hung a few feet above the group.

"The Harbough?" I said. "That was the boat my dad always talked about from his Navy days. How the heck did this picture end up in Bill's office?"

"So it was your dad then? That confirms what I thought. Look at the list of names along the bottom margin."

"Confirms what? What do you mean?" I asked, squinting to read the small font identifying the men. When I got to the third row of names, I knew: *Petty Officer 1st Class James Billings; Fireman Anthony Barnes; Seaman William Ordway; Seaman Arvil DuMot...* The list continued but my eyes couldn't move beyond my father's name, immediately following Bill's. I counted down the faces from the end and squinted at the two men near the middle. The faded photo was decades old and there were more than forty seamen crowding the eight-by-ten glossy. It was impossible to make out recognizable features.

"My God, Tina! Are you saying my dad and Bill served together on the Harbough? That they knew each other?"

"Well, that's what I was wondering, too," she replied. "When I saw the name DuMot, I didn't think anything of it. After all, there are a billion DuMots in America, right? But the unusual first name cued my memory and I started thinking about you. I recalled that you once said that your dad's name unusual, like Arden or Arvid."

"Arvil. Yeah, I remember telling you that," I said. "At a company picnic at Minnehaha Falls."

"At first I thought it was only a weird coincidence. The unusual first name with the last name of DuMot, I mean. But then I found something else in Bill's desk that made me wonder."

Tina lifted a large eleven-by-fourteen inch manila envelope from the pile.

"I found this in his bottom drawer. It's filled with weird little slips of papers with a date written on each one — Bill's birth date."

I pulled out a random slip. My heart skipped a beat and I couldn't catch my breath: *Willy — December 21 — 12*. I pulled out another one: *Willy — December 21 — 19*. And another: *Willy — December 21 — 7*. I didn't need to pull out any more. I knew what would be hand-written on each one. I quickly opened my wallet and found the slip with my dad's birth date written on it: *Arv — February 23 — Ø*.

As I stood comparing my slip to one from Bill's envelope, I realized that Tina must have been utterly confused. I explained everything about the letter I discovered under the neighbor's bush, then about the trip down to Mankato. The details began sounding strange — even to me — so I brought the story back around to evidence that my father might still be alive. But I cut myself off.

Holding the two slips side-by-side must have been the trigger I needed, as my memory suddenly reclaimed something I had been struggling with.

Tina jumped back as I yelled out, "**God, now I remember where I've seen this before.**"

I summarized a version of the events.

"It was in our family home in New Brighton — when I was seventeen, the year my father moved out of the house. I came home from high school one afternoon and headed into the kitchen for a snack. There was nothing unusual about sifting through the mail piled on the kitchen table, but there was one open letter hand-addressed formally to *Mr. Arvil DuMot*, with its contents removed. Arvil? Not Tommy, his common name that was on every other piece of mail. In fact, I couldn't recall ever having seen *Arvil* in print before. From hearing him tell it, he hated the name and kept it buried it in his past."

"As I reached for the refrigerator, I saw a small slip of paper lying across the corner of the stove. I assumed it was a shorthand reminder from my mother about starting dinner. Under terms of an agreement with my father, she typically scheduled real estate appointments during the hours I was in school. As I grew older, though, she agreed to meet with clients at any time of the day. I often found dinner instructions taped across a pile of food ingredients set out on a countertop. When I read the note, though, I was surprised to find that it wasn't my mother's familiar loopy handwriting. It was the same type of small handwritten note as these."

I stopped the story while Tina compared my slip to one or two from Bill's large envelope. I continued.

"I suspected that the little note probably came in the letter addressed to my dad. My mother must have opened it for some reason. There was a date written on the slip."

Tina interrupted.

"So it is likely that the date was the same date on this slip you found under your neighbor's bush? February 23rd. Your father's birthday?"

"Yeah, I guess so."

"And it was the first time you ever saw anything like it?" Tina asked.

I thought for a brief moment as I tried to bring something into sharper focus.

"Actually, no," I said. "Now that I think about it, there was one other time. It was about five years earlier, when I was eleven or twelve. Our family was just finishing up dinner. I thought we were all having a great time together until my mom said something nasty and began waving a piece of paper in my father's face. As usual, he headed for the nearest exit at a gallop, but not before ripping the sheet from her hand, crushing it into a wad and slamming it into the front hall wastebasket. Later that evening, I fished out a wrinkled business envelope and read the small hand-written slip of paper tucked inside. It had a date — which I don't remember — I'm guessing now that it must have been February 23rd. But more unusual, I recall that it had the word *'Arv'* on it. I later asked my mother about it. That was when I recall hearing for the first time that Dad's real name was Arvil, not Tommy."

"Was there number tacked onto the end of either of those notes?" Tina asked. "Like on these?"

"Probably," I said, "but I don't remember."

Under the dim lamp light, Tina brushing against my shoulder as we compared notes: *Arv — February 23 — Ø* in my left hand; *Willy — December 21 —19* in my right. The handwriting wasn't the same. I picked up *Willy — December 21 — 12*. Again no comparison.

I spilled the contents of the envelope across the desk and rustled through the pile.

"Tina look, these two don't match," I said. "And the paper used for some of these doesn't look quite as old. A few are in different handwriting. But it looks like whoever sent this one to Bill also wrote the one intended for my father, too. So something about these notes changed."

We both agreed there was obviously some connection between Bill Ordway, my father and the slips of paper. Beyond the similarities in handwriting, though, we drew a blank.

"What made you think that these little notes proved conclusively that there was some connection in the Navy picture?" I asked.

Tina shook the manila envelope upside-down and a folded letter slid out onto the floor. She picked it up and handed it to me.

> Willy;
>
> Thanks for your letter. Yes, I've thought about your idea, but I've given up trying to end this thing — or running from it anymore. Look what happened to Mickey's daughter. Jenny didn't deserve it. Sins of the father, I guess.
>
> I don't know, but I just think I'm right about this one. I think we have too much to lose. Remember the letter I wrote you across the back of our Navy picture, "either roll with the sea or break like the waves."
>
> All of this sure stinks, Willy. It stinks more and more every year. It seems like no matter what shots we play, it won't matter — he's the Skip and he has the hammer. We have to do the best we can to take care of our families. Your son Jason and my son Jack need

us to do what's right by them. So...let's keep rolling with the sea. — 'Tommy'

There was no date, so it was impossible to know how long it had been sitting at the bottom of Bill's desk drawer. I tried to recall my father's handwriting but drew a blank.

"What did he mean, Jack, he's the Skip and he has the hammer."

I explained why I thought it might be a reference to curling, then asked what she made of the letter.

"*Jason* was Bill's son," she said. "I put two-and-two together with *Seaman Arvil DuMot* in the Navy photo. That led me to assume that the *Jack* he mentions must refer to you. After reading it, I started wondering whether there was anything else I should be looking for that he may have kept hidden. I pulled apart the picture frame and found this."

I could barely read the fading pencil-writing across the back of the photo. It had the foundations of the same unique handwriting style as the previous letter, but there seemed to be several years of maturity separating the two. This time, though, I recalled the telltale way my father drew a little line through his letter Ƶ, to distinguish it from a 2.

> Willy;
>
> From little Gluek to the wide blue horiƶon, I wouldn't have made it through two tours of duty without you. You're like the brother I wish I had.
>
> Let's not be afraid of the future. We're the lucky ones. We can number our days. By my calculation, we still have about 11,000 of them remaining. We'll get this thing figured out, or die trying. We can either roll with the sea, or we can break like the waves. We have to do something with our lives besides looking over our shoulders.
>
> You have always been part of my life and I promise to make the most of it. We'll weather this storm together - from this day forward, Sincerely, 'Tommy'

"Bill doesn't have any close family members to give this stuff to," Tina said. "Not anybody who might want it, anyway. I don't want ProtoCommand to toss it in the dumpster. Despite what everyone around here thought of him, I liked him a lot. He gave me a big break and working for him meant so much to me. I know that your parents are both dead, so I figured you might like to have it."

"Well, like I said," I broke in. "I'm not so sure anymore that my dad actually is dead, but this might help me find out. It's a weird story isn't it? I mean, he's dead for six years then he re-emerges as a curling superstar — if curling can have superstars."

"Sure, they're called rock gods, aren't they?" she answered with a smile. "Amazing coincidence, isn't it? I mean, you working here and your boss turned out to be one of your father's old best friends."

"I don't think it was such an amazing coincidence after all, Tina."

I began putting the pieces into place for her, telling her of my brief foray to the Bay Area, ending with the fire in San Mateo. I wrapped up by summarizing my suspicions.

"So after years of a futile job search, my mother visits me in California and tells me that ProtoCommand is hiring in St. Paul. One short telephone interview later and I'm hired sight-unseen by Bill Ordway, one of the top men in the computer science field. Then I get assigned to an insignificant little subcontract where I can't possibly don anybody any harm. Amazing coincidence, my ass. It turns out my father knew Bill Ordway all his life. And that means my mother damned-well knew him, too."

"But then the fire at the banquet hall killed her," Tina concluded.

"Not before she was able to pull the strings to get me a job back in the Twin Cities," I said.

Pulled the strings. What a perfect metaphor. Funny, I was beginning to think that I actually had some measure of control over my life. The truth was, though, I had been played like a marionette. But why the secrecy about it all? Other parents help their kids get their first job, or buy their first car, or get their first mortgage. Why didn't she talk to Ordway and help me get a job right out of college? Why did I make an ass of myself out in San Francisco starving for a year? Bill was apparently my father's friend for years, but I was still the first one to get the axe when the Boeing program was cut. Why was any of this descent into personal hell even necessary?

"This is only a few small items, Tina," I finally said. "You could have mailed them to me. Why did you want me to sneak down here? It could have waited."

She could tell I was angry and I hoped she didn't think it was directed at her.

"Well, Jack," she said. "There's something more you need to see. Stuff I couldn't mail to you or bring to your house. When I was cleaning out Bill's desk yesterday, I noticed this little slide-out writing desk that pulls out from under here."

She slipped her fingertips beneath the lip of the desk top and slid out a retractable wooden writing board, about fifteen inches square and covered with a colorful history of doodles and notes.

"He must have written his telephone notes on it whenever he didn't have a notepad handy," she said. "This desk is only three years old. I remember helping the janitor put it together. Most of the scribbling is just vendors' names I recognize, but there are some other names, too. Look at this one."

Tina pointed to the name and telephone number of the Grand Forks police department, hastily written and nearly completely covered over time by several scribbles added in blue, black and red Sharpie. Near one edge of the board was a bordered list that stood out by itself.

I pulled the table lamp over to the desk so I could read everything more clearly.

"Your dad's name is written here, again," Tina said, pointing to the line near the bottom.

~~Pete, Medora~~
~~Freddy~~, ~~mom~~
~~Hank Stenner~~
~~Mike~~, ~~Franny~~, ~~Jenny~~
Me, ~~Tanya~~, ~~Jason~~
Ary (Tommy), ~~Melinda~~, Jack 651-555-0124

The *me* on the list must refer to himself — Bill I mean. *Tanya* was his wife. *Jason* his son. Bill and Tanya were divorced about ten years ago. Tanya got remarried out in Seattle. Bill got in touch with her again for Jason's funeral a few years back. She died of a heart attack about a year and a half ago."

"Maybe that's why her name is crossed out, too," I ventured.

"Jack, was your mom's name *Melinda*? She's dead. And look, her name is crossed out, too. I don't know any of the other names but death seems to be the only common denominator among the ones I recognize. I thought you should see it for yourself. Does any of it make any sense?"

"No," I said. "It doesn't make sense, but I'm beginning to see some other connections between Bill and my dad."

I tapped my fingertip on a couple of names at the top of the list.

"*Pete* and *Medora* were my paternal grandparents. They're dead and their names are crossed out, too. I was just at their gravesite out in western Minnesota on New Year's Eve day. I don't know any of the other names. *Mickey* might refer to the *Mike* in that old letter to Bill. And *Franny* may have been Mike's wife; *Jenny* their daughter. Something must have happened to her, because she's crossed out. Same with *Freddy* and *mom* on this line. Tina, was Bill's mom remarried to a man named Fred by any chance?"

"Yes, he talked about Freddy a lot. He never mentioned his biological father, though."

"Ok, so now Bill's parents add up, too," I continued. "And look, my dad's name Arv — his nickname was always *Tommy*. For some reason Bill put it in parentheses and his name isn't crossed out. It may be one more reason to suspect Dad's still alive. Do you recall? Did he ever come here to visit Bill?"

"Not that I'm aware of but Bill had vendors and customers coming in and out of here all the time. Does this list have some kind of dark side to it? Why would he keep it on a writing board, rather than a flash drive he could hide somewhere?"

"Because using a memory stick leaves traces on the hard drive," I reasoned. "And they can be lost or stolen. Entrance to this building was under guard until a couple of months ago. If he was trying to hide it from someone, this would be the toughest place to get at it."

"Bill was a computer genius," Tina replied. "He could have encrypted it."

"Encryptions can be broken. Particularly if he knew someone here at ProtoCommand might want it. I don't understand any of this."

She touched my arm gently.

"There's one more thing I think you need to see."

Tina moved the lamp near a small coat closet in the corner of the office. She slid open the vinyl accordion door and shined the light into the small space. Across the length of the rear wall, in large, anguished red letters were scrawled the words, **Please, God! Give us back the hammer!**

"Now that you've explained the reference to curling, it makes a little more sense," she said. "I know it wasn't there in late November when I came in here one afternoon to retrieve his coat for him. I wouldn't have missed something this obvious. That poor man. I think he was scared to death about something. I worked alongside him every day and didn't understand. I must have been asleep not to see it."

"Yeah," I said quietly, thinking of Bill's weekly telephone calls to my team down in the fishbowl. "I guess we all just slept through his darkest hours."

I helped her pack the last box of items, while explaining in greater detail the clues I was beginning to assemble regarding my father. I started with the banners in the curling club and the newspaper article, and finished with the scant information I discovered on the Internet. When I got to the part about the pipe cutter tool in my basement, I tugged down my sleeve to hide the light scar still evident on my wrist.

"I don't know why my dad walked out of my life, or why he may have faked his death back in 2002," I finished. "And now I need to find out why he's on a list with all these dead people."

"Jack," she said pointing to the board, "your name's on here too."

"Yeah, I know," I said. "For whatever reason, Bill was keeping track. Now his number came up. If my father is still alive, I'm linked to him in some way."

Tina looked at her watch.

"We better get a move on before managers start showing up to get some quality time away from their families."

Walking down the first-floor hallway toward the side exit, I screwed up the nerve to admit that my wife had left me and my life was a wreck. The lies and excuses all came out sideways. Although I tried to spare the details about LaVon's affair, Tina gave me a comforting smile and took a scientific wild-ass guess.

"Yeah, very good perception," I confirmed.

We exchanged cell phone numbers and I suggested that we get together for lunch sometime during the week. She agreed and said we could discuss more about what to expect with her pending unemployment and job search.

"What are you going to do with all of Bill's things?" I asked.

"His car is parked around back. The company allowed me to keep it there until we figure out what to do with it. I'll store whatever I can fit in the trunk. The rest I'll take out to his townhouse. I still have the keys."

Tina and I walked back out to the parking lot mostly in silence. I held the framed Navy photograph and the large manila envelope in my right hand, while squeezing the desktop writing board under my left armpit. In my hip pocket was an old rolled up copy of the Montevideo American News, which Bill had used to line the bottom of a drawer hiding a half-empty bottle of gin.

"I'll bet my dad grew up with this newspaper, too," I rationalized.

It has been said that facts are stubborn things. As withdrawn and cynical as I had become about my life, I had learned to place my trust in measurable facts. To be sure, the facts weren't always comfortable, but there was always some comfort to be found in using them to shape my world. Suddenly, a new set of facts were beginning to emerge, changing the back-story of my life. The 19th century English author Thomas Haliburton once wrote that innocence is always unsuspicious. But my innocence was gone forever. Everything I once thought I knew about my family had become suspicious.

As I pulled my car onto the street, I glanced into my side mirror to see Tina softly waving with her fingertips, surrounded by a neat stack of boxes filled with Bill Ordway's death. Scattered haphazardly across the rear seat behind me was the scant hope of my father's resurrection.

Michigan Rink - Gold	**Minnesota Rink - Silver**
Lead: Jim Coventry	Lead: Paul Stenner
Second: Dale Harder	Second: John Mistovich
Third: Steve Talbert	Third: Mickey Bellows
Skip: Norm Thunger	**Skip: Freddy Schade**

Fifth End

Norm Thunger's Michigan men were taking their full allotment of time to discuss an aggressive strategy to come back from a 5-2 deficit. By getting only a single point in the fourth end, his rink was at a distinct disadvantage. Minnesota would regain the last shot for the fifth end and could begin slowing down the scoring. Keeping the house open with no points scored would be just fine, as they would be happy to waste an end and retain the hammer heading into the sixth.

As the end played out, one conservative shot followed the next. As a Michigan player lay down a rock in the house, a Minnesota player was content to knock it out of play. Freddy Schade would have the final option of taking a single point with a cold draw with the hammer, or simply riding out the game with open ends; keeping the hammer until Thunger finally capitulated with a handshake.

But it was also clear that Freddy was losing interest. On several occasions, his teammates had to pry his attention away from his son sitting with two friends in the fifth row. He didn't like it when his young, brooding, hand-picked alternate had elected to sit in the crowd rather than on the players' bench. "Let him sit with his friends," his teammates finally argued. "The kid is only a teenager and not likely to be used in the match anyway."

"What the hell's going on, Freddy," John Mistovich asked with an angry tone as Schade stepped into the hack. He stared down the ice at his opposing counterpart Norm Thunger's #7 rock sitting at the front center of the eight-foot ring. It should have been an easy target but Schade seemed so distracted that his teammates weren't convinced.

"You're spending more time looking up at the crowd than down at the sheet," Mistovitch said, leaning over his broom, preparing to sweep whatever shot Freddy would eventually send down the ice.

"Shut up and get your brooms ready. I'll clear off that son-of-a-bitch's rock. Don't worry about it."

But Freddy didn't clear off that son-of-a-bitch's rock. In fact, his shot ended up curling several feet short of the target and slid harmlessly out of play. It was an unexpected break for Michigan.

Thunger took advantage by placing his second shot — #8 — slightly shorter and about two feet right of his first. Schade would have to use the hammer to split a narrow gap or draw around to the middle.

As the Michigan rink gathered again on the edge of the ice, the players followed Schade's eyes into the crowd. Two police officers could be seen talking to the three teenage boys. Freddy walked toward the seats but a steward quickly warned him about the clock.

With a flash of anger, he calmly stepped back into the hack and delivered a heavy shot that sailed wide, coming to rest against the back edge of the house. Michigan had stolen two unexpected points without the hammer; closing the gap to 5-4 heading into the sixth end.

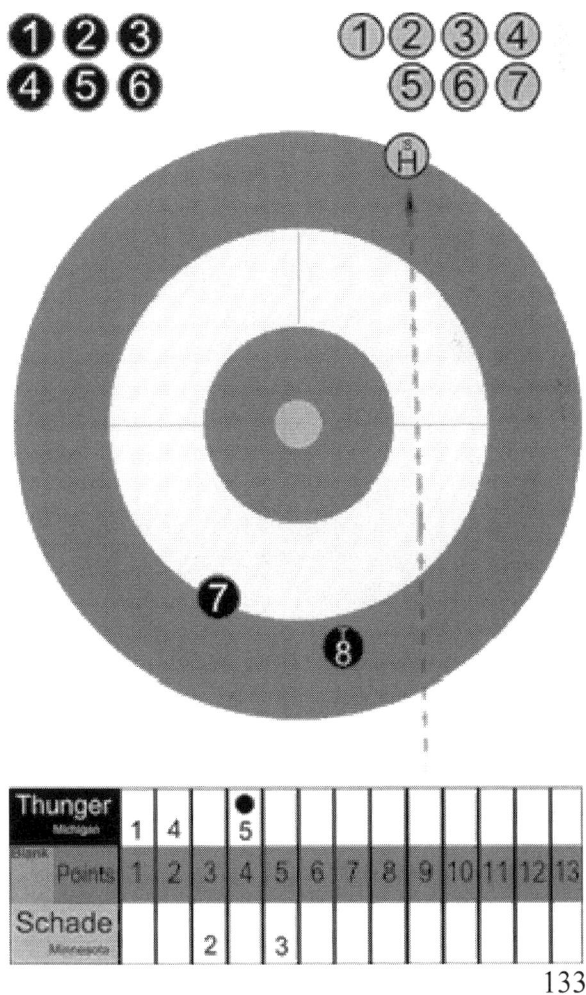

Sunday, January 27th, 2008

The week after meeting with Tina in Bill's office, I concentrated on every scant piece of evidence I could find or imagine about my father's possible whereabouts. For the first time in my life, I was able to tolerate the unbearable cold and dark of a Minnesota January.

Evidence? Is that what I was calling it? Evidence of what? The official proof of his death still heavily outweighed any formless expectation that he might actually be alive. The deeper I got into my search, the more I began questioning what it was I was really hoping to find. Answers to why he walked out on my life? An opportunity to wrap my arms around him with a hug? Or an opportunity to punch him in the nose?

I suddenly began feeling a sense of self-inflicted urgency about it, too. I looked down at Bill's writing board for the thousandth time and read the list of names again — every one of them dead. Everyone, that is, except the two most important names; mine and my father's. Some died years ago. Some died fairly recently. I was certain that, somehow, the names tied together all the little bits and pieces of information I had been gathering. But how and why?

The answer may not be lying on the dinette table in front of me, I reasoned, but it's probably not too far beneath the surface, either. I considered hiring a private detective but quickly dismissed the possibility when a few local agencies quoted seven hundred dollars per day — plus expenses. I didn't have seven dollars per day — plus expenses.

Following my mother's death, my first course of action was to investigate whether she carried any life insurance naming me as the beneficiary. There was none that I could turn up. My second step was to join with one hundred sixty-three other plaintiffs, including LaVon, in a group-action personal injury lawsuit against the owners and operators of the Flanders Banquet Hall. Our lawyer talked of getting us enough money for early retirement. However, our group was forced to settle for an insignificant amount when the insurance company proved the fire was started as a criminal act by a disgruntled ex-cook; negating much of the property owner's liability. LaVon blew through her nine thousand dollar settlement in about a month. My money went to paying off medical bills for myself and my mother, transporting her body back to Minneapolis and burial expenses. My final hope was to file a wrongful death lawsuit on behalf of my mother's estate, claiming personal loss and distress resulting from her suffering and death. But the family of another victim had quickly settled their own claim for less than thirty thousand dollars. I wasn't able to prove that I relied on my mother's income, so I was left arguing for emotional pain. Even my lawyer rolled his eyes. I accepted a quickly-arranged settlement of twenty-one thousand dollars — of which the attorney took a generous cut for fees and expenses. It all sounded so rational when LaVon suggested that we use the remainder of the lump sum payment to clear off her student loans and personal credit card debt prior to our wedding.

It came as a surprise to me when I learned that after a lifetime in a successful real estate career, my mother's assets amounted to her Volkswagon Passat, her mortgage-free house in South Minneapolis and some capital gains savings remaining from the sale of the New Brighton rambler. I was powerless to prevent her former divorce attorney from draining her bank account for the legal fees she still owed him dating back several years. Although the amount he was awarded was still several thousand dollars short, the leech agreed that forcing me to sell the house and car to pay him off would be more blood than even he could suck.

Even if I had been sitting on a pile of money, though, it wouldn't have mattered. I knew LaVon's attorney would eventually get around to calling about the divorce. I would be required to give a full accounting of every penny. Nearly a month had passed since she dropped the bomb on New Year's Day and things remained eerily quiet from Mankato. But there was one thing I wouldn't back down about: I was going to force her to make the next move.

I turned my attention to thinking things through rationally. What tracks would a living person leave, without being aware of leaving tracks? I started by following the money. After all, the man had to eat.

I called the Minneapolis Local Pipefitters Union #539 to ask about his pension. Their records showed that he cashed out his retirement annuity in 1998. He was one of the last union members allowed to cash-out before they disallowed the practice. It was one more piece that could have fit a pattern. He would have known the union was ending the buyout policy. It may have led to his decision to leave home when he did, in order to take advantage of the lump sum. It wasn't like him, though. Money was something he neither worried about nor focused on. Besides, his total payment after taxes only came to ninety-seven thousand dollars. I was puzzled about why he would take a lump sum, until I realized that a monthly annuity check would have to be mailed somewhere and it would leave a paper trail. No matter how frugally he tried to live, he would certainly have burned through the cash within five or six years. So okay, I speculated, to supplement his money, perhaps he traveled around the cashspiel circuit to pick up some extra scratch whenever he could.

I contacted the Minnesota Department of Revenue, the IRS and the Social Security office but was informed by each that the information was confidential. Whether he was dead or alive, they wouldn't tell me anything. I then called the Minnesota Department of Motor Vehicles to request public information about vehicle registration. It was an uphill battle but I was finally connected to a clerk who told me that no one named Arvil DuMot had registered a vehicle in Minnesota since 2000. His last known address on record was in 2001, a P.O. box in Mankato. That would be about the timeframe he started curling at the Mapleton club, I thought.

I looked at my atlas and realized I would need to extend my search. In order to put together a team made up of other Minnesota curlers it was logical he must have remained somewhere in the five-state region. I called the neighboring states' DMVs with no results. When I checked with the two bordering Canadian provinces, I learned that in January of 1999 he was listed as the buyer of a 1994 Ford Bronco. His name also appeared on the title of an Airstream travel trailer a few months later. In both files, his address was listed only as Lake Wasaw, Ontario. His name was on the titles but he never officially licensed the vehicles for the road.

"Lake Wasaw, Ontario?" I thought. I searched GoogleMaps. *"My God, Dad, what the hell were you doing up there? You hated the cold."* I was able to locate the little town but there was no curling club listed in the nearby area. Assuming he had to practice to maintain his skills at a national level, he must have driven across the border to the nearest U.S. club in International Falls several times each week. It was one more lead that was several years old, but it might give up a name or two.

I called the International Falls Curling Club but the woman had no information for me except that he had never been registered as a member. She said that some members occasionally talked about seeing him at bonspiels around the state, but nothing concrete. The call turned out to be another cold, dead end about a cold, dead man.

The only further option I could think of was to contact every county courthouse in the Upper Midwest, to check whether there were any other files on record. There were eighty-seven counties in Minnesota alone. Add to that the number of bordering counties in neighboring states and I could easily be looking at calling more than one hundred courthouses, probably requiring two or three phone transfers at each one. I knew it was an impossible mission that would likely bring me very little further along the timeline.

I started asking myself again what I was really driving at. I shouldn't have been interested in putting together a history of his travels and travails after he left home. Instead of looking back, I needed to remain focused on the present and immediate future. I finally admitted to myself that I needed to find the living, breathing *him,* not his footprints or his shadow. If he was out there, I could find him. I just needed to work the equation backward by figuring out why he went into self-imposed exile in the first place. As for everything else, hell, we could get together over coffee someday.

I pulled the wooden writing board in front of me once again and drew up a list to make sense of the notes scribbled across its surface. Like an archaeologist, I began digging through the historical layers of names and phone numbers from most recent on top to the oldest scribbles beneath, covered over by other numbers, names and colorful doodles. After a few hours, I compiled about thirty contacts, as well as a few additional annotations that were directly related to Bill's job. I congratulated myself on my impeccable logic. Since I knew the desk was only about three years old, everything written on the board would certainly be fresher than anything the DMV or a county courthouse would have provided.

I looked at the long list and figured the majority of the names were legitimate vendors and salesmen who would be part of the daily comings and goings of any business organization. Calling each one would lead to more tangents that would ultimately get me nowhere. I needed help and I immediately thought of Tina Bucholz. With her insider knowledge, I could cut to the chase. After all, she worked just outside of Bill's office for years. She would certainly recognize the names of people who popped in and out on any given workday.

It had been more than a week since I had left her waving goodbye on ProtoCommand's sidewalk. Despite our promises to get together for lunch, we had left each other alone. I was tempted to call her but I didn't know how to re-break the ice. I knew she was unemployed and I wasn't sure whether she immediately moved back with her family, but it was worth a shot. I opened and closed my cell phone several times before getting up the nerve to punch in her number. I was surprised when she answered on the second ring.

"Hi, Jack," she said before I could identify myself.

"Caller ID. I hate that about cell phones, Tina." I chuckled. "Well, you're out of work now. How does it feel?"

"Well, you know," she returned. "Not too bad, I guess. The timing was right for it. My apartment lease runs out at the end of this month.

I'm thinking of moving back to Pipestone — in with my parents for a while. How are you doing?"

"Say, Tina," I said, ignoring her question. "Could I trouble you to stop by my house sometime in the next day or two to check something for me? Or maybe we could just get together over lunch somewhere. I've been tracking down information about my father and I'm trying to decipher the notes from Bill's desk board."

"Will tomorrow work?" she answered. "What's your address?"

Monday, January 28th, 2008

Tina knocked on my outer porch door at about 1:30 the following afternoon. I found her standing in the yard brushing the fresh layer of snow off my sham Brinks Home Security sign. She gave me a knowing wink and shook her head with mock indignation.

At the dinette table, I handed her a Coke and we spent a few minutes in small talk. It was the first time she had ever been unemployed and wondered how much money she should expect for jobless benefits. When I showed her my most recent unemployment check, she wasn't happy to see the number on the bottom line.

"How do they justify taking out taxes? she asked. "It isn't earned income, is it?"

I changed subjects and took a few minutes to explain the swath of notes and website printouts scattered across the table, overflowing onto the nearby kitchen countertop. She agreed with my conclusion that it didn't make sense to track down someone by sniffing out clues that were arguably five or six years old. She looked at the writing board and started scanning through my list, pausing over each one methodically as if trying to put a face with a name. As I had hoped and suspected, in most cases she could.

Within an hour, she was able to identify most of the names and included a brief explanation of the person's connections to Bill Ordway and ProtoCommand. Initially, I tried to save her the trouble of fleshing out every name. I stopped, though, when I realized she was using the opportunity to seek closure with the company. I was somewhat jealous that nobody had offered me the same courtesy.

I wrote down the few names she didn't recognize or remember. They would be my jumping-off point. When she finished, I had a manageable list of about a dozen names. Our conversation swung around to what the boxed list of crossed-off names could possibly mean. Tina admitted she had been giving it some thought.

"The more I think about it, Jack, the more I realize there might be some connection between Bill dying and your father still being alive. It's easy to think that it all must add up somehow."

"That's where my head is going, too," I said, "if our suspicions are correct."

"Well, yes," Tina said. "*If* our suspicions are correct, Jack, and *if* your father is really still alive. You need to find out."

"Well, there's something else I'm discovering, Tina. Yes, I need to find him, but not only because of that death list. He's been out of my life for years but suddenly I feel that I need him. I can't explain it. My heart is fighting with my head. For the first time, I want my heart to win this one. I feel as if I'm dangling at the end of a rope."

"Dangling is a terrible position to be in," she said. "If you're really that close to the bottom, just let go and get your feet back on the ground, so you at least have a foundation to push off from."

"I guess that's what I'm doing," I answered. "I need him to be part of my life now. I don't understand why."

She reached out with her slender, soft hand and gently stroked my shoulder.

"I think I know why," she whispered.

We couldn't assume that our paranoia about murder and death was the only possibility for the list. We knew we had to look at every other potential reason my name was included. We decided to write up every fantastical conjecture. Was Bill simply keeping tabs on former classmates and their families over the years? Were the names old Navy shipmates and family members? Did he owe them all money? Did they owe him money? Were they all members of the VFW, the American Legion or some other social club he may have belonged to? No — My grandparents' names wouldn't be included. Were the names all former neighbors of his from back in Gluek? No — His mother and step-father's name were included, too.

We finally decided there could have been any number of reasons, some of which bordered on the absurd. We settled on the most logical ones, based in large part on which possibilities were the least laughable. Without having access to legal records, though, death remained the only common denominator we could find.

I was growing more and more convinced that a connection existed between the list and my father's decision to disappear into his unknown world. If he was still alive, it was easy to assume he was running and hiding from imminent danger. But Tina pointed out some obvious non-sequiturs. First, no danger with a shelf-life of more than a decade could be considered imminent. It was too difficult to believe that he successfully looked over his shoulder, behind every bush, and around every corner all those years. Second, if he was trying to run and hide, he could have found a way to contact me somehow. I wanted to believe that he might even have needed my help now and then. Finally, if staying incognito was his only chance to survive, why would he surface for something as brazen as curling championships?

"Anything might be possible," I finally said scanning the lists. "But we're missing the connection about why Bill didn't also run and hide if he knew his life was in danger, too. He was scared enough to climb into a dark corner and scream for help across a closet wall. But he lived and worked out in public all those years? That list of dead people goes back decades, but all of a sudden he self-medicates himself to death? It doesn't make sense."

We looked again at the names on the list and Tina had an idea.

"Let's see how many of these names match any first names I didn't recognize on the vendor list. Maybe it's a place to start."

It was a good idea, but it only led to more confusion when we found the very common name Mike listed three times among the scribbles and doodles. We moved on to other possibilities.

"There is no way of knowing how these people were connected in life," I said. "So what about finding ways they may have been connected by death? What do you know about Bill's ex-wife and son? Anything peculiar about their stories?"

"Nothing too peculiar," Tina replied. "You know that Jason died in a hunting accident when he was thirty. Tanya died of a heart condition a couple of years ago."

I thought quietly for a moment and realized there was something I had overlooked.

"You said Bill died on the evening of his birthday?" I asked. "That's a damned rare thing to do, isn't it?"

"Well, the medical examiner said possibly as late as early the following morning but yeah, basically his birthday. It happens."

I tapped Pete and Medora's names on the list.

"My grandparents each died on their birthdays, too. Their fifty-sixth birthdays to be exact."

An idea began forming in my head.

"How old was Bill?"

"Well, his birthday was December 21st. He was in his mid-fifties, I guess. I remember he told me once that his wife was a couple years older."

"And when did Tanya die? Do you remember the date, or at least the month and year? We can look up their records if we need to."

Tina's eye grew wide.

"Jack, I remember it was in early June. Let's see, it would have been June of '06."

I pointed down at the writing board and tapped the list.

"Tina, look. First, we have my grandparents dying exactly on their fifty-sixth birthdays, but two years apart. Their names are crossed off. My mother passed her fifty-sixth birthday just a few days before she came out to California to visit me — where she died. Name crossed off. You say that Tanya would have been in her mid-fifties. Is it too much of a stretch to think it might have been on or near her fifty-sixth? If Bill died on his fifty-sixth, we may have found an undeniable connection. For whatever reason, people on this list are dying — or getting murdered — each when they turn fifty-six years old."

Tina used the nail of her little finger to quietly trace the list of names on the writing board as she thought for a moment. I could almost see the glow of her thoughts.

"Calm down, Jack," she finally said. "Not everyone on this list was fifty-six. Jason wasn't. We're jumping to too many conclusions about everyone being dead. We don't know anything about Mike and Franny or Hank."

"I'm listening," I said.

"Look, Jason — dead —was only thirty. And if Mike and Franny were mutual friends of your dad and Bill, then their daughter Jenny — dead — must have been only about our age, too.

"Okay," I agreed, "But the number of times fifty six comes up is just too weird not to be more than just a coincidence. It's not as if these people were in their nineties."

We took a quick break to share another drink and sat quietly for a minute as I doodled on the legal pad, thinking.

"According to the groundskeeper at the cemetery, my grandparents both died in suspicious accidents. In fact, he said the townspeople around there *still* talk about it. Here's what we have. Jason died in a hunting accident while separated from his party. Bill's wife Tanya died of, what, a heart attack you said? My mother died of a stroke after getting injured in a fire. Bill died of an accidental drug overdose. So okay, every death appears to be an accident or natural medical causes. But they could all have been arranged with enough careful planning, couldn't they?"

"I don't know, Jack," Tina said. "This is a bit of a stretch. How many years ago did your grandparents die? Nearly forty? I know Bill's step-father Freddy died sometime around 1972. Your dad's letter mentioned Jenny's death, so we know it was before your dad died in

2002. And your mom died several months later in that same year. Bill's wife, Tanya, died in 2006. Bill just died a couple of weeks ago. We'd be talking about a serial killer tracking down a disconnected group of victims for nearly four decades."

"Disconnected group?" I said with a touch of incredulity. "Tina, Bill wrote those names on a list and then drew a boxed line around them. By definition, names on a framed list have some kind of logical connection. Murder, natural causes or otherwise, these names are anything but disconnected!"

"Don't get upset, Jack."

"Yeah, sorry," I said. "I don't mean to. This is scary as hell if we're right, but I think we're on to something and it might explain a lot."

"That's what I mean, Jack. Even if we can draw nice straight connecting lines between the names and the deaths, let's not allow ourselves to get carried away. Your emotions are getting ahead of your evidence. Not everyone on the list was necessarily a murder victim. You need to slow down and think this through rationally."

"You sound like one of my old philosophy teachers explaining why he graded my A+ term paper a C-," I laughed.

"Look, I'm talking about a psychopath who has years to follow each victim, until he knows their patterns and lifestyles. He sets up every murder to look like an accident and covers his tracks completely. The deaths are taking place years and miles apart. There's so much time and space between them that the local authorities can't possibly find a connection, especially if they don't know they should be looking for one."

"Rational, but I'm not ready to jump completely onboard yet."

"Maybe I'm wrong but what else do we have, Tina. If I'm right, I think there must be an obvious connection that Bill and my dad would have known about — or the list wouldn't exist. Or the Navy photo. Or the letter. But, God, I'm sure it has something to do with their fifty-sixth birthdays. That would help explain some things about my father."

A thought suddenly occurred to me. I rushed to the dinette table and spilled the contents of the large manila envelope onto the floor.

"Tina, we don't know what these little slips of paper with their birthdays and the dash numbers mean. Some of these slips look older than others. Bill might have been saving them over the years. I found my dad's inside a business envelope mailed nearly a year ago. Let's see if the dash numbers on the end could mean anything."

We knelt together on the floor, our thighs, hips and shoulders occasionally brushing each other's as we arranged the little papers in a row. Eventually, the trail ran the full length of one oak floorboard in the bare center of the living room. As I suspected, there were no duplicates, with the dash numbers ranging from —37 down to —1. To complete the string, I tacked on my dad's slip with the zero to the very end.

We rose to our feet to get a broader perspective. Over the length of the sequence the changes in paper and handwriting seemed to follow a vague evolution. The larger numbers were written on hand-cut spiral notebook paper, changing eventually to card stock or heavy linen paper before finally morphing into precisely cut heavy, bright white business letterhead. Tina noticed that several numbers toward the beginning of the sequence were missing, — 33 through — 26. I surmised that Bill had been receiving and collecting the slips on or near his birthday every year. If I had calculated the dates correct, the slips would have dated back to around his nineteenth birthday. The missing numbers could possibly have been the six years he served in the Navy with my father, during their late teens and early twenties.

"My dad must have received them every year, too," I said. "Maybe he just didn't bother to save his. Tina, do you think it's possible these things were sent as warnings? If they were, what a lousy way to celebrate a birthday."

"Yeah, a real curse, I suppose," she answered. "But think of what a blessing it could be to have an annual reminder that our days are numbered. Imagine how fulfilling it would make our lives."

I looked at her with a quiet wonder.

"Where do you acquire that level of serenity?" I asked. "Can you bottle it for sale? We're sitting here talking about someone playing God with people's lives for forty years and you still find an up-side."

She looked confused and then her face broke into a shy smile.

"I didn't say any of this was a good thing, Jack. I just think we could all use a reminder now and then that we shouldn't take our lives for granted. I think that's why Bill hung all those training certificates and awards on his office wall. They weren't there just to satisfy his ego. He wasn't like that at all. He was trying to teach us that there is a right way to do things and we should dedicate ourselves to doing it. Every time any one of us walked into his office we could have learned something, if we had only bothered to listen. Remember what your dad wrote on the back of the Navy picture, *"We have to do something with our lives."* So, Jack, were they cursed with a lifelong death sentence? Or were they blessed by knowing their appointed hour? That's all I'm saying."

"Yeah," I answered as I tried to look past her black bangs and peer into her dark brown eyes, "but you say it so well."

I was disappointed when she quickly knelt down again and brought our attention back to the slips of paper.

"Jack, look more closely at how the handwriting changes on some of these? Look at this end of the line. The handwriting from the highest numbers down to here appears to change only a little over time. I think we can assume they were all written by the same person."

She scooted across the floor on her butt. "But, look — it changes dramatically down here at this end."

I knelt next to her again, deliberately bumping my shoulder into hers. We picked up various papers to examine them in better light. It was clear that the change in style across all five of the final slips was from the same hand. Following our assumption that the dates corresponded to years, it meant that beginning in 2003, a second person was responsible for writing the slips and mailing them.

"Whatever this thing turns out to be about, Tina, it doesn't involve you," I said quietly. "My father and I are on that list. You're not. This is my problem."

I realized I was speaking to her as if she were a child.

"I mean, it's great that you're willing to help and all," I quickly added, "But none of this concerns you."

"But it does concern me," she said quietly. "Bill was like family to me. In fact, he really stepped in as the only family I had after I finished college."

"Like your own father, huh?" I added.

"No, never like one of my parents," she responded. "He never tried to control my life. Not the way my parents did, anyway. In some odd ways, he became more like an older brother. My dad and I didn't get along very well, so I moved in with my aunt before I finished high school. She's the lady I was visiting when Bill died. Whenever things got a little rough, she would say, *"We are each where we are supposed to be, and we're on time."* Well, Jack, I think this is where I'm supposed to be right now."

"You've been alone for a long time?" I fished.

"That morning we were in Bill's office," she continued, "I didn't tell you the whole story. I got involved with his son, Jason, soon after I started at ProtoCommand as an intern. He was in pretty deep with his girlfriend back in North Carolina but he promised he was trying to end it. Her drinking was becoming a real problem and he didn't want things to get to the point of marrying an alcoholic. I dated him whenever he flew into Minneapolis to visit his parents during the baseball offseason, but he could never find a good enough reason to break off the relationship with Hillary. When she started realizing that he was trying to end things, she entered a series of chemical dependency programs. He felt so guilty about making her go through recovery alone that he never told her about us."

"From what I understand, very few of those rehab programs work the first time through," I said.

"Yeah, I told Jason that giving her a crutch was the last thing she needed but he felt stuck and responsible. I understood that. She lived on the outskirts of Charlotte, so I suspect he liked the idea of having a girlfriend near him during the long baseball season."

"I'm sorry to hear that, Tina." I offered.

"So I kept waiting through all the promises. He said he was going to give it one more season to see if he could make it to the Major Leagues. He knew that if he couldn't make it at age thirty, he never would. He wanted to work with his dad but he didn't know anything about computers or programming. When I suggested that he should live in Minneapolis during the off season, he said that he and his father needed to figure out some things first. I didn't understand what problem they had between them. They sure seemed to be very close to each other."

"But you kept waiting?"

"Well, Jason didn't make the Majors and he was at the end of his minor league contract. Trading a career minor leaguer was almost impossible. He was getting ready to move up here at the end of the season. Then his girlfriend announced she was pregnant. I finally accepted the fact that there was no future in it for me. Bill was aware of everything and we both had a good cry in his office. He didn't like Hillary. He was looking forward to having a grandchild, of course, but we both suspected she got pregnant on purpose."

She paused for a quick smile before continuing.

"It's been quite a few years since Jason died and I'm just starting to get over it. Now I have to get over losing Bill, too."

She blinked back a tear.

"So you see, Jack, this really does concern me, in more ways than I'm able to express right now."

I looked at her and thought about the times my co-workers and I stepped all over our penises whenever she stopped by the fishbowl window to gave us a soft smile and a genuinely friendly wave. Now here she was, sitting on the floor next to me, just a kiss out of reach; lost, lonely and vulnerable. It would have been the easiest thing in the world to wrap her in my arms and make love to her among those damned slips of paper scattered across the hardwood floor. But she wasn't like any other woman I had ever met. I couldn't imagine how to make the first move.

I jumped up to pour her a glass of wine and we moved over to the living room sofa, where we spent the next couple of hours sharing stories of two lives that had occupied the same parallel plane for so many years, yet rarely intersected. With no conscious agenda on my part, the conversation came full circle. We found ourselves once again talking about how important it was to find my father.

A sinking thought suddenly occurred to me. I retrieved my dad's letter and the Navy photo from the dinette table and returned to sit close to her on the sofa.

"Look at this letter again," I said. "He says, *'I've given up trying to end this thing, or running from it.'* That sounds like a man who's telling his friend that he's at the end of his rope."

"And that adds more evidence that we may be right," Tina said, taking the Navy photo from my lap and flipping it over. "Look again at what he wrote to Bill on the back of this picture. *'We're the lucky ones. We can number our days. By my calculation, we still have about 11,000 of them remaining.'* Jack, it's possible that from the very beginning, they knew there was some odd connection between all these deaths over the years. Every time they received one of these slips in the mail, it drove the nail a little deeper into their coffins."

"Tina, didn't you say that Bill didn't have much of a life after Jason died? That his work became everything to him? He might have been hiding behind his work and his office doors, trying to figure out what to do next. Maybe that's what Jason meant when he said they had to figure things out before he could move back up here. Imagine what it would be like knowing that your execution date was drawing closer one day at a time. Sitting behind that desk every day must have been like his own personal Purgatory."

"No, not his Purgatory," she answered with a tone of introspection. "More like his Gethsemane. But, Jack, lots of people receive a diagnosis of terminal cancer. They go through the stages of grief and dying but they don't necessarily start screaming for help on closet walls. And inmates on death row come to terms with it."

"I'm sure many do," I said, "but we don't know the internal depth of fear that terminal patients or dead-men-walking feel. Or what bargains they make with their god in their final days. Give the inmates a magic marker and those prison walls might be covered with anguished scrawls."

"He watcheth every sparrow fall," Tina said quietly.

"Yeah, but he catcheth not a single one," I smirked.

I pointed down to the slips of paper.

"My guess is that Bill received another one of those slips just before his birthday last month, a day or two before he died. Possibly with a dash zero written at the end, like the one I found for my father."

"Bill could have run and hid," she said. "I wonder why he didn't."

"You mean like my father?" I interrupted. "And live like a ghost? Forgetting about his wife and kid..."

Tina placed a finger to my lips, interrupting my next words.

"Don't judge him so harshly, Jack. This whole thing may be nothing but a crazy theory."

She held up her empty wine glass.

"After another glass or two of these and I might start agreeing that you're right. Any refills?"

"Tipsy after just one glass?" I thought silently. What a refreshing change from LaVon's all-night binge marathons with her friends.

"Sure," I answered, taking the glass and retreating toward a kitchen cabinet. "I rarely drink the stuff. It's from my wife's hobby cupboard. I should have poisoned it a long time ago."

"Shuush," Tina said quietly. "Instead of trying to make me hate her, why don't you let me judge for myself. I think you said her name is LaVon?"

"Not much to tell," I said flatly.

"Well, I'm not driving anywhere until the wine wears off," she said. "I'm listening."

"Well," I started, "she was the youngest of four daughters born to second-generation German immigrant crop farmers Cyril and Laura Bever. Speaking German as her second language around the home came as natural as popping open a can of Budweiser at lunch. By the time she was in her junior year at the local public school, she was the last remaining daughter who hadn't escaped her father's heavy hand and his love of all things fermented. Her dad was already over sixty when LaVon entered high school. The family farm hadn't turned a profit in years. Like every other farmer in America, though, the Bevers had leveraged their land values to the hilt before the bottom fell out."

"How did she end up in Minnesota?" Tina interrupted.

"When her maternal grandmother died and left their family an old homestead house near Mankato, her parents got out from under their pile of debt by turning the farm over to the bank. They moved three hundred and fifty miles further north and took over the house. Moving north, however, was not the escape route that any of LaVon's older sisters had taken and certainly not the direction she had in mind, either. But for her, it was the last flight out of hell."

"To Mankato? Last flight out of hell?" Tina chuckled, surprised.

"Well, considering where she came from, the highway maps made Mankato look as if it was just a quick Friday evening jaunt to Minneapolis. It didn't take long for her to learn, though, that Highway 169 got icy during the long Minnesota winters and often slowed to a stop through the small towns. To her disappointment during her high school senior year, very few of her new friends were willing to make the unnecessary trip to the Twin Cities. In their small town minds, Mankato had everything they were looking for in boys, toys and joys. Besides, big city bouncers took their jobs seriously and her friends' parents were a great deal more involved with raising their kids than Ma and Pa Bever."

"So how did you end up meeting her?" Tina asked.

"Late in her senior year, LaVon learned that she had been accepted to join one of her older sisters at Arizona State University. It was going to be her final escape. Before the end of the school year, though, her mother was diagnosed with non-Hodgkin's Lymphoma, so LaVon's imprisonment was destined to continue. *"I'm not a nurse, I'm a farmer,"* her father complained. Her only real choice was to attend nearby Minnesota State University, as she continued to look after her mother. For better or worse, her parents went along with letting her live independently, initially in the Kappa Kappa Iota sorority house as an education major. Later, she shared an apartment with roommates. As she pressed on toward her teaching certification, she focused on the injustice of watching her sisters discover lives of their own. As the final months of her college years passed, she reduced her contact with her parents, eventually relegating her visits and phone calls to brief discussions about her mother's health. In time, even the smallest amounts of face-time with them became more than she could handle, so she ended the relationship, altogether."

"Yeah, I guess I can understand that," Tina said.

"Anyway, one of LaVon's roommates at MSU was Bussy Steiger, an education major whose only real career goal was to score a job that promised her a six-hour school day and summers off. Her real name was Bertha but she took on the nickname Bussy as a young kid. She had been raised in New London, Iowa, so she had something in common with LaVon's past. The empathy they exhibited toward each other created an immediate bond of sisterhood."

"And they're still friends?" she asked.

"Oh, yeah. They knew the shortest Saturday route to every Twin Cities bar that conveniently forgot to check IDs. Although they pretended to take turns being the designated driver, both ended their college years with two underage DWIs and a handful of juvenile court offenses, including one each for lascivious acts — a reduced charge from solicitation. LaVon's behavior proved to be completely alien to her parents' Roman Catholic expectations. Her father finally ex-communicated her from the family, but by then it was academic."

"So, that still doesn't explain how you two met."

"She came out to the Bay Area to attend a wedding that happened to be at the same banquet center my mom and I were visiting for some old man's birthday party."

"That would be the banquet hall fire you told me about?" she interjected.

"Yeah. Afterward, LaVon returned to Mankato and I moved back to this house. We stayed in touch and saw each other whenever she came up to the cities. Both of her parents died within a few short months of each other. Her mother succumbed to complications of the Lymphoma. Her drunk father drove his car over the edge of an overpass. LaVon learned about her mother's death through one of her sisters. She screwed up enough sympathy to sit at the back of the church at the funeral Mass but skipped out early without speaking with her sisters. Her dad's fatal car wreck made the Mankato newspaper. She didn't care. Her three older sisters inherited the house and sold it to pay off her parents' bills. With little fanfare, the Bever family unit just sort of dissolved into history."

"And Bussy?" Tina pursued. "Was she the one you were visiting in Mankato when this whole search started?"

"Yes" I continued. "After LaVon graduated from college, the knot between LaVon and Bussy began to unravel. LaVon eventually agreed to move in with me; more because she needed a place to stay rent-free than anything else. Bussy completed her teaching certificate but ended up staying in Mankato and went to work as a daytime dispatcher for a small taxi company. It was about as far from the teaching profession as she could get. For the next couple of years, she was a frequent Saturday night guest on our sofa. Her trips to the Twin Cities slowly tapered off, though, and eventually stopped altogether when she started dating one of the local cabbies at her work. LaVon's trip down to Mankato for the holiday sorority party was a way to rekindle a fire that seemed to be dying a little more with each passing year. I wasn't so sure it was a great idea to try to keep the relationship going, but I agreed to go along for the ride."

"And now you're ready to throw in the towel with her?" Tina asked. "Jack, she sounds like she's a live cinder at heart. Certainly there must be a spark there that's worth blowing back into a flame."

I looked at her, not knowing how to explain the hurt and betrayal I felt because of the affair with Tony Perkovich.

"Yeah," I finally said, "she's a hot coal, all right."

We sat in silence for several seconds before she spoke again, "See what I mean, Jack. Everyone has a story."

Tina saw how uncomfortable the conversation was becoming, so she changed the subject.

"So, how do we account for your name and the dead young people on the list?" she asked.

"I suspect we need to consider the misfortune of being related by birth," I responded. "And now my father and I are the last men standing. I'd sure like to know if he thinks about me now and then."

"Oh, I'm sure he thinks about you often," Tina sighed. "Now...we've had enough self-pity for one evening. If this curler guy is your father, you said he uses a first name that he hates, Arvil, and your old nickname, Firpo. Come on, Jack, a moniker like *Arvil Firpo*? Now there's a name you couldn't miss in the newspapers or on television. Have you considered that he might *want* you to find him, if you just start paying attention? He's been out there entering national championships for the past several years. There must be a real good reason he hasn't contacted you."

My stomach suddenly growled. I realized it was nearly eight o'clock and we had talked straight through the dinner hour. We discussed going to a local restaurant but decided to order a pizza. While waiting for it to arrive, I told her more about my childhood and teenage years living with my mother.

When the doorbell finally rang nearly an hour later, I gently lowered her sleeping head onto a sofa pillow and covered her with a tattered blue blanket. As I stepped quietly toward the stairs to go up to bed, I turned to take a final look at her red stockings extending over the arm of the sofa. Would I find her there in the morning? Or would she be out of my life forever?

Tuesday, January 29th, 2008

I was disappointed but not surprised the following morning, when I tiptoed down the stairs and found the ragged fleece blanket folded neatly on the sofa. Tina's car was gone from the front of the house and there were ten bucks set on top of the unopened Dominos box.

Had I blown my chance? She was one sip over the line with her head nestled on my shoulder. But if we had gone upstairs together, I knew that neither of us would have known what to do with the left over feelings in the morning. In my own way, I was too raw and distrustful about LaVon. And in Tina's own way, she was coming to terms with her own emptiness after losing Jason and Bill. Neither of us was ready to ride out an emotional rebound.

I was surprised at mid-morning when she called my cell phone to tell me about some phone calls she had already made. She explained that she woke up sometime after midnight and felt clear-headed enough to drive to her apartment. She thanked me for a nice evening and for *"not, um...well, you know, Jack."*

"You may have noticed that I took the lists we drew up last night," she said. "I wanted to start chasing down some of the names I didn't recognize. If you're looking for your legal pad, I have it."

No, I hadn't noticed, but I couldn't admit that I hadn't noticed anything except the empty sofa all morning. I hadn't even bothered to make a cup of coffee or walk out to pick up the morning paper yet.

"Remember the name and phone number of the Grand Forks Police Station written on the board?" she continued. "Well, I called them first thing and introduced myself. It was awkward, but I tried to explain everything without sounding like a nut. After a few phone transfers, I talked to a man named Paul Gombrich. When I told him I knew Bill Ordway, he paused for a long moment, then said, *'Find Ruude'* and hung up immediately. I called him back right away but he said we couldn't talk. All he said was that I needed to find Ruude. Sam R-U-U-D-E. He warned me not to call back and he hung up again."

I caught myself staring at the wall.

"What did you just say?" I asked.

"Find Ruude," she repeated. "Sam Ruude. That's about it. Maybe he's the key to all of this."

Find Ruude. Something was banging inside my head? *Find Ruude.*

Like lifting a manhole cover, light rushed in to fill the dark recesses of my memory. I suddenly made the connection and was transported back to my mother's hospital room in 2002.

"Tina, remember I told you I was at my mom's bedside when she died in the hospital out in San Mateo?"

"Yeah, what about it?"

"Find Ruude. Those were my mother's final words. But at the time, I thought she was calling LaVon rude for the comments we were making about her at the party the previous night. When I tried to interject, my mother yelled, ***'No! Ruuuude!*** *Find...Ruude.'* Don't you see, Tina? She was trying to tell me to find a man named Ruude. It

must have been Sam Ruude."

I struggled to remember what else happened that long-ago afternoon. She had yelled, shaking a frustrated fist at me. Was that significant? And why find him? Did he have information about my father? Suddenly, more particles began filtering through the haze. I recalled something my mother said in my apartment before driving to the ill-fated party at the Flanders. She said there was *"something we need to talk about."* Did she plan to tell me about all of this?

"Even your mom's clenched fist had a story," Tina said. "Jack, you have to call out to California to try to locate the nurse on duty that night. If she's still around, she might remember or know something. You said your mom died of a stroke? Are you sure? Or was it like Jason's hunting accident? Or Bill's accidental overdose?"

"Whoa," I said. "I'm supposed to be the suspicious one here?"

"I'm starting to feel weird about this, Jack. I'll continue to follow up on the three guys named Mike on our list. They might actually be legitimate salesmen that I didn't know about. If one of them is dead, though, maybe there will be a surviving family member or someone else who might be able to share something."

"No offense, Tina" I said, "but you have an innocent nature that allows you to take people at their word. Sometimes it pays to be a cynic. There's something beneath the surface of all of this. There was a reason that cop in Grand Forks wouldn't talk to you. We may have to be careful. Let's call the police or FBI about it all. I'm not a hero."

"Yeah, I'm way out of my comfort zone, too," she agreed.

"Christ," I sighed, rubbing the back of my neck. "What's going on here? I wake up one morning a month ago, walk out to get the paper and without blinking an eye my life changes forever. My dad used to say, *'You never know what's going to happen when you get up in the morning.'* Well, I always made it a point to know. But this isn't about controlling facts and figures. It's about a bunch of uncontrollable randomness. Now I'd like to push this genie back into the bottle, but I can't. What if I can't ever figure this out and I can't find him before he gets us both killed. God, six months ago my life was perfect."

"Perfect?" Tina laughed into the telephone. "Jack, six months ago your parents were both dead. You were working sixty hours a week and still failing at your job. You were married to a cheating wife who played you like a fish for your money. So in your world, how exactly do you define *perfect*? You say your life suddenly changed without blinking. Well, that's because zombies don't blink."

"Okay, okay," I said. "Lighten up. You're right. I'll call the FBI, but what do I tell them? That we discovered a list of ten or eleven people, whom we know are either dead or soon might be? They'll say the obituaries list five times that many names every day — and they all die in alphabetical order."

"Just start at the beginning, Jack. Tell them you think you have some evidence that a murder has been committed."

"Tina, we have no evidence connecting anything to a murder. Except for my dad committing a federal felony by *possibly* manipulating a death certificate, what crime has been committed? And how do we know that anyone is really in any danger? Every one of those deaths has likely received the Good Housekeeping Seal of Approval by the local medical examiner."

"Well, you're certainly not saying that everything about this can be explained away by sheer coincidence," she said. "But you're right. We don't even have any positive proof that your dad is still alive."

"Again with the we?" I thought.

"OK, Tina, if you're really willing to take the risk of helping me, I'll accept your time, energy and probably some of your money. Hell, we might even make a good team. I'll start by calling the local FBI office. You start by chasing down the names on the writing board."

"Jack," she said emphatically, "Before we hang up, there's something I want to say. I know you *think* you're all about measuring facts and figures, but you're too emotionally invested. Whatever this is about, some of it can't be charted on a graph or measured with a yardstick."

"Fine, I'll use an abacus and a slide rule," I tried joking.

"My point is," she continued, "you'll never be able to discern the difference between a wishful hope, a cynical doubt and an actual fact. We'll follow your wishful hopes and cynical doubts whenever we don't have anything else to go on. When it comes to following the actual facts, though, I'll keep my head screwed on straight. Deal?"

"That feels like a punch in the gut, Tina. But we'll try it your way."

After hanging up, I immediately called the local Minneapolis FBI office to explain my story. After several transfers and a lengthy time on hold, agent Craig Tomlinson picked up the phone. He listened quietly to my bumbling before relaying that he started as a young detective in the Minneapolis office in 1984. Although he wasn't personally involved in any investigation involving my father, he vaguely remembered the on-again, off-again discussions about it throughout the 1980s and into the '90s. After a few more questions, he said he wouldn't discuss it any further. He recommended I call a retired friend of his. Former agent Doug Chimny had been a field agent in the Minneapolis office for nearly thirty years. He was always the go-to guy for inside information throughout the various departments. He had recently retired after a series of run-ins over budget cuts and inflated expense reports.

Tomlinson gave me Chimny's home number in Iowa and added a cryptic aside, "I shouldn't be telling you this, but Chimny will be more than happy to air the Bureau's dirty laundry. He also does a little private-eye work on the side. He may be a good asset for you."

I immediately called Chimny's number and he answered on the second ring. I learned in a hurry that he was still angry with the Minneapolis FBI and *"those jerks in accounting up on the fourth floor."* It had been more than six months since he was escorted out the front door in a flurry of swearing, legal threats and waving fists. He still hadn't emotionally recovered from the Bureau's generous offer to retire or face federal fraud charges.

"Those piss-ants have no idea what it takes to protect your ass in the field," he finally concluded.

Chimny's discontent was my good fortune. He offered to tell me anything and everything he could recall.

I asked every question I could think of about my father, a possible relationship with Bill Ordway and the previous FBI investigations into the string of unusual deaths.

"There was nothing unusual about any of those deaths from what I remember," he corrected me. "And seven or eight deaths over fourty years does not necessarily make it a serial murder. The only sure thing is that it works out to be a string of bad luck for the dead guys."

Apparently, my father and Bill had made damned fools of themselves for many years with repeated phone calls and letters to the FBI and local police departments throughout the Midwest. By 1989, everyone's frustration and anger had reached a boiling point. Despite FBI orders to cease and desist, neither of them would let it drop. After haranguing local detectives, county coroner offices and other authorities for years, my father was eventually arrested in 1989 for interfering with an investigation.

My mind drifted back to when I was eleven or twelve years old but I couldn't remember anything about the incident. My parents must have handled it quietly. But Chimny's information led me to speculate about why my father always disappeared from the curling club for hours at a time between my games at junior bonspiels. He was probably off to the local police station or court house.

Chimny snapped me back to the present.

"I recall that the facts in the case never quite added up," he said. "The senior agent who took over the investigation officially closed the file in late '02 or early '03. When did you say your father died? In '02? So, the dates work."

I told him about Bill recent death. He feigned interest but said there was no way those sons-of-bitches at the Bureau would ever reopen the case on such circumstantial speculation.

"An agent named Carl Stringer was the senior investigator through most of it," he continued. "I remember him talking about that list during department briefings and hallway discussions. Over the years, Ordway or your dad would call periodically, whenever anyone with some connection or another turned up dead. They claimed they could predict who else was going to die mysteriously over the coming years. I mean, yeah, the investigation team could never explain some of the weird coincidences but I don't recall ever hearing any specific evidence that would prove a crime. If there was any, the Bureau would have found it. That was a pretty damned good group of men they had working on it. They must have figured there was enough behind it to keep the investigation alive for as long as they did, though. Whenever somebody on the list turned up dead, Stringer's team investigated with local authorities. But nothing ever came of it. I guess the local coroner's report always proved more convincing."

"So, I'm on my own with this one?" I asked out of frustration.

"Look kid," he continued, "even if I investigate Ordway's death or your father's whereabouts, I can tell you what I'm going to find. There will be a perfectly plausible explanation for everything. In your dad's case, he might have run away from your family because mental illness set in. You haven't seen him in how long? Ten or twelve years? Crazy people walk off into the woods sometimes and never look back. In Ordway's case, I can tell from where I'm sitting that he probably overdosed on his meds. There simply isn't any proof of anything."

"But there must have been other predictors they were pointing to," I pressed on. "Why were the names on the list in the first place? You don't believe it was just coincidence."

"I'm not sure, kid," he said. "Remember, I wasn't officially part of the investigation."

"What happened to the team? Maybe I can track them down."

"Well, there were three guys as I recall," he said. "Stringer, Samualson and some new guy. I remember that Stringer got himself killed on duty in early January of '01. Samuelson, died in a small plane crash heading down to Aruba for a fishing trip a short time later. Just a few weeks after that, the new guy disappeared into the blue. As far as I know, there's still a federal warrant out for his arrest."

Chimny's chuckle caught me off guard.

"A federal warrant? Why?" I interrupted.

"Oh, he just took off with a few million dollars in cold, hard, unlaundered cash from a drug sting he was heading up, that's all. Nobody has seen or heard from him since. I'm not sure I ever knew his real name but I recall that some people around the office called him Bizmo. I guess because he was originally from Bismarck."

"That would have been in March or April that year? Back in '01, maybe?" I asked.

"Yeah, around then," he confirmed. "It was a week or two after Samualson's plane went down, so I think early spring would be about right. After working on that investigation for more than a decade, the whole team imploded overnight. The Bureau never put another unit back together. It lay dormant until they closed the file a year later."

"They assigned a new guy to a major drug bust like that?"

"Well, he wasn't a rookie," he explained. "He worked in the Denver office for several years before transferring to Minneapolis. The chief thought he was good enough to put on the setup. The sting involved two separate Mexican drug rings bringing cocaine north along the coast into Vancouver, across the Canadian heartland into Winnipeg and then south into the states through the forests in Northern Minnesota. The FBI and DEA worked together to set up a bogus three-way deal. It was arranged to take place in International Falls but it never pulled off. Federal marshals were waiting in the wings to make the collar but one of the parties never showed up."

"This Biszmo person did all that by himself?" I asked.

"No, I didn't say that," he replied. "Word around the office was that he must have worked with someone. Somehow, some innocent go-between got involved. Apparently, they worked together to cross-up everyone and they were able to exchange our marked bills for the dirty drug money. It was all the stuff of a good international crime novel. The whole thing left millions of dollars worth of egg on the Bureau's face. I hope it was enough money for everyone involved, though. With the feds and Mexican drug lords on the hunt, they'll be living in caves the rest of their lives — if they're not already dead, that is."

"You said you can't remember his real name?" I probed. "Any chance it could have been Ruude?"

"Hm. Well, the guy was only at the Bureau a few months before the whole thing went down. I never worked directly with him. But yeah, now that you mention it, the guy's name *was* Ruude. Some wise-ass named Saul...no Sam Ruude. There is probably still a price tag on his head. Even if there isn't, you don't want to be connected to this mess, kid. If you know something about him, step forward."

"No," I said. "I don't know anything. I'm just trying to learn more about my dad. I came across Ruude's name somewhere. I figured he must be related to the FBI investigation somehow. I think he may know of my dad's whereabouts."

"Well, Sam Ruude disappeared with unmarked millions of dollars, a surveillance van full of very advanced equipment and several years of FBI field training," Chimny said. "If the FBI never found him, you certainly won't."

"Can I call you if I need you to chase down some information for me?" I asked.

"No, don't call me on this one," he said quickly. "Everyone involved in that investigation is either already dead or soon will be. Let me have your phone number. If I think of anything else, I'll call you."

I gave him my cell phone number and immediately called Tina to relay the information. We agreed that there must have been a connection between the deaths of the FBI agents, Ruude's disappearance and the investigation into the possible murders. We put the facts together. When Ruude's partners died during the investigation, he probably realized his life wasn't worth much, either. He knew too much and he would be next. He figured it was worth taking a gamble and hit the road running. When the opportunity arose to clear out with a lifetime supply of other people's money, he jumped at it. But run where? Over the subsequent years, even the FBI with their network of agents and federal resources gave up looking for him. How could two inept fools like Tina and me possibly find him? We figured the answers must lie somewhere other than the scant evidence scattered across my dinette table.

"Bill kept a lot of notes," I said, "but he probably didn't write down everything. Is there any chance we missed something in those boxes we packed out of his office that day?"

"I locked most of it in his car trunk. I could look again," Tina said. "I moved his car out of sight, back at the rear of the offices by the loading docks. It'll probably sit there until spring when Mr. Nehmer and I finish up the probate issues. Whatever didn't fit in the car, I brought back to my apartment."

"But you still have the car keys?" I asked expectantly.

"Right. I never turned them over to the receptionist and the company has never called to ask me about them."

"Anything still out at his townhouse that might be worthwhile looking through again?" I asked.

"Well, I can look," she answered, "but I'm sure there's nothing new we'll find there. After Jason died, Bill pretty much moved his life into his office. Mr. Nehmer and I went through his house and inventoried everything for probate. And I mean everything. There's nothing there but some clothes, kitchen stuff and furniture."

I was amazed that she still referred to him as *Mr. Nehmer*, even after he stood to walk off with nearly a half million dollars, which arguably should have been hers.

"I think we'll need to look through all of his boxes again," I said.

"Well, we can do that Jack, but we should also suspect that your mother was involved in investigating this, too. Any chance there might be information at your house that you don't know about?"

I looked over at the old bedroom door. Inside, I knew I would find piles of her personal belongings. Boxes of kitchenware, books, clothing and old files and reports lay heaped and scattered across the double bed, on top of the dresser and jammed everywhere along the walls; exactly as LaVon and I had left it all, more than five years earlier.

"OK," I said, "you start by looking through the boxes you have access to at your place. I'll poke through what's left of my mom's junk around here. We'll contact each other when we've gone through everything and then compare notes. We'll take a drive together over to ProtoCommand to check out the boxes in Bill's car. But first, I'll follow up on your suggestion to call the ICU nurse who was on duty the night of the fire."

"Ooh, this is getting good," Tina said. "We'll be just like detectives in those old black-and-white movies on television."

"Yeah, that's us," I said. "William Powell and Myrna Loy. *The Thin Man*. All we need is a terrier."

Wednesday Morning, January 30th, 2008

I awoke the next morning, eager to start looking for concrete answers to our abstract questions. I knew that asking the San Mateo Medical Center to retrace shift records dating back five years would be a stretch. After hearing several exasperated sighs and explicit imperatives, I finally reached a woman who mistook me for a lawyer pursuing a medical malpractice lawsuit. When I realized I was actually getting somewhere with my questions, I decided to run with it.

Through her spitting invectives, I learned that the ICU nurse on duty that distant evening was C.C.N.S. Gloria Thorson, who had long-since transferred to a part time job in the hospital's home health care services unit. When I asked to be connected, however, I was refused.

"Do your own damned dirty work if you're trying to sue us for saving the woman's life!"

"But you didn't save her life," I retorted, just as I heard a loud click and dial tone on the other end of the line.

My next phone call found me connected to nurse Thorson at her desk in the basement of the medical center. She remembered the fire, but couldn't recall working with any particular injury patient. When I explained some of the details, it jogged her memory.

"Oh, yes, I do remember," she said. "One lady was redirected here because of our heart center. Was that your mother? I'm sorry.

"Yes, that was Mom," I replied, trying to sound sincere. "It means a lot to me that you remember. She was admitted through your emergency room about ten o'clock the evening of the fire and placed under your care in ICU. She died at about three thirty the following afternoon. You were off duty at the time of her death."

"Yes, that's right," she added. "My shift started at eight p.m. back then and I went off duty at nine the next morning."

"Great, so you may be able to help me," I continued. "Apparently, my mother had a brief conversation with her nurse some time during the night. I'm hoping that you were that nurse.?"

"Well yes, as a matter of fact, I do recall the conversation," she answered. "I remember having to wake her up to give her meds. She was scheduled for some tests the following morning. It was about midnight, I think — yes, it was! It was just before she suffered a severe stroke. She wanted to know whether anyone had stopped by the front desk to visit her. I told her that she wasn't allowed visitors. She grew quite agitated. She demanded that we wake her up if anybody asked to visit her. I explained our visitor policy on the ICU but assured her we could arrange something if a family member came onto the floor."

"That conversation doesn't sound like anything unusual," I said.

"It wasn't so unusual," she answered, "but then she asked me to get her address book from her purse. She asked me to write down some information as she read it to me. The only paper I could find handy was the corner of a paper towel from the wall dispenser."

"I'm surprised you remember it so clearly," I said.

"I almost lost my job over it," she replied. "I wrote up the entire incident in my shift report. And it was a good thing I did. When she had a cerebrovascular accident — a stroke — later that night, I had some explaining to do. The doctors wanted to know whether the incident could have upset her enough to cause it."

"Do you remember what she asked you to write? A name, maybe?"

"No, not a name. It was some numbers or something. Probably a phone number, but I know it wasn't a name. I do remember thinking that it was odd information to be asking a nurse to copy down in the middle of the night."

I was onto something and tried to remain calm, "A phone number and a street address? What did she do with the paper?"

"I didn't say it was a street address. In fact, I remember that it wasn't. But I don't remember exactly what it was, except that it was a very long series of numbers. It was ages ago. She could barely speak above a whisper. It was hard to hear what she was saying and it was very confusing. After writing it down, she made me read it back to her twice — to make sure I had everything exactly right. Then she took the paper from me. That was the last I ever saw of it."

"What did she do with the address book?"

"She tucked it back into her purse and asked me to put it back with her personal belongings."

I paused for a brief moment to think. Why would she want the information copied out of her address book and then keep the paper? Of course! I recalled my mother reaching out and shaking her clenched fist at me over the bedrail. When I didn't understand what she wanted, she even reached toward LaVon. With her last remaining strength she was trying to give me something crumbled between her twisted fingers. It could only have been the torn piece of paper towel with Sam Ruude's contact information on it. Her final words, *"Find...Ruuuude!"* echoed in my head again.

"Gloria, I just realized that I never collected any of her personal items after she died. She was wheeled down to the morgue right away and I immediately made arrangements with the hospital to have her body sent to a funeral home in Minneapolis. I know it's been a long time, but if the hospital might still have her purse and personal property, I'd like to get it all back."

"Oh, that happens all the time on ICU," she replied. "When a loved one dies unexpectedly, family members are so upset they often forget to handle the small details. But the social workers on staff usually tie up the loose ends pretty well. I don't think we would still have her personal items after so many years, though. The hospital would have boxed everything and forwarded it to the funeral home with her body."

"What about personal items she was wearing, like jewelry. Or even something she may have been holding onto, like that piece of paper," I begged.

"Everything would have been boxed up and shipped with your

mother's body or sent to next of kin, but I suspect that a rumpled corner of paper towel would likely have been discarded as trash."

I gave her my cell phone and home phone numbers in the event she thought of any other details. I hung up and immediately called Bronson Funeral Chapel in New Brighton. The director assured me that my mother's property would certainly have been turned over to me as part of the comprehensive all-inclusive burial plan I purchased. When I assured him I never received any of her personal items, he excused himself for several minutes before returning with an apology.

"Well, Mr. DuMot, you're in luck. We have a box labeled for your mother that was in a storage closet downstairs, along with several other boxes we've accumulated over the years. I'm very sorry for the oversight. We're going to have to review our procedures."

"No, your comprehensive all-inclusive plan is fine," I said. "I recall that someone from your office called and left a message about making arrangements to pick up the box. I never bothered to return your calls. Don't blame yourself or any of your staff."

"Well, I can drop it into the mail to you right away."

"No," I stopped him. "A package will take about a week to get here. I don't really need the items. I'm just searching for some specific information. Could I ask you to open the box and describe the contents of her purse if you have a minute? I'm looking for something I believe she might have been carrying with her when she was admitted to the hospital where she died."

I heard him spill the contents across his desk and jingle his fingers through the items; describing the contents one piece at a time.

"Let me see...a silver brooch, a pair of gold hoop earrings with a sliver of amethyst, a gold watch..."

The brief description of the items brought back a vivid reminder of what my mother had been wearing the night of the fire.

"Nothing else?" I asked desperately. "I need to know everything that's in the purse. It's a long shot, but I'm hoping there's a small address book. Check all the pockets. It's terribly important."

"Oh, here's something. Two credit cards...no, wait. Not credit cards. They're plastic hotel room key cards."

"Hotel room keys? Which hotel?"

"Two different hotels, actually."

"Just a minute, so I can write them down."

"Well, it's just two St. Paul hotels. I'm sure you can remember their names."

"A dull pencil is still better than the sharpest mind," I responded.

I wrote down the hotel names and asked him to keep rummaging.

I could hear him unzip and unsnap various pockets and pouches on the exterior and interior of the purse.

"OK," he said, "Yup, I've found the address book. It was lodged under the lining at the bottom."

Then, figuring it might be the most exciting moment of a funeral director's career, I added some urgency in my voice.

"Great, Mr. Bronson. Thanks. Now, this is really important. Could I ask you to look up a name and phone number in the address book while I have you on the line? I'm specifically looking for the name Sam Ruude. R-U-U-D-E. Could you check under R and possibly S for Sam?"

He flipped through the letter R. It was no surprise that he found only names and numbers for the local offices of ReMax, RealtyWorld and one or two other small real estate brokers my mother would have kept in contact with. He checked the S listings but found only Southside Realtors and a few names of old family acquaintances.

"Please keep looking," I implored. "I'll take anything."

He quickly turned the pages and read off dozens of other names. My heart skipped a beat when I heard him read Bill Ordway's name as one of the entries under the letter O. I implored him to continue. I knew I was asking for a lot of his time but I could also sense that he was sinking his teeth into the hunt.

"Here's something unusual, under the letter N," he said. "No names, but there's a phone number. It's a 406 area code. Then below it on the next line there's a strange eight-digit number."

I copied down the information as he read it to me, then asked him to continue looking through the book, page-by-page.

"Oh, here it is again under the letter W," he said. "No phone number listed this time. But there is a — let's see...one, two, three...four...a nine digit number."

"Huh," he finally said. "This is interesting. In each case, the series of numbers are broken up with haphazard dashes and decimal points."

He read the series to me again, verbally inserting the appropriate punctuation between the numbers. Whatever it was, it certainly fit the nurse's description of odd and unusual. I was certain that it must have been the information my mother was trying to hand off to me in her death throes. When I was satisfied that there was nothing more I could use, I thanked him very much and told him I would stop by sometime to pick up the personal belongings. I knew I would never follow through. It would stay boxed up forever.

I quickly looked up the 406 area code on my laptop. It covered all of Montana — a very big and very empty place.

I held my breath as I carefully double-checked the numbers. They clearly weren't street addresses. The nine-digit number could have been someone's Social Security number but the digits weren't spaced in the typical 3-2-4 pattern. Either or both series could have been the combination to a lock, but the decimal points didn't belong. When I entered the complete series directly into the Google search field, no results returned.

I removed the hyphens and decimal points and keyed them into Google again as whole numbers. For one of the series, I received a site listing for catalog numbers for products manufactured by a Taiwanese clothing company. I figured it wasn't likely to be anything my mom would have been so desperate to tell me about.

I then compared the phone number and the two alpha-numerical series against anything written on Bill's writing board. The randomness of his scribbling made it impossible to keep track. I gave up and decided to call Tina once again to explain everything and asked her to compare the 406-phone number to the lists we had written on our legal pad. When she couldn't find a match, she was skeptical about my conjecture that the numbers may have been some kind of private coded information.

Tina had been following up on the three *Mikes* listed on the board and had already made several phone calls.

"Two of the *Mikes* were vendors from different circuit board companies," she said. "I remembered one of the jerks from a sales call he made to the office about a year ago. He apparently remembered me, too. I hung up on him when he started hitting on me again. The other Mike I talked to used to sell alumina oxide ceramic substrates for hybrid circuits. He told me he's out of the tech industry now but he has a nice life insurance policy I might be interested in checking out."

"Maybe you should keep his number," I chuckled.

"Anyway," she continued, "ProtoCommand got out of circuit boards when the whole industry started to go off-shore in the late '90s. I'm not sure why Bill kept the names of those vendors, unless the company was thinking about re-entering the market."

"And the third *Mike* on the board?"

"The third Mike is dead, Jack. The phone number connects to a drug treatment center up in Thief River Falls. The man at the front desk remembered someone named Michael Bellows, who typically went by the name Mickey. When I asked whether Mr. Bellows may have had a wife *Franny* or a daughter *Jenny*, he was certain it was the same guy. His roommate found him dead from suicide back in 2001."

"Did you ask if it was on his fifty-sixth birthday by any chance?"

Tina was silent for a second before adding, "Yes, as a matter of fact, I did, Jack. And yes, it was the evening of his birthday."

There was more.

"The guy recalled that Mike — or Mickey — was a widower who checked himself into the center after failing out of a series of recovery programs throughout northwest Minnesota. He said he had no family and no place else to go. He was incoherent most of the time and talked about being responsible for his daughter's *murder*. The director called the police after one particularly nasty outburst, but nothing ever came of it. His only personal belongings were a few clothes and an old photo of a dark-haired high school girl. Probably Jenny."

"Yeah, he sounds like he's the guy on our list." I said.

"But did you hear what I said, Jack? He called it *murder*. It could mean that Mickey believed the same thing that your dad and Bill did. People on that list aren't dying in accidents or from natural causes. They're getting murdered. What are we up against here? Do you think we should chase down his former drug counselors? Maybe they remember something from the sessions."

"Even if they kept notes, I'm not sure they would be allowed to talk to us, Tina. But I came up with some better information than that to go on."

Michigan Rink - Gold	**Minnesota Rink - Silver**
Lead: Jim Coventry	Lead: Paul Stenner
Second: Dale Harder	Second: John Mistovich
Third: Steve Talbert	Third: Mickey Bellows
Skip: Norm Thunger	**Skip: Freddy Schade**

Sixth End

After handing two unnecessary points to Michigan in the fifth end, Freddy Schade knew he better get his head back into the game. The Grand Forks police who had been in the arena had stayed only a few minutes before evaporating into the crowd, but it was enough to shake his nerves. Schade's Minnesota teammates didn't need to say anything about the distraction, even if they had dared. The looks on their faces and their general demeanors on the ice.

Freddy was living up to his usual reputation. Everyone who had ever curled with, against, or near him knew Schade's oft-repeated joke. "Teamwork is three other curlers doing what I tell 'em to."

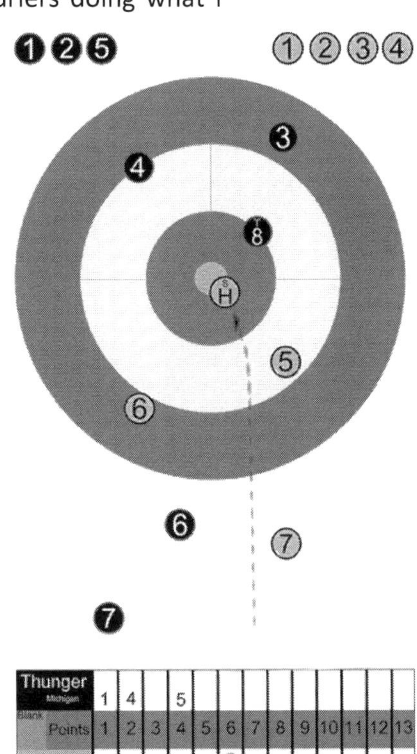

But whatever else he may have been, Schade was nothing if not sensible. Moving on to the championship game could give his family some level of public empathy for whatever might lie ahead.

Slinking low in the hack, he tried to concentrate on his last shot. With Norm Thunger's #8 rock lying on the rear edge of the four-foot circle as shot-rock, Freddy calmly slipped the hammer onto the button to win the sixth end with a single point.

Heading into the final third of the match, Minnesota could breathe a little easier with a 6-4 lead, but a desperate Michigan rink would get the hammer back for the seventh end.

Wednesday Afternoon, January 30th, 2008

After hanging up with Tina, I returned my attention to the odd series of numbers the funeral director had given me over the phone. I needed to figure out what they may have had in common with the 406-phone number. Just as important, why had my mother entered them in the address book where she did?

Could they have been Social Security numbers of prospective real estate clients? Or lockbox access codes to homes on the local market? Real estate file numbers, perhaps? Legal case files held over from her divorce? Were they possibly dial-in access codes for long distance phone cards? They didn't look like any numbers I had ever seen.

I dialed the phone number and a woman's electronic voice clicked in to request my access code. Apparently, I was on track. I quickly dialed the eight-digit series, 46-46-25-89, but the line remained silent, as if waiting for more. I hung up after a few seconds and dialed the phone number again, this time entering the nine-digit series, 101-04-34-83. Again nothing more than hollow silence, as if begging for more information. I pushed the pound sign but the woman's voice returned to scold me for making an invalid entry. I looked at the numbers and remembered that Tina had warned me about discerning wishful thinking from cold hard fact. OK, I thought. Think of this as a computer program. Garbage in, garbage out. I hit the hotkey on my laptop keyboard to open a resident notepad program and began typing. *"Now from the beginning, Jack,"* I thought aloud.

Line 1: The phone number prompted me to enter the access code, so I knew I got that much right, at least.

Line 2: The individual series of numbers were written down separately in Mom's address book, one series under the letter N. The other under the letter W.

Line 3: Both series of numbers included hyphens and decimal points, breaking up the series into subsets of various sizes.

Line 4: Entering the hyphens and decimal points would make no difference on a telephone keypad.

Line 5: Entered individually, neither series of numbers was immediately rejected by the system Therefore; the system seemed to be waiting for more information.

Line 6: Conclusion — I needed to enter additional information into the code, beyond the digits of the combined series of numbers.

I suddenly remembered that the nurse said my mother had read each of the numbers as a long series. What if the two series needed to be combined to form an awkward seventeen-digit series? I combined the two numbers: 4646258910104 3483 and redialed the phone number. At the voice prompt, I entered the full string of numbers but the combination was still not what the system was expecting. OK, I thought. I don't have any more information to tack on at the end of the series, but what if I need to start it with something, or throw something in the middle somewhere? I looked at the telephone keypad and counted off letters on my fingers. The letter N corresponded with the number six; the letter W with the number nine. Not much of a secret code, I thought, but maybe it was good enough.

I dialed the phone number again. When the voice prompted to enter the access code, I keyed in the number six for N, followed by the corresponding eight-digit series, then the number nine for W, before continuing with its corresponding series. I heard a distinct click and an answering machine suddenly whirred to life. I was in! I put the phone on speaker and turned laptop to transcribe the message. It was the memorable timbre of my father's voice.

> **"Hi, Jack;**
>
> **You found this message. That means you have everything you need. You probably already know that there is no turning back from here.**
>
> **We have done everything we can, but after all these years, we can't find a way to make sense of this. Everything we have tried only ends in more pain and loss. I can't even explain any of this to your mother. Not without stirring up something that is best left unstirred.**
>
> **At the tone, leave your current e-mail address. Please enunciate clearly and spell it out correctly two times and then hang up immediately. You cannot leave a message nor call back to be reconnected.**
>
> **Soon, you will receive an encrypted e-mail message. You will recognize the access code to open it. Trust your gut, Jack, but trust nothing else. I wish I could tell you more but we can't take the chance. Not even here. When you get the message, follow the instructions. Trust no one, Jack. No one.**
>
> **I love you and miss you very much. I'm sorry, but there is no other way."**

How was I supposed to *"enunciate clearly and spell it out correctly two times"* with my voice choking with tears? I finally composed myself enough to leave my e-mail address exactly as he requested. As I started to say more, the machine cut off immediately. I I *did* try to call back, but was not reconnected.

I read and re-read the message several times. *"I'm sorry, but there is no other way,"* I repeated to myself. Those were my mother's words when he left home. *"I can't even explain any of this to your mother."* That meant my mother was still alive when he recorded the message. Of course! That's why she came out to California. She must have known she was in danger, too. She had planned to tell me or ask for my help, but the fire interrupted everything. Then, when she wasn't sure she would come out of the hospital alive, she asked the night nurse to write down the code for me. What did the message mean, *"That means you have everything you need*?" I didn't feel as if I had *anything* I needed. And what did he mean, *"Trust your gut, Jack, but trust nothing else*?*"*

I sat trembling for several moments. Was this more evidence that he might really still be alive? Things began adding up. I thought back to my mom's over-reaction to those little slips of paper received in the mail so many years earlier. She must have known they were intended as some kind of a warning. Dad could never take the chance of telling us everything because it would have dragged us in. I began to suspect that even her death might have been by careful orchestration. Poisoned in the hospital, perhaps? More than five years had passed since her deathbed attempt to tell me the message was waiting for me. Dad wasn't 56 years old yet. Only 52, when he still considered himself relatively safe.

I turned my attention to the hotel key cards. Like most women, mom made a habit of swapping out her purse every spring and autumn. If the cards no longer had a purpose, she would have discarded them rather than transfer them each season. Maybe she was staying at the hotels during a transition period before moving into this house, I thought. But she certainly would have called to tell me about her plans. Neither did it make sense that she would stay at a Ramada for a few days before transferring to a nearby Embassy Suites.

When I phoned the hotels, neither desk clerk was excited about tracking down room records dating back to late summer of 2002.

"Do you know what you're asking?" one asked. "We had a different registration process before we put in this new system in '04."

"But I really need you to try. Can you at least put me in touch with someone who could provide some information?"

The woman gave me the number to the Ramada corporate headquarters in New Jersey, where I eventually learned that my mother had checked into the St. Paul Ramada on Saturday, August 17th, under her maiden name of Melinda Ann Singleton, initially for a five-day stay. However, she never formally checked out. They were able to find her records only because she had reserved the room using an old MasterCard.

I had a somewhat easier time learning more about her move to the St. Paul Embassy Suites, where she checked in the following day, Sunday, August 18th, and remained for five nights on the same credit card. Again, she never formally checked out of the room.

I stared at an open space on the wall, as I recalled the circumstances of my mother's visit to the Bay Area in August that year. Even through the haze of more than five distant years, things were becoming clearer. It was the reason she inexplicably sold the house in New Brighton and moved to South Minneapolis. She was on the run and trying to hide. Despite her change of address, she must have known she continued to be in danger. That had to be it. Checking into two different hotels virtually simultaneously was a further effort to throw someone off her scent. When she called to inform me she was coming out to San Francisco, it was a final act of desperation.

I shook my head vigorously to prevent myself from thinking any further about the banquet hall fire that caused her death. It was all beginning to make sense as the questions rolled through my head. Did the killer follow her from Minneapolis all the way to that banquet center? Was it him who picked her up off the floor and induced the heart attack or stroke? Did he start the fire? Four other innocent people died that night because they followed me blindly. Was their stupidity just collateral damage?

Whether real or imagined, the evidence was all stacking up, including her odd excuse to attend a stranger's birthday party, her weight loss and her nervous fumbling with the car keys. Even renting a car from an off-brand rental car agency should have been enough of a clue. I never even questioned why she chose to spend the extra money to take a small private flight into San Carlos Airport in San Mateo, rather than a commercial flight into the main San José International. It would also explain her tearful outburst at my kitchen table, and why it was so important that I accompany her to the party that evening. I recalled that she said she wanted to discuss something with me, but I never gave her the chance. Yes, everything was adding up and I felt terrible about it.

I realized that Tina was right about something, too. I needed to stop judging my father so harshly. There was a reason he couldn't just call or write me — or simply tap me on the shoulder as I walked into a grocery store one day. He must have known that whoever was on his tail would use him to get to me, too. Was that what got Bill's son killed? Did Jason know too much? Could that also have been what Mickey Bellows meant when he said he was guilty of *murdering* his daughter, Jenny? Did she try to get involved? It was the only plausible theory I could think of. As long as I remained ignorant of everything, I was safe. But was it already too late? No wonder my parents never said a word. *"I'm sorry, but there is no other way."*

Maybe I couldn't show my calculations on paper, but I felt confident that I had solved for *X*. I was growing convinced that the entire equation had become as much about saving my own life as it was about finding my father. What would I have done if I had been in his shoes; living year after year with hopelessness and futility descending like a fog day-by-day? So, in his late forties, he left the family to give himself time to figure out how to become a non-entity. Over the next several years, he became a mere apparition who chose to materialized only for brief moments at a time, only to dissolve invisibly back into his world...whatever his new world may look like.

His sham accident and falsified death certificate would have been the final necessary steps to convince the killer that he needn't bother to look any further. Then he pulled off his phantom act long enough to feel safe enough to resurface using an alias nickname that only I might recognize. Of course, curling would have been the one thing — sadly, the only thing — we had in common that might catch my attention. There may have been other clues, but I wouldn't have noticed. .

I may have been correct about some of it, all of it, or not a stitch of it. But it was what I wanted to believe. It was a brilliant plan and I welled up with emotion thinking of how well-conceived it had all been. Tina was right. After so many years, he probably began to wonder whether I was even capable of looking outside of my own dining room window to search for something bigger than myself. After years of comatose apathy, I was finally waking up and feeling alive again. Brick-by-brick, I would build on the foundation of hope.

Part IV

Revelation

January 30th through February 5th, 2008

I pushed open the door to the old first-floor bedroom as far as the clutter inside would allow and squeezed into the dark interior space. Most of everything in the room remained tucked and wrapped in the original moving boxes, including a few with beige packaging tape still sealing the flaps, just as my mother had packed them.

I quickly recalled the first time I stepped into the house upon returning to Minneapolis for the funeral. When I finally broke through the locked rear door with a painful blast of my right shoulder, I was surprised to discover the clutter of crates and personal articles scattered across the living room. It had been nearly a year since my mother bought the house and moved in, but the majority of her clothes and personal items remained unpacked. I recalled thinking that it just wasn't like her to live in such a disorganized clutter. To make room for myself moving in that day, I shoved everything off to one side, too lazy to remove them any further than I had to. When LaVon joined me a few months later, we lightly poked through many of the boxes but decided it would be easiest to leave everything packed as it was. We moved it all out of sight and mostly out of mind.

I had no idea what I might be looking for in the bedroom and felt overwhelmed by cartons stacked floor-to-ceiling on all sides. I started along one wall nearest the door but soon realized that the only option was to haul everything out to the living room, where I could sort the items according to general category. I emptied the bedroom and arranged the boxes in such a way that allowed some sense of organization. As I finished searching through each one, I repacked it as best I could but there always seemed to be one or two items that wouldn't fit neatly back in place. To save time, I started a pile of miscellaneous items out on the front porch; lying to myself that I would schedule a local charity to collect it all later in the week.

I soon realized I was facing an unmanageable task. The boxes were bringing back a lifetime of childhood memories of our old house in New Brighton. A cracked plate. An old coffee mug. A book here. A souvenir knick-knack there. Every object was an heirloom of suburban kitsch, which still somehow filled a dark corner of my memory. In my mind, everything I touched belonged stacked in a kitchen cupboard, folded into a linen closet or placed neatly on a living room shelf. I felt as if I could walk right to its exact location, pick it up, drink from it, play with it, or read it. Unexpectedly, I could remember the number of square inches it once occupied in my youth. *"Funny that I should remember where it all once belonged,"* I thought. *"When I was a kid, I needed help finding my school books every morning."* But there in my living room, every box-flap I pulled back dug up a time capsule of colors, textures, smells and experiences; none of which I could ever remember burying.

During the week that followed, I balanced my time between poking away at a job search and searching through every container, dresser drawer and pocket of my mother's belongings. I couldn't find anything that gave me any further clue about my father's whereabouts or why-abouts. When I was satisfied I had looked through everything — twice — I repackaged the boxes into a disorganized mess and haphazardly propelled the containers once again into the small bedroom. As I bounced the last small box onto the old mattress and pulled the door closed behind me, I wondered whether Tina had hunted down any further information from her own safari through Bill's belongings.

As I began dialing, I suddenly realized that she and I were caught uncomfortably in that nebulous gap between friendship and relationship. Well, at least that's where I was stuck, anyway. God only knew where she might have been stuck. Before punching in the last digit of her phone number, I hung up and took a moment to think about what I intended to say when she answered. All the signs pointed in the right direction. She smiled, nodded and laughed in all the right places. But Tina wasn't like LaVon. There was nothing about her that let me know what I should do next. I hadn't heard from her for several days, but she may have had a good reason for not calling me.

I punched the keypad and she answered on the third ring. I quickly relayed the conversation with my mom's night nurse and how it led to the old answering machine message and the two hotel keycards. I finally caught my breath and asked her whether she had discovered anything new or meaningful.

"No," she answered without elaborating, "I haven't had a chance to look through Bill's boxes yet."

I found myself jealous of whatever else may have occupied her time for so many days. Didn't she know how much this meant to me?

"I don't mean to pressure you, Tina," I said. "It's just that I'm running out of time and I need to get moving. The national curling championships start in a week and a half. If I can't find my dad and stop him, it'll be suicide for him and murder for me. Realistically, I think that leaves me less than a week."

"I'll try to get through everything tonight," she said with a sigh. "Didn't you say there were still some things down in your basement and maybe in your garage or attic you could also look through?"

And that was about all she said before we hung up. Nothing about calling later just to chat. Nothing about getting together for dinner and a movie. Nothing about wanting to sleep with me that night. I was deeply disappointed in her sudden indifference.

In the basement, I picked through the pile of items scattered throughout the furnace area, tossing each piece aside to get to the next. The smaller items, including the picture frames, I set on top of the nearby water heater. I was over-tired and over-frustrated by Tina's response. I was no longer even certain whether I was looking for evidence of my father's whereabouts or just hoping to find a reason to call her back to thaw out her sudden cold shoulder.

Most of the pile included larger items, too heavy to haul back up the rickety stairs. It was a wonder how I got them down the stairs in the first place. Things seemed a little promising, though, when I slid a short steel file drawer out from behind a broken desk chair. Inside were several hanging folders with copies of real estate sales sheets and purchase offers. Most dated only as far back as 2001. Any one of the dozen or so files could have been important, or none of them could have meant anything at all. I set the handful of files on top of the picture frames and quickly sorted through the remaining items. Emotionally exhausted, I clomped noisily back up the steps, tossed the small pile on my dinette table and flopped down on the sofa, where I slept until morning.

I wasn't able to read through the files the following day until I returned from a second job interview with a new company starting a contract programming business out in the western suburbs. I was impressed with some of the business partners' ideas but I was nagged by the fact that the company was a startup. I had been through a half-dozen interviews and was getting comfortable with the process, but this one was different. I couldn't tell whether the owners surrounding me at the conference room table were conducting an honest job interview or simply picking my brain. When I inquired about the hiring timeframe, the entire tone of the conversation suddenly changed. When one of the men suggested the group take a short break, I used it as an excuse to end the conversation. It was a job I needed and wanted, but my heart wasn't in it. I apologized and excused myself from further consideration. Until I was at peace with myself, hiring me would be a waste of their venture capital funding.

Over a lunchtime sandwich at the dinette table, I flipped on the Internet to research the files I had retrieved from the steel cabinet. I wanted to discover whether the listings were legitimate business transactions for prospective clients or perhaps properties she was interested in buying herself.

The sheets that included Polaroid photographs listed common, single-family houses on common, single-family streets in the single-family suburbs. They were the kinds of listings my mother excelled at; selling to young married couples who needed an extra bedroom and bath for their growing families. It wasn't likely she was looking at any of those types of properties as a potential hiding place. There would have been a paper trail a mile long. Secreting herself away too far out in the open would have been too dangerous. The listings must have been a legitimate part of her waning real estate career.

One of the manila file folders, however, was particularly intriguing and I read through its contents several times. The five or six individual handwritten sheets included general descriptions of acreage and property prices in communities throughout the Midwest, but included no photographs or specific street address information. I looked up the township listed for the properties and learned that each was located in a relatively remote area. Most of the acreage was in Northern Minnesota but five were scattered throughout the Dakotas and several more in Wisconsin or Iowa.

Altogether, there were twenty-six properties ranging in price from fifteen thousand dollars to more than a quarter million. But there were no page headings to give any indication of what the listings could mean. I dumped the papers onto the recycling stack building up on the corner of the table. So that was that. I had searched through every available box and pile in the bedroom, basement and garage and came up with little more than a wrap up of my mother's life in real estate.

I pushed my laptop and pile to one side and lowered my tired head on my sore arms. At table level, I saw the old picture frames lying beneath several items from the basement. I carefully selected one from the bottom of the stack and looked at the faces of my young father and his two friends. I felt myself fighting back tears as I carefully removed the photo. I recalled that the faded five-by-seven inch color picture had once been a constant fixture on the bookshelves of my childhood, where I ignored it completely. I squinted more closely to determine whether one of the young men might have been Bill Ordway, but it was impossible to tell beneath the low brims of their ball caps shading their faces. Along the bottom margin, hidden beneath the shiny metal frame all those years, some young hand had written the names *Tommy* and *Willy* at the feet of the two boys standing to the left and right sides of the trio. My initial suspicions had been correct; it was Bill Ordway with my dad in the picture. The unidentified teenager in the center appeared to be the tallest and most mature of the three, by at least a year or more. Some long-lost high school friend, I guessed. I turned over the picture to discover that someone had used a dull pencil to write the date in large print across the full length of the back; *April 24th, 1969*.

"Damn it, where are you, Dad?" I yelled into the faces. "I'm in this with you now. I'll find you and we'll end this thing somehow."

Wednesday Evening, February 6th, 2008

As the kitchen phone rang for the third time, I let it automatically go into the voice recording. I heard LaVon's familiar recorded message interrupt the ringing with our voicemail greeting, "**Hello. We won't come to the phone right now, so leave a message.**" When recording the message, LaVon had carefully chosen her words. We *won't* come to the phone, rather than *can't* come to the phone. It was an accurate description of our attitude toward incoming calls. The majority of the time, we ignored the ringing and let the phone go directly to voicemail, figuring it would just be a bill collector. Though we hardly ever used our landline, we almost always gave out the number as our primary contact. We just didn't bother to answer it.

The recorded message ended with a beep and I was surprised to hear an elderly woman introduce herself with a thick Midwest accent, "Hello, Jack DuMot? This is Mary Coventry calling from over at the U.S. Curling Association."

I quickly picked up the receiver and announced I was on the line.

"Oh, hello, Jack. This is Mary Coventry. I work for Dan Graber at the USCA. He told us about your phone call last week. You know, asking about Arv Firpo. I didn't think twice about it until I was working on some paperwork today and ran across Arv's name. Sorry to call you in the evening but I thought it would be the best time to reach you. I remember Dan said you sounded a little desperate."

I thought back to the phone conversation with Dan Graber but couldn't recall sounding particularly desperate.

"I had an idea which might help you," she continued. "I was doing some background checks for the playdowns and started remembering some things about the first time I ever talked to Arv."

Mary gave a rambling explanation for why she called. One of the members of the rink, John Paulheim, had faxed in the official registration form, listing Arv Firpo as the Skip. For contact information, he used the same P.O. box and phone number listed on old registration forms from the previous few years. Out of curiosity, Mary tried to call the phone number to track him down but, of course, the line was out-of-service. She then took the liberty of calling the Duluth post office to track down the owner of the post office box but the information was confidential and the rental had been discontinued several weeks earlier. Finally, she called Paulheim back to ask some sneaky questions.

"Apparently, Arv asked all the players to meet at the Hibbing club late in the evening of Thursday, February 14th. Mr. Paulheim said the unusual time raised some eyebrows."

"Why?" I asked. "Because the 14th is Valentine's Day?"

"Oh, heavens no," she laughed. "I've never met a curler yet who cared about such nonsense. Well, at least my husband never did. It was the late hour that was so troublesome. Arv asked them to meet at the club at eleven o'clock — p.m. Plus, players typically don't arrive until the day prior to the start of the matches. That would be Friday the 15th this year. If Arv had called to register himself, I would have told him you were looking for him."

"Maybe Paulheim will tell Firpo I'm trying to find him," I said.

"I'm sure he would but I doubt that they'll talk together much before the 14th in Hibbing. Arv just doesn't work that way."

"Well, thanks for trying, anyway, Mary. It sounds like you know him."

"I do a little," she said. "About seven or eight years ago, he called here to register for the national senior playdowns in Eau Claire. It must have been his first nationals, 'cuz I had never heard his name before and I've been around curling for a *loooong* time. He was very excited. As I was looking for a pen to fill out the entry form over the phone with him, we got sidetracked onto another conversation. I found that I really liked him so I asked whether he had any family members I could sit with during the matches. He said he could only hope his family could watch him play someday. He even talked for a couple of minutes about his son who had spent some time in junior curling."

"He really cared that much?" I asked, trying to sound noncommittal. "Do you still have that old registration form on file?"

"No," she replied, "we put everything online a couple of years ago, but we didn't bother with anything older than five years."

The phone grew quiet for a moment. Then she floored me.

"If Arv Firpo is your father, Jack, you need to know he cares."

"I don't know if he's my father, Mary. As far as I know, my dad never curled and I was only in junior curling for one year. That would hardly have been the highlight of his life. It certainly wasn't the highlight of mine. Besides, records show that my father died in 2002, so Mr. Firpo couldn't very well be my dad, could he?"

"Well," she continued, "if you're still trying to find Arv *Whoever-He-May-Be* before the nationals, I have an idea that perhaps you hadn't thought of. Even the great Firpo can't stop practicing for six weeks between major championships and expect to play well. He would need to get in some competitive practice. So I started looking at a calendar of bonspiels throughout the Midwest. There are several scheduled at clubs in Minnesota and one in Bismarck this coming weekend. Entering one of these 'spiels will be the last real chance he'll have to practice before Hibbing. I thought you might want to call the clubs and ask for the list of registered names. We've heard that Arv quit the 'spiel circuit and went completely out of sight about a year ago, after last year's championships. But you never know, he might figure he needs the ice time."

She read off the club locations throughout Minnesota and added the Bismarck Curling Club as an outlying possibility. It was generous and heart-felt, but she was wrong; I *had* already thought of it.

During my initial discussion with Dan Graber at the USCA a few weeks earlier, he explained how Firpo typically went about the process of registering for bonspiels. It was usually not a problem finding players willing to join him, especially when the registration fee, hotel room, meals and beer would be bought and paid for. The Vice Skip — or Third — would then register the rink and list all the other players as TBD, to be determined. If the pre-registration required names, he would list the players but write down a false name as Skip. It was an *impossible* long shot. There were likely to be dozens of rinks registered for each of the bonspiels. Even if they had the names of every player, there would be no way to know which one individual Skip's name might be the alias he used.

The deception allowed him to remain competitive while giving him a chance to come up for air in the curling world, even if it was only a few hours at a time during a scheduled match. He must have realized that if club members knew he was scheduled to play, the news might get around that the great Arv Firpo would be available for autographs.

"Thanks, Mary," I said, jotting down the club names.

I thought of the dead FBI agents who had investigated the case.

"Don't get involved in any more of this, okay? I appreciate it, but I'll handle everything from here. It's not that big of a deal, really. What the heck, if I can't find him soon, I'll see him up in Hibbing. Does anything exciting ever happen at the large national championships? I mean anything besides world-class curling."

"Well, occasionally the celebrating gets out of hand," she

answered. "You know, a few scraps between zealous spectators and fights in the local bars during the evenings. But the USCA is proud of the way we handle things. We're a first-class organization and we expect things to stay pretty quiet. We don't want a repeat of 1969."

I took the bait, "Did something bad happen in '69?"

"Well, it wasn't the USCA," she continued. "There was a different bunch calling the shots back then — the American Curling Union. They thought of themselves as the governing body but they eventually went defunct, and for good reason. Since the USCA took over running these things, we've had a long string of good luck and I don't want to jinx it. '69 was the year a drunk driver ran down the North Dakota boys, the night before the championship match up in Grand Forks."

"Grand Forks? What happened in Grand Forks?"

Tina's call to the Grand Forks police was racing through my head.

"Well, the rink from Bismarck had just won the semi-final match earlier in the day. The boys were out celebrating at a local watering hole that evening. They came out of the bar just before midnight and some young punk ran them down on the sidewalk. It was hit-and-run, but they found the VW bus a few blocks away a couple of hours later."

"The entire team? My God!"

"Yeah, it shook the curling world. Most rinks usually have some fans traveling with them to national playdowns. Some young kid in the Minnesota group must have gone out partying. He was driving through town going about fifty-five in a pedestrian area when he swerved onto the sidewalk. I don't remember much, except that one of the best curlers in the world was killed. John Skinner. I seem to recall that someone else may have died, too, or at least suffered some pretty serious injuries."

"Were any arrests made?"

"Yes, they investigated and arrested the kid the next day. He had a rap sheet a mile long. He was a half-crazy sixteen or seventeen year old. They picked him up at the arena, as I recall, and brought him down to the police station. I don't know whatever happened to him."

"Weren't his parents with him?"

"I don't know, but I suspect not. I can't imagine any parent letting a high school juvenile delinquent go unsupervised to a curling championship a couple hundred miles from home. Alcohol can flow pretty fast and loose. I never heard whatever came of the kid."

"So how'd the playdowns finish up? Cancelled?"

"Oh, no. Remember, it wasn't the USCA running that show. The two losing rinks from the Saturday semi-finals matches played each other Sunday morning in a new semi-finals match, to see who would take North Dakota's place in the finals match Sunday afternoon."

"Cripes. Were people okay with that decision?"

"Not hardly!" she chuckled and then added, "For curling fans, that was the biggest crime of all. My husband at the time, Jim Coventry, threw Lead rock for the Michigan rink. The replay game started at eleven o'clock on Sunday morning and people were upset from the first rock to the last. It was pretty tense in the arena. I remember police crawling all over the place. Heck, at one point late in the match, the Minnesota players even got into a brawl with each other. Who would have thought there was anything to fight about in a curling match, but that Skip of theirs was such a pill."

"But a pretty good curler?" I asked.

"Yeah, but nobody would ever admit to his face," she answered. "But I suppose we have to be honest after all these years. He was one of the best ever. He brought them that far in the nationals. During the match, he made one of the greatest curling shots you ever wanted to see. But for some reason, police took him in for questioning about the accident right after they beat our Michigan boys."

"Was he charged with drunk driving, too?"

"Like I said, I'm not sure how it all ended with him. All I remember was that he didn't play in the finals match later that afternoon. The Minnesota guys ended up using their alternate as their Lead. It didn't matter. Schade had a great rink and won easily enough, anyway."

"Schade?" I repeated? "As in Freddy Schade?"

"Yes, have you heard of him?"

I asked Mary what she knew about Schade and the other men from the Minnesota rink. Except for Schade's nasty reputation on and off the ice, she never heard anything more about him until years later when she started working for the USCA. He was the stuff of legend.

"Quite an unsettling Sunday afternoon, huh?" I ventured.

"Well, that semi-final replay turned out to be a great match. The emotions carried over throughout the championship match later that afternoon, too. I don't know how those Minnesota players got through it. That poor young kid they brought in as their Lead couldn't get any of his shots in play. He finally figured things out, though, as I recall."

"But you don't think things were handled well?" I concluded.

"No, I guess not," she sighed. "Whenever playdown rules come up for discussion, I'm quick to remind the committee that I was there in '69. I warn them never to allow that kind of decision again."

I was getting more curious.

"What should they have done?"

"I don't know," she answered. "Maybe the buzz throughout the crowd that day was right. They probably should have awarded the championship to North Dakota, but let the other finalist — the Wisconsin rink — represent the U.S. at the World's in Scotland a few weeks later. That, or maybe just awarded the championship to the Wisconsin guys, or both teams."

"Would that have been okay with guys from Wisconsin?" I asked. "Just to give it to them like that, without playing for it, I mean?"

"All the rinks were emotionally drained because of the accident, Jack. I think Wisconsin knew they couldn't have beaten Skinner's North Dakota boys. Three or four years ago, I ran into a man who played on that Wisconsin team. He said they would rather have conceded that match in North Dakota's honor than lose to Freddy Schade the way they did."

"Even after nearly forty years, he still felt that way?" I asked. "Well, I doubt another tragedy like that will ever happen again."

"Look," she said. "Fergus Falls is one of the clubs holding a bonspiel this weekend. I would recommend you go up there. Talk to an old rink rat named George Penski. My ex-husband spent a few years in western Minnesota before moving to Michigan, where I met him. That's how I got to know George and his wife Maggie, through a long distance friendship. I know Arv has stopped by the Fergus Falls club to play and visit a few times over the years. George always brags that he knows everyone in that family."

"Well, he doesn't know me," I replied. "I'll certainly talk to him. I hate to ask this, but do you think there's any way I could contact your ex-husband, to ask him some questions, too?"

"That one's going to be a little tough," she replied in a somber tone. "He moved to Florida after our divorce in '91. We stayed in touch for a good many years but he suffers from advanced Alzheimer's now. I haven't tried to talk to him since about '05, but he didn't know who I was."

I ended the discussion with an apology.

"Look at how late it is and this is a long distance call," she said after a second or two of silence. "I've gotta let you go. Well, it's like you said, Jack. If nothing else, you can be sure Arv will be in Hibbing to meet up with his rink. You can catch up to him then."

As I hung up, I knew I didn't have that long. We would both be convenient targets the minute we arrived in town. I needed to buy more time for both of us. I couldn't count on digging some rogue FBI agent named Sam Ruude out of permanent hiding. I didn't even have a clue why I should be looking for him.

I decided that George Penski would be my best bet for explaining some of the cloudy connections about 1969. I pulled a yellow legal pad in front of me and sketched a line to chart the associations that were beginning to add up. Up to that point, all my information dated back thirty-eight years to my grandfather's death in 1970. No, I thought, now I can start earlier. The 1969 national curling championships were held in Grand Forks and Bill Ordway's stepfather Freddy Schade was in the picture somehow. I decided that I would call the Fergus Falls club the next morning and start asking some very specific questions.

As usual, I ended my evening by checking my laptop e-mail and cell phone for any messages I may have missed. My e-mail box was empty but there was a text message on my cell phone from Tina, asking me to call her immediately.

Without checking the clock, I quickly redialed Tina's number.

"Jack, hi," she said, with a noticeable lightness in her voice. "I'm sorry if I sounded distant with you when you called earlier. I spent the day worrying about a job interview that turned into a train wreck."

"Yeah, I've had a few of those myself," I said. "Don't worry about it. I'd be lying if I said I didn't wonder what was wrong, though."

"I've looked through all of Bill's boxes in my apartment and even checked his townhouse again," she said, "but I can't find anything peculiar. Heck, everything might mean something — or it might mean nothing at all. There's just no way to know."

"What about the boxes you stored in the trunk of his car?" I asked.

"No, I didn't get over to ProtoCommand to check those. But do you really think we need to? Bill had a lot of interesting things in his personal items. I'm not sure any of it will help, though. I think everything you need for finding your father is spread out across that wooden board."

"I'm sorry if I sounded like I was expecting you to dig into everything right away, Tina," I said sincerely. "I've learned something interesting that I think is worth checking into, but we...I mean I...just don't have enough time left. I need to make some phone calls to curling clubs. If I get the information I'm counting on, it could mean a lot of windshield time between now and next week. No pressure and no expectations, but it would be great if you wanted to join the ride."

"Hmm," she said with a smile in her voice. "Sounds like a road trip. I can't think of a better way to take my mind off my financial worries right now. I'll be over first thing in the morning."

7:30 a.m. Thursday, February 7th, 2008

The following morning, Tina was standing on my front porch before I finished my first cup of coffee. She stepped through the door into my living room and shivered stiffly for a moment as she soaked up the immediate warmth emanating off the nearby radiators. She was wearing white fur-topped boots and white sweatpants under a white ski parka. A golden-yellow scarf was wrapped loosely around her neck and a light-orange stocking cap was pulled low over her ears and forehead, covering her black bangs. Rosy pink cheeks and coral lipstick completed the startling impression of a five and a half foot candle flickering in my entryway. As she began pulling off her mittens, she pressed a bag of bagels into my hand and tossed a rolled up gob of something onto a nearby lamp table.

"I think this used to be your morning newspaper," she said. "I found it laying in your curb gutter. You should call the Star Tribune and complain."

"Yeah, I've thought of that," I said. "Guten Morgan, und wie gehts dir?"

"Ooh, German. Impressive," she said. "Mozart's language of love first thing in the morning. Have you been drinking already?"

"No. Never quite this early," I laughed.

"Well, ça va," she added. "Je vais bien."

"Ooh, French," I said. "The language of feisty independence. Do you speak it fluently?"

"Actually, fairly well," she answered. "I picked it up somewhere along the way."

We sat together at the dinette table and I explained the real estate files I discovered in the basement, as well as the phone call I received from Mary Coventry at the USCA. I also showed her my makeshift time chart and asked whether I was missing any possible branches or points of interest that I should be adding along the main line. She reminded me of her call to the halfway house in Thief River Falls and the information about Mickey Bellow's death in 2004.

I opened a website of a directory of the various curling clubs that I would be calling and she pulled her chair closer to mine, to get a better view of the screen.

I opened another browser and brought up an outline sketch of the Midwest.

"Minnesota is a big place," she said. "We can't get to all six clubs, Jack."

"Yeah, it's even bigger if we tack on the Bismarck club," I added.

"But we can check out some of them, at least. Since this Penski character will be at the Fergus Falls club, we can start there and then move on to three or four other clubs throughout that area of the state."

Tina pointed out that an insider at the Chippewa County Courthouse must have agreed to help falsify my father's death certificate in 2002. She insisted it would be important to go back to Montevideo to check things further, since we were heading toward western Minnesota, anyway. She reached across me and my eyes followed her manicured pink fingernail, as she outlined a sensible driving route from right to left across the screen.

"...and then we could head west on Highway 7 to the Maynard cemetery to ask a few more question," she concluded.

As if asking permission, I interjected that I'd like to check out the old DuMot family farm in nearby Gluek, too, as long as we would be in the area. I couldn't explain why it was important, so I rationalized that an old neighbor might offer some important information. Tina nodded and agreed knowingly, deciding that we could probably spare an hour or so. Finally, we would drive fifteen miles further west to the records department at the courthouse in Montevideo.

Lying down there at the end of her slender finger, the entire plan made perfect sense. She said something important about arriving at the courthouse by closing time, but I couldn't divert my attention from the back of her creamy-smooth hand. She paused for a second and I drifted back down to earth, just in time to hear her utter something about driving north along Highway 55 to Fergus Falls, arriving in time for the bonspiel check-in at the Gateway Curling Club late Friday afternoon. With any luck, every rink would have a game scheduled that evening. We would know immediately whether Arv Firpo appeared among the registered players. We briefly discussed the remainder of the schedule, but agreed to hold off on firming up additional plans until we had a chance to meet with George Penski.

As she leaned toward me to get a clearer view of the screen, the sharp ends of her neatly trimmed jet black hair pricked and tickled my bare arm. For the first time, I noticed the musky scent of her skin lotion hovering over the keyboard, as if descending from heaven. I paused for a moment and looked downward at the side of her face, with her right ear within easy nibbling distance. When she suddenly glanced upward to ask why I had stopped mid-sentence, our eyes locked for an eternity. She took my left hand and I waited silently, as she traced the pale indentation still circling my finger where my wedding band had once been. Was she trying to erase it? Or was she reminding me I was technically still married? A second or two later, the curtain came down with a thud.

"It's not even seven-thirty in the morning," she said softly. "It's too early to be thinking what you're thinking."

"Too early?" I dared to ask. "Or too soon?"

"Let's get back to finding your father."

"Oh, yeah," I said. "Him."

We enjoyed a bagel and cream cheese over a cup of coffee while reading the paper together and checking my bookmarked news sites. When I opened the London Times page, however, she apparently had seen enough. She pulled the laptop toward her and took some time to finish a Sudoku, explaining her deductive process as she worked.

After a few minutes, I asked what she had planned for the remainder of the day and whether we could start out at the break of dawn the next morning. I jumped up to look out at the narrow strip of sky visible through the dining area window. The morning sunrise was still low behind the houses but was painting enough light to reveal a high, wispy haze overhead.

"It hasn't snowed in a while," I said. "We're pressing our luck. We don't know what kind of weather we might get blowing through western Minnesota this early in February. It's pretty flat up there."

I stopped when I saw that Tina had joined me by my side at the window and was shaking her head in mock disgust.

"Whenever Jason visited here from North Carolina," she laughed, "he always asked why people in Minnesota are so obsessed with the weather."

"I'm not obsessed," I defended myself.

"Look," she pointed, "the sky is light, just a few winter clouds, and it hasn't snowed in a week. Instead of marveling at it, you're worried that a blizzard might come barreling out of Fargo at any minute, straight down I-94 like a bat out of hell."

"Yeah," I chuckled. "I guess you're right. Minnesota television stations treat a two-inch snowfall as a license to print money. I guess we are a little obsessed with bad weather up here, aren't we. But be fair, I'm just saying that we might lose some time tomorrow if a storm rolls in."

Tina pinched my lips closed with her fingertips, then sealed them with a pantomime zipper motion.

"Well, it's still early today," she said. "Why wait until tomorrow? There are a few frozen crystals falling, but nothing that looks like the blizzard of the century. I haven't heard that any bad weather is coming our way. I'll leave my car parked in your back alley. Drive me to my apartment to get packed and we can get going right away. We could be out at that cemetery and to your dad's old farm just after lunch. Maybe even get to Montevideo to check the records before the courthouse closes late this afternoon. That will give us tomorrow morning to drive the remainder of the way to Fergus Falls and find Penski before the *bonspiel* starts tomorrow night. We never know. We might need the extra time."

"Well, it sounds great," I said, "except it leaves out one important part. I want to make sure every base is covered and that means looking through the boxes in Bill's car. We might find something that will save us quite a few tanks of gas. I was hoping you could give me his keys so I could sneak over to ProtoCommand tonight and bring everything back here for a quick look."

"No problem," she said. "But we don't have to wait until tonight and we don't have to sneak. I carry his keys on my key ring. I don't want to forget where I put them when the probate court finally calls. I'll just call the company and tell the receptionist that I'm stopping by to pick up the boxes. To sound more convincing, I'll also tell them I'll be back over the weekend to move it off their property. I'm sure they'll be happy to hear that it's finally getting taken care of without them having to lift a finger. We can look through everything and get on the road right away. That puts us out at the cemetery in Maynard at about one-thirty, I think."

She was speaking rapidly and I was starting to sense her nervousness about what all of this could mean. Standing next to me was a beautiful young woman who had pulled herself out of bed at six a.m. to drive across town for breakfast with a condemned man. She understood the danger but also knew there was nowhere I could turn for help. She was coming along for the ride and I had to work hard to contain my excitement. It was as if she was a butterfly that suddenly landed on my hand; surprising, beautiful, whimsical, and fragile. It was so tempting to snatch her up in a net and call her mine forever. But I knew she would have flitted away the instant I tried to pinch hold of her wings. She wasn't mine to keep. She would only feel safe with me as long as I respected her space with gentleness. Unfortunately, I also knew that tenderness and gentle emotions coming out of me were likely to be thin on the ground over the next several days.

I moved my car around front to make room for hers in the back alley for the weekend. In my backseat, we crammed in everything that remotely related to our search. It wasn't much, but every list, photo, chart and note might prove to be something we would need once we started talking to people. Tina stood outside the car for a moment, holding the photograph of my dad and his two young friends. She used the back of her knit mitten to flick off a wayward snowflake.

"This guy on the right — labeled Tommy — he's your dad, right?" she asked. "You said his name is Arvil. How on Earth did he get from a name like Arvil to the nickname Tommy?"

"I've never been sure," I answered. "I once heard some convoluted story about a British soldier who saved an old family member's life during the war. I think the soldier's surname was Arvil, though, not his first name. Some guy named Peter Arvil or something like that. From Manchester, I think. Thus, he got stuck with the name Arvil, to honor the old soldier. But my dad must have decided that Tommy worked just as well, I guess."

"You think? You guess? A little weak on the details, aren't you, Jack?" she said, shaking her head in disbelief.

"I'm not sure I have any of the story straight," I admitted, "but it would explain a lot. Maybe I made up the whole thing in my head somewhere over the years. He's my father and I get to believe anything I want about him, don't I?"

"Well, Jack, when it comes to believing stuff about our parents," she said, "maybe we're all graduates of MSU — Making Stuff Up."

"Dad once complained that he was the only one in the world stuck with the god-awful first name of Arvil and he hated it."

I held up the old Navy picture and turned it over to read the inscription written across the back.

"See, here at the bottom, he wrote, *'We'll weather this storm together - from this day forward, Sincerely, Tommy.'* It sounds as if he decided to use the name Tommy when he left the Navy."

"Even if you learned the true story about your father and how he got his name," she said, "would it matter?"

"No, it wouldn't," I admitted. "I guess we all hang onto the stories we want to be true."

She waved the photo of the three young men in front of me again.

"Is this the only picture you have? This is an old grainy photo of teenage boys. You haven't seen him in years. If he is alive, are you sure you'll recognize him if he shows up at one of the curling clubs? You're going to have to tackle and shackle him to get him out of town quickly. You don't want to kidnap the wrong guy."

"Very funny," I said. "He's my dad. I'll know him at a molecular level."

I finished arranging everything in the car for a comfortable trip while Tina stood shin deep in snow and called ahead to

ProtoCommand. When she saw me squint and lean my ear in her direction, she started repeating the receptionist's words for my benefit.

"Joe Nehmer called from Omaha? When? A couple of days ago? Are you sure it was Mr. Nehmer? Is he in town? No? Okay, well, you know that Bill's car is parked out back and the trunk is still full of boxes from his office. I'll be there in about an hour. Don't let anyone call the police if they see me back there, okay. Thanks, Bye."

We discussed the call for a few minutes, but didn't know quite what to make of it. Why would Joe Nehmer call about the car? The property was still tied up in probate and he wasn't scheduled to fly back into town for nearly six weeks. Even if he wanted to pick up the boxes or the car, he would need to connect with Tina for the keys. She immediately tried returning his call, but settled for leaving a message. We finished packing the car and headed to her apartment complex. In less than twenty minutes, she was making room for her small suitcase in the rear seat and we were back on the road heading toward ProtoCommand. *"She's low maintenance,"* I thought to myself. *"This keeps getting better."*

En route to the company, I asked her to switch on my laptop and search for a nearby WiFi signal to check for e-mail messages. Depending on how far afield our search would take us, we might not return to the Twin Cities until late Monday afternoon. If an employer wanted to reach me about a job interview, I needed to be on top of it and respond immediately. When we could find no reception out on the road, we pulled into a Caribou Coffee. While I was at the counter getting a cup to go, Tina logged into the free Internet.

"No messages for you," she said as I set my cup on a table near the gas fireplace in the rear. "Do you mind if I check mine? Maybe Mr. Nehmer sent an e-mail."

Tina spun the laptop toward her and read a short message from her mother. The family was disappointed that she was thinking about staying in the Twin Cities rather than returning to Pipestone. They were happy she had met someone. *"Me?"* I wondered silently. They understood, of course, that job opportunities were better in the metro area, but everyone had been looking forward to her moving back home in time to see her sister, Sophie, graduate from high school. They even had the old bedroom ready.

"You don't sound thrilled about the idea of moving back home," I said. "Any lingering issues with your parents?"

"Mostly things are fine," she said. "My sister is keeping Dad busy. I see her making some of the same mistakes I made. But I've changed so much. Some people kind of get stuck, as if the four years of high school were the best years of their lives. That wasn't true for me, but I'm not so sure about Sophie. I couldn't wait to move on. Some of my old friends are still sitting in Pipestone — as if something large is going to happen for them. Not that it's a bad place to sit. It's a great town. A lot of people love it and so would you. But my friends haven't outgrown going to the same bars and parties on Saturday night. That could have been me and I hope it won't be my sister. My father was worried crazy about how I was starting to live my life and he didn't handle it very well. My mom complained that it was affecting the whole family. I argued that everyone should mind their own business, but now I see that they were mostly right. With Dad, though, there was more to it than just trying to keep me out of trouble. It was as if he was counting on me for something, like I was a co-parent in the family. I used to yell at him, *'I'm your daughter, not your wife. I have my own life.'* I'm sure that was pretty hurtful to my mom. He shouldn't have ever slapped me around like he did, though."

"What do you mean? Are you saying he beat you?" I probed.

"Just once, but it was enough. He was waiting in the kitchen for me when I came home really late one night. I think he must have been drinking a little bit, which wasn't like him at all. He grabbed me by the collar and screamed, *'Some people learn by repetition. Others learn by impression. I've told you a hundred times, now I guess I'll just need to make an impression.'* I had never seen him like that and I was too scared to yell for my mom."

"It started in our kitchen, carried through the dining room and ended in our living room. Just as I reached the front door to escape, my mother finally tackled him. I broke my wrist when he slammed the door on my hand."

"It sounds more like he slammed the door on your childhood, too," I added.

She paused to show me a faded scar on the back of her left wrist. "I spent the night in the emergency room and the next two days in the hospital. From there, I moved directly to my aunt's house a few miles across town. I was out of school for two weeks until the bruises healed."

"But you and your dad made up over time?"

"Well, it took a couple of years of me being away from home to attend college in St. Paul. But, yeah, my dad and I finally made up — to the extent we needed to, anyway. He's terribly sorry for the way he acted that night and feels awful about what it did to our family. But I never did move back in with them. When I told them I lost my job and was coming home, they were really looking forward to putting our family back together. But I doubt that moving back into my old bedroom could do that."

I broke in, "Was he ever abusive to anyone else in your family?"

"Not that I was ever aware of. Mom and I have a great relationship. I think she would have told me if he ever abused my sister. I'm not making excuses for my dad that night and I would never say that any domestic violence victim deserves it. But the truth is, I was guilty of committing some forms of abuse long before he was. I knew I was loved but I just didn't feel as if I had any relevance in the family. I mean, my parents were well-respected and an important part of the community. My dad was even mayor for a couple of years back in the early 1980s. He seemed to need a lot of attention from us, but I never understood it. I drifted in and out of our family life throughout my teenage years. I remember he once said, *'Tina, you linger like a vapor in the air. Sometimes it's like perfume, but other times it's like bad gas. You surround our lives but you're not part of us anymore. You're here for a moment but then you just blow away. We don't know how to reach you.'* I told him that even a fart served somebody some good. Now I think Sophie is feeling the same way."

"He called you a fart?" I asked, recalling that LaVon had once used a similar metaphor to describe my presence in her life.

"Not really. But what did he mean by that, Jack? That I blow away? Just because he didn't understand me doesn't mean I wasn't there."

"He didn't say he didn't understand you," I corrected her. "He said he couldn't reach you. There's a big difference. He may have understood you completely. He might not have liked what he understood, though. Maybe he was the same way when he was a kid. I think he was expecting something that you weren't capable of giving — or at least you didn't know how to give him what he was expecting. You were only eighteen."

"Yeah," she continued, "I was young and dumb. On the other hand, I know I did nothing to try to reach him halfway. I left it entirely up to him to try to reach me. How self-centered was that? Why did I think it was totally up to him to come looking when he needed whatever comfort I could provide. He was a good man, a good husband for my mom and a good provider for our family. But you add all those up and you still have all the insecurities and frustrations of a father. I didn't allow for that. I had been slowly neglecting him and withdrawing my love and respect for years. Even when I was able to overlook his flaws, my friends were more than happy to point them out for me. Looking back on things, it's pretty amazing how much your friends define your worldview when you're that age. He didn't deserve that — any more than I deserved to be slapped around the house that night. So who was guiltier of the greater abuse?"

"He was," I said. "You were just a teenager and..."

"And what, Dr. Phil?" she shot back. "At that age it's all supposed to be a one-way street between parents and their kids?"

"No, but I think you can be forgiven for acting a little self-indulgent as a high school senior."

"There it is again," she said, rolling her eyes. "The Oprah-fication of America. I've watched my parents try to deal with Sophie a little differently than they dealt with me, but I'm not sure it really matters. Every parent will tell you that raising kids is as much nature as nurture. Children don't come with an instruction manual and parents aren't born with special knowledge."

"So Sophie is burning the blue flame, too, huh?"

"Not the same way I did," she responded, "but yeah, in a way. As I watch her get a little older, I can see her do so many stupid things. About a year ago, she was arrested with some friends for underage drinking. I drove down to support my family and realized that she was copying a lot of my old behavior. Sophie's a good student — better than I was — but she's looking for relevance, too."

"Parents are supposed to accept and encourage their kid's individuality and magically know instinctively how to keep them on track. You know...let them trash their room. Trust them to make the right friends. Let them make their own decisions. It's supposed to be healthy for them to test boundaries. That's like saying, 'Pour 'em their first beer, but hope they don't like the taste.' Well, unfortunately, some kids do like the taste. I certainly did. So, where does encouragement end and no-boundaries begin? A kid doesn't always understand the parents' game plan. My family was lucky. We could turn to my aunt. Everyone — including my dad — agreed it would be best if I moved in with her. Every family should have an outlet to defuse the anger and settle down the hormones that way. Or maybe we should just lock high school kids in a gym for four years and let them out only when they're ready to act like adults."

"But you were only eighteen," I tried again. "You didn't deserve to get beaten up."

"Yeah, that's exactly what Bill said when I relayed this story to him once. He said he could forgive anything and everything out of people, but he couldn't forgive anyone who ever violated me that way."

"So, when your father came up to the cities, Bill never met him?"

"No," she said. "I didn't dare let him. I'll never say my father had a right to act that way. In fact, the only thing he beat into me that night was three more years of anger and confusion. I have sincerely apologized to my family for the worry I must have caused them back then. Things are better between us now but we all carry around a heavy burden of guilt. Dad has apologized a thousand times but he knows he can never pull back those fists he threw that night. I never lifted a finger to fight back but it has turned out that he's the one who really took the beating. He never did it before or since. Now I can't bear to watch him live with his shame."

"One of my teachers at the U once said there are only two ways to motivate people: fear or guilt. You either behave a certain way because you are afraid of the consequences or..."

"Or you act out of love and respect," she interrupted with a smile, "because you would feel ashamed to let the person down. My aunt says the same thing. She jokes that it's the difference between a Midwestern Lutheran and a Roman Catholic."

"Maybe she had the same professor," I laughed. "He was about that old. Shame is a powerful thing."

"Yes, Jack. It is. And you may need to remember that if we find your father."

9:30 a.m. Thursday, February 7th, 2008

We pulled onto the ProtoCommand property and I immediately commented that the parking lot seemed terribly void of cars for a mid-week morning. It should have been filled corner-to-corner by that time of the day.

"Doesn't anyone work here anymore?" I asked.

"Not hardly," Tina answered. "That's why I moved Bill's car to the back by the old loading docks, out of sight and out of mind. Nobody can see it sitting abandoned in the empty lot day after day."

I followed Tina's directions to the narrow rear alleyway running full-length behind the building. With the snow plowed high on either side of the narrow driving lane, it was difficult to figure how she could have found space to park the car. It wasn't until past the halfway point that I finally saw the front bumper of the gold Chrysler Sebring convertible protruding from behind a rusted-out dumpster.

"I'm surprised they still bother to plow out this narrow pathway," I said. "Do people park back here?"

“They keep it plowed for the rescue trucks in case of a fire or other emergency,” Tina said. “Whenever it snows, management complains that it cost an extra three hundred bucks to clear out this useless old alley.”

“How did the truck drivers get back here to offload at the docks and turn their rigs around?” I wondered.

“They couldn’t,” she said. “A lot of the younger truckers just dumped their pallets onto the parking lot at the side of the building. So, management finally closed these docks and moved them over to the new building annex.”

Tina suddenly gasped as I slowly rolled to a crawl in front of Bill’s car. She jumped out and began running toward it even before we came to a complete stop. As I stepped out and walked toward her, it was obvious what had animated her into such a quick reaction. It appeared as if someone had jimmied open the latch and emptied the trunk of nearly everything. Only a deflated spare tire, an old tire jack and a half-gallon of blue wiper fluid remained inside.

“Did you have anything locked in the front or rear seats?” I asked.

“No,” Tina said. “I didn’t want any of the boxes left out in plain sight. Who could have known there were items in the trunk, Jack? Do you suppose Mr. Nehmer flew back into town and broke into the car when he couldn’t reach me for the car key?”

“I doubt it,” I said. “He’s getting Bill’s money. Why would he care about a few of his personal items, too?”

We did a quick walk-around inspection, but could find no other damage. The console radio and the dashboard GPS were still in place.

“It wasn’t neighborhood kid, either” I concluded. “Whoever did this was only after the boxes.”

“And it looks like they got everything,” she added. “But what exactly did they get?”

“Well, it’s like you said, Tina. Bill’s stuff might have meant everything...or nothing. But if someone was trying to cover all the bases like we are, starting with personal belongings he kept locked out of reach in his office all these years would make sense. Someone either knew — or guessed — there were boxes hidden in his car trunk.”

I looked at the ground for possible tire tracks. Not enough snow had fallen to separate any fresh tracks from the dozens of previous snowplow tracks in the mix. I wasn’t sure what we would have done if we *had* found a fresh set of tread marks or footprints, anyway. We were both too scared to start being a hero. Tina flipped open her cell phone to search for the number to re-dial the receptionist. A thought suddenly hit me and I snatched at her hand quickly, knocking the phone to the ground.

"Hey!" she yelled, jumping back. "What the hell, Jack?"

"Sorry to be so dramatic," I said, reaching down to pick up the phone and checking to make sure it wasn't dialing into a number. "I just realized that somebody may be on to us; intercepting cell phone calls."

"Oh, come on, Jack," she said. "I told the receptionist we were coming. Maybe she asked someone to come out here to empty the trunk...for whatever reason."

"Really?" I said. "By jimmying it open with a crowbar? The car's been sitting here all this time. They knew you and Nehmer were dealing with the probate courts. Besides, they had twenty-five years to sift through Bill's personal junk in his office. Why would it suddenly be so important to wreck his car to get to it all?"

"Okay, I think you're right," she said. "The receptionist didn't care about his boxes. But come on, Jack, somebody intercepting my cell phone calls? That's stuff for the CIA. No one has that kind of technology available to them."

"No," I said, "you're probably right that no *one* person does, but someone working at a technology corporation might." I pointed to the building to make my point. "Do you really think it was just a pure coincidence that someone got here just before we did?"

"We don't know that it was *just before* we got here," she said. "It's always possible it was Mr. Nehmer. It might have been anytime in the past several days."

"It's possible," I reiterated, "but if he couldn't reach you, why wouldn't he ask someone in the building, or tell the receptionist he was flying into town. Also, I'm back to thinking about the damage to the car again. It's tied up in probate. He wouldn't have taken the risk of breaking in...not with Bill's life savings practically in his hip pocket already. It's worth double-checking with him, though, just to make sure. Keep trying to call him...but we'll use a payphone somewhere."

"Oh, God, Jack. This is my only phone. I've been using it to talk to you about Bill and your father for the past two weeks. If someone's been tapping in, he knows I'm in this with you."

"Well, I tried to warn you that I didn't know where this was heading, Tina. But yes, I think you're probably in it for keeps now, too. Let's start by getting out of here, where we can stretch out our thinking. I don't like the idea that someone might be watching us from any one of these windows. We'll get to a pay phone and call Nehmer until we reach him. Wouldn't it be a relief to hear him apologize for giving us a scare like this?"

We hustled into my car and quickly drove around front of the building and out onto the main boulevard. It was several blocks before we found a gas station with a drive-up payphone.

Tina looked up Nehmer's number on her cell phone then quickly turned it off and dialed the phone through her open passenger-side window. He answered after a handful of rings and confirmed that he had never called the company, nor visited Minneapolis in connection with Bill's property. From Tina's half of the conversation, I could tell his curiosity was aroused enough to ask several more questions. She reassured him politely that everything was okay and hung up without discussing any damage to the Sebring.

We sat quietly for a minute, watching several cars come and go at the rows of gas pumps. I couldn't decide what to do next.

"We should call the police to report it..."

"Report what?" Tina interrupted with a flash of tears in her eyes. "That someone stole boxes of Bill's personal items before we had a chance to break into his car and steal them ourselves? That would raise too many questions from the court, which I'm not ready to answer, Jack. I'm not even supposed to have a set of keys to his car or townhouse. Mr. Nehmer and I both signed affidavits saying that we turned over everything to a trustee. I'm out of work and I really don't need a legal matter hanging over my head. I don't have Bill Ordway to fall back on anymore and neither do you."

That stung. I looked at her and wondered why her genuine empathy and gentle bravado had suddenly disappeared. I knew she was scared, but so was I. Neither of us was thinking straight. I pulled the car forward several feet into an empty parking slot and left the engine idle while we considered our options. There was no going back. Going forward might lead to any number of dead ends, but it was our only choice. We both agreed: We could trust no one and we could talk to no one without possibly putting our lives — and possibly the lives of others —in danger. Whoever took those boxes was after the same thing we were. It was a sickening feeling. We were playing a new version of fox and hen with someone who had been playing by his own rules for nearly forty years.

"Jack," Tina said with some hesitation. "If he's intercepting our phone calls, wouldn't he know your whereabouts? He must know you are aware of him. Why hasn't he killed you, like he may have killed Jason and Jenny when they tried to get involved?"

I thought about what she said for a moment. Then reached behind me and pulled the wooden writing board onto my lap.

"Well," I said, "he knows we're looking for my father and he knows Dad and I are the final two names on his list."

"Right," she responded.

"But he must also know you're in this with me," I continued. "So I'm afraid you're probably on his target list now, too, Tina. He'll follow us right to my father, which is exactly what he wants. Maybe we should separate and get you out of this mess."

"Do you see, Jack? This is exactly why I said that I'll do the thinking," she said. "Let's assume we're right about all of this. That means this guy has been sticking to his basic plan for four decades. He has killed everyone who has tried to get involved in finding him. If your father really has successfully evaded him over the past year, it has changed everything."

I sat silently and looked into her eyes. My confusion must have been evident. She spoke again when she realized I wasn't tracking with her logic.

"If his plan is to use one of us to get to your father, it's not going to be me," she explained. "He only needs you. But I know too much already, so he can't let me go now."

"Let's not panic about him chasing us all over the country," I said. "He doesn't really need to do anything except wait for my dad to show up in Hibbing next week. If we're right about all of this, he takes years to plan his executions and has always managed to cover his tracks. It wouldn't make sense for him to blow his cover now by trying to kill us out in the open, after only a few days of planning."

"Don't expect rational behavior from an irrational person, Jack. If you and your dad are the last ones on his list, he won't care about sticking to his game plan. He's just trying to finally win the game."

"That's a comforting thought," I said sarcastically. "But he can get to us later. I think we're the ones with the tight timeline, not the killer. We need to find my father and stop him from going to Hibbing."

"And that's exactly what I'm saying, Jack!" she said, shaking her fists in front of her in mock frustration. "This is why people joke that you can buy a woman's brain for half price — because it's used. Let's assume the killer knows that we have been investigating everything the past couple of weeks."

"Judging by the empty trunk, I think that's a safe assumption," I said, feeling wounded and misunderstood.

"Okay," she continued, "now let's look a little deeper into that empty trunk. Your dad's murder has been planned for years. Probably decades, in fact. There are only two names left on his list. That means the killer is only inches away from getting away with the whole thing.

We're his only threat. He needs us out of the picture — before or after we have a chance to get to your father — he doesn't care. In fact, we probably understand the circumstances and evidence more than Jason or Jenny or the FBI investigators ever did, so he needs us deader than he needed any of them. Even if he kills your dad in the next half hour, we already know too much. It doesn't matter if it's today, in Hibbing next week, or crossing a street in Pipestone ten years from now. The only way it will ever end for him is to get rid of everyone associated with the list."

I finally understood her point.

"And that includes you now," I said sadly.

"Yes, that includes me now," she answered with a quivering whisper.

"God, I'm sorry I got you involved in this, Tina," I sighed. "I don't know what to do next. Christ, is any of this real?"

"And that will certainly be the hardest thing of all," she replied. "Not knowing what is real and never being absolutely sure of the truth. But this is part of everyone's true story, Jack; our never-ending search for whatever it is that keeps us moving forward."

"Yeah," I said. "Ironic, isn't it? My father has been out there somewhere in a barren wilderness he created for himself, while I was living safe and comfortable in my own little world. If only I hadn't walked into that curling club and looked up into those damned rafters. We wouldn't be involved in any of this right now."

"Right," she snapped back. "Yes, he may be hiding. In fact, he may even really be dead. But maybe — just maybe — he found at least one wonderful place in his big, wide, borderless world that isn't so barren — a clean, white sheet of curling ice, where he can hitch his sense of purpose to every shot he makes. Whether he's dead or alive, Jack, it doesn't really matter. You need to search for him. You need to find him so you can come in from your own wilderness."

"What do you mean come in from my own wilderness?" I asked. "Sometimes I can't tell where you're coming from, Tina."

"Jack, you're the one who's been hiding all these years, not your father. Sure you were safe and comfortable hidden in your shrunken little world, but a barren wilderness can come in all sizes and shapes, including a suburban cul-du-sac and a little old brick cottage on a quiet neighborhood city street. I think you feel it, too. What was it you were really looking for up in those rafters at the curling club in Mapleton that evening? And that Mankato newspaper article you read that morning? Sure Arvil Firpo is an unusual name, but there could be a thousand in the world, and who's to say they aren't all great curlers?

And what evidence was really in that pipe cutter tool you found in your basement that night? Then, when I called that evening to tell you I had discovered some little tidbits about your father, you were willing to crawl out of bed at six o'clock the next morning — on a Sunday — to come running."

"That's not fair," I protested. "You asked me to come down to Bill's office. You were the one who found the photograph and the letters..."

"Yes," she interrupted. "I asked you to come down to pick up an old black and white picture and a letter that I believed you might appreciate as a memento of your parents. I thought the items might mean something to you. Hell, I sure got that part of it right. There was a lot more between the lines of that letter than I ever saw coming. And that writing board in Bill's desk? My God, man, you ripped that thing out of its tracks with the passion of the crucifixion. I know how big Minnesota is, Jack. When you left your wife down in Mankato, you drove a hundred and fifty miles out of your way to get to that little cemetery in Maynard. You had to prove or disprove it for yourself that your dad was never quite as dead as you thought he was?"

"I just wanted to..." I started, but choked myself off.

"Jack, there's more to you than what you have become," she continued. "Living is one thing. But you weren't alive. There's a huge difference. I walked out of Bill's office with my arms full of boxes that Sunday morning and I knew exactly what was packed into each one. You left there with only a few scraps of paper and other pieces of junk in your hands, but how much more were you carrying in your heart?"

She was absolutely right. A long silence was the only appropriate response and she was kind enough not to break it with meaningless chatter. She left that up to me.

"So we shake off our fear and search for my dad, whether he's really out there or not?" I asked.

"Yep. Until we find him — dead or alive," she said. "We don't have a choice anymore. We're on the same page now, Jack. So let's turn it. We can't take the chance that this isn't all very, very real."

"Okay, but we stay attached at the hips until we find him," I scolded.

"Let's get attached at the heart before we get ourselves attached at other parts of our bodies," she smiled back.

Michigan Rink - Gold	**Minnesota Rink - Silver**
Lead: Jim Coventry	Lead: Paul Stenner
Second: Dale Harder	Second: John Mistovich
Third: Steve Talbert	Third: Mickey Bellows
Skip: Norm Thunger	**Skip: Freddy Schade**

Seventh End

Teams were getting a firm understanding of how to relate to the changing ice conditions. Minnesota's 5-1 lead after three ends had been slowly whittled away to a narrow 6-4 margin.

With the hammer in hand and three of his team's rocks already nestled closest to the button, Michigan Skip Norm Thunger exhibited an uncharacteristic display of greed with his final shot. Rather than pushing his final shot harmlessly out of play and taking the certain three points, he instead hoped to slip it through a narrow gap to pick up a fourth.

With the rock tracking perfectly toward the center of the house, Thunger remained on one knee at center ice to soak in the cheers, but momentarily forgot his responsibilities as Skip. Hearing no guidance from his captain, Vice Skip Steve Talbert was uncertain what to call out for sweeping instructions. Thunger could not react quickly enough to the magnitude of what was about to take place as his rock slid several yards in front of him.

The sweepers lifted their brooms and began strolling leisurely ahead of the moving stone, as if escorting it under arms into the Rose Garden. As the rock slid beyond the hog line, it suddenly picked up a small speck of broomcorn frozen to the ice, causing the shot to careen wildly to the right.

The Michigan rink reacted in horror as their rock twisted off sharply and thumped into an otherwise meaningless rock. Minnesota's #3 rock was knocked forward as if it had eyes, coming to rest nearly dead-center of the button. In less than a few seconds, for the want of a few slow strokes to clean the ice of invisible debris, Michigan watched three certain points vaporize before their eyes. Schade's team had stolen a point without the hammer.

The crowd buzzed with disgust at the role that dirty ice would play in the outcome of the match. "The game should never have been played in the first place. No! They can't let that junk stand. It can't be possible that a rink might go on to play for the national championship because of a loose piece of broom straw. These playdowns are cursed."

For the Michigan rink, the psychological blow only darkened the pall hanging over the arena. Players on both sides knew it in their bones that they should be in the stands watching the North Dakota rink handily defeat Wisconsin for the championship. To determine a winner this way would highlight the unbearable injustice. Three Minnesota players saw the look of despair on their opponents' faces and understood the anguish. Three Minnesota players — but not all four. Stenner, Mistovich and Bellows immediately walked over to their Skip.

"Shut up, Freddy," Paul Stenner said before Schade could utter a word. "That shit should never happen to anybody. Least of all those guys. Least of all in a game like this."

Schade raised his broom as if to take a swing, but something in the crowd caught his eye. He jogged quickly toward the bleachers, where his son was standing and cheering. Next to him, nearly a year older and a head taller stood his constant companion and best friend, eighteen year old Arv DuMot. Freddy scanned the angry crowd. He wasn't concerned for his son's safety; Willy and Arv had proven over the years that they could take care of themselves. But where was that other young punk who should have been with them?

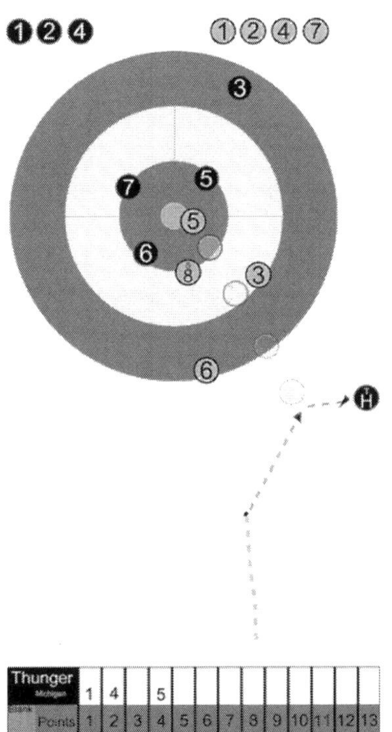

Early Afternoon Thursday, February 7th, 2008

We pulled into the parking lot of Holy Savior Lutheran Church in Maynard a few minutes before one o'clock, just as the sun finally broke through the thin layer of high clouds overhead. With the exception of a small delay waiting for the police to clear a fender-bender at a new, unfamiliar traffic circle on Highway 7 near Mayer, the two and a half hour trip had moved along quickly.

Along the route, Tina went crazy exchanging text messages among various friends, which I figured must have numbered in the dozens. Before leaving Minneapolis, we had mutually agreed that texting would probably be a safe method of communication. I regretted the decision almost immediately. When she wasn't tapping her keyboard with her thumbs, she was trying to figure out how to set up the GPS unit we impulsively retrieved from the dashboard of Bill's car. In our haste to disconnect it, however, neither of us thought to open the glove compartment to search for an instruction manual. She managed to get it to light up when we plugged it into the 12v jack on my console, but while driving at sixty-five miles an hour I couldn't take my eyes off the road long enough to make sense of the array of knobs and buttons. I finally convinced her to leave it alone and we would look at it together, if we decided we ever really needed it. I tried to remain politely silent, but my curiosity finally got the best of me as we turned off the highway and headed south on a small road toward Maynard.

"Why don't you just call and talk to the person?" I asked with a light chuckle. "Who's on the text conversation with you?"

She looked at me momentarily as if starting to answer, but then turned her head forward and stared through the windshield for several seconds.

"It's okay," I said. "It's really none of my business."

How I wished she had said something. Anything would have been better than leaving me tethered to my jealous curiosity. *"Oh, it's just a friend, nobody you know,"* might have been a welcome response. Instead, I watched her quietly turn off her phone and slip it into her purse, then change the conversation to something vague about the bleakness of the wintery landscape.

"God, I don't know what to do next with this girl," I thought silently.

We were the only car in the church parking lot as we sat for a minute looking at the old Chaska yellow brick façade. On either side of the double-door entry stood two roughly carved jamb statues of angels with improbable features. Chiseled into the pointed faux-gothic arch above the large entryway doors was inscribed: **Herein, Faith Abides.**

"I didn't really look at it closely when I was here on New Year's Eve," I said. "I don't recall the brick being quite so yellow. Probably more direct sunlight today, that's all."

Tina stepped out of the car and I followed her across the front of the building toward the cemetery. Despite two or three inches of new snow that had fallen, I could still detect the impressions of old footprints. Clearly, nobody had set foot in the graveyard since Knoblechner and I plodded our way down through the headstones several weeks earlier.

I took her by the hand and began retracing my previous path down the hill toward the DuMot family plots. To my surprise, she pulled back and walked back toward the front sidewalk.

"I'm cold," she said. "I can see the gravesites from up here. We're not going to learn anything new out here. I'd love to see the inside, though."

She was right, of course, but the change in her demeanor and general withdrawal over the course of the three-hour trip was difficult to understand. It made me nervous and I hoped that she wasn't regretting coming along. I calmed down when I saw her smiling as she climbed the steps and discovered the front door unlocked.

I hurried after her into the narthex and we walked together into the gray, quiet space of the sanctuary. The early afternoon sunshine bled a mosaic of colored light through the three tall stained glass windows along the south side facing the cemetery. Well, the sunlight was shining through two of the windows, anyway. The third window, tucked into the rear corner, may once have helped illuminate the interior space, but no longer. Decades before, a pine tree planted for the greater glory of God had overgrown its landscape enclosure and smashed tightly against the outside of the building, robbing the window of the critical bright sunlight needed to raise Lazarus. Three figures in the scene stood dark and brooding against the thick cluster of branches outlined against the exterior of the glass. What should have been hundreds of vibrant colors instead blended indifferently into various shades of murky gray.

Posted on the wall placard to the right of the pulpit were the hymns for the order of service. It was impossible to say whether the numbers remained posted there from the previous week, or from five thousand Sundays ago. Tina speculated that they were probably intended for the coming Sunday service — something that had never occurred to me.

"I always thought it was strange that an American flag should hang in a church," she said, pointing to the stars and stripes displayed prominently behind pulpit. "God didn't draw borders on the planet. People did."

Hanging against one wall was a colorful quilt, with a different historical scene from the congregation's history stitched onto a white square in each corner.

"This is all very much like stepping back in time two hundred years," I smirked. "What is it that people pray for when they come here, to stop the world and let them off?"

"Well in a way, I suppose they do," came a man's gravelly voice from near the entry. Tina and I spun around, startled. It was Knoblechner. We hadn't heard him coming up the stairs from the social hall below the sanctuary.

"For many people, son, this place is their final freedom and their last refuge," he continued. "So yes, some people do want time to stand still for an hour or two every Sunday. People need to believe that at least one thing in their lives is constant and timeless. "

"You mean they think God wrote the Bible then died," I said, not expecting a reply.

"Something like that," Knoblechner said.

I suddenly realized the old man might not remember me.

"Hello again, Mr. Knoblechner. I'm Jack DuMot. You may recall that I was here at the end of December. You showed me my grandparents' headstone...down the hill at the bottom of the cemetery."

"And your dad's marker, too, as I recall," he replied. "I thought I recognized you. It's good to see you again so soon. And who is this pretty young lady?"

I introduced him to Tina, who extended her hand with a polite hello and a gentile, genuine smile. She pointed at the hymn board, picked up a thick book from a pew and looked up the first number.

"How Great Thou Art," she chuckled. "That was my old aunt's favorite hymn. Great. Now I'll have that tune stuck in my head all day."

"Oh, so you know that one?" Knoblechner said. "How about you, son? Anything about any of this feel familiar to you?"

"I've vaguely heard of the song," I said. "But except for funerals and the occasional wedding over the years, I've never spent much time in church."

"Then don't be so critical about those who do," Tina admonished.

I was feeling outnumbered and tried to defend myself.

"I've always thought that religion is a crutch."

"Ah, so you have complete faith in your doubts, do you?" Knoblecher replied. "Somewhere along the journey we all find ourselves needing a shoulder to lean on whenever we come up limping. But you're right, young man. Religion is a crutch. For some of us, it's even a wheelchair or a gurney. God doesn't have a problem with that. Why do you?"

Tina smiled at him and agreed with a slight nod.

She hummed the hymn lightly as she wandered through the rows of pews toward the stained glass windows. When she reached the window toward the front, nearest the pulpit, she asked in a loud whisper whether I thought Bill Ordway once attended church there, as a kid growing up in nearby Gluek. I wondered the same about my father. As she neared the center window, her white parka and sweatpants suddenly exploded into numberless colors radiating through the glass from the bright outdoor sunlight. She paused for a moment to hold her arms out to her side, twisting them back and forth as if to soak up the tones and hues across every inch of her body, now bright with tinted highlights.

"Look, I'm Joseph," she said, laughing and spinning around quickly several times, as if to model herself. She stopped with a disappointed look, however, when she realized that the obscure reference was completely lost on me.

"Oh, you know," Knoblechner said coming to her rescue. "From the Book of Genisis — Joseph and his coat of many colors."

She reached out toward me, "Here, come over and stand in the light with me, Jack. It's like a fantastic dream."

"Yeah," I said quietly, taking her hand, "and with you, any dream will do."

Just as quickly, she fell silent and motionless; looking down toward the windowsill at her waist. She reached out to touch a large, blue octagonal piece of glass that made up a large segment of hem at the bottom of Judas' robe. I watched as she gently caressed a metal nameplate attached to the recessed sill. Standing close behind her, I wrapped both arms around her waist and clasped my hands loosely together at her belt buckle. She leaned back and slipped the top of her head perfectly under my chin. I breathed in the sweet smell of her hair for a few seconds, as we swayed lightly side-to-side, absorbing the invisible rhythm of the colors.

Looking down at the windowsill again, I half-whispered the words written on the brass plate: ***The Betrayal of Christ, in memory of Freddy and Cynthia Schade by their loving son Willy, 1972.***

"If 'Willy' is Bill Ordway, then this must be referring to the *Freddy* and *mom* crossed out on the list," I said. "When Mary Coventry called from the USCA, she mentioned an old curler named Freddy Schade. You said Bill's stepfather's name was Freddy, didn't you? I guess that answers your question about Bill attending church here as a child, anyway."

She broke away with a gentle *"Yeah, I guess so"* and moved further down the wall a few more feet, where she stood for a moment in the vibrant glow of lights streaming through another window. It was a scene of a man sticking his finger into the spear wound in Jesus' side. The colors and style appeared to be from a different era and by a different designer.

"Doubting Thomas," Knoblechner explained from behind us. Tina followed his lead and provided me with a brief explanation of the story. Knoblechner explained that the window had been donated in 1964 by the sons and daughter of John and Dorothy Reismuller.

I started walking in the opposite direction toward the dark window in the rear corner. As I passed the center *Betrayal of Christ* window again, something about it recaptured my attention. I wasn't sure what I thought I saw, but something drew my head toward the upper half of the scene. It was one of those momentary, fleeting peripheral visions, like spotting a profile of Richard Nixon in a cloud; then losing it forever when you try to point it out to someone standing nearby.

I turned back to Knoblechner, who had taken a seat in the last row of pews. We discussed the window for a moment and I explained that both Tina and I once worked for the *Willy* who had donated the window. I asked about the circumstances of its installation. He knew very little of the story but recalled that it was the second of the three windows to be installed. He recounted a brief history of the building, gleaned from various pages of a fundraising calendar sold for the congregation's centenary celebration in 1994.

In the early 1960s, the original clear-glass windows were in leaky disrepair and needed replacing. The women's guild sponsored a sale of quilts and handwork to raise money to have stained glass installed, but fell far short of the money needed. But the Reismuller kids commissioned the first window in 1964, which the pastor dictated should go nearest the pulpit in the front. Times being what they were for local farm families, the two remaining clear glass windows on that wall remained in place for several more years, until Bill Ordway donated the center *Betrayal* window in 1972.

"What can you tell us about that one?" Tina asked, pointing

toward the dark *Lazarus* scene in the corner.

"It's the most recent," he replied. "But I can't tell you anything more about it. The church council was ordered to keep it anonymous. I don't remember ever hearing who commissioned and donated it. The one elder who did know died unexpectedly shortly after the council approved the installation."

Tina gasped and Knoblechner took her hand.

"Nobody much cares for it, so they allowed the tree to continue to grow to block out the light."

Taken as a whole, the three disparate scenes were neither uplifting nor inspiring. Apparently, the local farmers just didn't think God was much fun to be around. Knoblechner added that a family of stained glass artists in western Minnesota created and installed all three windows, across two or three generations.

I stepped closer and squinted in the gray light, trying to read the gold letters lightly etched into a brass plaque at the base of the dark window: ***To the Family of Peter and Medora DuMot, 'Thy brother will rise again.' John, 11:23***.

"They were the words Jesus spoke to Martha after hearing that Lazarus had died," Knoblechner clarified.

Tina joined me by my side.

"Do you think your father might have donated it?" Tina asked. "If he's still alive, I mean?"

"Odd sort of gift to a God he never seemed to care too much about," I answered. "But who else would have? Since it's so recent, it could be more proof that he's not dead. It's too bad the light can't shine through it from the outside."

"I'm sure it will someday," she replied. "Nothing stays hidden in the shadows forever."

"Yeah, I suspect you're right, Tina, but it's an eerie scene and quote to commemorate your family with, isn't it?"

"And that's why the building and operations committee won't let me cut down that tree," Knoblechner said. "Some people believe there's a story in that glass. Whenever I bring it up at council meetings, many elders say they would rather remove the window than the tree. Until someone gives us something better to replace it with, though, we just leave it there as dark and gray as the story behind it."

Knoblechner gave us a brief tour of the building and explained as much of its history as he could recall. When I realized the time had somehow slipped toward mid-afternoon, I explained that we still needed to drive the final twenty-five miles to Montevideo in time to check on some details with the records clerk. I asked him if he knew the directions to the old DuMot farm in Gluek. We would be heading back to Highway 7 and could continue for a few miles further into town. He told us our best bet would be to stop at the Cenex station and ask the attendant.

"Jake Highwheeler runs the station in the winter months. Summer months he operates a big dairy operation out near your grandparents' old place. From what I understand, he may have bought out a parcel of the land and annexed the acreage eight or ten years ago for some extra pasture or feed crops. Some of the old buildings might still be standing. You can probably see your dad's old house, anyway. You can waste a lot of time driving up and down those roads when every square acre of plowed field and pasture land looks the same covered up by snow. But I'm sure Highwheeler will know those country miles like the back of his hand."

Tina objected and mentioned the time it would take to get to the courthouse, but Knoblechner agreed that it would be worth our while to take a quick drive out to the old homestead.

"If you find the place, you might want to see if there's a For Sale sign posted along the road," he added. "I was at the courthouse fairly recently and I understand someone was asking about buying some of the land. Maybe Highwheeler has parceled some of the acres up for sale again."

At the Cenex station, we learned that Knoblechner didn't have his facts completely straight. When I introduced myself to Highwheeler as Tommy DuMot's son, it drew only a confused stare. When I added that I was Pete and Medora DuMot's grandson and explained that we were looking for the old farm property, a nervous look crept across his face. He stammered a polite hello and quickly admitted that he had never legally purchased the DuMot homestead land. In fact, he had simply *appropriated* it by conveniently moving a barbed wire fence post here and there. After all, he complained, the land had grown overrun with weeds, which were beginning to migrate onto his farm fields. The best thing for it, he argued, was to let his cows keep it nibbled down. He only intended to continue using the land until the farm was reclaimed by the unknown owner or put up for sale by the county.

"Look," he said, "I didn't mean to just steal it. I'd like to buy the land but I just never knew who owned it. I've checked several times over the years. It's still in the DuMot name, for God's sake. When I read that Arv died, I kept waiting to see whether it would stay in the family. After so many years of never hearing anything, I finally figured the damned fool probably never took care of the legal paperwork. So I watched for it to come up at auction. Eventually, I realized that it wasn't likely to go on the market, so I moved some fences. Some neighbors asked how I got away with it, but they accepted my story that I had a private agreement with your family. Things have been quiet about it now for several years. I'd like to keep it that way. I want to do things legally. If it's your property, son, I'd be happy to pay you for the ten or fifteen acres of good summer pasture I use along the road."

"Which road is that?" I asked. "We're heading into Montevideo to the courthouse and I thought we might drive by and take a look at the old place. I've never seen it."

He wrote down the address and sketched a small map of the road grids running north out of town. By his reckoning, it was about seven miles to the old property. Tina checked her watch and reminded me that seven miles in one direction meant seven miles returning, as well. When Highwheeler said that it was pretty easy to get confused on those long narrow roads, it sealed our decision. I agreed that we would need to postpone looking for it until we had more time. I stuffed the note paper into my pants pocket and bid goodbye.

"I'm sure I'll be in touch in the near future," I said. "Don't worry about moving the fences back on my account. As far as I'm concerned, you can farm the whole damned place."

We settled into the car and Tina checked the road atlas for approximate mileage to the courthouse. The time was slipping toward three o'clock. Assuming the records office remained open until at least four-thirty, we wouldn't have a problem.

As we continued west on Highway 7 and neared Montevideo, I wondered aloud whether we were close to a WiFi signal. We pulled into the parking lot of a local convenience store and Tina gave an excited little squeal when two or three bars flickered to life along the bottom tray of my laptop screen. She checked my account and announced there were three messages posted to my inbox. The first two were routine employment rejection letters.

"The third message is in your junk bin," she said. "The subject line is a bunch of gibberish and symbols."

"It's probably one of those spam ads offering to enlarge one of my body parts," I said. "Which I assure you, doesn't need enlarging."

"I'm sure," she replied with a smile.

"Funny," I said, "but I shouldn't be getting any spam. My filter is set too high. What do you mean gibberish and symbols? Like Cyrillic or Chinese? Or just bad English grammar like from Indonesia or the Philippines?"

She turned the screen in my direction so I could get a quick glance. I reached down to hit the delete button but my hand froze above the key. The symbols had a definite pattern, unlike anything I had ever seen before. I copied the gibberish to a Word document and saved it in my documents folder.

"I'll figure it out later," I finally said. "For now, let's keep moving."

We pulled back onto the highway but I couldn't stop thinking about the message. I finally gave in to my curiosity and asked Tina to pull up the document again. As I stared at the tangled lines of symbols, Wingdings and punctuations marks, I lost my concentration on the road. Tina suddenly shrieked and yanked at the steering wheel, narrowly preventing us from drifting over the centerline and into the path of an oncoming car. I flew headlong into panic mode and ripped her hand off the wheel, struggling to regain control on the frosty road. The car fishtailed several times as I instinctively pushed the brake to the floorboard. Tina yelled at me to let off the brake, but it was too late. Our momentum pushed us into a sideways slide and I over-compensated to the right. We spun once around in a complete circle and drifted onto the shoulder, where our wheels sunk into a rut, jerking us violently. We skidded and bumped along for two hundred or more feet until we slammed to a stop; the passenger side of the car pushed up at an angle against a plowed bank of snow.

I looked over and found Tina staring down from a foot above me, gaping with her mouth open gasping for air, a death grip on the dashboard. Our steep angle felt as if we were in real danger of rolling over, so I moved ever-so-slowly to unbuckle my seatbelt and open my car door. When I found the angle of the car made it impossible, I lowered the electric window and wiggled my way outside. As I lay there on the shoulder, I realized with relief that the car was undamaged and in no real danger of tipping. I called to Tina to climb out, but her passenger side door was jammed against the heavy pile of snow. I heard her unclick her seat belt and watched as she wiggled around the interior. A few seconds later, she tumbled out through the open driver's side window, as well; spilling out on top of me.

We lay there quietly for a moment, catching our breath, before simultaneously bursting into laughter. I knew I was holding a very precious thing in my arms and I was overcome with wonder when I found her gazing at me and smiling about our near-death experience. It took only a few seconds more to realize what was about to happen. There on that icy shoulder of State Trunk Highway 7, on the outskirts of an isolated town in the middle of frozen western Minnesota prairie farmland, one abandoned, wounded young man was about to be kissed by a beautiful, confident, intelligent young woman. And I had every reason to believe that the young man was going to be me.

"Will you two get a room?" came a sarcastic, pitchy voice from behind our car. "Or at least find a stretch of county road where nobody has to watch."

From some distance away, a pimply-faced driver from a nearby farm had pulled over when he saw our car tipped onto the snow embankment. With callous disregard for my obvious disappointment, Good Neighbor Sam rushed to our side. No-doubt he expected to live large as the local hero in the next day's edition of the town newspaper. To his obvious disappointment, however, he quickly surmised that would both recover quite nicely from our near-death experience, thank you very much.

In an instant, Tina was up and on her feet, blushing and brushing dirty snow from her white sweatpants and parka. She quickly straightened her hair and gave me a cute little *ahem,* as if I hadn't noticed the unwelcome interruption. In another instant, I was also up and on my feet, dodging for my life as I stumbled awkwardly into the traffic lane. When I regained my bearings, I realized what was happening right before my eyes.

Sure enough, there on that frozen shoulder of State Trunk Highway 7, on the outskirts of an isolated town in the middle of frozen western Minnesota prairie farmland, one young man did get kissed by a beautiful, confident, intelligent young woman. But it wasn't me. When the young man offered the use of his pickup truck winch to pull our *"little foreign car"* back onto the highway, Tina gave him a bear hug, grabbed his face between her cold wet hands and planted a long playful kiss full on his mouth. It wasn't just any kiss, mind you. It was *my* kiss. I had been struggling mightily to figure out how to get to first base with this girl. All farmer-boy had to do was rush to the rescue expecting to save her life. Go figure.

Within a few minutes, the kid winched us clear of the snow bank and helped us brush the snow off the passenger-side door and windows. Tina thanked him with another kiss and we pulled slowly back onto the road. As we got back up to speed, she picked up the conversation as if nothing at all had happened.

"So, what was so interesting about that gibberish e-mail message that nearly got us killed?" she asked.

"I don't know, Tina. There was something about it that caught my attention. I want to check it out more carefully."

I drove another mile and pulled off the highway into a business section on the eastern edge of town. I stared at the document, trying to bring the jumble of letters and symbols into mental focus. I had seen a thousand similar spam messages from foreign senders, typically sent out in the millions to test live e-mail addresses prior to starting a spam advertising campaign. This one, however, appeared to be clearly different, yet vaguely familiar. The spacing of the individual characters and groups were structured as if they belonged in a grammatical sentence. It took another few seconds before I realized it wasn't gibberish at all. My mind flew back to the phone message from my dad, *"You will receive an encrypted message. Don't worry, you will recognize the code."* Like a veil being lifted from my eyes, I recognized it as the same familiar encryption that Bill Ordway had developed to be used by the members of the LightTect project. We used it to routinely exchange secure programming data with each other on evenings and weekends. Tina agreed that it looked like encoded language, but wasn't prepared to blindly accept it as anything more.

I had followed my father's directions on the answering machine message and left my e-mail address, but I never thought for a second that it would matter. More than six years had passed since he set up that machine somewhere in Montana. If this e-mail really was from him, it meant that he listened to the tape, heard my voice and knew I was finally searching. If it was from him, it meant he still cared enough to follow through. If it was from him, it meant we could meet each other half and find a way forward together.

"It would be great if it's from your father," she said, "but the odds are out of this world against it, don't you think, Jack?"

"We're in luck!" I yelled, ignoring her. "I still have Bill's decryption program and some old protocol codes stored in an e-file."

In my heart and in my head, I knew the old access codes on my hard drive wouldn't work, though. When I noticed Tina gently shaking her head, I realized that she knew it, too. It was one of Bill's policies to change the decryption sequence the last workday of every month.

"If this message is from my father," I said, "why would he say I would recognize it if I couldn't open it? He wouldn't have been able to predict when, if ever, he would send it to me so many years into the future."

"I think that's not altogether true," Tina corrected me with a hesitation in her voice. "All those years, your dad must have stayed in contact with Bill, maybe to find the killer...I mean. Why else would he know about the code program in the first place? It's possible that he may have known exactly when Bill would cut you loose from ProtoCommand. In fact, this moment may have been planned from the day you were hired, Jack...or the day you were born."

I poked around with a couple of old decipher codes before giving up.

"Well, I tried all the old codes I still have on file from ProtoCommand," I said. "Do you happen to remember the last encryption code Bill wrote, before the LightTect program was shut down? Maybe that's the one we need."

"Right," she said sarcastically. "I wrote it down, memorized it and then ate the Post-It note. Sorry, Jack, but Bill made it up from scratch every month."

She paused for a second and I could see in her eyes that a spark was beginning to ignite her memory.

"No," she said, "I take that back. He didn't make it up from scratch every month. I think he used some kind of a system or formula from month-to-month. Once, when he needed to come up with the new code at the last minute, he pulled out his pocket calculator. Then he asked me to read a list of numbers he had written on a scratch pad on his desk. As I read the numbers, he punched them into the calculator. Then he read a new six-digit number to me — right off the calculator — and asked me to make sure you guys had the new code number prior to leaving for the weekend."

"Yeah, thanks for ruining about a thousand weekends for us like that," I joked. "Look, we'll have to figure this out later. Right now, we've got to get to the courthouse in time to talk to some people about the death records."

I showed her my computer screen with a full list of previous LightTect access codes filling the screen.

"Here are Bill's protocol code numbers dating back several consecutive months of last year. I'll drive while you see if you can figure out a formula he might have used or a pattern to the numbers. If you find something, maybe we can get inside my father's head."

Michigan Rink - Gold	**Minnesota Rink - Silver**
Lead: Jim Coventry	Lead: Paul Stenner
Second: Dale Harder	Second: John Mistovich
Third: Steve Talbert	Third: Mickey Bellows
Skip: Norm Thunger	**Skip: Freddy Schade**

Eighth End

Mid-way through the eighth end, the Leads and Seconds had done their jobs by laying down guards and keeping rocks out of the way. Now Michigan's Third, Steve Talbert, knew what he had to do with his shots. He needed his first shot to clear out whatever Minnesota Third Mickey Bellows left in the house. His second shot would require a little more finesse.

Bellows did his part by laying up his #5 rock shallow in the twelve-foot ring, guarding the center and forcing Talbert to throw a heavy rock that would clear out the middle once again. The shot needed to strike a glancing blow with enough weight to push the Minnesota rock out of play, then peel off harmlessly to the other side of the house and hopefully stick around as a counter. It would be one less rock for his Skip to worry about later. Leaving the center open for the final two shots of the end would virtually guarantee that Michigan could pick up at least one point with the hammer.

Talbert's shot struck true, hitting Bellow's #5 at the four o'clock position. The shot had enough weight to push the opposing rock from the center and out of play and then peeled about a foot to the left. Michigan couldn't have asked for more out of their twenty-six year old rising star. Minnesota's Bellows would have to use his second shot, #6 rock, to clear it out with little to gain but to force his counterpart to repeat the peel and roll. Bellows took Talbert's #5 out cleanly, leaving his own rock in its place.

Talbert responded in kind, making his second shot as true as his first. Same weight. Nearly the same result. His rock struck Bellow's #6 on the nose, sending the Minnesota rock forward and out-of-play with a burst. His own #6 rock now lay as the only rock of consequence, leaving the center set up perfectly with the Skips due to shoot next and Michigan with the hammer.

Freddy Schade cursed that he had been forced into a corner. Taking out Talbert's #6 rock was his only chance of minimizing the potential damage Thunger could do with the final shot. Knocking Talbert's #6 off the center wasn't a tough shot. No, not a tough shot at all. If he could strike hard enough, and at the correct angle to keep his own rock in the area, it would force Thunger to waste his first shot removing it from play.

As Schade crouched in the hack, teammate Paul Stenner looked down from his sweeping position several feet ahead of him.

"I don't know what the hell's going on up there in the seats with your kid," he said, "but damn it, Freddy, we need to keep 'em down to one point this end. Keep your head in the match. You need to take out their rock and keep yours around the center."

Freddy stood up and took a step toward Stenner and Mistovich.

"Listen," he said, "we're going to win this game. I'll see to it. But in the finals against Wisconsin this afternoon, I don't expect to be there. You guys will have to go with the alternate as Lead. Bellows, you'll have to take over as Skip."

"I don't even want to know what you're talking about, Freddy," replied Stenner. "But whatever reason you may have for pulling out, we'll plug in that punk DuMot kid. We've got him listed. Hell, nobody's likely to let the first few rocks stay in play anyway. All the kid needs to do is plant his shots out front to get in the way."

"And sweep," added John Mistovich.

"Yep, that's why we brought him. That young felon is one hell of a sweeper," Stenner continued. "Matter of fact, Freddy, we won't lose anything by losing you."

From his Vice Skip position in the far house, Third Mickey Bellows watched the conversation for a few seconds and quickly slid down the ice to join the group.

"What the hell are you discussing down here, Freddy?" he asked. "We've called the shot and we're running out of time. Get into the hack."

Stenner pointed toward the boys in the crowd.

"Freddy was just telling us that you may have to finish the championship game against Wisconsin this afternoon as Skip. You okay with that, Mick?"

"To hell with the game against Wisconsin," Bellows hissed back toward Schade. "We haven't won this one yet."

But Freddy's attention was once again back in the seats, this time watching the police and two tournament stewards lead his son's friends away by the elbows. Willy looked down toward the ice with a tight smile and pantomimed a zipper motion across his sealed lips. Freddy returned the smiled with a quick wave, calmly stepped back into the hack with the #7 rock and just as calmly missed his shot wildly to the left; watching it slide through the back of the house. Bellows kicked it off to the side in disgust.

With Michigan's #6 still lying as the shot rock, Thunger chose to use his first shot to try to split the house. His shot crashed several feet too early and hooked too far right as it neared the front edge of the house; clipping a Minnesota guard that wasn't hurting anyone.

"Damn it," Thunger said to his teammates. "Schade's miss gave us the opportunity to double up the points, but that brick I just threw means we're back to trying to grab a single point for the end. Hell, I'm sorry boys."

"Let's see how the end plays out, Norm," Harder said. "From the looks of things, Schade is just as likely to miss his second shot, too."

Freddy stepped into the hack with only one option and one remaining chance to possibly steal a point or two from the end. But his mind and body were no longer acting as one. His shaking hands betrayed a nervousness that his teammates had never seen in him before. While leaning over their hovering brooms, Stenner and Mistovich looked toward each other and shook their heads imperceptibly. It came as no surprise when Schade's second rock, #8, missed its intended target again, this time with just enough weight to come to rest harmlessly at the back edge of the house. The miss miss gave the Michigan rink the reprieve it needed. Thunger calmly dropped into the hack, sprung out and slowly drew the hammer onto the front edge of the four-foot circle, coming to rest a few feet from the Michigan #6 rock that had proven so elusive for Freddy. The two rocks gave Michigan two unearned points they desperately needed heading into the ninth end, trailing just 7–6.

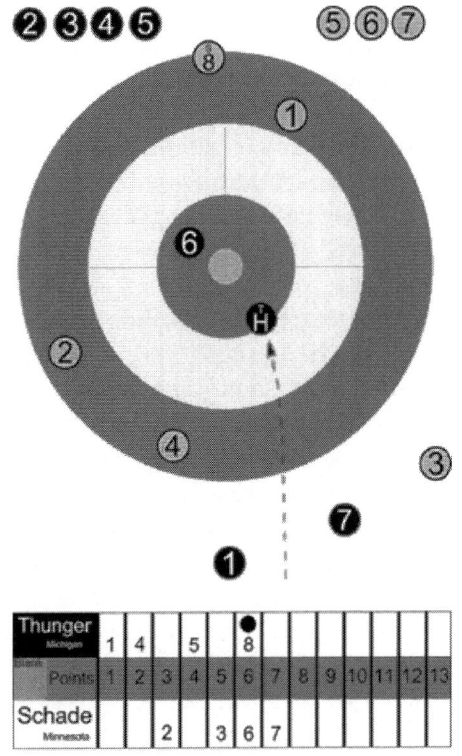

Thunger Michigan	1	4		5		● 8							
Blank Points	1	2	3	4	5	6	7	8	9	10	11	12	13
Schade Minnesota			2		3	6	7						

Late Afternoon Thursday, February 7th, 2008

We arrived at the Chippewa County courthouse in Montevideo at 3:45 and quickly made our way to the records department. I rushed to the counter and began to speak, but a young lady silently pointed toward a small red machine mounted on a table by the entrance. I pulled number 41B and showed it to Tina with disgust. She responded that there were only a handful of people in the waiting room and pointed to the lighted display above the counter, which suddenly flashed to 40B.

"Oh, good," she said, "we're next."

"Yeah, I hope we still have time," I said. "They only offer service until 4:30."

"I always like being *next*," she continued. "So many people like to be first in everything, but I never cared much about being first. I always like being next."

I stared at her incredulously. "Huh? What the…?"

"Sure," she continued, "being first is over-rated. It's over and done with before you even know it. But being next comes with a little rush of excitement and anticipation. When someone says, 'Okay, who's next?' you get to raise your hand or step up to the counter. It's like waiting behind the curtain to go onstage to perform."

While my mouth was still hanging open, a soft chime sounded above us and the electronic sign changed to 41B. I quickly stepped up to the counter and explained to the clerk that I had been to the records department on New Year's Eve, but wanted to ask some further questions regarding my father's death certificate. An older gentleman joined the young lady and explained that it was highly unusual that I was allowed to look through the records at all. Typically, people ordered copies online or by fax, then photocopies are mailed after the check clears.

"All right, so I'm here to order a copy," I said. "Now let's discuss what will be more cost-efficient for your county. You can send me away today, then run my check to the bank tomorrow morning and hope it doesn't bounce. When you get your money, you will process my order through your archaic ordering system and roll off a copy on your mimeograph machine. Then you can mail it to me by snail mail."

The man tried to interrupt but my blood was up.

"Or, you can simply let me pull up a chair next to you while you call up the microfiche on your computer? When I was here last month, the nice young lady behind this counter knew intuitively that my twelve bucks doesn't begin to cover the cost of processing a mail order copy of a certificate. Even so, I'll bet your medieval process keeps you and about four other people working on the county taxpayers' dole, doesn't it?"

From behind me, I felt Tina tug at my elbow as she hissed through pursed lips.

"Jack! Jack. It's Okaaaaeeey. Let it go-ohh."

The man continued to stare at me, then looked around the room to see that no one else was waiting in the chairs. Finally, he asked me which record I was interested in poking through. He quickly opened the door and ordered us to follow him down the hall into the records room.

As we stepped into the room, he closed the door behind us and introduced himself.

"I'm Terry Wissen," he said. "I think I might know what you've come to find."

"What do you mean, *come to find*?" I asked. "We're not even sure what it is we're looking for."

I explained as much as I could about searching for my father, including my questions about his death certificate and cemetery plot. As I talked, Wissen loaded the e-files on the screen and lines of text rolled down in a blur. He slowed the scroll to a crawl until one specific certificate suddenly filled the screen. I began searching for some questions to ask, but I was stuck. When Tina realized that we were getting nowhere with me at the helm, she stepped in.

"Mr. Wissen," she started, "you moved through the other files awfully fast. Can we trouble you to back up a few files so we can see what other death certificates look like from 2002? Just pull up anyone's."

Wissen looked at her sideways and started fumbling with the mouse and keyboard. He suddenly lowered his head and spun in his chair to look at me.

"That won't be necessary," he said. "We have been entering death certificate information using a word processor program since the late 1980s. You saw for yourself that your dad's certificate was filled out by hand."

"So, why the difference?" I asked, confused. "Out of many hundreds of files, why is his entered by hand?"

"I think you suspect the reason," he answered quietly. "Because it's bogus. Or at least, I think it is."

"Faked?" I asked. "Who would have access to these files nearly six years ago? You, maybe? That's a pretty big risk for a mid-level county office worker to take, isn't it? That's gotta be, what, at least a gross misdemeanor or possibly a felony charge? To falsify a death certificate, I mean."

He stammered for a second. I could see in his face that I had it figured correctly.

"Look," he answered as he stood up to pace the room nervously, "I knew it would come back to haunt me one day. First of all, I didn't falsify the document. It was a long time ago. Some balding middle-aged man came in here one day and asked for a blank death certificate form. I told him that, by law, they were controlled by the county coroner. Then he offered to pay me a thousand bucks in cold, hard cash on the barrel head. A thousand dollars! For a blank form and no receipt. It was only about a month after Christmas and I needed the extra money to pay some family bills. I rounded up a form and had it available for him the next morning. He returned later in the afternoon with the certificate filled out by hand. It was signed and dated by the county coroner. He said he wasn't going to do anything with it. He just wanted it on file, where he promised me it would sit forever undisturbed."

Wissen stopped briefly and pointed again at my father's certificate filling the screen, indicating the date of death as February 10, 2002.

"Forged by the medical examiner?" I asked.

"I double-checked the signature at the bottom against other certificates on file," he continued. "It was Doc's handwriting, all right. Not forged. Then the stranger showed me the local newspaper story about the rollover car accident that had occurred a few days earlier. He assured me that nobody would ever discover the truth and he would make it worth my while to keep it that way. I figured he was probably right about that. We have thousands of records on file here, going back over a hundred years. Once in a decade, some reporter might request to look into details about some dead big-wig from the 1930s, but other than that, nobody bothers checking."

"So you went along with the fraud and filed it away?" I confirmed.

"Well, fraud is a pretty strong word," he said. "When I continued to protest that I could lose my job and pension, he said the last thing he wanted was to get me in trouble. He didn't want the publicity that would come with it. If I lost my job, he would take care of me. He asked me to take the certificate and file it and forget it. Then he gave me a thousand dollars cash — all in twenty dollar bills, I recall — and walked out of here. I never saw him again."

"Oh, hell, I don't blame you for taking the money," I said

sarcastically. "I mean, how often does a dead man walk in here to offer you a stack of money to keep your mouth shut?"

Tina sat down and scrolled the cursor across the screen playfully. I looked at the certificate one more time before telling Wissen he could close it down. This time forever.

"Don't worry, we won't say anything. I'm just trying to find out whatever I can about my father. I don't know what to believe."

We talked for a moment about the official process of recording a death with the county. Tina then reminded me that we also needed to check land records before the courthouse closed for the day. Wissen walked us down the hall to the county recorder's office smiling, apparently very relieved that he had emerged unscathed from the secret he had been carrying with him for half-a-dozen years.

In the land records office, we were introduced to a young man and I explained what we were looking for. Wissen hung around the room to overhear wherever else the conversation might lead. We learned that Highwheeler was correct when he told us about the DuMot farm property. Sometime in early 1907, the eighty-acre homestead property came into the DuMot family name when my great grandfather, Charles, migrated south to Gluek out of Moose Jaw, Saskatchewan, as a young man. It remained in the family until 1971, when my widowed grandmother, Medora, deserted the property and moved into town. She officially transferred the title into my father's name in October of the following year.

But that's where the timeline grew a little fuzzy. I realized Dad must have been a young man in the Navy at the time he assumed ownership of the farm, no more than twenty-three or twenty-four years old. He was in no position to continue farming it. Why not sell the property, instead of letting it go into disuse. Perhaps he leased the land to neighboring farmers to supplement his mother's seamstress and laundry income in town until her death. That sounded like something I wanted to believe, until Tina reminded me that Highwheeler had farmed the neighboring land all his life. He would certainly have had first opportunity to lease it, but hadn't said anything about it.

The clerk retreated to the back of the room and returned with another file. It was a record of tax assessments and payments.

"You said your dad died back in '02?" he clarified, pointing at a record. "Nobody ever came in to claim the property or enter it into probate. That happens occasionally with these smaller farms around here. The original farm generation dies off, but by then, the adult children have established roots in the cities or out of state. They don't want flat, dusty, plowed land they don't know what to do with. After two or three years, the county finally catches up with things and nobody is willing to pay the taxes owed. So the land reverts to us for a sheriff's sale. In the DuMot farm case, though, the taxes are current, so there's nothing anyone can do."

"What do you mean the taxes are current?" I asked with a surprised pitch in my voice. I spun the file around to see for myself, as if I knew what I was looking at.

"So, you're saying that someone has been paying taxes on the land every year? Who? My dead father?"

"I didn't say it's your dead father," he replied. "I don't know who it is. But someone does. Comes in here and pays it off in cash, too."

Wissen stepped toward the counter and looked carefully at the file. We paged through the papers in the manila folder and found copies of tax receipts dating back several years. In each case, the name and address lines were left blank. Only the amount due and the amount paid were included on their appropriate lines. In large black ink, **PAID** was stamped boldly across the front of each. The forms were initialed in black by one office clerk or another, including Wissen's own initials on many. I could only wonder how many more thousands of dollars my father had to pay to keep that little secret quiet over the years.

I asked whether there were any other records on file which might help me learn something more about the farm or my family's history. Tina was more precise and interrupted to ask specifically to see family birth records, dog licenses, building permits — anything that might shed light on whether we could track him down.

"Well, between the courthouse, the library, and the county historical society in the basement, we have about sixty-six different municipal departments here in town," he replied. "All the files are open to public access and I promise you there is no shortage of department managers, clerks, academics and self-proclaimed enlightened experts, who will be ready to interpret and elucidate every record."

I was realizing that I had misjudged Wissen. I was beginning to appreciate his acerbic tone and sardonic attitude toward his profession. Tina, however, felt he was directing his frustration at us.

"Mr. Wissen," she said, "we just want some answers to some questions that are very important to us. We have a right to ask, don't we?"

"Yes," he replied. "I'm sorry. There's probably a lot of interesting local history you could dig up about the DuMots, but I'm not sure any of it would uncover what you're really trying to find — even if you spent a lifetime. Look, it's almost closing time and tomorrow is Friday. We're open to the public again at nine o'clock. It's quiet time of year. Stop by in the morning and you can start requesting files and documents through the official process."

"Yeah," I said, "someday I may have the time and inclination to do that. Last time I was here, I was digging up a ghost. Now I think there's a body missing from the grave. Thoreau said it best, I think, 'It's not what you look at that matters, it's what you see.' And we've seen enough."

Tina and I thanked the clerk and began walking down the hall toward the main lobby, escorted by Wissen. As we reached the exit, I turned to shake hands and apologize for my initial rudeness.

"Well," I said, "thank you very much. It wasn't everything I was hoping to find, but the tax records are proof that my dad is still a warm body out there somewhere."

Wissen looked back toward the recorder's office with a quizzical look on his face, then back at me. He pulled me off to a quiet corner and Tina followed.

"No," he whispered, "those tax records don't prove anything. I'm the one that supervises that office. Most days, I work in the recorder's office. I told you, after that man came in with that death certificate that day and bribed me to keep my mouth shut, I never saw him again. I swear. Ever since that day, I've been scared he would walk back in here and blow the cover off of everything. Believe me, I would remember the guy if I ever saw him again. We only get a handful of cash tax payments in here every year, usually in pennies and nickels from some pissed off libertarians, which I have to approve for payment."

"Then who walks in here to pay the taxes in cash year after year if it isn't my father?" I asked.

"Or conversely," Tina quickly corrected me "if your dad *is* the one who pays the taxes every year, then who was the man who brought in the sham death certificate?"

I had an idea.

"We can call the coroner," I said. "What's his name? Doctor Mark O'Brian, wasn't it? Whoever brought in that death certificate either forged it very well or somehow got the good doctor to fill it out and sign it. Does he still live around here? He'll know."

Wissen shook his head.

"I'm sorry, Jack" he said. "O'Brian was killed several years ago. He and two or three local cops were called to the scene of a suicide at a farmhouse several miles east of here. They were inside investigating and the whole place suddenly went up when the propane tank exploded. By the time the fire trucks arrived, there was nothing left of the house or the bodies."

Tina jumped in.

"Jack! I remember it," she said. "It happened late one night back in late 2002 or early '03. It made the morning news. I remember that Bill called me at my apartment to ask if I could pick up a newspaper on my way into work."

I thought of the list of names on Bill's writing board and recalled there was one name we couldn't account for.

"Mr. Wissen," I started. "Can we trouble you to look up whether the suicide victim's first name was Hank? I'm afraid I don't know his last name. Just Hank...or Henry."

We returned to the records room where Wissen brought up more files on the screen and scrolled down until he found what he was looking for.

"Well, I'll be a horse's ass," Wissen said, as the certificate filled the screen. "As a matter of fact, his first name was Hank. Henry Stenner. He was the relative of a local celebrity, of sorts. His cousin was Paul Stenner. Paul was a champion curler back in the late '60s. He got out of competitive curling and worked that farm for several years. I curled with him for a few years at the Montevideo club years ago. Paul's rink would win the club championship just about every year. About seven or eight years ago, though, he moved away. He either died or went off to some place in Europe, as I recall. Local gossip had it that he suffered from serious depression. It sometimes happens on these large farms. No neighbors nearby. I imagine it's a damned lonely life."

"Do you remember how the explosion happened?" I asked, afraid of the answer.

"No, not much," he answered. "That happens to propane tanks and underground gas lines sometimes, when the pilot light from the hot water heater or furnace ignites a leak. If it's a full tank, it'll blow like a five-ton bomb."

I felt a sick, nervous feeling beginning to fill my stomach and my heart was pounding. Wissen grew quiet for a moment, thinking.

"Say," he asked, "how did you know the man's first name was Hank? Did you know him?"

"No" I said. "I didn't know him. But I'm afraid my father did."

Thursday Evening, February 7th, 2008

Before leaving the courthouse, we asked the main receptionist to recommend a nearby restaurant that might offer WiFi service. In the short drive between our Highway 7 spinout and the courthouse, Tina hadn't been able to figure out the access protocol needed to decipher the encrypted e-mail message. I counted on killing the next hour or two over a warm dinner while we worked on the code. At some point during the evening, though, I knew we would have to confront the reality of checking into a hotel room. I was relieved to learn we were only a block or two away from the main business district where we would probably find WiFi service in any of the local cafés or bars. The lady also suggested that we leave our car parked in the courthouse lot and walk to town, rather than circle the blocks to find a rare parking place on the main drag during the dinner hour.

I left Tina standing in the warm entryway while I retrieved my laptop and satchel full of notes from the car. When I returned, I found her on the courthouse stairs, sending a short text message.

"Shit, it's going to be a cold walk," I complained. "I hate Minnesota winters."

"Yeah, growing up I always did, too," she replied. "Then I came to realize there are only three ways to handle winter around here: endure it, enjoy it, or evade it. Since I could never afford to be a snowbird, I figured I might as well learn to enjoy it."

"Well, I've tried to evade it and it didn't work out so well," I said. "And I've never felt like a better man for enduring it. Some year, I'll have to try to enjoy it, I guess."

As we walked toward town, the pewter gray afternoon dusk quickly descended into the dark of the early evening. I finally worked up enough nerve to take Tina's soft, warm mitten in my chapped and cold bare fingers. Apparently, it was all she had been waiting for. She pulled us to a stop, turned and kissed me gently on the lips.

"I think you needed that," she said.

"Yeah," I sighed, "I think I did, too."

"I also think you have been worrying about how we're going to handle things tonight at the hotel," she continued. "So let's put the problem to bed right now — pun intended. I'll tell you what big plans I have for tonight."

She smiled shyly.

"Oh, you will?" I laughed. I tried to kiss her again, but she pushed me away playfully.

"Yes, Jack," she continued, "I will if you'll let me. Look, we have to assume that someone has been following us from the cities. We need a name for him, something other than *the killer* or *the murderer*. Let's call him *Skip,* since that's how your dad and Bill referred to him in the letter."

I chuckled but agreed, "Yeah, okay, *Skip* works."

"Well, *Skip* doesn't know what we may or may not have discovered in the courthouse," she continued. "We need to stay close together. If we separate, we will each be twice as vulnerable. So...we are going to find an inexpensive motel here in town tonight and get a double room. That means two individual beds. You will sleep in one. I will sleep in the other; where we will each sleep warm, safe and comfortably — through the entire night."

"That's it? That's your big plan?" I asked.

I wasn't sure whether my face registered disappointment, shock or relief, but it didn't matter. What she said next brought my heart to a standstill.

"Over dinner tonight, I will tell you more. Some of which you won't like. In fact, you probably won't understand it all. But it's only fair that you know."

I wanted to put up a false complaint about waiting for dinner to learn her darkest secret, but thought the better of it.

Within a few short minutes, we were stepping through the entrance doors of The Monty Café, where I stopped at the cash register to ask whether a password would be required to access WiFi. The waitress looked around cautiously as she scribbled something onto the corner of a napkin and slid it over the counter toward me with a wink.

"This is supposed to cost you five dollars," she whispered.

Hanging our coats on a hook near the front, we ignored the *please wait to be seated sign* and walked past several empty tables to seat ourselves in a quiet booth toward the rear. Another waitress chased us down to inform us that the section we were seated in was closed. After following my mocking look around the empty room, she nodded and sighed with resignation and handed us two menus.

Over coffee and cocoa, I cast my line into the cold rolling sea, hoping Tina would bite. What did she mean when she said, *"I will tell you more?"* What was it she could possibly tell me that I *won't like* and *probably won't understand*? She could see that my intestines were twisting in the wind, but she changed the subject.

"Jack," she started, "there are a few things that happened today that I don't understand."

"Just a few?" I scoffed.

"Yeah," she replied, ignoring my tone, "a couple. First, you seemed to take it pretty much in stride about the death certificate and the tax thing. I had a thousand questions I would have asked."

"Well, I guess there were some more things I could have followed up on," I replied. "But I just don't think someone who knows about the inner workings of government departments, old history stories and land plats can really give us the answers we're looking for."

"Okay, let's start with your questions," she said. "Then we'll get to mine. What other questions would you have asked?"

"Well, Tina," I started, "when we left the church and drove over to the Cenex station in Maynard, who do you suppose Highwheeler was talking about when we asked him about the farm. He said he figured 'the damned fool never took care of the legal process.' That didn't make any sense."

"Well, I didn't give it much thought, but I suppose he was talking about your father."

"But he said that after he learned my father died, he kept waiting for the damned fool to take care of the legal matters. First, why would he expect my dead father to take care of the legal process? Second, I told him who I was. I don't think he would refer to my dad as a damned fool right in front of my face. Nobody would do that."

"Well, as a matter of fact, you might," she said. "But I see what you mean. Was he suggesting that someone else in the family should have taken care of the taxes and title transfer? That would be you, Jack, I suppose. In a roundabout way, I guess he was calling you the damned fool, then."

"Maybe," I said. "But not likely. Until I walked into that building, he didn't know I existed. But there's something else that's bothering me even more. Did you get a good look at my dad's death certificate? I remember that my mom called me in California to report that he died on my birthday, February 6th."

At that, Tina interrupted.

"Oh, my goodness! That was just yesterday wasn't it? Sorry I missed it, Jack. Happy belated birthday."

"Thanks," I said. "I completely forgot about it myself until we were at the courthouse and I saw the date on the certificate."

I continued to explain my confusion.

"The coroner filled in the date of death as February 10th, a full four days after the date of the accident reported in the local news article. The death certificate clearly said that he was pronounced dead at the scene. If my dad was holding a gun to the man's head, doesn't it seem likely that he would make sure the date was correct?"

"Yes, he would have," Tina confirmed. "It's possible that it wasn't your dad who brought that death certificate to Wissen that day. It might have been someone who just wanted to make sure your dad looked good and dead — on paper, anyway."

"To cover some tracks," I suggested, folding my napkin between my fingertips nervously.

"Or to create a dead end," she suggested. "Getting the details exactly right may not have been important for him. Either that or he didn't know the exact details."

The waitress arrived with our soup and I used the interruption to enter the WiFi password. The signal was weak, but sufficient to open e-mail. Tina's inbox was empty, but I had two messages. One was the encrypted message I had received earlier that afternoon, which I intended to begin working on. I caught my breath for a moment when I saw the second message was from LaVon. I debated about whether to tell Tina, but decided to quietly save it in an archive file and return to it later. I was with a beautiful young woman for whom I was beginning to develop some real feelings. Even better, I was sensing she felt the same way about me. Whatever it was LaVon had to say could wait until later that evening. Or maybe the next day. Or maybe for never.

I clicked open the encrypted message again and quickly scanned the page. By the syntax of the occasional commas, periods and exclamation points punctuating the coded gobbledy-gook, I determined that it was written by someone who spoke English as their primary language.

On the back of a clean napkin, I wrote down the six old encryption codes remaining in my files from the previous spring and summer. For the next hour and a half, Tina and I worked through every possible mathematical formula we could think of to figure out what pattern Bill Ordway may have used to develop the new code protocol every month. The numbers all included six digits, all beginning with seven and ending with a lower case letter, which I already knew designated the first letter of the appropriate month, *j* for January, June and July, *a* for April and August, and so on. From my memory of the code progressions over my years at ProtoCommand, it was safe to assume that the first number referred to the year. I distinctly remembered the sequences once started with a five then progressed to a six in 2006, then moving on to the number seven as we entered '07. I was grateful that Bill kept parts of the formula simple. The sequence of five numbers in the middle, however, appeared to be completely random. Tina suggested that we start to think like a grizzled fifty-five year old man rather than young millennials.

"Okay, let's think." I said. "So what else would Bill and Dad have in common? Both were born around this area, right? Local ZIP codes, maybe?"

We applied the three local ZIP codes to the number sequences to see if we could determine a pattern, but came up dry.

"Both were in the Navy," she said. "Anything from that we can work with?"

I went on the Internet and searched for everything we could think of having to do with Navy serial numbers, but drew another blank. When our waitress approached us for the fourth time to ask about more coffee or cocoa, it was obvious we were beginning to overstay our welcome.

"I'm sorry," I said. "We got involved in this puzzle and lost track of time."

I could tell that she was trying to get a look at the dozens of mathematical calculations we had scribbled across our legal pad. Without elaborating, I politely turned the pad in her direction and showed her the list of numbers; explaining that we were searching for some connection to the Navy. She looked at the napkin carefully.

"Oh," she said, it might be the military Julian date," she said. "Julian isn't really the right word for it. It's really just an ordinal calendar to keep track of the days of the year. Today's Julian ordinal date is 8038. It's not just Navy. The whole military uses that calendar system all the time. My dad is retired Air Force. When I started managing this place, he taught me to use it for scheduling because it eliminates confusion and possible errors."

"How so?" I asked.

"Like, if I made a mistake and scheduled somebody to work Thursday, February 18th , but the 18th is actually a Wednesday. It eliminates possible confusion. When everyone works off the military Julian system, you can't get the days of the week screwed up. For example, 8038 — I want that person to work on the 38th day of 2008. Period. I don't care whether it's a Thursday or a Wednesday."

Tina and I looked at each other and shrugged. It made sense. The formula would have to be cryptic enough to confuse people, yet simple enough for Bill to keep track of in his head. And it certainly would have been a formula that could be tracked over time, as well.

We proved the theory against our list. The first four numbers in each series increased by a factor of thirty or thirty-one. Altogether, the numbers on our list tracked perfectly with the '07 calendar on my screen. We were onto it, but we still needed to figure out how my father would have predicted the final two numbers.

"He said you would know how to break the decryption code," Tina said. "And he was right as far as we've figured it so far. It can't be impossible, right?"

The waitress topped off my cup and politely told us that she could only give us a few more minutes unless we ordered something. Tina picked up the menu and asked for two pieces of apple pie. It wasn't what the lady had in mind and she stomped off.

"It must have something to do with numbers that your dad and Bill would have been familiar with, Jack," she continued. "Their old Navy boat number, maybe?"

I looked through the pile of notes in my satchel, not sure what I expected to find. When I came to the large manila envelope, I pulled out a small number of slips.

"Bill would have been hauntingly familiar with the numbers on these slips as they drew down toward zero," I suggested. "If he did rely on the dash numbers to determine the code, it would have been a monthly reminder, like some sort of self- flagellation."

Tina aligned the slips as best she could across the small table space.

"Look at this." I said. "Here's one of Bill's slips for — 6. That would have been from six years ago. Could it be so simple that the — 6 stands for the month?"

I watched her tick off the numbers with the nail of her index finger. But none of the sequences ended in 6, 06 or even 60. She looked doubtful that we were on the right track.

"Look at this, Tina!" I exclaimed. "It may be a huge stretch, but let's try something. You said that Bill's birthday was December 21st, right? What's twenty-one plus six?"

She tilted her head to one side and cocked an eyebrow at me sarcastically.

"Oh, sorry," I said, embarrassed, "Yeah, I guess I can do the math myself. Check the list of numbers. Do any of them end in twenty-seven?"

None did, so we tried subtracting the — 6 from twenty-one. Yes! The access code assigned for the month of June, 2007, ended in fifteen. *715115j*. I felt as if I was showing off as I tested it out by opening an old project file that I recalled working on over the summer.

"Great!" I yelled, turning the heads of the two or three patrons who had entered the café. "We've cracked it!"

I felt myself smiling widely.

"It doesn't prove everything yet, Jack. It may just be pure coincidence."

I went deep into my ProtoCommand archive and pulled up an encrypted project file from the months April through September of '07.

"Now let's subtract other corresponding month-numbers from twenty-one and see if we hit on the other numbers on our napkin."

My excitement grew with each calculation as each sequence opened a file from its corresponding month.

"Done." Tina said. "Now let's open your dad's message."

"Well, it's February," I replied aloud to myself. "So I'll subtract two. Does it work? It should, shouldn't it?"

I saved the e-mail file to the encryption program file and entered the Julian date and the formula number, *803821f*. The program didn't blink.

After a minute of sitting motionless, silently thinking, I reached into my hip pocket and pulled out my wallet, as if getting ready to pay for our meals. The waitress rushed to our table, "You can pay for that at the front checkout," she scolded as she wiped down the adjacent table.

I searched through every compartment and card slot in my wallet, but it wasn't there. I pulled out the thin stack of bills and handed the money to Tina, then frantically shook my wallet upside down and watched as the clutter of contents spilled across the table. I frantically picked through every scrap of paper and fleck of lint. In front of me lay years of tiny scribbled notes and jotted-down reminders, including phone numbers I would never call, websites I would never surf, titles of books I would never read and names of people I would never talk to. With a few quick jerks of my hands, I spilled out a decade of useless tidbits of a life spent deceiving people into thinking I actually cared. The one thing I didn't wanted to lose, though, wasn't among the rubbish.

"Only ones and fives?" Tina complained as she wetted her fingertips and flipped through the money.

"Who steals my purse steals trash," I smirked.

Tina held up a bill.

"They're starting to print new designs for some denominations," she said. "Have you seen one of the new twenties yet?"

"No, I'm married, remember?" I replied. "I never saw any of the old ones."

My head was deep inside the nether regions of my empty wallet, trying to remember when I had removed it and where I might have left it lay. My fingers were probing into every credit card slot, poking into every empty photo cover and scraping behind each hidden flap. Search as I might, it was no longer there.

"Hello. Earth to Jack," Tina said, waving her hand in front of my face. "What are you looking for?"

Suddenly, the small dingy slip of paper flipped off one of the bills in Tina's hand and fluttered end-over-end slowly to the floor. With a gulp, I lunged to catch it, as if saving it from shattering into a thousand pieces, as if it were hand-blown Murano glass. Tina could only stare wide-eyed as I wiggled my way upright in the booth, clutching my hand close to my chest. *Arv — February 23 — Ø.*

"It's all starting to make some sense," I said. "I'm beginning to understand. This slip of paper wasn't meant as a warning *for* my father. I may be wrong, but I think it may have been mailed to me *from* my father. It's the missing piece. He said in his recorded message that I have everything I need and that I've seen the code before."

"You never did tell me everything that he said in that message," she said, as she began sorting the contents from my wallet into a single pile in front of her.

"You won't need any of these scraps and notes from your billfold anymore, will you?"

"No, I guess not, why?"

She held her open purse below the table's edge and swiped the artifacts of my life into its dark, gaping mouth. I was already too distracted entering the access code and opening the decrypted e-mail message to care. Everything she had emptied into her purse already belonged to yesterday.

I slid my computer screen to one end of the table so we could both read the message. A second later, the coded symbols blinked into action and a single page of content appeared. I read the first couple of lines and forced my eyes to fall to the bottom of the screen. To my surprise, it wasn't my father who had sent the message, after all.

Michigan Rink - Gold	**Minnesota Rink - Silver**
Lead: Jim Coventry	Lead: Paul Stenner
Second: Dale Harder	Second: John Mistovich
Third: Steve Talbert	Third: Mickey Bellows
Skip: Norm Thunger	**Skip: Freddy Schade**

Ninth End

Skips in championship matches often work to keep scores low by employing a conservative strategy. Generally, this means keeping the guard zone and house free from unnecessary rocks for as long as possible into each end. The strategy, of course, is to use their final shots to take a point or two or, at worst, leave the end blank. It isn't unusual to see a ten-end championship match finish with a score of 6-5. In years past, the 'open house' strategy may have proved useful, but it also meant there was very little premium placed upon the first few rocks. Often, the Leads' and Seconds' opening salvos resulted in laying down a perfunctory guard rock, followed by the opponent's obligatory takeout shot to remove it from play. To be sure, the Lead's and Second's shot always required accuracy, but the bottom line was that their primary job was to sweep.

In 1991, the World Curling Federation ushered in an international rule change known as the Free Guard Zone. It revolutionized the role of the Leads and Seconds. Simply put, any of the first four rocks lying in the zone between the hog line and front edge of the house cannot be removed by any player. The rock may be bumped or moved within the area of play but it cannot be struck out of play by an opposing team before the fifth rock of the end.

Occasionally referred to as the Moncton rule, named after the Canadian city in which it was conceived, the rule proved to have the impact most of the curling world had long hoped for. With the stroke of a pen, all sixteen rocks on each end could actually count for something, even when Skips played the most conservative strategy. Following the rule change, the Leads needed to be more careful about the accuracy of their rocks landing within the free guard zone. The opposing Lead must deal with it as it lay; either curl around it or 'tick' it a few feet off to one side. With the rule in place, finesse on the handle of the rock became just as important as finesse on the handle of the broom.

But for the men on the ice at the 1969 ACU national playdowns, the rule change was still an unforeseeable two decades into the future. Neither Skips Norm Thunger nor Freddie Shade needed to concern themselves with avoiding early guard rocks. If the opposing Lead lay down a long guard, your Lead was free to knock it out of play. If another guard rock replaced it, take that one out, too. It was as simple as that. For Freddy Schade, it was the style of curling learned at his father's hip. If he could get Mrs. Freddy Schade to see things his way, it would be the brand his stepson Willy would bring to championship tournaments someday, as well.

Mrs. Freddy Schade was Cynthia Ordway of Gary, Indiana. As a young teenage girl, Cindy had every reason to believe her life was bound to turn out better than it eventually would. Not even her father's periodic bouts with dark depression could dim the light that glowed from the family's dining room table every night. When he attempted suicide and was consigned to a mental hospital, her mother could no longer hold it all together and their world crashed around them. County social services agreed to remove the fifteen year old girl to the foster care of a generous family while her parents worked through a range of treatment plans.

As foster parents, the Thistleton's deserved nothing but respect and kindness in return for their efforts, but Cindy was completely unable to cope with her new reality. After three attempts to run away, all parties finally recognized that the arrangement couldn't possibly work. When she turned eighteen, she was emancipated and returned to live with her mother. Less than a year later, Cindy realized there was no hope of recovering the family so she struck out on her own. A year later, she learned that her father's body was found floating in Lake Michigan. Her mom continued to live in the family house for a short while but eventually returned to her own childhood home in Alabama. Cindy could only hope that her mother would finally rediscover the happiness that the family once shared before her father's mental illness left him unable to cope. Someday, Cindy swore, she would move to Alabama and make sure of it.

Cindy signed on as an underage barmaid at a blue collar pub on Chicago's south side, where she met Seppi DiFranco. Two years living with the illegal Italian immigrant were hard on her body and spirit. To supplement their income, Seppi would often force her to get out there to 'peddle your pink and white.' Even in the best of times, her life remained a damned-sight worse than the childhood she had enjoyed with her parents in their home on the south shore of Lake George in northern Indiana.

By the date of her nineteenth birthday, she was pregnant and broke. She was afraid to tell Seppi for two reasons. First, he did not have the temperament for fatherhood. More important, she doubted the baby was his. It could just as well have been the child of any of the countless, untraceable men that he forced her to spend her afternoons with. She needed the roof over her head for as long as she could keep one there. The way she figured it, whether it was his child or not, he was responsible for the pregnancy. At four months along, she could no longer hide it. When Seppi caught on, he told Cindy she could stay with the baby only as long as she paid the rent on his basement apartment lease.

A little more than a year after little William Michael was born, one of Cindy's former clients showed up at their door, asking whether she was still open for business. Seppi overheard the conversation and went into a blind rage. Half-drunk, he struck out at anything that moved. Young William Michael made the mistake of toddling into the room at the wrong time.

Seppi grabbed him by the collar and flung him ten feet across the cramped room. He watched as the child came crashing down onto a table lamp, eyes twitching and body convulsing in pain from a broken ankle that would leave him with a lifelong limp. Cindy came running from the bedroom and tried to reach her young son, only to be caught by the throat by the enraged Seppi. After a minute of gasping for her last breaths and clawing blindly for anything within reach, her fingers wrapped around her only hope — a heavy plaster bookend set on a makeshift shelf above the sofa. A second later, Seppi lay on the floor with his own eyes twitching and rolling in their sockets and his head draining blood into a pool on the bare linoleum. A second later, Cindy had William Michael on the way to the emergency room and eventually to a shelter for battered women. The incident began a period of nightly stays at a series of emergency shelters throughout South Chicago.

For the next year, Cindy resolved to make a better life for her son but never — never again — would it come at the expense of losing a shred of dignity and self-respect to any man. As mentally ill as her father had been during her childhood years, he was lucid enough to teach her that much. Now she intended to live it. She owed him no less.

Eventually, she and her son were able to find a distant relative willing to take them in. For second cousin Milt Abeln, it suited things perfectly well to have Cindy and young William Michael move into his two-bedroom apartment in Juliette. Milt needed the extra little money Cindy could earn at a local coffee counter. Cindy needed a safe place for son until they were sure Seppi was deported safely back to Naples.

Several months later, in the winter of 1955, Cindy and William Michael accompanied Milt to the Midwest regional curling championships in Chicago to watch a rink from the Juliette Curling Club compete. The Juliette rink did well enough to get into the quarterfinals but it was a rink from western Minnesota that stole the show the entire weekend; led by a flamboyant, cock-sure thirty-five year old bachelor-farmer named Frederick Herman Schade. Cindy found Freddy's self-assurance and cocky confidence irresistible and a whirlwind barroom romance quickly followed. After a hastily-arranged wedding, Freddy Schade and new wife Cynthia and two year old 'Little Willy' could be seen driving west on Interstate 90 toward their new lives on Freddy's farm near Gluek, Minnesota.

As years passed, the bond between Willy and Freddy grew but Cindy made sure that she remained the dominant influence in her son's life. When the local elementary school teachers began noticing the young boy's aptitude for math and science, Cindy did everything she could to arrange whatever academic help the underfunded school district could provide. Freddy did everything he could to dissuade her. Freddy lost — as he would lose nearly every battle involving his stepson. It didn't matter. He had the boy's loyalty firmly by the heartstrings. He knew Willy would eventually leave the farm to attend a leading University but not for a few years into the future. Until then, Freddy could count on seeing him sitting behind the glass with his best friends at every curling league match, bonspiel or playdown; wherever his obsession might take them.

With a slim 7-6 lead and the hammer in hand, Freddy Schade intended to have his men play conservatively over the final two ends and that meant sacrificing every shot but his own. Michigan's Jim Coventry led with long guards, crawling seven or eight feet over the hog line and well-short of the house. Minnesota's Stenner removed them in turn, leaving nothing to chance. Michigan's Second, Dale Harder, dropped his first shot, #3 rock six feet into the house but far left of center.

As Minnesota's Second John Mistovitch prepared to step into the hack, Schade did everything he could to catch his attention from his place in the house at the far end of the sheet. He slapped the ice hard with his broom and wildly swung his arm to the side, indicating to the world that he expected all rocks to be cleared out neatly. To everyone's surprise, though, Mistovich ignored him, as well as the Michigan #3 rock. Instead, he placed his own #3 rock onto the left front-edge of the house, just inches inside the twelve-foot circle. It might have been a bad mistake but it wasn't lost on Freddy that it appeared to be deliberate. The crowd murmured for a second, then cheered as they realized what was happening. Rather than simply coasting to victory with takeouts and heavy garbage shots to the back wall, Minnesota was making a game of it and Freddy Schade was furious.

"What the **F** are you doing, Misty?" he yelled down the ice. "I told you to take out every rock. That means **every** goddam rock."

Mistovich didn't look up. Michigan's Dale Harder stepped into the hack for his second shot, but paused a brief moment to look over at the opposing Minnesota players.

"How the hell can you play for that son-of-a-bitch?" Harder asked softly before squaring his shoulders in the hack.

"We can't," Mistovich replied quietly. "And we're not."

Harder used his second shot to do exactly what everyone knew he would. He placed his rock nearly parallel to his first shot, about five feet inside the house on the far right side. It split the house, meaning two Michigan counters were laying roughly eight o'clock and four o'clock, nearly ten feet apart. As Mistovich returned to the hack for his second shot, Schade made it clear there was no choice but to clear out either one of Michigan's stones, since it was now impossible to knock out both with a single shot.

"You don't have the shot in your bag for this kind of double," he yelled as he retreated to his place in the house. "It's what you get for going rogue on me."

Mistovich looked down the ice between his two crouching sweepers out front of him and surveyed his possibilities. Freddy tapped his broom head on Michigan's #3 rock at the left side of the house. Mistovitch shook him off. Freddy slid to the #4 rock on the right side of the house. Mistovitch ignored him. Freddy flipped up his middle finger in the general direction of his players and walked over to the bench and sat down with a thud.

"You figure it out your goddam self, damn it!" he yelled. "You got us into this shithole; don't look at me to get us out."

The crowd booed at Schade's eruption and catcalls poured down from the seats. ACU official walked over to speak to him quietly while the public address announcer requested quiet in the arena. Stenner and Bellows stood upright and stepped toward Mistovich in the hack.

"Freddy may be right about this one, John," Stenner said. "We don't like the bastard either, but you put us in a hole with your first rock. You should have figured they'd split the house. It doesn't leave you with much. Take out one of their rocks and Mickey can take out the other with his first shot. Then we'll see how the deck stacks."

"No," Mistovich said. "We're going to show that asshole of ours that he's not the only one who can play this game. We owe those North Dakota boys more than heavy takeouts and goddamned blank ends. It's a beautiful game. Let's keep it that way."

Stenner and Bellows returned to their places several yards in front of the hack and waited. As Mistovich released his #4 rock at the line, he quietly told his sweepers to ignore any instructions Schade might give them.

"This rock won't need your brooms. Just clean the ice."

The crowd drew to a hush as Paul Stenner unexpectedly moved away from the path and allowed Bellows room to shuffle slowly forward as the lone sweeper, cleaning the ice ten or more feet out front. The baritone growl of the rock droned like a bassoon behind the metrical percussion of the sweeping. The whispered undertone of John Mistovich's trailing right toe on the ice added a resonance that steadied and tied together the entire composition. Unexpectedly, everyone in the arena was breathing in rhythm with the symphony played on stage before them.

As if materializing from the vapors forming above the ice surface, Paul Stenner suddenly re-joined Bellows in front of the path of the stone. He, too, seemed to understand what should happen next.

"It's on target," Mistovich said, still crouched low in his delivery position at center ice. "Just keeeeeep the ice clean. Don't sweep any distance to 'er."

Freddy had come off the bench and was jogging toward the moving rock. He could see that the shot was beginning to curl slightly left and come up short but didn't yet understand. It was dying too early and wouldn't slide beyond Mistovich's first shot already parked at the front of the house. Clearly, the shot again had no hope of knocking out Michigan's #3 rock without aggressive sweeping to keep it pressing forward. Worse, it would clog up the path toward the center.

"**Hard!**" Freddy yelled, running the final few steps to begin sweeping the rock vigorously. Instantly, Bellows swung his arm down and lifted Schade's broom head violently off the ice. At the same time, Stenner took hold of Schade's shirt collar and yanked it back hard, pulling him down and falling on top to pin him to the ice. The crowd broke into a loud gasp, followed by a spontaneous roar of approval as the rock slid harmlessly beneath Stenner's left foot, untouched and unimpeded toward its intended landing spot.

Schade came up swinging but Mistovich and Stenner just as

quickly tackled him and held him to the ice again. Stenner took Freddy by a knot of hair and forcibly jerked his head backward, leaving the angry Skip no choice but to witness the last two feet of the dying shot. The rock came to rest near Mistovich's first shot at the front edge of the house, less than a foot away on a parallel line to the immediate right. Schade fought himself free. His first instinct was to go toward Stenner for physically preventing him from sweeping the rock through to knock out the Michigan #3 — or at least harmlessly through to the back of the house. When he felt Bellows clasp him from behind, he turned toward Mistovich and screamed obscenities about ignoring his orders. Finally, he spun savagely on his heels and swung violently at any head that happened to be within range of his broom. Bellows ducked neatly and pushed him down to the ice.

"This is my last chance, you sons of bitches!" he screamed, jumping to his feet. "You're costing me my last chance."

"No," Stenner yelled back above the crowd's jeering, "it's the last chance for all of us and we're calling you out to win it or lose it — the way those North Dakota boys deserve."

Schade didn't understand, but he was too humiliated to care. He shook himself free, kicked his broom across the ice and walked toward the locker room.

"Finish it yourself and go screw yourselves."

As he neared the edge of the ice, though, he found two stewards and three uniformed police officers stepping over the hockey boards to greet him. He sized up the situation immediately and retreated toward the far side of the ice, where he once again picked up his broom and returned to the Minnesota bench amid a growing crescendo of catcalls.

"Okay," he spit through gritted teeth. "Now suppose you boys tell me what the hell's going on. I'm Skip of this rink and I deserve to know."

"Funny," Stenner replied, "we think we deserve to know the same thing, Freddy. But that can wait. If you want to finish this match, you're going to play by our rules. Or we walk away. Right here. Right now."

"You boys wouldn't be here right now if it wasn't for me," Schade growled.

"I suspect that's exactly what the police are saying right now, too, Freddy," Stenner said.

The crowd resettled itself into a low buzz as Michigan's Third, Steve Talbert, readied himself in the hack, preparing to take his first shot with his #5 rock. He yelled playfully at the Minnesota rink for quiet. Schade walked briskly toward the house at the distant end and hunkered down on the Skip's bench once again. Stenner, Mistovich and Bellows gave an apologetic wave to their Michigan opponents and rested their elbows quietly on their broom heads.

It was impossible for Talbert to figure out what Mistovich had intended with his two shots, other than to speculate that both had been unfortunate misses that fell short...or were intended as guards. But what are they trying to guard? Ten feet of empty ice in the center? The best he could figure was that they had both been delivered with too little weight and on the wrong lines.

He crouched low and lurched himself out of the hack, following his Skip's orders to release the shot with a hard swing needed to breeze it past the Minnesota rocks. His sweepers leaned on their brooms to keep it straight until the final few seconds and then allowed it to curl, where it drifted to a stop deep in the right-rear of the house. Michigan had three rocks laying for potential points, splitting the house right and left and deep. Certainly, Minnesota would need to waste their remaining rocks clearing them out, to make room for Schade's final shot.

Freddy was pacing the ice as Vice Skip Mickey Bellows stepped into the hack to prepare for his first shot with his own #5 rock.

"Do you see where we're going with this, Mick?" John Mistovich asked. "Do you know where we need you to put your shots?"

Bellows smiled. He knew.

"Do you really want to put this all on Freddy?" Paul Stenner asked. "Are we really ready for that?"

"He's been asking for it, fellas," Mistovich answered.

He looked up at the police and ACU stewards again. "Besides, I have a sick feeling that he owes those poor North Dakota guys and their families a hell of a lot more than just a good curling shot."

As Bellows squatted in the hack to align his shot, he only sent a fleeting glance down the ice toward his Skip. Freddy had resumed his position in the house and was hammering his broom head aggressively on the ice immediately in front of one of Michigan's rocks.

"**We'll start with this one! Take 'er out.**"

When he realized his shrieks were the only sounds to be heard throughout the arena, he suddenly fell silent along with the crowd.

Bellows ignored him. He picked out a spot of ice about sixty-five feet ahead as a mid-point target and pushed off smoothly with his right foot. As he approached the release line, he let the silver handle sift through his fingertips gracefully. Sweepers Stenner and Mistovich walked quietly in front, brushing the ice gently to keep it clean.

"**It's crashing early!**" Schade was yelling. "**Sweep 'er, dammit!**"

"Leave 'er be, boys," Mickey Bellows said softly, as he came quickly up and out of his slide; "Do you see what I want 'er to do?"

His two close friends did, indeed, see exactly what he wanted 'er to do, even if Schade nor anyone else in the arena did not. As the rock slid across the hog line and neared the front edge of the house, Michigan's Jim Coventry and Dale Harder stepped alongside ready to sweep it out of play in the event it drifted cross the T-line intersecting the center of the house. A second later, they knew it would not. They watched in disbelief as it crept to a slow stop at the front edge of the house, again on a parallel line with John Mistovich's two previous shots and just twelve more inches further to the right. The granite wall of Minnesota's shots now grew to include three rocks spaced almost exactly evenly apart; spread nearly four feet across the center front-edge of the house.

Although the narrow spacing between the rocks made it impossible for Michigan's Talbert to slip his second shot through the gaps, he reckoned there was still enough room on the right side of the wall to curl past and draw his rock to the center. It would be tight but he convinced his Skip he could do it. If successful, it would result in four Michigan counters scattered strategically throughout the house. Minnesota would only have three rocks remaining in its holster. Unexpectedly and inexplicably, Michigan had found itself with numbers in its favor. Putting a fourth counter behind the guard wall would virtually nullify any advantage Freddy Schade thought he might have with the hammer in hand.

Talbert's #6 rock was nearly perfect, curling beautifully to a stop less than one foot behind the center button. He knew that Michigan's Skip could be counted on to guard it with the next shot, making it nearly impossible for Schade to dislodge it. With only the two Skips' shots remaining, Michigan had every opportunity to steal multiple points from the end and leapfrog to a two or three point lead.

Minnesota's Bellows returned to the hack to throw his own rock #6. Immediately upon releasing his shot, a hum went up in the crowd. "He doesn't have enough weight. It isn't going to clear out one of the Minnesota rocks at the front. It's not heading toward any of Michigan rocks in the house, either! It's crashing early! It's heading toward the right. They need to sweep it hard to get it past and into the center! Their brooms aren't even on the ice. What the hell?"

Bellows stayed in his delivery slide nearly the entire length of the ice, keeping his eyes low and whispering encouragement from just a yard or two behind the rock. No need for sweeping instructions; his sweepers knew what to do.

As the rock crossed the hog line and began sliding to its final rest, everything grew quiet. Freddy's jaw dropped as the rock again came to a stop on the right side of the Minnesota wall, extending the parallel line to nearly six feet across the front of the house — but none lying within point range of the button.

For Michigan, it was a perfect — if incredulous — scenario. Four counters spread around the house and just two rocks remaining at Schade's disposal. Norm Thunger stepped into the hack with little question about what he needed to do. At the conclusion of the seventh end, he had learned his lesson about greed, when a stray piece of broom straw resulted in tossing away three certain points. That swing of misfortune remained the difference in the match.

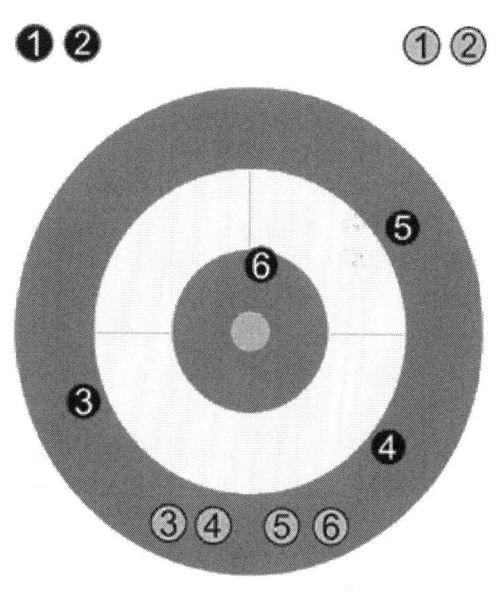

The Minnesota Wall, as it looked to Schade as he prepared to take his first shot with his #7 rock

Thunger pushed himself gently from the hack and started his shot down the center of the lane. With little sweeping required, his #7 rock came to rest in the guard zone, eight or nine feet across the hog line. It was not at all a usual strategy for a Skip to use his first rock as a long guard, but the setup of the rocks in the house dictated it. Thunger had placed it perfectly, making it virtually useless as anything except a nuisance in the event a frustrated Freddy Schade tried to clear out the house by going nuclear with his first shot.

Schade had no interest in discussing strategy with members of his rink. It was clear to him that they had set him up to fail. What did they expect him to do? Freddy decided that his only option was to go after one of the Minnesota rocks in the center of the wall, hoping to run it up and take out Michigan's #6 lying behind the button. With luck, his shot might bump to one side, leaving a wide enough gap to slip through and drop his hammer onto the button. As he saw things, it was his only hope, slim as it was, and it would all come to nothing if Thunger used his second shot effectively.

Standing with his right foot in the hack, Schade squinted toward the far end and was surprised to see Vice Skip Mickey Bellows lightly tapping the ice directly between the two Minnesota rocks on the left side of the wall.

"What the hell is he asking me to do?" Freddy asked, as much to himself as to his sweepers out front. "Turn the rock on edge and roll it through those two?"

"Just hit the shot he's asking you to make, Freddy," Paul Stenner replied bluntly. "We know what we're doing. Do you?"

There was simply no way to make sense of it but Freddy knew he was outnumbered. He jumped up from his crouch and pushed himself deftly, gliding on one foot toward center ice to get a better view of the spacing between the rocks. No way was it more than a rock wide. Nine or ten inches possibly but not the minimum of twelve inches a perfect shot would require. Besides, he thought, even if he slipped through on that side, there wouldn't be enough ice left behind the wall to curl his rock back toward the center. Furthermore, there were no rocks lying immediately behind to serve as a backstop. In all probability, a shot through the gap would simply drift toward the back of the house uselessly. None of it made sense.

Without saying a word to his teammates, Freddy returned to the hack, squatted and squared his shoulders as he prepared to throw the shot of his own choosing; intending to clear out as many rocks as he could. He lowered his eyes toward ice level and took a long, slow look at the pattern of rocks from a new perspective. Suddenly, it all made sense to him. Suddenly it all made sense to the Michigan players, as well. Suddenly, it all made sense to everyone in the arena, as people began rising to their feet.

As if a veil had been lifted from their eyes, the Michigan players could see and understand the lay of the rocks. Norm Thunger slapped his broom on the ice, wanting his first shot back. In fact, he wanted about four or five of his team's shots back. It was all so clear. While inexplicably ignoring Michigan's rocks splitting the house side-to-side and front-to-back, Minnesota had been sucking them in; setting them up for a double takeout; leaving Norm Thunger with just one final shot to fight back. It was a colossal gamble to put everything on Freddy Schade's final two rocks, but what the hell...the match was being played under colossal circumstances.

Whether Minnesota's rock placement was perfect enough, however, would be determined by Schade releasing a perfect shot to the left side. With sufficient weight and if struck at the perfect angle of approach, his rock would send two of Minnesota's stones forward at approximately forty-five degrees needed to knock out two of Michigan's rocks behind them. Equally important, Schade's rock would freeze solid at the point of impact just inside the edge of the twelve-foot circle. A shortened wall would still remain out front, limiting Thunger's options... to do what? Clear out a guard? Curl around everything to the center? Throw hard and break up the entire bunch and hope for the best. Even if that were successful, Schade could use the hammer at his whim to draw to the center.

Any way the Michigan men looked at it, a disaster was descending like a fog. Unless Schade missed with his first shot, Minnesota would likely take at least one point from the end. If the strategy worked, Minnesota could force Michigan to capitulate before heading into the tenth end. It all came down to forcing Freddy Schade into making one of the greatest shots of his life, then following it up with an equally great response to Thunger final rock.

"You sons of bitches," he whispered to his sweepers through the gritted teeth of a half a smile. "There's no way in hell I would ever have agreed to this shot. Now it's all or nothing. You put the entire damned thing on me. You set me up."

"Set you up?" Mistovich answered back. "Why, you're the great Freddy Schade. You said yourself we wouldn't be here if it weren't for you. Now we're giving you the chance to win this thing. You couldn't throw anything straight last night against North Dakota when they cleaned our clock. Now you get a do-over, Freddy. Isn't this what you wanted?"

"We're trying to win this thing the right way," Stenner added. "Any one of those players from the North Dakota rink could make this double if they were squatting in the hack right now. We made our shots. Those Michigan boys made their shots. Now it's your turn to make your shots. You think you deserve to be here? Prove it. It looks like the cops are watching to see whether you can prove it, too. Hell, you have a chance to make one of the most memorable shots in national championship curling history. This is why we're all here. If you don't think you belong here, then do the right thing. Let's forfeit so you can turn yourself in. They've been waiting for two hours and I suspect we all know why."

There was nothing more to say. Freddy stood a few feet behind the hack and looked down the ice again. He would need to start his first rock left of center, slip it past Thunger's long guard and hit his two target rocks squarely and at the correct angle. He knelt on one knee, set his broom under his arm for balance and nervously spun the rock several times to prepare its running surface. The crowd drew a collective breath as he rocked back in the hack, pushed out and followed his momentum forward.

The spontaneous cheer that rung the rafters as Schade hit the blue release line came a fraction of a second too soon. The sudden burst of energy raised the hairs on his arms and he felt himself muscle-up unexpectedly. The handle came out of his fingertips with perhaps a full turn and a half more rotation than intended.

Schade's immediate reaction was to start yelling for aggressive sweeping. After one or two warlike barks, however, he realized that his players were ignoring him. Serving as Vice Skip for Freddy's shot, Mickey Bellows had dropped to hands and knees in the house, peering between the target rocks and gently giving directions to Stenner and Mistovitch." Sweep. Clean. Up! Sweep. Clean. Off".

As Schade slid to a slow stop at mid-ice, so did his world. His eyes stopped following his shot and, instead, looked up toward the crowd. In the haziness of the moment, he could make out every face turned in unison toward the moving rock, as it crawled toward its target; every face, save one. One young set of eyes continued to glare in Freddy's direction, peering from the shadows beneath the low visor of a baseball hat covered by a sweatshirt hood. It was as if the kid somehow knew what was unfolding before him. Knew he was witness to a moment in history. Knew he was watching events which would one day affect the lives of so many people, as they were set in motion.

Freddy couldn't bear to keep his eyes tracked on the path of his shot, but he knew he didn't need to. There was nothing more he could do about the eventual outcome. Whatever now happened was under the control of his men and whatever forces of physics they could extract from their brooms. The reaction of the players on the ice and the audience rising from their seats would tell him everything. So he remained, instead, kneeling on one knee at center ice, staring back into the distant narrow eyes of the young village idiot of Gluek, Minnesota, sixteen year-old Tommy DuMot.

At the time, adopting a young eighteen-month old toddler from the Chippewa County foster care program seemed like a perfect solution for Pete and Medora DuMot. The parents expected to watch with pride as their three-year old son Arvil took younger brother Tommy under his wing as the two grew up together. In their happiest dreams, the two boys would eventually take over the farm as a team. They would marry and raise children of their own with proud Grandma and Grandpa living out their final days in a small house built on the property; helping where they could around the farm and watching their grandchildren grow to one day take over the farm themselves. It was the way things were done in good families all across Chippewa County and western Minnesota.

Within a year or two, however, the family realized there were deep flaws in their plans. Young Tommy was damaged goods, affected by fetal alcohol syndrome that was still so misunderstood and undiagnosed in the 1950s. Nobody expected or knew how to deal with the behavioral problems that the kid exhibited almost daily. The county didn't have an answer for a failed adoption, so the family did what it could to hold things together. By the time the boy was ten, older brother Arv was the only person in the world who could provide any kind of a steadying influence. Tommy clung to him and best friend Willy like a burr. People knew that you simply didn't get one without the others.

By the age of twelve, Tommy's teachers began recognizing telltale signs of psychopathic behavior as the kid retaliated for even the smallest perceived insults regarding his broad forehead, narrow eyes and angular facial features. By the time he entered eighth grade, every teacher and county social worker had him tagged with a soup can full of behavioral disorders, either real or assumed.

It was as if he knew he wasn't going to get away with pasting a classmate to the wall with a left hook, but he did it anyway. Often, his only bizarre explanation about starting a fight was that he honestly didn't think it would be wrong to swing a metal pipe across a classmate's back. More surprisingly, Tommy frequently expressed disappointment, confusion and even violent frustration when a teacher who witnessed an unprovoked assault didn't take his side. After all, he argued, the other kid desperately deserved some kind of serious ass-whipping?

As Tommy's problems became more pronounced, Arvil did what he could to find some space of his own, but with little success. Increasingly, he found peace in the company of his best friend Willy Ordway. When the pressure of his younger brother's behavior grew too great on the family, Medora would allow him to slip away to his friend Willy Ordway's neighboring farm half-mile to the west. The two would often spend quiet hours sitting in the solitude of hayloft, where the boys would frequently have permission to camp out overnight. It was Medora's way to help her son avoid the domestic wrath that was part and parcel of Tommy's adolescent and teenage years. During those times Arv was able to break away, the younger Tommy often escaped the family as well, disappearing for two or three days at a time before Pete or Medora called the police.

As he grew through his teenage years, the problems became worse and Tommy was a highlighted name on the Chippewa County juvenile court frequent offender list. A general sense of sympathy for the DuMot family increased throughout the community. Whenever there was the slightest disturbance or property damage on a farm in the surrounding countryside, the local constable, Mickey Bellows, drove out to the DuMot farm to ask a few questions. He generally found Pete and Medora confounded and distraught over their adopted son's behavior. It became common practice to simply arrest Tommy, untangle his lies and excuses, and hold him overnight until Medora agreed to sign for his release the following day. It was against county regulations to keep the minor in jail overnight, but the police and neighbors knew that it gave the family and townsfolk some short periods of peace.

After Tommy was suspended from the public school on the third occasion, he was assigned to a live-in program at the county juvenile center. A restless Arv came to a haunting realization: As long as his parents retained custody over his little brother, it would be impossible to escape the little town of Gluek. Nobody doubted that Tommy would someday become a ward of the St. Cloud State Penitentiary or the federal prison system. But until then, the safety of the entire family would be at risk whenever he was returned to the DuMot farm under the care of his parents. Figuratively, and often literally, Arv tied his younger brother to his waist and stayed with him wherever he went, including Grand Forks when Tommy was named as an alternate for the Schade rink in the national curling championships.

Freddy knew the kid looking down at him from the seats meant trouble. He could only hope that one day, his step-son Willy could get away from him alive, and without a criminal record of his own. Yet there sat the juvenile delinquent in the crowd, right next to Willy, staring hot needles of hatred across the open space, burning with judgment about the events that were transpiring around him.

Freddy felt his face grow red with anger. "Don't you dare feel contempt for me, you young punk," he thought. "You don't know the half of the torment you've put everyone through these past years and I'm not going to let you bury my son in your stinking world." Yet for all the hatred, Freddy could not look away. In a few hours, nothing the kid said or did would ever again make any difference.

Schade and his co-conspirators had it mapped out so perfectly.

They were confident the teenage Tommy would stay true to form. It was most predictable. Alone in a small room with the police, the kid was bound to fall into his usual bluster of anger, bewilderment and frustration. When asked for details about the previous night, he would be unable to explain anything clearly and consistently. On first telling, he would likely get the story almost right, saying that his brother and friend had left him alone as he slept in their Parkview Motel room, while they stole away by themselves for a night of underage partying. The cop's first questions would be straightforward and Tommy's answers would be quick and direct. He would probably say he heard loud, agitated voices, which woke him abruptly at some unknown midnight hour. He would confess to being confused and unsure of his strange surroundings in the hotel, so he lay still for a moment, listening to Willy's father talking rapidly and pacing the room. When Mr. Schade realized he was awake, he stopped and told him to go back to sleep. The next thing he knew, they were waking him to get ready to head to the arena for the eleven o'clock start of the curling match.

On second, third and fourth interrogations to clarify some inconsistencies, however, he would just as likely confess to being on the other side of town at the time of the accident, sneaking into the back door of a bar around midnight. Later, he might brag that he had spent the evening with a girl, whom he couldn't name, nor could the police locate. Finally, he would likely admit to riding with his brother in the back seat of the Schade's VW bus. Freddy knew that Tommy's inconsistent, convoluted and confusing alibis would be the break he needed. The betrayal was a perfect set up. Willy had agreed to corroborate the story that Tommy had snuck out of the room and hotwired the van for a late night drunken joy ride. That final version of 'truth' would serve as enough reason for the Grand Forks police to accept Freddy's version, especially after they checked on the kid's priors.

But Freddy knew that Tommy DuMot was a lot of things, but he wasn't stupid. The fetal alcohol syndrome affected the synapses in the brain, but it didn't render him brainless. Yes, the kid was untrustworthy, injudicious and lacked the common sense that God gave a goose, but he was far-removed from obtuse. The kid would know he was being set up, even if he would be unable to articulate exactly why or how he knew. After all, his older brother and best friend would never betray him. So who else would do it to him? From more than fifty feet away, Freddy Schade could see it in the kid's fiery eyes.

With a loud clunk, both target-rocks sprung forward at the intended angles, exactly as needed. The crowd broke into a roar as the silver #3 rock angled left and cleared out Michigan's gold #3, shoving it forward several feet and out of play. Simultaneously, Minnesota's #4 angled toward the right, pushing Michigan's #5 rock off the right rear edge.

His double takeout shot did its job and the Minnesota rocks would serve their purpose coming to rest inside the house. What had been sitting as four likely Michigan points just thirty seconds earlier had been reduced to a single #6 rock lying as shot rock in the center. The front of the house remained guarded by what remained of the Minnesota wall, along with Norm Thunger's ill-conceived long-guard lying helplessly several feet out front.

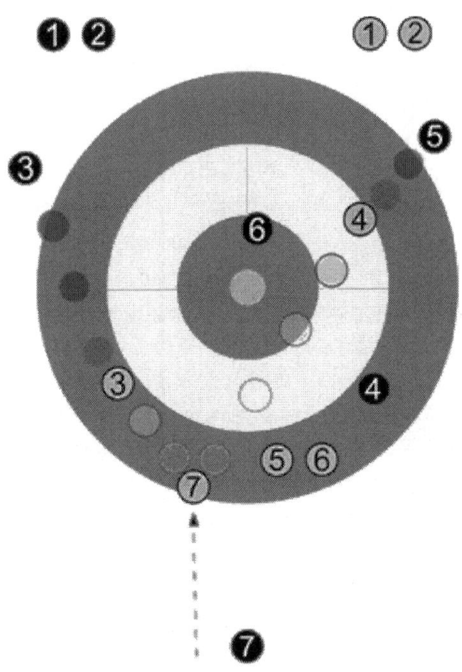

Schade used his first shot to raise two rocks from the wall at perfect angles for a double takeout

Norm Thunger took a moment to walk down to the house to observe and discuss the new pattern with his players. The crowd knew. No matter how much his Michigan teammates pointed and shook their heads, it would make no difference. Thunger's only real option to salvage the end would require clipping his shot off the edge of the Michigan #4 rock lying at the right-front of the house and rolling his rock left to come to rest near the button. If he could get the angle right, he could remove Schade's options to take more than a single point with the hammer. Michigan would regain the final shot for the tenth end, sitting just one or two points down; not insurmountable.

Thunger took his time returning to the hack, then slowly turned and faced his Vice Skip, Steve Talbert, at the far end. His sweepers knew the stakes. Stay too far left by three inches and the shot would clip the rock on the right side of the wall and roll off uselessly. Drift an inch too far right and he would hit his target #4 rock too flush, pushing it straight ahead and over the end line. Clipping his target rock on the right side to edge it toward the middle was too unpredictable and risky. He could maintain better control of his own rock's carom, speed and distance. Bouncing his shot perfectly off the inside edge of his team's #4 rock was the only real option.

As he released the shot, he gently turned the handle in a clockwise rotation, intending a slight left-to-right curl that would allow him to use the center of the ice as long as possible. He felt good about the delivery. He felt great about the release. He felt confident about the direction. Sweepers Coventry and Harder in front of him began working their brooms exactly at the right time and kept the shot heading on a straight trajectory until precisely the right moment. The final twenty-five feet would tell, all as the rock began swinging gently toward its target. As it crossed the hog line and headed toward the right side of the wall, it began its anticipated curl. Thunger barked the command his sweepers had been waiting for — **Off!** — and they raised their brooms and simply ushered the shot forward, as if walking a turtle on a harness lead.

The rock was moving slowly — but not slowly enough — as it approached the right edge of the wall at the front of the house. Its curl seemed on pace to avoid chipping the end-rock by the slight margin required. From his position behind the shot, Thunger could see that it was on its way toward striking his target perfectly at the eight o'clock position on the rock, as intended. But it needed to begin its death drag. Missing his targeted spot by just a half-inch, or hitting it with too much force, could be a disaster.

There was nothing more his sweepers or anyone else in Grand Forks could do. Throughout the arena, time and motion were suspended in a net of palpable tension as the shot crept forward. Minnesota's John Mistovich dared to avert his gaze for an instant and locked eyes with his opponent, Jim Coventry. Each knew they stood engulfed in that rare phenomenal moment they would remember for a lifetime, as it evolved inch-by-inch at their feet.

"It's a beautiful game," Mistovich whispered.

9:00 p.m. Thursday, February 7th, 2008

I stared at Sam Ruude's name at the bottom of the message for several seconds and then pulled the screen in front of me again without considering Tina.

"Hey, I was reading that" she said, quickly scooting around to my side of the booth and hipping me several inches further toward the wall. "What does it say?"

I read the message aloud:

Jack;

After all this time, I was surprised to hear you left a voice message on the answering machine. Your father always knew you would come calling some day.

It is important that we talk. Drive up to Alexandria and meet me at the Perkins Restaurant off Interstate 94. I will be waiting and watching for you at 12:00 noon sharp on Saturday, February 9th. Do not walk into the restaurant before precisely noon, nor a minute later. Request a booth in the rear of the restaurant. The lobby area will be busy for the lunch crowd.

Order something for yourself and request that the waitress bring you the check immediately. After exactly ten minutes, leave the table to head toward the restroom. Bring your check with you to the restroom. After exactly one minute, head directly to the checkout counter. Pay and leave the building as quickly as possible.

Drive back to Interstate 94 west, toward Fargo. At exactly 7.3 miles, you will drive under an overpass. Immediately pull your car onto the shoulder, get out and act as if you have a flat tire. Very shortly thereafter, I will pull onto the shoulder as if to offer assistance. You will drive us to a safe place where we can talk.

Don't screw this up. I will be watching you every step and the timing must be perfect. You have only one chance to get this right, Jack. Come alone and trust no one about any of this. NO ONE!   S Ruude

"Well," Tina started, "we still don't know whether your father is alive or dead, but we know there must be someone or something out there he's hiding from...or at least was."

"And it will finally explain why my mother wanted me to find Sam Ruude," I added.

She looked closely at the screen for a moment and continued, "Let's see. The message was sent just after three o'clock, when we were at the courthouse. He's been waiting about six years for this. Now he suddenly can't meet you until Saturday at noon? So, assuming he's been living on the run all these years, he can't fly into town. He'll have to drive. It sounds like he's coming in from out of state, don't you think?"

"As a matter of fact, yes, I think he's probably driving here from Montana," I said.

I explained the Montana 406 area code to connect to my dad's answering machine message.

"He instructs me to drive *up* to Alexandria," I continued, "that means he evidently thinks we're still in the Twin Cities and doesn't know we're on the road. Let's see, today is Thursday the 7th. The timing may be about perfect for us. We can head north to the Fergus Falls Curling Club to talk to George Penski tomorrow evening, Friday the 8th. We can spend the night in Fergus. Then we'll leave after breakfast Saturday morning to backtrack east down I-94 to Alexandria in time to meet him at noon."

I opened the Google Maps website. We checked to make sure we got the distances and driving times about right. The other two curling clubs we intended to visit by the end of the weekend were in Brainerd and St. Cloud, both within a few hours' drive of Alexandria...depending upon what Ruude had in store for us, of course.

"We better get out of here," said Tina, watching our waitress pointing toward us with an agitated finger while talking quietly to a bus boy near the kitchen. "We've been here almost three hours. She's probably worried about losing money if she doesn't get new customers into this booth."

"New customers? On a Thursday night in this town?" I said with a chuckle. "I'll leave her an extra dollar tip."

"Jack," Tina started again, but then hesitated. "When are you going to open LaVon's e-mail message?"

I had hoped she hadn't noticed that I had one unread message in my inbox. But she had obviously squeezed in a spare second to read the subject line and who had sent it. The fact that LaVon continued to have access to her school account from her laptop told me that she hadn't left her job completely behind. Apparently, she had taken a leave of absence. That would be just like her, I thought; keeping her options open for every contingency.

"Oh, I suspect I know what it'll say," I replied. "I'm not particularly keen on reading a message telling me that I need to hire a lawyer. She can sit and stew in her own juices for a while yet."

"It's been five or six weeks since she left you, hasn't it?" Tina asked, already knowing the exact date. "If she was just going to tell you to get a lawyer, don't you think she would have done so by now? Why don't you take a moment to read it?"

"Yeah, okay, you're right," I said.

I clicked open the message and scanned it quickly. On first pass, I didn't see the word lawyer or attorney anywhere, so I invested the time to start at the top.

"Well," I started. "I was wrong. Do you want me to read it to you?"

"If it affects us, then yes, I guess I'd like to hear it."

If it affects us? My heart gave an excited leap. Despite whatever it was she intended to tell me — some of which she said I wouldn't understand at all —she was still holding out the possibility of an equation that included the word *us*.

I read the message quickly and then once again more slowly. When Tina saw that I was scanning it for the third and fourth time, she lowered her eyes perceptibly.

"I'll just have to give it some thought tonight," I finally said before shutting down the screen and standing up to leave.

I held Tina's soft mittened hand the entire walk back to the car. We didn't say much. Frankly, I didn't know what to say or how to express what I was thinking. Whatever the next few days would bring, I was glad to have her with me. As we sat for a moment in the car, waiting for the heater to kick-start our chilly bodies, she surprised me.

"Jack," she began. "I should have told you this right away, but I'm not quite sure how things will turn out, so I held off. Now I think I owe you some explanations."

"Well, I've been on edge all evening."

After a long pause, she said bluntly, "I'm already in a relationship with someone."

Ouch. I shouldn't have been so shocked, but I was.

"A r-relationship?" I stammered. "How? No, I don't mean how. I can see exactly *how*. I mean *when*? You're always available when I call. You practically stayed all night on my sofa one night. You were at my door this morning at 6:30, for God's sake. You never talk about someone special in your life. You're not afraid to touch me or let me touch you. And now we're ready to walk into a hotel lobby and get a room for the night..."

"Jack," she tried to interrupt but to no avail.

"Tina, I've been thinking about this for weeks," I continued. "You don't give any indication whatsoever that you're in a relationship. Like I said, not that you couldn't be, but *when* and with *whom*? I mean, if you don't mind me asking."

"He's married," she said matter-of-factly, hitting me with it like it was the blunt end of a two-by-four, point blank and right between the eyes.

Over the previous couple of weeks, I had given a lot of thought to our relationship. Of course I realized that someone of her age, beauty, tenderness and vivacity was likely to be in a relationship. A steady stream of relationships, in fact. After losing Bill's son Jason so tragically, it was even likely that she rebounded from one to the next. I had hoped that she was finally ready to meet someone who was ready to take things to the next level. Someone who...well...someone exactly like me, to be precise.

"He...he's married?" I stammered.

"Well, technically, you're married, too," she replied, starting to cry.

She could tell I was at a loss for words, so she tried to speak through her tears.

"Cripes, here I go," she continued. "You're the one who should be upset but I'm the one crying."

I tried to be brave, "Well, so tell me about him."

She dried her eyes and smiled, as if she had been waiting an eternity to finally get to tell the story. She explained that she had been dating a department manager at ProtoCommand almost since the first week he arrived from southern Illinois, a year after Jason's death.

"An office affair? Oh, ick," I quickly interrupted. To my surprise, she chuckled and agreed with me. Within a few minutes, she filled me in on every detail.

Gary had been a good friend of Bill's for many years. She got to know him because Bill dragged him to business gatherings, company outings and private parties, many of which Tina was invited to attend, as well. He had left his wife and school-aged daughter behind when he moved from Decatur to the Twin Cities to take over the head of the ProtoCommand purchasing department.

"Well, that explains why I never heard of him," I interrupted. "Our department never had two dimes to rub together."

Three floors and a quarter mile of hallway between their offices meant the two of them couldn't interact much during the workweek. They occasionally slipped out together for lunch, always taking separate exits to meet at some distant restaurant, where they would be safe from prying eyes. She doubted that Bill ever became aware of the affair, although she was never quite certain. If he knew anything about it, he never let on.

"The texting I was doing on the drive out here all morning was with Gary," she admitted. "I'm sorry I was so rude about it."

She continued dumping everything off her ample chest. After several empty promises that Gary would talk to his wife and daughter, Tina was ready to quit waiting and move on; he wasn't. Finally, he did talk to his wife and he asked for an easy, quick divorce. But after waiting another six months, no official paperwork was yet in the works. Tina simply didn't know where she stood with the guy, or where the guy stood with his family.

"And then Bill died and here we are," she concluded. "It's like dating Jason all over again. I keep giving these guys so many fair chances. What's wrong with me?"

"Maybe you've just never found a guy who knew what to do with someone as great as you," I ventured. Although I was torn apart with disappointment, I felt surprisingly relieved about her revelation.

"If it means anything, Tina," I said after a moment. "You don't fit the part of playing the other woman."

"That's because I didn't know I was getting that role again when I fell so hard for him," she continued. "After the Jason fiasco, I swore I would never be that stupid again. Gary didn't tell me he was married until he let it slip while driving to work together one Monday morning. By then, we had crossed all kinds of lines and he had made all manner of promises. I tried to break it off with him right away — and I've tried several times since. We've painted so many pictures of our future together, though, that's it's hard to get that little picket-fence yard out of my head."

"And I was supposed to fit...where?" I asked. "In your hip pocket in case things didn't work out between you two?"

"That's not fair," she said sharply. "You've still got a wife you're carrying around in your shirt pocket, Jack. Remember her? You haven't told me what she wrote in that e-mail. Where is she? Tucked into bed somewhere in Mankato? I'm here with you. Right here. Right now. We don't know what's going to happen with any of this. That kiss back there by the restaurant — that was from my heart, Jack. If you give yourself a chance, you might just get the girl in this story."

"It's not as easy as I thought it would be for me either, Tina," I said quietly.

I reflected quietly for a moment about what to say or do next. I tried to sort out why I was feeling so confused. Maybe it was her honesty. Maybe it was her tears. Just as likely, though, it was my wife's e-mail message. LaVon had admitted that things weren't going well with Tony. She had always known he liked his beer, but his daily binges to forget his wife and kids were more than she had been prepared for. Apparently, he wasn't able to escape the guilt he thought he had left behind in Grand Rapids. "I spent my childhood watching my mother rip her life to shreds because of my drunken father. I'm not about to live that hell all over again." At the end of the message, she asked to move back home, hoping for a fresh start.

Tina interrupted my thoughts, "Was I right that night in your living room, Jack? I mean, was I right when I said you shouldn't judge people too harshly. That your wife has a story, too."

I thought back to the piles of letters and love notes I discovered in my basement, revealing that LaVon's affair had started before I ever met her and continued until the day she moved out.

"She's asking for a fresh start, Tina. How can we make a fresh start in a marriage that never left the starting gate in the first place?"

Tina leaned across and kissed me, then wiped a small tear from my right cheek.

"It's cold and late, Jack," she replied. "Let's get to the motel. We've come a long way today, in more ways than one. I want to take a hot shower, crawl into my warm pajamas and get a good night's sleep. Neither of us has to think about any more of this tonight."

Thursday Night, February 7th, 2008

While Tina was showering, walked back to the lobby and asked the desk clerk about available Internet service. I was told that the old couple who owned the place never thought the Internet was anything more than a passing fancy, so they didn't bother to pay for the expensive installation. I resorted to asking about a copy of a local phone directory. He gave me a look of distrust as he reached beneath the counter. Before handing me the book, he asked for promises that I would return it in good condition. I assured him that nobody beyond the confines of his time-warped motel had much use for the damned things anymore. With a wary look, he allowed me to take it outside under the light of the entrance canopy, from where he could keep an eye on his *precioussss,* and I could keep an eye on the door to our room.

I knew it would be a long shot that I might find listings for Fergus Falls businesses as far south as Montevideo, so instead looked up the nearest curling club in the region. The Granite Falls Ice Gardens lay just twenty miles away. I was confident that every club manager in the state would have the phone number to every other club. It wasn't yet ten o'clock, so I was certain to find someone still near the telephone as evening leagues wrapped up. As the phone rang for the third and fourth time, my mind recalled a vivid image of the little club in Mapleton, where this search had all begun. I recalled Tina's words, *"Jack, what was it you were really looking for up in those rafters that evening?"*

I was right with my hunch that all curlers know each other, or at least know of every other curling club. The woman answering the phone quickly gave me the number to the Fergus Falls club, as if she had it committed to memory. A minute later, I was on the phone with a man at the Gateway Curling Club, asking for driving directions and the schedule for bonspiel matches the following evening.

"Yes," he replied, "every rink is schedule to play one game tomorrow evening, starting at seven o'clock. But the club will be open earlier in the day for the after school program."

I thought I'd better check...

"Will George Penski be opening the club tomorrow afternoon?" I asked.

The manager seemed a little surprised that I would even have to ask.

"Of course," he chuckled. "As far as I know, old George hasn't missed in twenty years. He'll open at one o'clock, as always. But I can't talk now. The league matches are finishing up and I have to get the bar ready for the curlers coming off the ice. We'll see your rink here for check-in about six tomorrow evening, I suspect?"

"Oh, uh, no..." I started, "I'm not with a rink..." But I realized it wasn't worth correcting him. I had all the information I needed. "Yeah, looking forward to it," I concluded.

The next morning, we pulled out of Montevideo after returning to the Monty Café for a leisurely breakfast. We were both relieved that nobody from the previous evening was working the morning shift. Over eggs and toast, we double-checked my road atlas. Tina thought it would be interesting to take the smaller county roads north for a while, since we would have more than four crisp, clear morning hours to drive only one hundred thirty-five miles. As she traced the narrow black lines on the page, I wrote down the road numbers and highway names as she read them off. Finally, though, even her most manicured fingernail could find no other alternative than to reconnect to State Highway 59 near Morris. When I noticed a local farmer in the next booth craning his neck to observe which route we planned to drive, I asked some questions he was apparently dying to answer.

"Well, I don't recommend that you take the small county roads," he replied. "They get awfully narrow and slick this time of year. You'll be driving through some flat land up that way. That's the old Lake Agassiz glacial lakebed area. There's nothing to stop the wind. Hell, locals will tell you that the earth stops curving up there. We got a little snow last night, so you might see some light drifting across the roads, but it should be dry sailing. No blizzard."

"Dry sailing?" I thought to myself.

"Aw, no blizzard?" Tina said, shaking her head with a mock pout. "You look disappointed, Jack."

The trip north through large tracts of farmland proved spectacularly bleak and not nearly as interesting as we had hoped. Along the way, we took a mental tally of the dilapidated abandoned farmhouses that once housed two or three generations of farm families working the rich, dark soil lining the Red River Valley. As individual farmers retired with no progeny interested in taking over the chores, an opportunistic neighbor stood ready to buy out the acreage, hoping to become a 'corporate' farm. Much of the original family acreage spreading in every direction around us had long-ago become part of large enterprises of fifteen hundred acres or more.

En route, the conversation between us was often as sparse as the features on the landscape. Tina filled the awkward silent moments by occasionally fiddling with her cell phone. The leisurely pace allowed me to quietly sort through some unresolved thoughts still hanging from our conversation of the previous day, as well as what had transpired between us during the darkest hours of the night. The mysterious death certificate at the courthouse and Sam Ruude's message gave us a safe topic of conversation to start with, but we both knew what we were deliberately avoiding.

"Is Married Gary texting you," I asked, trying to keep the disappointed tone out of my voice. "Can't you tell him to leave you alone? Or can't you simply turn off your phone?"

I was perturbed and Tina knew it.

"It should be that simple," she said. "But I guess it's not going to be."

As usual, I didn't know what to say next. So, as usual, I said the wrong thing.

"And where does that leave us?" I asked.

Leftover pieces from the night lay scattered throughout the car, as if needing lassoing, corralling and branding like stray cattle. Tina's silence suggested that she didn't know quite what to do with her feelings, either.

"Jack, let's just forget all about it," she finally started. "I wouldn't take a million dollars to repeat what happened last night."

"And I wouldn't take a million dollars to change a thing." I added.

The events of the night in the motel room were still palpable between us. We left the car parked immediately in front of the lobby and carried our travel bags the thirty yards to our room on the lower level. Inside the room, we discovered that the yellow concrete walls offered poor insulation against the frigid winter night air seeping through the inch-thick hollow steel door. The temperature inside the room hovered around sixty degrees. In order to soften the hard, cold feeling of the room, I immediately turned the knob to start the radiator heat flowing and closed the curtain as best I could. We dropped our bags on the floor and Tina quickly claimed the first shower. I agreed and took the opportunity to go back to the lobby to call the local curling club.

When I returned to the room shortly after ten o'clock, I found Tina standing at the vanity sink in front of a steamy mirror. She was bent over, wrapping her wet hair in a dry towel. I took a brief second to study the way her hips stretched her pink flannel pajamas snuggly across her butt. Her body was so different from LaVon's tiny frame, which always seemed completely lost and difficult to define deep inside her oversized loungewear that doubled as pajamas. Just as I was thinking that Tina could stand to lose a few pounds, my libido informed me in no uncertain terms that her body was perfect just the way it was.

When she straightened up, I quickly diverted my eyes upward to see her smile at me through the steamy reflection. When I turned away, I noticed for the first time that she had sorted and separated our personal items onto the two beds. I hung up my coat, pulled some personal effects out of my travel bag and quickly brushed past her toward the inner bathroom. As I stepped inside, she caught me by the shirtsleeve and stopped me mid-stride. She seemed to want to say something but the moment apparently got in the way.

We stood for a brief second, looking into each other's blank, tired faces. Although it might have been the stinging effects of shampoo in her eyes, it appeared she had been crying. When she broke her gaze and glanced downward, I reflexively shifted to hide the bulge filling the crotch of my jeans. She pretended not to notice, but we both knew.

"I'm afraid I didn't leave you any hot water, Jack."

"Good," I said bashfully, quickly pulling the door closed behind me.

After the longest shower of my life, I slipped into a pair of boxer shorts and a gray U.S. Navy t-shirt and brushed my teeth quickly, trying not to glance over my shoulder in the reflection. When I couldn't help myself any longer, I was relieved to see that she had climbed deeply beneath her covers in the bed nearest the cold door. She was rolled over in the opposite direction, with her wet hair wrapped in a towel. I stared for several seconds, watching her body lightly rise and fall with the rhythm of her soft breathing.

I quickly flipped off the bathroom light and felt my way a short distance through the blackness to the edge of my bed. I crawled under the thin layer of covers and allowed my eyes to gradually grow accustomed to the darkness. Slowly, I could start to make out the soft whitish glow from her towel. I felt an unusual warm comfort knowing that she felt safe enough to fall asleep so quickly. "Good night," I whispered, but didn't expect a reply. Once again, I envied her innate capacity to find peace with whatever inner turmoil rocked her world. I certainly couldn't.

With everything that had erupted over the previous days and weeks, I found it difficult to fall into a deep asleep. Inevitably, my thoughts turned to Tina. What do I do with my feelings about her? What will she do about Married Gary? Do I owe my wife a fresh start?

Sometime around one o'clock, I was suddenly jerked awake when Tina gently slid her warm firm body under my covers and rolled tightly against me. Without a whisper, I raised my right arm and allowed her to lay her head in the crook of my neck and shoulder. Rolling on her side, she pressed her firm breasts against my chest and draped one warm leg over my bare thighs, sharing the warmth of her flannel pajamas. Slipping her warm hand beneath my t-shirt, she caressed my thin chest hair with her fingertips. I discovered her left hand with my own and we interlaced our fingers. Her damp hair smelled sweetly of fresh coconut shampoo and I craned downward to peck the top of her head with a soft kiss. We lay motionless and silent, allowing each other's empty hearts to slowly fill up.

Instinctively and against every fiber of the man I thought myself to be, I realized that I dared not move to touch or take her. I somehow knew that if we allowed a single ounce of desire to pass between us, it would have crushed the foundation we were building in stone. So we lay breathing softly, thinking our own thoughts about what the moment might mean. Within minutes, we were both sound asleep in each other's arms.

As the first rays of morning light slipped through the narrow crack between the curtain panels, I awoke and crawled from beneath my warm covers with a shiver. I felt an empty sadness when I realized that Tina had silently slipped back to her own bed sometime during the night. I stood for a moment, watching the gray silhouette of her blankets gently rise and fall. Across the foot of my bed lay her damp towel, the only evidence that her quiet visit hadn't all been only a sweet dream. I dressed as quickly and quietly as I could and stepped out into the cold pre-dawn air for a long walk. When I returned to the room a frozen half-hour later, she was dressed and packed and ready to head out for breakfast. She didn't ask where I had gone, nor for how long. It didn't matter.

Part V

Relevance

Friday Afternoon, February 8th, 2008

We pulled into the parking lot of the curling club in Fergus Falls about twenty minutes before George Penski's expected arrival at one p.m. For a quick lunch, I suggested a nearby Burger King but Tina volunteered to run across the street to a small grocery store, while I waited and watched for old George.

With fruit slices, cheese and crackers precariously balanced on the console between us, we distracted ourselves by toying with Bill Ordway's TomTom GPS device, hoping we could use it for whatever might remain of our road trip. We nearly missed it when a bent little man of about eighty years old climbed out of an old Jeep Wagoneer and limped his way toward the main door.

"That must be Penski," I said, turning off the engine. "Tina, when we talk to him, I'd like to just make this about my father; nothing about this whole Arv Firpo thing. I just want to find out what he might know about my family history."

Tina didn't understand my reasons. I started to refer back to my phone conversation with the local Minneapolis FBI and my brief discussion with Doug Chimney but ended by keeping it simple. "I just don't want any more people dragged into this. We don't need any more names added to that list."

She agreed and stepped out of the car to button up her coat.

"I thought you said he was a curler," she said, watching Penski fumbling with the building keys. "He doesn't look like he could play marbles."

"No," I corrected her, "the lady from the curling association said he knew everything about my family and that this curling club is his life. I don't remember whether she said he actually curled. I guess I just assumed he did."

We deliberately waited a few seconds until the old man stepped into the building, then another half-minute to allow him to get himself settled inside. We found him by the front desk, sorting the day's mail. After a quick introduction, we explained the telephone call from his old friend Mary Coventry at the USCA. To my surprise, he said he didn't remember her very well, but that she had called the day before to say that he should expect us to drop by. When I said I was looking for more information about the DuMot family, a noticeable smile crept across his face.

"I had a minor stroke back in '03, Jack," he explained apologetically as he opened a gray circuit box and punched several large toggle switches to turn on the lights above the ice. "Some of my memory for certain things ain't too good na'more. Still, I may be able to help. I hardly remembered Mary when she called. Until she reminded me of her husband, old Jim Coventry. Then it all came back to me. It's been awhile since I've talked to her. We had a real nice conversation."

"But you remember my father Tommy and the DuMot family pretty well, though?" I asked hopefully.

"Sure, sure," he reassured me. "I used to curl with your grandfather Pete, down in Montevideo. There were some damned good curlers in that family, as I recall. I remember the whole DuMot family."

"Well, that's why we're here," I said. "Do you have time to tell me more about them?"

"Hey," he said. "I'm an old man. Ordinarily, I've got nothing but time. But I've got a lot to do between now and the bonspiel tonight. Right now, I've only got about fifteen minutes to get the ice ready for the kid's school program while these lights fire up."

He winked at Tina as if he had said something so seductive that only an attractive young woman could possibly understand.

"You two go upstairs and find a place to sit down for a few minutes. I'll get these kids going and then we can talk. I'll have a little time before I start setting up for the bonspiel players arriving early this evening."

From our table in the upstairs bar room we could look down over all six curling sheets below us, each separated by a narrow walking platform. As the high-watt halogen bulbs grew gradually brighter, the vivid red and blue concentric circles at each end of the rink sprung to life in stark contrast to the brilliant milky-white ice. At the center of each sheet was a logo stenciled through the ice, each advertising a different local business sponsor. I pointed at a handful of bright blue and gold satin banners hung in the rafters.

"Those are the types of banners I saw down in Mapleton, Tina, where I saw Dad's name."

"You mean where you saw a name that you *think* might be his," she corrected me.

We watched as old Penski walked carefully backward down the ice waving a short hose attached to a water tank he held under one arm. As he swung the sprinkler-head back and forth, small droplets of water sprayed from the nozzle head and dispersed widely to cover the full width of each sheet.

"That's called pebbling the ice," I said, assuming Tina couldn't possibly understand the technical intricacies involved with sprinkling water. "In curling, the ice isn't smooth like a skating rink. Those droplets of de-ionized water will freeze to form small contours to give the surface a rough texture. You'll hear the rocks rumble down the ice because of the rough granite bottom sliding over the pebbling."

"But he's not doing it just so the rocks make that cool rumbling noise is he?" she asked.

"No, of course not," I answered, but then realized she was making fun of me. "No, I'm sure the rock would make some noise, anyway. But it rides along on the raised surface of the bumps. My father told me once that when he was a kid back in the 1960s, they didn't pebble the ice. I'm not sure when or why they decided to start pebbling it. Interesting to watch, though, isn't it?"

"I suppose," she said with a smile, "but not nearly as mesmerizing as watching a Zamboni."

"Yeah, but that's not a fair comparison," I laughed. "Nothing can compete with watching a Zamboni."

A few kids began practicing on the sheet below us. I explained that the concentric rings on each end are called the house and went over the rules about scoring as simply as I could. Tina smiled cheerfully at the low constant growling sound penetrating through the building as rocks crawled down the length of the sheets.

As more kids took to the ice, I tried to explain shooting technique, sweeping and scoring. My inability to articulate things very clearly finally brought my feeble attempts to a screeching halt.

"I think I've got it, Jack," she said, holding the palm of her hand up to my face. "It's just not that complicated."

"That's because you're only watching the rocks, young lady," George Penski's voice interrupted from behind us. "To really understand this beautiful game you need to understand what's happening in the time and space between the rocks. You have to get inside the players' heads."

He pulled a chair away from the table but didn't sit down.

"Well, anyway, it doesn't look like rocket science," Tina tried for a save.

"Well, it may be true that it's more of an art form," Penski continued. "But it's art as old as cave paintings. Historians have discovered rocks that prehistoric peoples in northern Europe used in some kind of ice game thousands of years ago. Inscribed curling stones have been found in Scotland dating back to the early 1500s. In 1824, the first club in North America was formed in Halifax, Nova Scotia. Here in the U.S., a doctor established a club near Detroit in 1832. One club in Milwaukee has been operating continuously since 1845. Today in America there are tens of thousands of curlers in nearly one hundred fifty clubs spread out across twenty-six states and more open every year. Did you know there are clubs in Miami, the Caribbean and Hawaii. Wisconsin has more clubs than any other state. Here in Minnesota, the St. Paul Curling Club is the largest club in the nation. There are uncountable thousands more curlers throughout Canada. Altogether, there are more than one and a half million curlers ranging from age five to ninety-five playing in more than thirty countries around the world. Curling is older than hockey, baseball, football and just about every other team sport you can think of. The beauty of it is that everyone can play. Brute strength means very little out there on the ice."

I curled for a year," I said, in a vain attempt to reclaim the conversation. "I didn't think it was such a big deal. You're right. Anybody can do it."

"See, like I said. It's great for everyone, including young inexperienced punks."

Ouch.

"That's what makes it so great," he continued. "But it takes more than just having a good time to reach the top. Most great curlers get there on their own, putting the pieces together one league game, one bonspiel and one championship playdown at a time. It's not like there are coaches, camps and clinics all over the place. If a kid wants to pursue a higher level, he really needs to go out and look for ways to make it happen. It takes individual hard work and the commitment of a lifetime."

Tina looked over at me.

"So, it's not something that — oh, let's say a fifty-two year old man could just decide to go out and get good at on a whim?" she asked.

"Well, it's possible, but there are a lot of things that have to happen. Champion curlers require the dexterity of a surgeon, the finesse of a gymnast and the grace of a ballerina. Athleticism is a key part of it, sure, but the best curlers need to be able to think, too. They need to read space and anticipate the next move, all within the context of physics. Not too many other sports require such a high level of insight combined with skill and athleticism to reach the top level. So, yes, in a very real sense you have to know a bit about rocket science, too. It's impossible for me to understand why it took the Winter Olympics until 1998 to add it to medal competition for the first time."

Penski pulled Tina up by the hand and I followed them down to the other end of the room. We found a seat overlooking sheet number five, where some older kids were milling about near the hack about ten feet below us.

"We'll watch these high school boys for a few minutes," he said. "They're good enough to get into the state junior championships this year."

"Most people think that the guy with the rock is the only one making the shot," he started, "but the entire rink will be involved. Let me explain what's really happening when the shooter gets into the hack. See the Skip down there at the far end of the ice? He has to take everything about the conditions and the lay of the rocks into consideration. Then he uses signals to communicate his decision to his players."

"Can't he just point?" Tina asked.

"Well, there's so much more to it than just the direction. He has to consider the curl he needs and the amount of *weight*, or speed, he wants on the shot. He also needs to think about where he wants the other rocks to more or less end up, too."

"And these other two guys with the brooms?" she asked, pointing further down the ice.

"The two sweepers have to be in place and ready to follow the exact instructions. When the shooter is in the hack and the sweepers are in position, they signal back that they understand the shot strategy and are ready to go. The shooter then squares his shoulders and aims his shot at the Skip's broom-head, down there at the far end. If the shot is perfect, it will end up exactly where the Skip expects it to."

"How does the shooter know how hard to throw it to get the shot right?" she asked.

"Well, for most recreational curlers, it's by touch and feel for the ice," Penski continued. "But now days, most of the champion curlers use a stop watch during warm-ups to get the time down. The Skip will yell out a time, like twenty-one or twenty-two. That will be the number of seconds the rock should take if it is thrown with the desired weight — or speed."

"Do they work as a team on every shot?"

"You bet. They have to be in constant communications the entire time, right up until the rock comes to rest."

Tina scooted her chair closer and rested her forehead against the glass. She pointed down to a rock that was slowly hooking to a stop, three sheets to our left.

"Does the shot always curve like that?" she asked. "Like throwing a curve ball?"

It was just the opening old George had been waiting for.

"Most shots take into account some amount of natural curl the last several feet as the shot begins to slow to a stop," he started. "Granite curling rocks don't curl because of aerodynamic physics like a baseball, though. A baseball pitch curves because nature abhors a vacuum. As the pitcher releases the ball with a tight rotation of the laces, lower air pressure develops on one side of the ball, usually along the bottom half. As the ball moves rapidly toward home plate, it will curve toward the side of the lower air pressure — downward— to prevent a vacuum from forming over that surface. As it moves further forward, more and more air releases off the side, causing the largest amount of break or curve to occur in the final few feet near the batter's box."

"Like the wing of an airplane?" she confirmed.

"Yes, in essence a baseball curves for the same reason airplanes fly," Penski continued. "The wings actually lift the plane into the air above them, searching to equalize the air pressure."

"Aerodynamics 101," I deadpanned.

Tina ignored me. "But you're saying that is not the reason a curling stone curves?"

Penski continued.

"As you might guess, a forty-two pound curling stone thrown at a slow pace doesn't react to air pressure. The actual forces that cause a shot to curl are still somewhat of a debate and a physics problem. Some scientists refer to the wet friction theory. First, you have to realize that the bottom of the stone's surface isn't actually flat."

"It's not?" I interrupted.

"No, it's actually slightly concave with only a flat narrow ring that touches the ice. I suspect the concavity helps amplify the rumbling sound. As the rock slowly rotates along its path, friction melts a molecule-thin layer of ice along the leading edge, which reduces the friction at the front. As the running surface passes over it, the layer of water refreezes beneath it. The trailing surface 'bites' into the re-frozen ice molecules, increasing the frictional drag at the rear and slowing its momentum."

"You mean like turning over a glass and spinning it down a wet table? It will curve in the opposite direction of the rotation?" Tina said.

"Well, you would think, but it turns out it curves exactly opposite of that, which perplexes a lot of curlers. As the shot fades to a stop, its forward energy can no longer overcome the frozen surface tension at the rear. The drag along the middle and trailing edge eventually takes over and forces the shot to curl as it starts to slow down."

Tina placed her open hand palm-down on the table and slid it along slowly, trying to emulate the curve of a rock as it crawls to a stop.

"Something like that," Penski smiled as he tapped the back of her hand gently. "Ice conditions change frequently as the game moves along. It's the Skip's job to determine where to set his broom head on the ice as a target for the player taking the shot. Fast, or *keen* ice, may reduce the amount of curl while *swingy* ice may result in a surprising amount of movement. Skips and players must continuously read the ice in order to adjust the speed of their shots and determine the amount of curl to expect. If the Skip gives the player a *wide broom* it means he is expecting a lot of curl. He will set the initial aiming point wide to the left or right of where he wants the rock to stop or strike another rock. A *narrow broom* tells the player that the shot won't move much. If a player delivers his shot directly at the Skip's target, the shot is said to be *on the broom*. If a well-aimed shot does not curl the expected amount, the Skip can be accused of giving the player *too much broom* or conversely, *not enough broom,* if the shot curls too much."

"Depending upon the space between the jumble of rocks scattered in front of the house, the Skip must also decide whether to play for a right or left-hand curl. Traditions on how to call for a specific curl differ around the world and even among curling clubs in different states.

"Some of those practice shots down there are staying straight," Tina jumped in. "Some are curling a lot."

"When a player gives the rock *too much handle*, it will rotate too frequently on its path down the ice, affecting the amount of curl. The *wrong handle* means the player rotated the shot in the wrong direction, in effect causing the rock to zig when it should have zagged."

She pointed to another kid stepping into the hack on the sheet to our immediate left. "I think he's getting ready to throw the rock? Does he have to deliver it in a certain way?"

"No," Penski said, "the rules are pretty forgiving about how to take shots, as long as you release the rock by the time you cross that first blue line out there about twenty-five feet. Some people even use a delivery stick like shuffle board."

"But there is a correct way, right," I clarified.

"More or less," Penski continued. "Let's just say there is an *athletic* way, with some variations between players. Now watch this kid down there. He's a right-hander. He'll set himself with his right foot in the *hack,* similar to starting blocks frozen into the ice."

Tina followed his finger as Penski pointed to the far end of the ice.

"See down at the other end? There's a hack down there, too, for delivering rocks back in this direction. Each time the rinks throw their rocks in one direction, it's called an end. Typically in league play at clubs around Minnesota the games will be eight ends. Four in each direction.

"Eight doesn't seem like enough," she said.

"Well, for championship playdowns, it's not. So they play ten."

It was perplexing to see that Tina was sinking her teeth into curling. She clearly found something in the game that I was never completely able to come to grips with.

Penski pointed down at the ice sheet beneath our table again. "Now watch as the kid comes out of the hack. From a low squat with his broom tucked under his left arm for balance, he'll launch himself forward with the rock. Notice how he doesn't just swing the rock back and forward like a bowling ball. He slides it to the rear, lifts his butt up a little, then thrusts out and follows directly behind the rock with his left sliding foot. Watch how he drags his right toe behind him for stability. His right trailing knee shouldn't touch the ice, although many beginners are referred to as 'knee curlers' for that very reason."

"It looks effortless," Tina observed. "Like the rock is pulling him forward."

"That's the way it should look, when it's done right," Penski affirmed. "It's actually the weight of the rock's momentum coupled with his push off that propels him forward to control the speed of the shot."

"Some of these kids look like they're just lunging and shoving," Tina said.

"Yeah, some are. Many novice players do heave their shots that way. At top levels of the sport, though, it is much more of a subtle art. Something far more athletic and controlled is taking place. As the player moves forward with the rock, he is adjusting his speed, balance and angle. He will make all necessary adjustments to keep everything under his control. At the release point, he will use his fingertips to gently urge the handle into a slow rotation to get the desired curl. Player and rock must each be where they are supposed to be, and on time."

As the kid released the rock, the two boys in front of him began walking quickly ahead of the shot with their brooms at the ready. Tina asked when the sweeping should start.

"That's up to the Skip down at the other end. He aligns himself with the shot and calls out sweeping instructions."

"And does the Skip ever get to shoot?"

"Sure, he usually shoots last and he better be the best shot. When it's his turn, the Third takes over as Vice Skip and holds the broom for a target. But make no mistake, the Skip remains in control."

"What does the sweeping do? Make it curve more?"

Penski chuckled.

"That's what too many people think," he said. "Actually, it's the opposite. Remember, the rock will naturally want to curl because of the rotation. Sweeping keeps the shot from curling too much or stopping too soon. The friction of the broom changes the structure of the ice crystals just enough to prevent the rock from biting in. With aggressive sweeping, the shot will typically stay in a straighter line. Strong, fast sweeping at the perfect distance out front of the rock can keep a shot on target for ten feet or more beyond the point it might otherwise stop."

"So the harder they sweep, the better the shot might be?"

"Well, usually good sweeping can make a difference, but the initial weight and direction of the shot is still ninety percent of its success. Sometimes, the sweepers use their brooms too much and the rock slides too far forward. Other times, they don't need to do anything except keep the path clean."

"So, players on both sides can sweep? The defense can try to sweep so it moves off target."

He pointed to the house below us and smiled, "No. See that thin gray line running horizontally through the middle of the rings? That's called the T-line. The defense isn't allowed to sweep an opponent's rock until it passes that line. Then they sweep hard to try to get it to slide out of scoring range or through the back side of the house."

I was feeling left out and looking for an opportunity to jump in.

"George, you said we should be watching the time and space between the shots. What did you mean by that?"

"Well," he started again, "for the casual observer, you can't really help watching the rock and the sweepers as everything moves in slow motion down the ice. For the first sixty-five years of my curling life, that's the way I watched and played, too. It was a great way to pass four or five nights a week. Then I got the chance to talk to one of the best players in the game who came to this club to play in a bonspiel several years ago. He opened my eyes to what is really going on each time he steps into the hack, whether other players know it or not."

"Take a look at the rocks scattered throughout the house at the far end of this sheet. The strategic possibilities on each end of the ice and across the course of a curling match are infinite. It makes no difference whether you have been curling for a lifetime or have never thrown a meaningful rock in your life — like Jack here."

I was really beginning to dislike the man.

"Hey, I told you that I curled for a year," I protested, trying to save face, but we all knew that anything I tried to add to the conversation would be laughable compared to Penski's insight.

"To make a difference in the game," Penski added, "every player needs to step into the hack with a specific purpose and a clear vision of success. Every rock on the ice is like people: Each has a life and a story of its own to tell. For every decision by the Skip, a thousand other options might have made more sense. Half the people in the crowd would have thrown the rock heavier; the other half would have thrown it lighter. With every stroke of the broom there are fifty armchair curlers who will call the sweepers lazy, but fifty more who would say they worked their brooms too hard."

"So, we're not just watching granite rocks bounce around those rings, huh?"

Old George smiled and continued, "Every shot is like raising a child, sweetheart. When you push off from the hack, it's like giving birth. Then, for the next twenty feet or so, you nurture your rock through youth and adolescence, constantly adjusting the weight, attitude and pressure by adjusting your hands, the drag of your feet, and the angle of your body. Everything you do must be nuanced and subtle. Push too hard and you over-correct. Shift directions too quickly and the shot ends up a confused mess, like so many teenagers today. As you approach the delivery line, you have one final split second to gently encourage, restrain, correct and adjust before sending it on its way into the world."

I rolled my eyes at the ridiculous metaphor but Tina cut me a disapproving look.

"It doesn't look like it takes a lot of effort to throw it that far," Tina said. "Those eight and nine year old girls down there are doing it every time."

"Well, it is a slippery ice surface," Penski chuckled. "Those girls could throw the rock a quarter mile if they needed to. It's not about how hard you throw it. It's how, when and where you bring it to a stop that matters. Stopping a forty-two pound rock dead on a dime across more than one hundred twenty feet of ice isn't a matter of distance. A successful curling shot is a matter of understanding and applying the right pressure."

"Pressure? Explain that one," I snorted.

"Players must apply the right pressure with their arms as they motivate the rock forward; the right pressure with their legs as they launch out of the hack; the right pressure with their trailing toe to control their sliding speed; the right pressure with their fingertips as they gently rotate the handle at the point of release; and the right pressure on the sweeping brooms as they move the rock along its path. It's all about controlling pressure, like being a good steam fitter or plumber."

"Like my father?" I thought. *"Where did that come from?"*

Tina pointed to a group of nine or ten rocks cluttering the house on sheet number four.

"That looks a little like a random checkerboard of scattered rocks," Tina observed.

"Well, I guess it might," Penski continued, "Curling has been called *chess on ice*, but it's an inaccurate analogy. In chess and checkers, players execute every move within a tightly controlled space and according to the rules assigned to each piece. In curling, pre-calculation is important, of course, but strategy and skill are subordinate to the natural laws of $E=mc^2$. At the highest levels of competitive curling, players will make some spectacular shots. Over the years, I've witnessed some of the most incredible shots you would ever want to see."

"It sounds as if it takes years and years to get good at it," Tina speculated.

"Well, thousands of people are good at it. But it's harnessing the intractable physics of energy, velocity, mass and friction that separates the champions. At some clubs with unlevel ice surfaces, even gravity comes into play. Experienced players at most clubs know that some sheets slope downward toward one wall or another. As the players line up their shots, they often confront a widely scattered arrangement of excellence, mediocrity and ne'er-do-wells cluttering the house at the other end of the ice. To win championships, competitive skill isn't enough. Players must take advantage of the intended and unintended consequences of an erratic combination of science, luck and randomness. It's controlling the bad luck and limiting the natural randomness that makes the difference."

"It sounds like a wonderful sport for spectators," Tina offered.

Something struck a chord and I chimed in.

"Yeah, my dad used to claim it's the world's greatest spectator sport."

"Oh, yeah?" he responded. "Then your dad has something in

common with many of the great ones, kid. Champion curlers watch and learn as much as they practice and play."

He pointed down to another kid who was ready to deliver a shot and continued, "After you release your rock at the line, you're putting it right out there for the entire world to love or curse as anyone sees fit. Like all of us, each shot is open to praise, ridicule or indifference along the way. The player's hopes, dreams and prayers for its future ride along with every slow rotation of the handle. As the rock gradually glides toward its destiny, it will be swept along by teammates who serve as its teachers, pastors, coaches, friends and family until the very end."

"All right, George, so every shot is relevant," I said. "So where does practice and skill come in?"

He looked at me incredulously. "Where would anybody be without practice to develop some level of skill? You need to develop muscle memory and the feel for the handle in your hands and the ice under your feet. Nobody is perfect, but nobody needs to be. Like everything else in life, it's as much about nature as nurture. Sometimes the ice doesn't cooperate. Sometimes the humidity in the air changes too quickly. Sometimes there is even debris on the ice. For a thousand reasons, some shots just don't go right. Every player makes mistakes and no player can overcome every obstacle no matter how hard he tries. What matters is how we deal with those miscalculations and natural obstacles. No matter how much we choke on one shot, the next rock gives us another chance at reconciliation and redemption. It's a beautiful game."

"Come on, George," I said with a mocking tone. "These guys aren't stepping into the hack thinking that way on every shot."

"No, maybe not," he sighed with clear disappointment. "But the great ones do." Then he added quietly, "I know Arv Firpo does."

Tina and I took a sideways glance at each other. It wasn't too much of a stretch to figure out that Mary Coventry had called from the USCA to inform him of the connection to Arv Firpo we were hoping to find.

"Do you think my...I mean, will Arv Firpo be here this evening?" I asked.

"No way of knowing," he replied. "There's never any way to know for sure unless or until he shows up. I suppose you hope to get a glimpse of him, too."

"Yeah, it would be fun to tell my grandkids someday that I saw him play," I said.

"We'll know tonight," Penski replied. "When Arv comes here to play, he doesn't do things the normal way. All of a sudden, you'll look out on the ice and he's out there playing Skip."

"Can't you set up the rules so he has to show ID or something when he checks in?" I asked, trying not to sound too interested.

"Ha! I heard that a club up north somewhere tried that a few years ago. He turned and walked out the door and hasn't returned since. He's quite a celebrity. Other players think it's an honor to get the opportunity to lose to him. Even a rumor that he might play at a particular bonspiel will fill the registration slots. Whatever reasons he has for living like a ghost are his own, so we let it go at that."

"Well, when can we talk about the DuMot family?" I asked.

"I'm afraid I can't right now, Jack. I'm sorry. I used up all of my time talking with this charming young lady. Now, I've got to get these kids going with their league matches. You two can hang around here for warmth, or come back tonight after all the teams start playing. Matches start at seven o'clock or a little later, by the time we get everything organized. If Firpo is coming, you'll find him out on the ice. We can talk more about your family then."

Penski walked back downstairs and gathered the school kids around him on the ice. He was clearly in his own element. I suspected that if he never had to leave the club to eat or sleep, he wouldn't.

"We should all have something we love with that much devotion," Tina said as we watched him animating his instructions. "That old man has spent his entire life preaching from this pulpit."

I recalled a favorite line I picked up from a medieval philosophy class during my junior year in college.

"Dio mi guardi da chi studia un libro solo," I said in butchered Italian. "God save me from the man who studies but one book."

Late Friday Afternoon, February 8th, 2008

Tina thought it might be interesting to stay in the arena and watch the youth league but I was too nervous about possibly meeting my dead father in just a few short hours. Although it was colder than bearable outside, I wanted to get some fresh air. We agreed to meet up with Penski again at about 7:15, after he was clear of his responsibility to get the matches rolling. Besides, if my dad did show up, I didn't want to chance running into him alone in the parking lot. In the event *Skip* had been following us, finding us isolated would be his best opportunity. As long as we stayed together, we were safe. The trick would be catching him immediately after his match, before he vaporized once again into thin air.

"Two days on the road and you're already thinking like a ghost," Tina chuckled. "I'm sure your father would be proud."

We filled the remainder of our afternoon walking the length of East Lincoln Avenue to check out the Fergus Falls main street, stepping inside often to take advantage of the warmth. On several occasions, I tried to open up a conversation about the previous night but Tina always managed to block it back, often returning the discussion to curling or George Penski.

"Did you catch something Penski said?" I asked, trying to sound engaging.

"George said a lot of things," she answered. "He sure knows a lot about curling."

"Yeah, he sure looks at the sport in a philosophical way," I concurred. "I'm not sure I buy all of that metaphorical and metaphysical junk he was spewing. A lot of people who don't know very much try to cover it up with pseudo-philosophy."

"He's the guru around here, Jack," she said. "Those kids and club members have probably learned everything they know about the sport from him. Probably some things about life, too. Some people actually do know their stuff, you know."

I could tell she was aiming her comments at me and I was grateful she chose not to say more.

"So, what did you think was so odd about something he said?" she asked.

"It was when he was talking about the curler releasing the rock at the blue line. He said the player and rock must each be where they're supposed to be and on time. Remember that night in my living room, when you told me your aunt used to say, 'We are each where we are supposed to be, and we're on time.'"

"Yeah, I do remember," she said. "I'm impressed that you remember it, though, Jack. Cute philosophical sayings...is that what it takes to make an impression on you?"

"I got that from my dad," I said, suddenly remembering one or two of his favorites. "I just never thought I would pick up on them, too."

We spent the next hour and a half commenting on the obvious as we came across mundane items of interest and disinterest in the various store windows. We stepped into Bella Cucina Café for a pizza, just as the afternoon light was fading into gray. I finally decided that I couldn't evade the topic any further.

"So, Tina," I dared to begin, "where are *we* supposed to be? And are we on time?"

"After last night, you mean?"

"After last night, I mean."

She took a large swallow of her diet cola and cleared her throat, but no words came out.

"We're going to have to talk about it sometime," I continued, "whether my dad shows up at the bonspiel this evening or not. In a few hours, we'll be checking into another hotel room. I can't face that until I figure out what happened between us last night."

"Between us, Jack?" she said, "I guess nothing happened between us last night, did it?"

It was as if she had been waiting and preparing for her opening all day. And probably, she had been.

"I thought it would be okay to come to you last night, completely honest and vulnerable. Nothing happened. You didn't — or maybe couldn't — respond. You fell asleep. I fell asleep. When I woke up an hour later, I moved back to my own bed. As far as I'm concerned, nothing happened last night. I'm trying to make a decision about us, Jack. I took a gamble. I'm sorry if I pressured you into something you weren't ready for. I guess we aren't there yet. Or at least maybe you're not there yet, that's all."

My knack for knowing exactly the wrong thing to say at precisely the wrong time suddenly reared its ugly head.

"You say I'm not there yet, Tina, but you're the one still trying to decide about Gary. What was I supposed to do last night? Hold both of you in my arms?"

"And LaVon, too," Tina shot back.

An awkward moment of silence later, she continued, "I was expecting to find something between us last night, but I don't know...maybe we lost something instead. I'm not mad. Just rejected and embarrassed. I'll get over it."

I was struck dumb. What corner of hell was this crawling out of? By my reckoning, I had done everything right. I thought it was a moment of pure discovery about me, about her...and about us. Whatever shape *us* or *we* might eventually turn out to be, I was determined to do things right. And that meant allowing the relationship to tenderize in its own juices. This was NOT going to be another LaVon story, born in an inferno of smoke and blaze, only to crash and burn when the sparks died away. No, ma'am. This time I was determined to do things right. We were going to start things with a flicker, blow on the embers with friendship, then stoke the fires with self-esteem and respect for each other. Or at least I thought we were.

That few minutes lying awake in that cold bed, soaking in the warmth of her flannelled body was the most tender, sexiest moment of my life. Was it really nothing more than a lost gamble for her?

I was at a loss for words and a tingle of frustration crawled under my skin. I began recalling the times LaVon and I struggled to get a firm toehold in the shifting sands of our marriage. *"You sooo love to fight,"* I once told her. *"Most people wouldn't cross the kitchen floor to get into an argument. You would cross a frozen lake and climb a mountain of broken glass in your bare feet to start a good spat."* But it would be disingenuous to say that I didn't get caught up in those scrappier moments, as well. To my surprise, I often did. Perhaps I even came to enjoy the emotional resuscitation from time to time.

But domestic hostility on LaVon's turf proved to be a foreign battleground for me; impossible to sustain the fight and hold the high ground. I was fighting guerrilla warfare in LaVon's own jungle and it wore me down. It came as an epiphany when a co-worker suggested that I was under no legal or moral obligation to come out loaded for bear for each attack. The next time LaVon and I re-engaged in one of our frequent skirmishes, I simply waved the white flag and withdrew to our front porch, much as my father used to do.

"I'm afraid I'm just not going to be much fun anymore," I once said as I gently pulled the door closed behind me for added effect. When I peeked back in through the window, she was kneeling in a fetal position on the sofa with her face buried in a cushion, sobbing uncontrollably. A flood of regret rushed through me. I had snuffed out the only flame that lit up her life. Perhaps Tony Perkovich was the lighted match that restored some of that heat.

But with Tina, I was getting a do-over and I was going to do it over right. Although I knew full god-damned well that I was about to say the wrong thing, I said it anyway.

"Tina, you were the one who made it clear about the sleeping arrangements last night. You know...you saw...how I feel about you. It took everything I had to respect you. If things had been different and I had been the one to crawl into bed with you, would you be feeling this way?"

We grew silent until I pressed forward with one final thought too far.

"You said we lost something last night. Well, I didn't lose anything and I don't think you did, either. I think I found something incredibly wonderful, holding you in my arms under those covers."

She didn't answer and we spent the remainder of the meal in tangible uneasiness. She finally broke the silence, "Jack, we have to settle something much more important than why we didn't make love last night."

"Do tell," I said with no lack of condescension in my tone.

"If you'll step back from your self-pity party for a second, you'll recall that more than our hearts are on the line here. We haven't even talked about what we're going to do if we find your father out on that curling ice tonight."

She was right, of course. I had become so fixated on searching for him that I never considered what I would do if or when I found him. What would my next step be after we came face-to-face? Finding him wouldn't change anything about the danger we were in. I had played the tape a thousand times in my head and it always ended with some variation on the same theme: I would give him a tear-filled silent hug, *"Oh, God, it's great to see you again, Dad."* He, of course, would hug me back and say, *"I knew you would find me, Jack. Just let me look at you. God, it's great to see you again."* But then the mental picture always faded to black as we held each other at arm's length and looked into each other's weepy eyes; our worlds once again coming back together.

"Let me put the question into clearer perspective," she added. "Good for you, Jack! You found him! Now what?"

"W-Well," I stammered, "I guess I'll try to talk him into coming somewhere private with us so we can talk things through and find a way to get us all out of this mess."

"And where do you suggest?" she asked. "A dark vacant parking lot on the outskirts of town somewhere? So *Skip* gets all three of us together in an isolated place?"

"All right, Tina," I said, embarrassed that I didn't have a better answer. "I get your point. Just because we find him doesn't mean we're in the clear. But what else do you suggest?"

"Look," she said, "your dad's been in a deep freeze, hiding for six years. You've been searching for him for — how long? Six weeks? Let's allow him to take the lead? Let's assume he knows you're looking for him. It could even be that Sam Ruude has contacted him somehow to tell him he'll be meeting us tomorrow morning. Your father shouldn't be too surprised wherever or whenever you happen to suddenly turn up in his life. Chances are, he's given this a lot more thought than we have. Maybe, for instance, eight or ten years more thought than we have."

"But I have so much to say to him, Tina. So much I want to tell him."

"So much to say?" she replied with a gentle smile. "Yeah, I

suppose you do. Okay, let's see how well you do. Tell me your next sentence after, *'Gee, Dad, it's great that you're not really dead.'* Go!"

I could have done without the sarcasm, but I knew she was right. If we somehow survived and if I ever did find him, I would need a lifetime of therapy. I could get a handle on why he walked out on my family. I could even admit that my indifference to him had something to do with it all. With Tina's help, I was even beginning to understand why he might have wanted me to find him, despite the danger. It wasn't his reasons that bugged me. It was his methods. If he could find the means to become one of the most popular men in U.S. curling, why couldn't he find the means to stay in contact with me somehow? If I had never looked under Crampton's bush or had never randomly stumbled into the Mapleton Curling Club, would I have been any the wiser?

Early Friday Evening, February 8th, 2008

We drove through the over-crowded curling club parking lot a few minutes before seven p.m. then settled for off-street parking down the block. Tina thought it might be a good idea to sit in the car a few minutes longer, if for no other reason than to finish our coffee and cocoa. In truth, we didn't want to go inside before we were certain the players would all be on the ice warming up or starting their games. In the event my father was still in the lobby and saw me, it would be difficult for us to make our greetings anonymously. Secretly, though, I knew that I wanted the chance to see him on my terms, hidden among the faces in the crowd. It would put me more at ease while steeling myself for whatever might happen next.

After a minute or two of silent fidgeting, Tina spoke.

"I didn't lose anything last night in that hotel room either, Jack. If I had really wanted to make something happen in that bed, I could have."

"In those pink flannel pajamas?" I asked with a smile.

"Yes," she smiled smugly. "Even in my pink flannel pajamas."

I smiled at her feminine bravado, "You know, Tina, women may find this hard to believe, but men aren't like old cars. We don't always start up with the crank of a handle."

"That's never been my experience with the handles I've cranked," she giggled. "All I'm trying to say is that I'm so sorry about all of this, Jack."

"Forget it," I replied. "I'm the one who should be apologizing to you. A few days ago, you were living the life of a happily unemployed Midwestern girl thinking about moving back home with your family. Now you're on the run, freezing your ass off outside a two-bit curling club and staking your life on finding a walking, talking dead man. Maybe we haven't lost each other, but we sure have lost our senses. So don't be sorry about any of this. None of it is your fault."

"No," she started, "none of it is my fault...but it's all my doing."

At a quarter after the hour, we walked into the club to find George Penski standing behind the registration table finishing up the final details of checking off names and counting the entrance fees. We remained near the chilly entrance area with only a narrow view of one small portion of the ice. From our vantage point, we could only see a handful of players milling around their rocks. Nobody resembling my father appeared to be among the players I could see. But I wouldn't know for certain until I was pacing back and forth in front of the plexiglass, carefully reviewing the players on all six sheets.

When George finally looked up, he gave us polite smile, nodded hello and waved us further into the warm lobby.

"Will you still have some time to tell me about my dad and his family?" I asked as nonchalantly as possible.

"You bet," he answered. "I'm looking forward to it. I'll be finished here in a few minutes. We can pull up a table in the bar upstairs again while the games are going on."

"Any chance Firpo showed up?" I asked.

One shake of his head told us everything we needed to know. "All the players are accounted for and are out on the ice. I've been here since everyone started arriving about five o'clock and haven't missed a face. Arv never walked past me."

I can't honestly say I wasn't relieved, although I can't describe my disappointment, either. I told Penski that we would be upstairs and took Tina by the hand as we walked through the lobby. About ten minutes later, he pulled up a chair and joined us at our table.

"Your father never told you anything about his family?" he started. "He never told you about your grandparents?"

"Nothing much. Just that they died when he was a fairly young man. I know they were farmers down south of here, in a small town called Gluek."

"I know Gluek," he continued. "Your grandparents Pete and Medora took over that farm from your maternal great grandparents. They worked it pretty hard for a lot of years but things started getting tough for those little homestead plots. Things changed so quickly for those small grain elevator towns. That's why I sold out when I could."

"What can you tell me about their deaths?"

"Yeah, they died," he said. "That's the best way to say it, I guess." He stood and walked over to the glass wall and gazed down at the games taking place on the sheets below.

"Something is wrong, Tina," I said quietly. "He either doesn't remember much or he doesn't much want to talk about what he does remember. Do you feel it?"

"Yeah, Jack," she whispered, "but I'm surprised that you feel it, too. You're getting better at this whole *humanity* thing we have going on here."

George returned to our table and stood pensively behind his chair for a brief moment, as if trying to figure out where to start. Finally, he walked to the bar to order a beer and offered to buy us a drink, as well. When we all settled in again, he seemed a little more at ease.

"Your grandparents were good hardworking farmers," he started. "They were good family folks, too, but that Tommy, whew, what a firecracker. I'm sorry to say that Jack, but he was just no good. From the moment he could make sense of things, that kid was nothing but trouble for the family and the whole county."

I looked incredulous. "He was a trouble-maker as a kid? I didn't think anyone could ever say that about him. I always figured him as the straightest arrow in the quiver."

But the old man wasn't smiling. Tina caught the serious look on his face and gave me a quick glance.

"What kind of trouble are you talking about, George?" she asked. "Drugs and alcohol? Violence? Robbery?"

"All of that and more, young lady. Everybody wondered how Pete and Medora could put up with him. He'd get into some real trouble and Pete would bail him out and beat the piss out of him to try to straighten him out again. Pete oughtn't have done that, but it made no difference, anyway. A week or so later, the kid would be back in one jail or another."

"But he disappeared from town at some point?" I asked.

"Yeah the cops busted him for something real serious. Seems like it was in the Dakotas somewhere, but I don't recall for sure. It was about that time that I sold the farm and moved here to Fergus, so I never kept track. Besides, one year starts running into the next with me now. It could have been the 1960s or it could have been last Tuesday."

"Serious trouble? How serious?" Tina asked.

"Oh, I'm afraid I don't recall what it was, honey. Pete and Medora should have given him back to the people that screwed them out of their money."

"Given him back?" I scoffed. "What do you mean given him back? Give him back to where?"

"You really never heard this about your old man? Your grandparents took him in as a foster kid — when he was just a toddler," he answered. "It was sometime in the mid-1950s. Then they adopted him after a couple of years. That's when the trouble started. Everyone would have understood it if they had just called it quits and given the kid back. I guess I'm not surprised that he never told you."

My mind was reeling. My meek and humble dad being arrested for anything more than J-walking just didn't add up. Foster child? Adopted? It just wouldn't have been possible for my parents to keep this quiet from me all those years. Particularly through their divorce when my mother was so furious with him. The thought of him being physically beaten by his father was more than I cared to hear.

"No redeeming qualities at all?" I asked sullenly.

"Only one that I recall, son," Penski answered. "He was a great curler. Yes, sir, one hell of a gifted curler. In my book, that's saying quite a lot, no matter what other problems he may have had."

Tina must have seen that I was growing agitated. She began asking some questions that I wouldn't have thought to ask.

"Tommy was a good curler?" she asked. "How good, George. Tell me...I mean tell us more about that part of him."

"Not much to tell," he continued. "Montevideo used to have a great club. We had some of the best curlers in the state back then, and that meant some of the best curlers in the country. There wasn't much on TV in the fifties and sixties. All the men in small towns spent their winters drinking, bowling or curling. A lot of us did all three. Pete and Medora were known at clubs throughout western Minnesota. It was only natural that any DuMot kid that came along would be a curler, too. Hell, that family was as regular as clockwork on league nights. Curling was the only thing that seemed to keep Tommy focused. As I recall, that local rink of his made it pretty far up the ladder at junior playdowns for about five years until..."

"My father never said a word about any of this to me," I interrupted.

"It's all news to me, too," Tina said. "I mean, Bill must have been part of that world, too. He never told me anything about curling when he was a kid."

"Bill?" Penski asked in surprise. "You mean Bill Ordway from Gluek? You knew Willy, too? He was a pretty good junior curler, himself, but not as good as the DuMots. I think that was a pretty big disappointment to his stepfather."

"His stepfather?" I cut him off. "Could that have been a guy named Freddy Schade? Mary Coventry at the USCA told me a little about him."

"Hey, who's telling this story?" he asked, surprised. "Yeah, Freddy Schade. Cripes, now there's a name I thought I'd never hear again. In 1968 or '69 — no, it was '69 — I was in my early forties and curling at the top of my game. I was slated to be the alternate — the fifth man — on a rink that made it all the way through the regional playdowns. I never got into any of the games, though. Schade was the Skip who put the team together but he never liked me much. He said I didn't play aggressively enough. He complained that I thought too much about my shots. That I was too careful. As if those qualities are bad things, huh? Anyway, he was outvoted somehow and I made it as an alternate for the playdowns. A week before the nationals in Grand Forks, though, I got myself busted up pretty bad and couldn't travel."

"What happened? A farm accident?" I asked.

"You'd think, wouldn't you?" he continued. "No, nothing quite so heroic, I'm afraid. We were practicing during the regular men's league one night. The old Montevideo club didn't have any of these fancy raised walkways between the sheets like clubs have now. They just put a narrow strip of carpet down. You had to be careful not to step too far sideways onto the ice. There weren't as many lawyers in those days, so clubs didn't worry so much about safety. While I was clearing off some rocks, a young punk on the next sheet made a shot with enough weight to take out the side of the building. It rolled off another rock and headed toward our sheet. It skipped right over the carpet strip and I couldn't jump out of the way fast enough."

"It took your feet out from under you, huh?" Tina asked.

"Hard enough to knock me ass-over-noggin," he continued. "I woke up in the hospital that night with a concussion and my left foot in a cast. When it came time to select a new alternate for Grand Forks, Schade nixed some older curlers with more experience and went with Tommy. I recall that Mickey Bellows was furious about picking the kid. Bellows was a cop on the Montevideo police force. In fact, I think he *was* the Montevideo police force back then. He knew the kid's track record and made no bones about how much he disliked him."

"Jack, did you hear that?" Tina said. "Mickey Bellows. That's Mike Bellows from the Thief River Falls rehab center. Could that be the reason he was on the list?"

Penski continued, "Anyway, Tommy couldn't have been more than a young seventeen years old at the time, but Freddy loved his *no-*

guts-no-glory style."

"I'm sorry you never got your big chance, George" Tina said.

"Hell, it wouldn't have mattered, sweetheart. Schade wouldn't have let me sweep out his locker during those championship playdowns. I knew that."

The three of us grew pensive and quiet for a moment. Tina traced her fingernail along an imaginary line on her napkin and drew a few more invisible doodles. She appeared to be calculating something in her head. So was I.

"It's all starting to make more sense to me now," she finally said.

"There's not much more I can recall," Penski continued. "Let's just say that your grandparents were good people, Jack. You said that Tommy joined the military after everything was all over, eh? We always wondered what ever happened to him after doing his stretch. I recall hearing that some kids from town enlisted toward the end of Viet Nam. I guess that would make sense that your dad followed those other boys in there. For misfits back then, it was join or jail. The military must have straightened him out though. Here you are; his strong, handsome young son with a beautiful young lady on your arm. I'll be damned if he didn't turn out all right, despite everyone's worst predictions."

Tina smiled. I couldn't.

"You said 'after doing his stretch.' So my dad eventually ended up spending some time in jail?

"He certainly must have, son. It was something big. As I recall, though, he came back to live on the farm for awhile under Pete and Medora's supervision, waiting for prison. I never heard where he ended up doing time or for how many years, though."

"But you don't recall what he was arrested for?" Tina asked.

"I'm sorry, honey. I can't recall my own kids' names half the time."

No wonder my father never said anything about his younger years, I thought. Who would have? I ran a timeline in my head. In jail until — when — maybe nineteen. In the Navy for six years and then he met and married my mother when he was twenty-six years old, where I was eventually added to the story. My calculations may have been off by a year or more, but some things just didn't fit snuggly enough. I couldn't account for a few years. If nothing else, though, it explained why Dad never attended college: He likely never finished high school. I figured he must have completed his GED while in prison or in the Navy. Somehow or another, though, he got accepted to the union's apprentice pipefitter's program.

"So what more can you tell me about my grandparents' deaths?" I asked. "I understand there are still some unanswered questions."

"No, the questions have all been answered," he said. "But there are always conspiracy nuts out there. You'll find them in every small town — and in Dallas. You've heard that your grandparents both died on their birthdays?"

"Yup," I said. "An old guy at the cemetery pointed it out to me."

"That must have been old Eddie Knoblechner," he chuckled. "Christ, he's been the gravedigger around those parts since they buried Moses."

"My grandparents each died on their fifty-sixth birthdays," I went on, "exactly two years apart. So what do you think? Are the deaths suspicious? Or just pure coincidence?"

The old man appeared to be dazed and a little tired. "That was a long time ago, son, and those were tough times for our little farm town. I don't remember anything about it anymore. Since my stroke, I've been diagnosed with some Alzheimer's, too."

"I feel like I have more questions now than when I first walked in here this afternoon," I said, disappointed.

"Look, I'm sorry, son," he replied. "And I'm busy this evening. I've got to get back downstairs to the bonspiel. The players will be coming off the ice and I'll need to set up the next matches. This bar will be hopping and we'll need all the tables to seat everyone for food and drinks. That's where the money is. Tomorrow's Saturday. I'll be here in the morning at eight o' clock. Losers' bracket games start at nine. Stop by and we'll talk some more. Stick around and you'll see some pretty damned good curling between now and Sunday afternoon, even if Firpo isn't here."

"No, I'm afraid we have to pull out pretty early to get over to Alexandria tomorrow morning."

"It sounds like you're running all over the place," he said.

"We suspect that Arv Firpo isn't his real name," I admitted. "When he comes around here, don't you recognize him from years ago, when he may have curled using a different name?"

"You mean his real name, like your father, Tommy DuMot?" Penski asked.

"Well, yeah," I said. "I guess it wasn't too hard to figure out why we're so interested in him, huh?"

"Well, as I said, I have a bit of a memory problem. So many years have passed since our old glory days down in Montevideo. No, I've never recognized him after all these years. You have to remember that when I knew his family, I was already in my thirties and forties. Tommy was just a sixteen-year-old kid. Even then, I never really knew him personally but everyone knew *of* him. People change a lot in forty years. Firpo never told me he knew me from way back then. With my memory all shot to hell, I never recalled his face. I never put Arv Firpo and Tommy DuMot together, though. But it makes perfect sense, now that you mention it. I'm not sure whether to say anything next time I see him, though. If I had his shady background, I'd want to change my name, too. He may stop coming by if he discovers I'm on to him."

"Yeah," I said. "From what I'm learning about him, I think you're probably right."

"Oh, I don't know," Tina jumped in. "It makes sense that he stops by to talk to you about the things he loves, Mr. Penski. You're like a curling god. He probably isn't too proud of his past and doesn't want to talk about it with anyone. But with you he can talk about the things that are important in his life. We're not sure about any of this. As you can tell, we don't even know what questions to ask. That's why we're here. We're trying to find out."

"But we can't just hang around here talking to you and waiting for him to show up," I added apologetically. "No matter how certain you are that he'll eventually return, just sitting in one place and waiting is no way to find him. We'll never know what hour of the day or night he might walk through the door. I'll keep searching."

Penski policed our empty beer cups and dropped them into the trash bin near the bar and disappeared down the stairs.

"A dead end," Tina said. "I guess that means our search will live to see another night, huh?"

"No," I said, "it wasn't a dead end. It led us down a road we never imagined. I can't believe Penski was talking about my father, Tina. He couldn't have been. It's the second or third time I've heard somebody refer to the *whole DuMot family*. He said Tommy was a foster child before he was adopted. It didn't sound as if my grandfather was that kind of a saint. People trying to make a go of a small farm in the late 1950s just wouldn't see any profit in taking on a young mouth to feed. They might take in a teenager to help with the chores, but certainly not an emotionally unstable toddler just out of diapers. Not without a compelling reason."

"What compelling reason?" Tina asked.

I thought for a moment, "A compelling reason like a family. Maybe my grandfather was really the kid's illegitimate father. Or maybe my grandmother couldn't have children and pined for a family."

"You're stretching it, Jack," Tina said. "Just because you don't like the idea that your dad was a hoodlum doesn't mean he wasn't one. As a teenager, he may have been every bit the juvenile delinquent George said he was. People change. I changed. Maybe he did, too."

"But George was surprised to learn that Tommy followed the other boys into the Navy," I continued. "He specifically said, *those other boys*."

"Yeah, maybe he meant some of the other kids in town," Tina answered.

"Maybe," I replied quickly, "But I don't think so. I think we know who they were. One would have been Bill Ordway. The other would have been an older brother, Arvil. Who I am beginning to believe is really my dad — not the younger Tommy."

I crunched the numbers in my head and drew a line and some dates on the back of my napkin. Based on the timeline we had been following, the years and dates suddenly didn't quite add up for the younger Tommy to be my father. But the numbers worked perfectly for Arv, a couple of years older.

"I saw you doing the numbers earlier, too, Tina. You see it, too. It explains so much."

"No, it doesn't make sense, Jack," Tina said. "Why wouldn't your parents have told you any of this? If you're so sure of yourself, let's go down there and ask George one more question. It's a simple yes or no. Certainly his memory is still good enough to tell us whether the DuMots had two sons."

We pushed our way through the gathering crowd of players coming off the ice. Tina avoided the crush by remaining near the trophy case as I looked for Penski. I found him yucking it up at the bonspiel bracket board as he posted the winners and losers. I got his attention and he agreed to step aside for a moment.

"I thought I made it clear," he said. "Yes, your father had an older brother, Arvil. He was a great kid. From what I recall, he was at least two years older."

I called Tina over to hear what Penski had to say.

"Everyone in town knew that Arv and Tommy were inseparable. They were like alter egos, like Yin and Yang. Arv was sociable, willing to walk among people, talking and sharing stories. It was as if he wanted to be part of us. He seemed to know that he needed to earn people's respect. Tommy was the unapproachable one. He wasn't arrogant really; just more aloof when he was around people. When he wasn't on the ice, he would just sit at a table upstairs in the snack bar with a cigarette dangling from his lips. Even as a teenager the kid was already a pack-and-a-half a day smoker. Hell, it seemed like everyone was a heavy smoker back then."

"Was Tommy just insecure or misunderstood, maybe?" Tina asked, still wanting to believe the best in him.

"There was no way of knowing for sure," Penski said. "You couldn't approach him to get a handle on him...unless it was to sit at his table to share a smoke. Then he would act like your best friend for about ten minutes. We'd look up from the ice and see him in the upstairs bar like he was sitting in a cloud, observing things from on-high, judging everything about us. It's like I said, the kid was a great curler but he expected people to respect him just for being there. People were afraid of him but nobody could ever really get to know him. Nobody except Arv and Willy Ordway, anyway. Tommy didn't seem to care if anyone liked him. He just demanded their respect."

"How did Bill — I mean Willy fit into things?" Tina asked.

"Well, then there was the third corner of the triangle— Willy Ordway. He seemed to tie everything together. If you wanted anything to do with the DuMot boys, you knew you had to deal with Willy. Those three boys lived for each other. You didn't see one without the others. At least until Tommy was arrested and sent up."

Tina continued.

"George, you said that Jack's grandfather used to physically punish Tommy. Any chance Tommy got revenge?"

"Well," Penski replied, "like I said, he was the most convenient one to blame at the time of Pete's murder, but the timing was all wrong. It was our understanding that he pleaded guilty to something pretty serious. You have to remember, after the curling season ended in those small farming towns, nobody saw much of each other over the spring and summer. After harvest one year, when the club opened again, all three boys were gone. The only thing we heard was that Arvil and Willie joined the Navy after Tommy got sent up. It wasn't the kind of thing you asked the family about some Sunday morning after church lets out, you know."

"So, he would have been in prison when my grandparents died a couple of years later?"

"Absolutely," he answered. "No question. The police investigated in case there was foul play, but farm accidents happened all the time back then. The cops didn't have much to go on. I don't suppose they looked very hard. It may have smelled like murder, but it looked like an accident. That was enough to close the case for a little county sheriff's department with only a handful of cops on the payroll. I recall that the feds came around and questioned a few of us, but nothing more ever came of it. Eventually, everyone had to accept that your grandparents' deaths were quirky accidents."

"And you never heard from Tommy again?"

"No," he continued. "Nobody ever heard from any of them three boys again. Well, at least until now. Explain it to me again, son...If your dad is Arv."

"I once thought I had it figured out, George" I said, "but now I'm not so sure about anything."

"Well, son, if Arv is still alive, and if he is your father — not Tommy — well, I wouldn't necessarily be any too proud of that fact, either."

"Why? What do you mean by that?" I asked, but he was already several feet away and waving me off with the back of his hand.

I followed him for a step or two, begging for a few extra minutes until joined me at my side.

"That's enough, Jack," she said, as we watched him disappear into the crowd. "I think we got everything we're going to get out of him. He may know more about your family, but I don't think he knows anything more that will help us."

Tina held my arm as we made our way back to the parked car. Neither of us knew quite what to make of what we had just learned.

"Okay," she said, "so you know you have an Uncle Tommy that you never knew about. From the way George sounded, your parents must have had good reason never to tell you. But at least it tells us who may have been paying the property taxes on the farm all these years."

"Yeah, maybe," I said, "but apparently nobody is living on the property."

My mind was racing through George Penski's revelations.

"Tina, George said that Tommy was arrested for something very serious back when he was a teenager. Something serious enough to get a seventeen-year old kid charged as an adult. The lady at the USCA said there was an accident at the national championships around then. One entire team was run over by a van driven by a deranged teenage drunk driver. She mentioned that Bill's stepfather was the Skip of the Minnesota rink that year. The way George was talking, I think Tommy may have been that kid arrested for the DUI and homicide accident. Nobody in town ever learned what happened afterward the arrest. Tommy must have been sent to prison for several years."

"How does any of this tie to your dad now?"

"I'm not sure, but if Tommy was the alternate on the team that year, my dad and Bill would certainly have made the trip to Grand Forks with him. If the three boys were inseparable, it's even possible all three were connected to the accident somehow. That could be the tie-in."

"No wonder George said you shouldn't be too proud that Arv is your father," she added.

We approached the car and I fumbled for my keys to unlock the doors. Tina checked her cell phone one final time and quickly thumbed in a text message, then dropped the phone into her purse and climbed into the passenger seat. I brushed a light layer of frost off the windshield and slid behind the wheel. While the engine warmed for a moment, I reached into the back seat and pulled out my father's old letter to Bill.

"Okay, so you have a long-lost uncle, along with your long-lost dad," she said. "He must have had his reasons for acting so wild back then, don't you think?"

"He may not be so different from my father or any of the rest of us. Maybe getting into trouble with the law was the only thing that gave him something to get excited about in a little town like Gluek. The writer Susan Sontag once wrote, *"Existence is no more than the precarious attainment of relevance in an intensely mobile flux of past, present, and future."* It's a big world. It's immeasurably bigger than I ever wanted it to be. Out here, it seems to be getting bigger every day, in fact. We can't really hide from it and it's too easy to get lost in it. I guess we all try to manage it by finding our own relevance somehow. For Tommy, it may have been tipping cows and burning down the neighbor's chicken coop. For old George Penski, it's running that curling club back there."

"For me, it was Bill Ordway," Tina said.

I suddenly pictured myself sitting with LaVon at our little green dinette table, nibbling a late-evening snack together. Though it was less than three-hours away down Interstate 94, James Avenue seemed a world removed from Gluek or Fergus Falls — or Mankato — and wherever else this search would take me.

"And I used to believe it was sitting in my little brick house trying to make sense of the world," I acknowledged. "You were right, Tina. This is part of everyone's true story. We never give up the search to understand what our lives mean."

"You are right, Jack," she said as we clicked our seat belts and pulled away from the curb. "I can promise you we never do."

Friday Night, February 8th, 2008

After a quick drive through town searching for an available motel, we decided that our best option would be to backtrack to Interstate 94 toward Alexandria, about forty-five miles southeast. Reaching behind her to pick up the manila envelope from the rear seat, Tina pulled out a sheet of paper and flipped on the visor reading light. She studied the photo closely for a full minute or more before speaking.

"I don't know, Jack. You may be right. I guess you could make all the pieces fit into place if your dad is Arv and Tommy was his younger brother. Every piece that is, except why your dad would assume his brother's name."

"Well," I answered. "I can't answer that one, but it sure seems to fit, doesn't it?"

"In this photograph it looks like these boys were all in their mid- to late-teens. So this may actually be your dad with Tommy and Bill."

"I think we can assume it is. The back of the photo says the picture was taken in April. If I'm right about the connection between Tommy and the drunk driving incident in Grand Forks, though, it's perplexing. Penski said the kid was in my grandparents' custody on the farm, waiting for sentencing. The playdowns would probably have been about mid-February...maybe as late as the beginning of March. If that is Tommy in the picture, what was he doing on a road trip in April. What were any of those boys doing on a road trip in April? They weren't out of high school yet."

"Spring break?" Tina suggested.

I could only laugh. "To Milwaukee?"

We decided to drive the entire distance to Alexandria before following a highway sign pointing up an exit ramp toward a handful of hotels. We selected the Kensington Runes Motor Inn, where we had our choice of rooms on the lower level. After checking in, we moved our car to an open space immediately in front of our room door. I hoisted our travel bags onto my shoulder for the short carry inside. To Tina's surprise, I also gathered everything from our backseat and dumped the entire pile across one of the twin beds inside the room.

"Well, I guess that's where you'll be sleeping tonight," she chuckled.

I sat on the bed and began sifting through the papers and notes. I felt certain I was on to something about Tommy and Arv DuMot, even if Tina still wasn't convinced. I intended to take all night, if necessary, to review everything in the pile. I didn't expect to find any further information about my father's whereabouts, but I hoped to at least confirm that Tommy was the one arrested at that tournament.

As Tina showered, I organized every note, printout, list and other piece of evidence we had assembled. I slid over to the desk and signed onto the motel's WiFi connection. I looked again at the pile scattered in front of me, wondering where to begin. My eye happened to fall first on the phone number to the Grand Forks Police Department, scribbled near one edge of the writing board. I decided I would call them first thing in the morning. If I could have them check arrest records or at least put me in touch with Detecive Paul Gombrich, I would be in business. Forty years wasn't an eternity. The DUI hit-and-run must have been one of the most memorable tragedies to occur in Grand Forks. Perhaps someone could tell me the name of the kid arrested on that terrible night.

I heard the bathroom door open and Tina say softly, "Are you going to keep me warm tonight, Jack?"

I looked up to see her standing in a silky, deep-red nightie, pulled tight against her figure; the hem extending mid-way down her thighs. I could smell the lotion on her arms and legs. After her reaction from the previous night, I had every reason to expect her to come out wearing a gunnysack, facial mud and hair curlers.

"You packed this along with you?" I said in surprise, reaching out to pinch and roll the hem between my thumb and forefinger.

"It folds up pretty small," she said. "I was hoping to find a good use for it. After last night, I thought I'd go for something a little more stimulating than flannel. Do you like it?"

"Yeah," I said, allowing my hand to follow the contour of her slender waist. "It'll look great lying on the floor."

I pulled her onto my lap and gently kissed her ears and neck. When my hand found her thigh and buttocks, I quickly discovered she was leaving no room for doubt. "Are you going to tell me exactly how we're going to handle things again tonight?" I whispered into her ear. "Or is it my turn to tell you?"

I walked her over to the empty bed and pulled back the covers to allow her to slip beneath the double blankets for warmth. I started to undo my shirt but stopped when I looked toward my father's life organized in neat heaps on the other bed. Tina sat up and gave an exaggerated sigh.

"Oh, hell, Jack? Now what is it?"

"I'm sorry, Tina. But I've got to get through all of this stuff flying around inside my head. In the morning, I'm going to call Gombrich again at the Grand Forks Police."

"Gombrich? You mean the cop I talked to on the phone?

Remember, he wouldn't tell me anything."

"Yeah, if I can get him to say more than what he told you, maybe we'll learn something."

"Do you really need to, Jack? I mean, if the *Skip* is..."

"To hell with the *Skip*," I blurted out. "I don't expect you to understand this, but I don't think I'm going to be much good to either of us tonight — or anytime soon — until I get through this thing with my father."

"You'd be surprised how much I actually do understand it, Jack," she answered. "Believe me. I know you have to do what you're doing. You're welcome to wake me up when you're finished. I'll be here."

I leaned over to kiss her lips and pulled the blanket tightly up under her chin.

"I don't think I'll be able to concentrate much on my old, dead father with you lying here wearing that," I said with a smile.

"Okay, then I'll take it off," she said, throwing the covers aside and quickly jerking her nightie up and over her head, exposing her nude body. I quickly grabbed the hem and pulled it back down in front of her; just as quickly re-covering her with the blanket.

"God, Tina, I swear, if I didn't have so much crap on my mind about tomorrow..."

"What about tomorrow?" she asked. "We have no idea what Ruude will tell us tomorrow. Have you even given any thought to that?"

"Maybe that's something I'll find out by looking a little deeper into all of this," I said. "Now that I know there's twice as much that I should be looking for."

"Or only half as much," she reminded me.

I kissed her again.

"Christ, I don't believe I'm doing this," I said as I stood up from her bed and hovered over her.

"Christ, I don't believe you're doing this, either," she replied, but then added with a cute smile, "You're starting to get to know yourself, Jack. That's a good thing. You probably won't find it as much fun as getting to know me tonight but still...getting to know yourself is a good thing."

I returned to the edge of my own bed and began sorting through my notes again. Within seconds, I heard Tina click off her bedside lamp. A minute later, I could hear deep breathing arising from her darkened side of the room.

Sitting cross-legged on my bed, I began sifting through the clues and evidence for the hundredth time, holding out no hope that I would finally discover something new or different about the real Tommy DuMot. I spent the greatest amount of time researching the 1969 curling championships to determine whether any news items might be available on some obscure historical website. To my surprise, I discovered one small item that had never surfaced before. As George Penski said, Tommy was listed as the alternate for the Minnesota team that played Wisconsin for the 1969 national championship. Mike Bellows was listed as Skip. There must be some mistake, I thought. Mary Coventry and George Penski both confirmed that Freddy Schade was the Skip, but his name was nowhere on the list for the championship game. After another hour of searching, I could track down nothing further about the match or the terrible accident. Shortly after two a.m., I accepted the inevitable: There simply wasn't anything more to learn.

I reassembled everything into their proper envelopes and folders as I thought about how great it would be to crawl into bed with Tina and take her up on her offer. But I knew that something wasn't right. Something wasn't settled and it had nothing to do with the clues and evidence in my hands. Tina and I had gone over everything too many times. We had pushed ourselves beyond the evidence.

What was it Tina said before she drifted off to sleep? *"We have no idea what Ruude will tell us tomorrow."* She was right. Why was I assuming he would tell us anything? What relevant information could Sam Ruude possibly have for us after all these years? We didn't know why my mother or Paul Gombrich tried to tell us we needed to find him. It might have been a warning as much as a clue. We didn't know anything about him except that he was a rogue FBI agent who made off with millions in a drug ring's cash. It appeared my father may have been in on the sting, but I couldn't be positive of even that much. Why did Ruude care if I ever found him? And why the cloak and dagger meeting at the restaurant?

For the first time, I realized that we needed to make a serious decision: Do we continue this search on our own and hope time doesn't run out? Or do we meet with Ruude in the morning and hope for the best? We had been warned not to trust anyone. But if we followed through on meeting Sam Ruude in the morning, we would have to.

Before closing down my computer, I re-read the short e-mail message from LaVon.

Jack — I'd like to talk about us making a fresh start.

What was happening to me? Lying just three feet away was an open invitation to crawl into bed with one of the most beautiful, intriguing women I had ever met, yet there I sat re-reading an e-mail from my unfaithful soon-to-be-ex-wife, now part of a distant past and another world. I looked over at Tina. During our short time together, I found her to be warm, gentle and well-meaning. She was safe, comfortable and more important, comforting. Her youthful enthusiasm and sensuality had no rough edges. Everything about her appealed to me from the neck down. Beneath the polished surface, though, I often sensed that she drifted to some distant place, where she disconnected for a time, only choosing to re-engage on her own terms.

LaVon, on the other hand, was hard-edged and cool to the touch. Her heart and intellect were open and out there for anyone. Entry into her world, though, came with an edgy attitude that few people could stand up to. Everything about LaVon appealed to me from the neck up. When she was in the room, she was all present and accounted for; ready to connect with an incisiveness that cut to the bone. But she often left her victims to bleed out.

There was nothing about Tina that cut, scraped, chaffed, bruised or even rubbed the wrong way. I recalled a particular philosophical class discussion during college: If you were given a pill that guaranteed you would never suffer another itch for the rest of your life, would you swallow it? At the time, I argued that I certainly would, and would probably take an extra one for good measure. Tina was that pill — guaranteed to never cause another itch or irritation. But after spending time alone with her, I was no longer so sure that scratching an occasional itch isn't a great feeling now and then. If LaVon was like poison ivy, Tina was like a shot of local anesthetic.

And me? What was I like? *"You're like a stale fart"* LaVon had once said. I tried to imagine how different this search would be with LaVon by my side — before discovering Tony Perkovich hiding in our basement, anyway.

I unbuttoned my shirt pocket and pinched out my wedding band. I twisted it onto my ring finger and nestled it comfortably into its familiar indentation. Out of old habit, I spun it around a few times between my thumb and forefinger, then pulled it off and stuffed it into my jeans pocket.

I switched my laptop to sleep mode and undressed. As I lifted the covers to slide next to Tina, I knew my body wasn't rising to the opportunity. *"What the hell is going on with me?"* I thought. Rousing her from sleep in a useless attempt at sex would only add to her rejection of the previous night. Nor did I need any further humiliation. I dropped the covers and sat on the edge of her bed, thinking again about George Penski and *the whole DuMot family*. Once again, I could only hope she would understand in the morning.

I stepped back over to my bed and stirred my laptop screen back to life. I read LaVon's message one final time before moving the cursor to type out my reply.

> **LaVon; I'm on the road. I suspect you still have your key to our house. We can sort this out when I get home.**

I toggled the cursor down another two lines and added:

> **I think you should know — I'm with a former co-worker you may remember meeting once or twice, Tina Bucholz. We're searching for my father, but I'm finding more of myself.**

I looked over at a sleeping Tina, wiped away the flicker of a teardrop creeping into my left eye and clicked the send button. For several minutes, I sat naked and shivering, staring into the screen and watching my soul drift away with the words.

Michigan Rink - Gold	Minnesota Rink - Silver
Lead: Jim Coventry	Lead: Paul Stenner
Second: Dale Harder	Second: John Mistovich
Third: Steve Talbert	Third: Mickey Bellows
Skip: Norm Thunger	**Skip: Freddy Schade**

Ninth End — Freddy Schade's Last Shot

As Norm Thunger's last hope clicked the side of his target, the Minnesota players aligned themselves quickly behind the T-line, brooms at the ready. The direction and angle of deflection had been perfect. Thunger's #8 rock bounced toward center, as intended, but his miscalculation of weight gave Minnesota its only chance to keep it out of the scoring zone.

More than any other reason, Freddy Schade had selected Paul Stenner and John Mistovich for their unmatched abilities on the thin end of a curling broom. The way Schade played the game, and the way the game was played in 1969, meant that the Leads' and Seconds' shots filled a specific role. It's not that rocks #1, #2,#3 and #4 never counted; Skips just didn't have the luxury of expecting them to count. Players on the front end were often selected more for their dexterity and athleticism required for sweeping.

Most top-flight players in championship playdowns were also Skips of their own rinks during their club's league season. Freddy Schade would have none of that nonsense in the players he recruited. Neither Stenner nor Mistovich had ever Skipped a game in their curling lives. Both had been playing together for more than five years as Lead and Second at their Breckenridge club. When their rink beat Freddy Schade to win a late season bonspiel the previous year, Schade was quick to ask them join him for a run at the national championship. Freddy saw two things he liked in them. First, they could handle their brooms in tandem like no two sweepers he had ever seen; and second, they weren't frustrated Skips who would second guess his aggressive, intimidating style of play throughout the match.

As the rock inched across the T-line and entered the back half of the house, Bellows screamed, "**Hard!**" and Stenner and Mistovich sprung into action, sweeping furiously just an inch in front of the path. Together, the long wisps of straw swishing in opposing directions melded into a blur of piston-like efficiency without a stroke wasted between them.

The Michigan teammates could only stand by helplessly, watching as their Skip's rock crawled deeper and deeper toward the rear, swept ever-forward with practiced precision by the their opponents. Where Thunger wanted his rock to stop — where it should have stopped — it didn't stop. The friction transferring from the whirl of brooms changed the ice surface, making the path in front softer and warmer; driving the rock's momentum forward as if on a feeding frenzy. With each additional inch forward, it became more obvious that it wasn't going to stop in time. Six more inches to get it out of scoring range. Four more; three, two…brooms up!

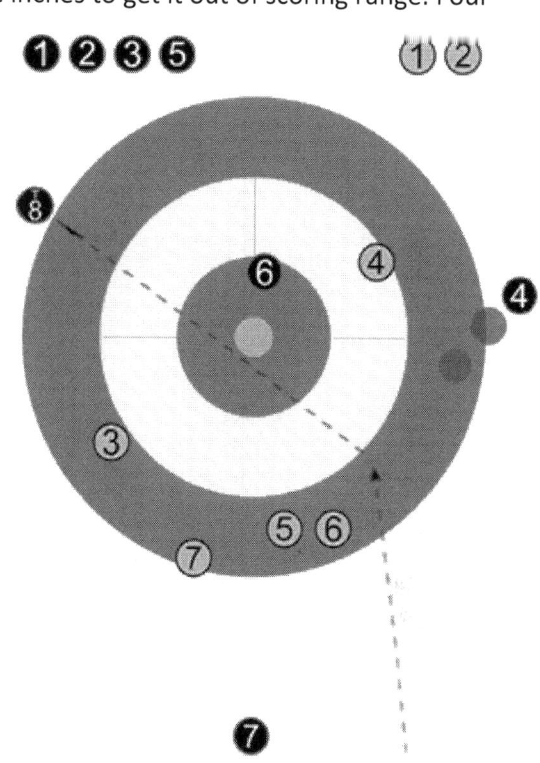

Michigan Skip Thunger's #8 rock was swept out of scoring range by Minnesota sweepers Stenner and Mistovich

Stenner and Mistovich had done it. Michigan's last chance to prevent a disaster finally came to rest just outside of play. It was only up to Freddy Schade to use his final shot to clear out Michigan's lone #6 rock still resting as the shot rock, an easy target sitting on the four-foot circle directly behind the button. Executed correctly, the simple draw around the right edge of the wall to remove it from play would give Minnesota six points for the end and a seven point lead going into the tenth.

Freddy called his men together for a quick conference near the hack, "They're still lying for the single with their #6, but it's deep enough in the house. I can start my shot wide to the right of the #7 guard out front and curl around our wall. It'll bump their #6 out of play nice and clean. But where's the fun in that? I'd rather raise one of ours to clean theirs out. Maybe bump up our #5. Put some mustard on it. Use the hammer to make a real showy statement, you know?"

Stenner, Mistovich and Bellows exchanged wary glances. Freddy looked into the faces of his players and saw their disgust and frustration.

"Either way, I can make the shot and we get six, that'll finally put this one to bed," he said. "I'll let it be your call. If I could give any one of you boys the shot, you know I would. The way you played this end, you deserve that much. What'll it be? Curl around it or let me raise one of our rocks forward to take it out with some flair?"

Curl around it; came the unanimous decision, in unison, "We set you up for your glory shot with your first rock, Freddy," Stenner said. "And that was one more glory shot than you deserved. We don't need another circus shot here. Let's just come home to the tenth end with a big lead. Thunger's boys played a hell of a game under these conditions today. You want to do the right thing? Make the takeout with your own rock. You don't deserve to walk out of here with anything more than a pair of handcuffs. Make your clean take-out and let's put this mess to bed. Oh, and you'll be on your own for this one, Freddy."

Schade milked his time walking back the length of the ice. After making a great show of stretching and loosening his arms, he finally turned and stepped into the hack, expecting to find his two sweepers in front of him. But the ice was vacant. Instead, Stenner and Mistovich were sitting on the players' bench, chatting it up with the Michigan rink. Rather than standing in the house at the far end, giving hand signals and tapping his broom on the target rock, Mickey Bellows had ambled over to the ACU stewards to explain why the remainder of the Minnesota rink would be sitting this one out. Schade caught his attention and pointed to the house but Bellows gave no indication that he intended to step in. Schade stood erect again and began to yell something to his players but stopped short when he realized it would make no difference. They had meant what they said, "You'll be on your own for this one, Freddy."

Only two people in the building realized that Freddy Schade was squatting in the hack for the last time in his life. He had been hitting clean takeout shots since he was a ten-year-old boy playing in the junior program at a suburban club in Chicago. There was no question that he could make the required shot. But why should he? Missing would give Michigan the single point it needed to move into the tenth end with the score tied. It would put off the inevitable with the police for another few minutes and give him more time to think. From Freddy's point of view, squatting low in the hack and staring at nothing but a jumble of rocks at the far end of the ice, missing the shot on purpose was a no-lose proposition; and it was something his treacherous teammates hadn't counted on.

Win or lose, though, there was no way the authorities were going to allow him to play in the championship match to follow. He knew this was likely to be the last time he ever curled on a national stage. But there was someone else in the arena who also knew that this was likely to be Freddy's last hurrah. Eighteen-year old son, Willy, had made his way down to the edge of the ice and began hollering above the crowd noise for his dad to call time out. After a few sharp yells, Freddy relented and requested thirty seconds to talk to his son. With no objections from the Michigan Skip, the officials obliged.

"Funny, isn't it, Dad," Willy started. "You've lived your life in a twelve-foot circle. You always say the house is big enough to do things your own way in curling. You make some shots, you miss some others, but you can still come away with the points at the end. Well, we're at the end, Dad, but it's not a twelve-foot circle anymore. It all comes down to a few inches. There's no room for slop. Make your shot. Leave me with this last shot to remember. More than anything else, when we walk out of here today, I need to know that you didn't let curling down, too."

Adding the word 'too' stabbed Freddy in the heart. He tried to find the words to answer but couldn't. He looked into his son's misty eyes, then into the faces of the DuMot boys seated above him in the stands. Hit or miss with the shot, it would only be a short time before young Tommy would be thrown to state authorities to be placed at the mercy of the Grand Forks County courts and, likely, the North Dakota Department of Corrections. After all, the small gathering of friends and neighbors in the back room at the Gluek bar room that night back in late February had agreed: The juvenile sociopath freak Tommy DuMot had to go. Finally putting him out of everyone's misery before he hurt or killed someone would be the best thing possible for long-suffering Pete and Medora DuMot, as well as the entire town. But what to do about Tommy's older brother, Arv? "Well, he's a good boy with a promising future. Let's just leave him out of it, if at all possible."

Freddy tussled his stepson's hair and returned to the hack without a word. With no broom to serve as a target and no sweepers to correct any errors, he aligned himself facing slightly toward the right of center and pushed off. At the release line, he gently removed his fingertips from the handle with a slight rotation. Twenty unselfish seconds later, his rock curled superbly around the rocks remaining at the front of the house and clicked the Michigan #6 rock squarely out of scoring range. The final tally for the end left the Minnesota rink with a 13-6 lead; nearly impossible to overcome.

Schade's first inclination might otherwise have been to leap up, running down the ice with fists pumping. That afternoon, though, his only response was to look into the crowd to find his son standing once again next to his life-long friends.

He slowly walked down to the opposite end to talk to his team.

"I guess you boys have figured out some things about that little incident last night," he said. "There's a chance I won't come out of it all right. That may have been the last rock I ever throw. That wasn't exactly the swan song I had always pictured for myself."

Paul Stenner placed his hand on Schade's shoulder and said something barely audible above the buzz of the crowd.

"Go turn yourself in, you son-of-a-bitch. We're up by seven. We don't want to see your ass holding a broom if Michigan comes out for the tenth end. If they don't concede, we'll play to an open house without your genius to lead us. We'll use that punk DuMot kid you handpicked for Lead in the championship game. What goes around comes around, eh, Freddy?"

Schade started to walk unsteadily toward the officials and the three policemen who had been waiting near the side of the arena. He abruptly stopped and retreated, as if he had changed his mind.

"Tommy won't be around to step in," he said quietly. "You'll have to go with the older DuMot kid, Arvil. He's damned near as good anyway. Nobody will ever know the difference."

Freddy hefted his broom onto his shoulder as if it weighed sixty-five pounds and gave a sarcastic wave to the crowd. When everyone in the arena could see that he would not be returning for the tenth end, Norm Thunger and his Michigan players extended four friendly handshakes to concede the match.

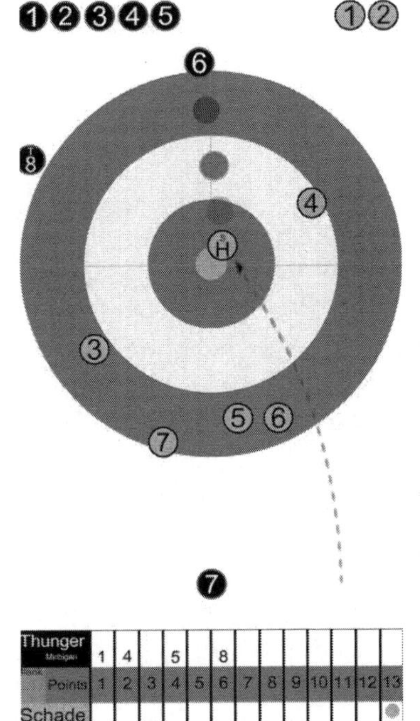

Thunger Michigan	1	4		5		8							
Points	1	2	3	4	5	6	7	8	9	10	11	12	13
Schade Minnesota			2		3	6	7						9

Part VI

Reduction

Saturday Morning, February 9th, 2008

I woke earlier than Tina and lay quietly, trying to decide whether my body and spirit could conjure the necessary forces to crawl under the blankets with her. I finally admitted to myself that it was hopeless. Search as I might, my thoughts were nowhere in the room. I let her sleep as I showered, shaved and dressed for whatever might come of the day.

Half-hour later, I had my hand on her bare shoulder, shaking her gently awake.

"Tina. Tina."

"Oh, jeeze, Jack!" she said, "What time is it? I fell asleep before my head even hit the pillow last night."

"Yeah, I have that effect on women," I replied. "It's a little past eight-thirty. I figured you needed to sleep in. I thought we should grab some breakfast, though. The lobby is only serving until nine o'clock. If you want to eat something, we should get going."

Tina kicked off the covers and slid her legs over the side of the bed. I was embarrassed to see her seated facing me full-on, with her nightgown twisted up high around her mid-section. She gave me a devious smile as she pulled it down tastefully to cover her bare bottom half.

"See what you missed."

She pulled the blanket around her and let it trail on the floor as she brushed past me to the bathroom. "So, did you discover anything new last night?"

"No, I'm afraid not," I said, "but I'm looking forward to talking to Gombrich later this morning. He must know something. There's some reason Bill wrote the Grand Forks police phone number on his writing board and there's some reason Gombrich told you to find Sam Ruude. Somebody up at the Grand Forks station must know the name of the boy who was arrested — or at least they'll have records."

"I think it's a mistake," she yelled through the door. "If you discover some things about that night, then what?" She stepped out to the vanity mirror to apply a light dusting of makeup. "How will that help you find your dad?"

I couldn't decide which bugged me more: the manner in which she asked the questions, or her reasons for asking. In truth, it wouldn't do anything to help me find my father, but this was my family history we were uncovering. If we could start answering some questions along the way, we never knew where it might lead. Besides, I might never find him. Learning about his past was becoming as much the purpose of my search as actually finding him. But I couldn't expect her to understand that.

Over a light breakfast in the lobby, Tina returned to the discussion, "Jack, you have to decide what's more important right now. Finding your father before we all get killed; or trying to solve a mystery that even the FBI couldn't solve after so many years. This isn't as if we're trying to figure out whether Colonel Mustard did it in the library with the candle stick. This string of murders is still going on. If you start asking a ton of questions, more innocent people are going to get hurt. Whoever the *Skip* may be, he has proven that he's capable of anything and everything. Don't piss him off, Jack. Please don't piss him off. I wish you wouldn't call Gombrich again. It might open a can of worms that we can't close. We need to stay out of harm's way. When we find your dad, he may know how we can all work together to end this thing."

"Well, I suppose you're right," I responded after a few seconds, "But if the *Skip* is Sam Ruude, then no more harm can come from calling the Grand Forks police to find that out. If he isn't Sam Ruude, *Skip* might be watching us from across the parking lot right now, anyway."

When we returned to our room, I ran through the list of instructions Ruude wanted us to follow when meeting up with him out on the highway, "The timing is perfect, Tina" I said. "Remember, we're supposed to wait at the restaurant table for ten minutes before driving out to I-94. While you wait at the table, I'll make a quick call to Gombrich from the payphone in the lobby. It won't be traceable and I'll keep an eye on everything to make sure we're both safe."

After two hours of watching mindless television, I asked Tina if she minded if we were to check out and leave about half-hour early. "There's a stop I want to make before meeting up with Ruude." I picked up the GPS unit and tossed it onto her bed beside her. "I found some good installation instruction for this thing on the company's website last night, but I still need someone to explain it to me. That Radio Shack across the way should be open by now. I'd like to stop in and ask some questions about getting it hooked up. It might be handy for the rest of the trip. The sales clerk might know how it works."

We checked out of the room and pulled into the strip mall parking lot a minute later.

"Yeah, it's a TomTom XL. Sure, we sell these," the young store manager said. He turned the unit over in his hands a few times and held it under a light to read the manufacturing label on the back. "This model is from last year but they all work pretty much the same."

He showed me a similar device and explained the keypad and display. When I asked him if I could see an instruction manual, he opened a box from the lower shelf and pulled out the folded booklet. "This unit is almost exactly the same as yours, but this year's model. I can't give you the instruction book but you're welcome to page through it. I can photocopy any of the pages you think you might need to get yours up and running."

Most of the instructions covered installation wiring and an explanation of features; information I really didn't need. I came to two or three pages that were a concise step-by-step layout of how to get it working.

"Assuming that Bill had this thing linked and synced," I said, "I think I see how we can get it to work. Tina come here and take a look at..."

But Tina had already pulled out her cell phone and had wandered to a distant corner of the shop, where she stood with her back toward us. I sighed and gave the clerk the page numbers I needed photocopied. A minute later, he returned from the back room with pages seven through thirteen, reduced to fit across a single sheet of paper.

In the car, I re-opened and read the encrypted e-mail message from Sam Ruude. His instructions specifically told us not to enter the restaurant until precisely twelve noon, but didn't say anything about sitting and waiting outside. Within minutes, we were reversing into a parking spot along one side of the property, where we could watch the coming and going at the front door. We spent the next several minutes carefully sizing up any man we saw entering the building alone. Finally, Tina suggested that I watch the door while she would keep her eyes scanning the sidewalks approaching the building. During our vigil, we saw five or six middle-aged men enter the main door, any one of whom might have been Sam Ruude.

12:00 Noon, Saturday, February 9th, 2008

At one minute to twelve o'clock, I made a last second decision to throw my laptop into its satchel to carry into the restaurant with us. I opened the glove compartment and shoved in the GPS unit, our sunglasses and a few other loose items accumulated on the shift console, to keep everything out of sight.

"We'll leave the car unlocked, in case we have to make a quick run for it," I said. "I don't want to leave any temptations lying in plain view, though. Should we put everything in the trunk?"

"I don't think anybody will care much about the boxes and papers," Tina replied, "but I'll cram our travel bags onto the floor behind our seats."

At noon sharp, we nervously walked into the lobby and approached the front counter. While waiting to talk to the head server, I dared to sneak a peek toward the back of the restaurant, where I hoped to get a glimpse of Ruude. The configuration of the tables and room dividers made the sightline impossible. I suspected he would have known that when he chose the location.

We pretended not to notice everyone who approached the front cashier, but we knew that any one of the customers in line to pay might have been him. When it was our turn for seating, I asked for a booth near the rear, just as the e-mail message had instructed. With a friendly nod, the server picked up two menus and we followed him toward the back, exactly according to plan. I couldn't help but wonder whether he was in on the whole setup. About six steps into the main seating area, however, Tina suddenly tugged at the strap of my satchel, nearly pulling it off my shoulder. I turned around to see her pointing toward the sign for the ladies room a few yards away.

"I'm nervous as hell, Jack" she whispered. "I know we're supposed to order and wait a few minutes first, but I have to pee really badly. I'll join you at the table in a minute. It'll give you a chance to scope things out. Just order a hot cocoa for me."

At the table, I ordered a cup of coffee and cocoa and scanned the room. At the front cashier counter, I could see five or six people milling about, but none appeared to fidget the way we expected Ruude to behave. After another futile minute, I realized that he must have already made his exit as soon as he saw that we had arrived on time. We would have to take our chances meeting him out on the interstate, just as he intended.

When the waiter returned with our drinks and asked for our food order, I asked whether the front lobby had a pay phone I could use. It proved to be a miscalculation on my part. Management had removed it a year earlier when cell phones became ubiquitous. "Sorry, always out of order and too much hassle to get the thing serviced."

I looked at my watch and grew concerned about the length of time Tina was taking in the restroom. It had certainly been four or five minutes. It wasn't an unusually long time, I reasoned, but longer than I had expected under the circumstances. I brushed off the waiter and asked him to return in a few minutes.

No payphone meant that I would have to take a chance using my cell phone to call Gombrich. I pulled it out of my inside coat pocket and tapped in the digits to the Grand Forks police. I was immediately told that the records department was closed on Saturdays and I would have to call back on Monday morning. I asked a few follow up questions and learned that I would need to request the arrest record in person or in writing. I went to plan B, pretending I was an old friend of Detective Gombrich….I would be blowing through town later that evening but didn't want to surprise him.

"Detective Gombrich? You mean *Lieutenant* Gombrich?" she replied. "He isn't a detective."

I was caught off guard by her response.

"He isn't?"

"Apparently, you were never a very close friend," she said. "He's been on a leave of absence for the past six months, recovering from back surgery. Right now, he's down in Florida scoping out places for retirement."

"That's impossible," I said. "My friend just spoke with him about a week ago. Are you sure we're talking about *Paul* Gombrich?"

"There's only one Gombrich here," she answered. "I don't know who you are, but I know Paul. He's my brother-in-law and he hasn't stepped foot in this office for months. But he's due to be back at his desk Wednesday, next week. You can call him then. Can I help you with anything else?"

I hung up and sat for a minute, thinking. This didn't make sense. Why would Tina say she talked to him if he hadn't been in the office for months?

I looked at my watch and it was nearing ten minutes after the hour. No matter how full her bladder may have been, there was no way it should have taken that long. I was worried and scared. I walked to the woman's restroom until an elderly woman exited. I asked whether there was another young lady inside, possibly freshening up her makeup.

"No, I was alone in there," she said.

"Can you go back in and check?" I asked frantically.

"Well, I could be wrong so see for yourself," she said, rudely holding the door wide open.

"See, I had the place to myself, I assure you."

The three stalls were wide open and unused. In the reflection of the large mirror I could also see that the entire room was, indeed, empty.

I flew into a sudden panic. Without creating a commotion, I walked quickly from corner-to-corner throughout the various seating areas. I even poked my head into the kitchen and took a few steps inside before being just as quickly escorted out. When my search turned up nothing, I stepped out onto the front walkway to see whether she had become frightened and slipped outside to hide in the car. She was nowhere. She was gone.

I returned to the table and tried to figure out what to do next. Staying together — attached at the heart — as she put it, was the only protection we offered each other. Separated, we would both be easy targets. Despite Tina's hesitation, I had trusted my gut instinct that it was necessary to meet with Sam Ruude. My gut instinct was wrong. Now her dead body would certainly be found emerging from beneath the melting snowpack in some farm ditch come springtime.

I sat for a long minute, staring in the direction of the restroom doors, retracing and justifying every action I had taken from the moment we stepped into the restaurant. I hadn't taken my eye off that area of the room for more than a few seconds. Although I couldn't directly see the restrooms from my vantage point, anybody entering or leaving would have passed directly through my line of sight. Certainly, a young woman escorted out under gunpoint or physical duress would have been immediately obvious. It didn't make sense, unless...unless Tina had never entered the restroom in the first place.

I pieced together the events. She was walking behind me as we passed the restrooms. I had one eye on the waiter in front of me and the other eye looking past him as I followed him toward the far corner. In a crowded, noisy restaurant anyone could have grabbed her by the arm as she stepped toward the ladies' room. In the few seconds it would have required me to walk twenty more feet to our table, Ruude could have whispered in her ear to *shut up or die* and spirited her away by the elbow, as if he was nothing more than a middle-aged man escorting his trophy wife out of the building.

I flipped opened my cell phone and began scrolling through the directory until I found her number. I punched the key pad and let it ring several times before it went into her voice mail. I didn't bother leaving a message. Instead, I turned my attention to what to do next. With Tina no longer with me, I knew it would be suicide to follow through with the original plan to meet Ruude out on the highway. It was nearly a quarter after the hour and I was already five minutes behind his schedule. It was time to drive out to meet him, where he would find me walking around my car inspecting the tires, just as he directed. He would calmly drive along side, pull out a gun, shoot me in the head then dump my body next to Tina's. He might even throw down an old handgun to make it appear to be a lovers' suicide pact.

I thought briefly about calling the police to report her abduction but realized that I had no evidence to prove anything. My father and Bill Ordway had spent years trying to make their case to the Minneapolis FBI. What could the Alexandria police department possibly do that the federal government couldn't? Tina was an adult. There were no witnesses to any crime. For all they would believe, she simply didn't like my company and walked out of the restaurant after an argument. It happened to men every day. To men like me, twice a day.

I could only surmise that Ruude had laid out the entire scheme with the purpose of separating the two of us. My only remaining options were to stay calm and stay on the run. With Tina out of the picture, though, there would be one less problem for him to take care of after he tracked me to my father.

12:15 p.m. Saturday, February 9th, 2008

I set a ten-spot on the table and quickly pointed it out to the waiter as I hurried toward the exit. I pulled the car out of the lot as quickly as possible and headed toward the interstate. I didn't know where I was headed yet; I just knew I needed to think. At the top of the entrance ramp, I pulled over and reached into the back seat for my road atlas. It was then that I first noticed that Tina's travel bag was absent from the pile. Not mine — only hers. I reached into one of the boxes of notes and felt the thickness of a few of the manila envelopes with my fingers. None of my notes or lists seemed to be missing. I pulled open the glove compartment and was relieved to find everything intact. Then I noticed her sunglasses were missing, as well.

I thought for a moment, trying to figure it all out. It didn't take but a few seconds for the light to come on in my head. Tina hadn't been abducted, after all. She had quickly snuck out of the restaurant, grabbed her travel bag from my car and jumped into a car with — who else? — Married Gary. It had to be. It could only be. When I told her I intended to call Gombrich, she was strangely averse to the idea. She would know that I would learn that she had lied to me about ever talking to anyone at the Grand Forks police. I surmised that she had been staying in touch with her boyfriend the entire trip and it was even possible that he had been following a few short miles behind us the entire time. One text from the hotel room while I wasn't paying attention, and he would swoop in to rescue her. She must have messaged him while I was talking to the clerk at Radio Shack. A minute later, he was at Perkins, ready to pick her up from right under my nose. It all fit; the entire escape plan required split second timing and good thinking on her part. Damn, the girl was good.

Everything fell into place except how she knew to refer to Sam Ruude's name when lying to me about the phone call to the Grand Forks police. Perhaps she had heard Bill Ordway talk about him? Perhaps, even, she contacted the FBI before I did? For whatever reason, she chose not to tell me. It was the *'for whatever reason'* part that was killing me, though. I couldn't help but wonder whatever else she had lied about or had chosen not to tell me.

I looked at my watch. Although I had missed my expected arrival time to meet up with Ruude by several minutes, I still thought it necessary to get myself killed. I was pissed off and knew that he may have been the only remaining link to ever finding my father. Also, I knew I might be wrong about Tina. If there was any chance of finding her alive, it would only come by sucking information out of Ruude.

I sped west as fast as I dared, carefully counting the miles and tenth/mile posts as they blurred past my window. It turned out that the 7.3 distance came at the end of a long entrance ramp, more than a hundred yards beyond a county road overpass. At least Ruude was good enough to scope out a safe place to pull over.

Per instructions, I stepped out and walked around the car, examining a tire as if preparing to fix a flat. I left the engine running and the driver's side door slightly ajar, in the event I needed to make a fast get-away. As I was stooping down for added affect, a late model Toyota Camry with Ohio plates came at me full speed down the entrance ramp, angling to a stop immediately in front of my front bumper. Before I could react, Ruude was out of the car and pointing a gun at me from within the long sleeve of his overcoat. He gestured for me to get behind the wheel of my car. A second later, he was sliding in beside me, while deftly tossing his black leather sack onto the back seat in a single motion. It was as if he had pulled the same maneuver a hundred times. With the gun pointed at my ribs, he reached over and calmly turned off the ignition and removed the keys.

"You're late. Don't worry, I'm not going to hurt you. I need you alive. I've been driving all night to get here. Why the hell would I hurt you now?"

"W-what do you want?" I stammered.

He returned the key to the ignition and cranked the engine to start.

"Drive."

"Drive where?" I asked.

"Just drive."

Sam Ruude was a lean and tall man, a narrow face and a thick gray mustache. Even beneath his Bozeman Feed and Fertilizer baseball cap I could tell that he was nearly bald. His faded blue jeans were worn thin on one knee and his red-checked flannel shirt completed the picture of a western farmhand. For a touch of realism, he even smelled as if he hadn't showered after working in a barn for a week. It struck me that he may have been living and working on a ranch. He spoke very little, but enough to make me wonder about his northwest Minnesota accent, straight out of the movie Fargo. Then I remembered that Doug Chimny called him Bizmo, possibly because he was originally from Bismarck.

"You're late," he said again. "But I've been waiting for you for five years. What the hell is another five minutes?"

I wasn't dead yet, so I began feeling more confident.

"Well, you'll understand that I had some trouble getting here," I answered. "How the hell did you pull that off back there? Where's Tina?"

"Back where? At the restaurant, you mean? I never stepped foot in the restaurant. That scheme was just to make sure you had a specific starting point — for timing purposes. Who the hell is Tina?"

Then he seemed to catch onto something, "Oh, God!" he yelled. "You weren't stupid enough to bring somebody in on all of this, were you? What part of **trust no one** didn't you understand, damn it?"

For added emphasis, he looked over his shoulder as if to make sure no one was following.

I started to answer but realized that he probably really was in the dark. I believed him when he said he still needed me alive. I decided that he was probably more nervous than I was and he would tell me everything, if I could just keep him talking. In return, I would tell him nothing unless I needed to.

I started bravely, "You go back all the way to my mother's dying words. What do you know about all of this and my father?"

"I know that you're in more danger than you think," he replied. "As for your father? Well, since we'll be spending some time together, you might as well know everything. I may be able to confirm some things that you are already figuring out. As for where the hell he is, well, that's the two million dollar question that you and I are going to answer together."

"Two million dollars?" I interrupted. "So he was the one in on the drug bust double-cross I heard about. I suspected he might have had a hand in it somehow."

"At the time, I thought that my half of the take would be enough," he continued. "But, well, bad investments into wine, women and song...things haven't turned out. Now I don't have much left and no way to get more. I'm still young. I want the other half of the money — his half — or what's left of it, anyway. You're going to help me find it before he buries it in some ditch forever...or pisses it all away, like I did."

We drove around the Alexandria chain of lakes region for nearly three hours, stopping often to leave the car parked for fifteen minutes at a time then driving again for another half-hour before repeating the pattern. Ruude spoke very little, other than to order me to turn down every road we could find and often doubling back. For the most part, I assumed it was to shake anyone who may have been following us. Other times, though, I sensed that he simply didn't know what to do next. As the afternoon grew late, I grew tired and irritated.

"What do you know about the long string of murders?" I finally asked. "Are they related to the Grand Forks DUI accident in 1969? Are they even connected?"

"Oh, they're very much connected, all right," he said. "If it makes you feel any better, I was the only one on the FBI team who believed they were connected. One murder after the next, years apart, the names on the list kept coming up dead. There was too much of a coincidence."

"Your old partner Doug Chimny doesn't seem to think so," I said. "When I talked to him, he said all the evidence points to random deaths. He just thinks the case is cursed."

"In the first place, Chimny was never my partner. He was never anything more than a two-bit punk assigned to investigate second-rate immigration cases for the Bureau. Now he's a damned bounty hunter who's been a pain in my ass for ten years. This isn't just a series of unfortunate coincidences. Hell, you know that."

"Yeah, hell, I know that. And in the second place?" I asked.

"In the second place, the murderer is still out there trying to wrap this up. There's only two people in the world who have ever known how to reach me. Your father and Ordway.

"Bill Ordway is dead," I interjected.

He sat silently for a moment before replying, "Dead?"

"Yeah, he died several weeks back. Not sure from what. A bit of a mystery."

He took a brief moment in silence to soak it in and then continued, "Well, I shouldn't be surprised. He contacted me in mid-

December to tell me there was an attempt on his life. Somebody got into his medication. Poison again. Pretty much the same MO used on Jenny Bellows back in '04. But Ordway knew what to watch for. Sure enough, the killer got sloppy and left some tracks. Bill caught on but kept it to himself until he could contact me. But, in the end, I guess it didn't matter."

"What did Ordway want from you after all these years?" I asked.

"He wanted me to help him find your dad. He was scared and he had every reason to be. He said his time had come. He wondered why your father had abandoned him. I felt sorry for the poor bastard, but he did it to himself. I told him Tommy ran, he should have, too. But he never did. He thought everything would work out."

It dawned on me that Ruude still referred to my father as Tommy, rather than Arv. I took a chance and tested the waters without giving anything away.

"So, okay, what do you know about my father's nickname, Tommy?" I asked.

"That was the only name I ever knew him by until 2002, when he told me his real name was Arvil. When I asked him where he picked up the nickname, he said it was to honor his brother. I don't remember...killed or MIA in Vietnam, I guess."

"MIA in Vietnam?" I asked, astonished.

"Yeah," he answered, sounding a little flustered, "But like I said, I don't know for sure. Your father never said another word about it. Who knows and who cares? His time is past due."

"Yeah, who knows and who cares?" I said, trying to sound unfazed.

Although he said he would tell me everything, he certainly didn't know very much more than I already knew.

"And now that you're involved, you're the final name on the list," he added.

"You sound so sure Dad's still alive," I said.

"Well, I was absolutely sure up until five years ago when I set up everything with Chippewa County to falsify his death record."

"So, you were the one who helped him," I stated. "And I suppose you set up the propane explosion to blow the coroner all to hell, too?"

"That was just a little something unexpected I threw in for the hundred grand your father paid me," he said. "But first I had to set up everything out at the old farmhouse, to draw him out there. There was no way that son of a bitch medical examiner was going to keep his mouth shut after he drank up that first ten thousand dollars I paid him for his signature. That's the problem when you use money instead of a bullet. Dollar bills just don't make a lasting impression. But your father insisted."

"So you killed some old farmer just to draw the coroner out into the open?"

"No," he said. "He wasn't just some old farmer. That was Hank Stenner. Somehow, he was connected to the others on the killer's list."

I reached behind me and pulled open an envelope with the list of names from the writing board. I read Hank Stenner's name, listed near the top and crossed out.

Ruude continued, "I figured the killer would get to him, too, same as all the others. In '03, Doc O'Brian found me and said he wanted more money for keeping his mouth shut. The ten grand wasn't enough. So I came up with a plan that involved the death list. I went out to Stenner's farmhouse and found the old guy dead — by more than a day or two, from the looks of things. Gas asphyxiation. It might have been suicide, but it also might have been a new MO. The place still reeked of fumes. With the propane tank right outside the rear window and an old fuel-oil tank sitting half-full in the basement, it couldn't have been easier. I jiggered a timer and called the police to report that I discovered a suicide on the property. I stayed hidden while the cops walked around the place, looking in windows for whoever might have made the phone call. When they saw Stenner's body propped up dead at his kitchen table, they called for the medical examiner. When he arrived and everyone stepped into the house, I nuked the place from my roost out in the old henhouse."

"And the two cops who went up in the explosion? What did they have to do with anything?"

"Collateral damage," he said coldly.

"So Dad didn't have anything to do with it?"

"Nada," Ruude replied. "As a matter of fact, he went ballistic when he found out. He said he was through with me. Said he never wanted to see or hear from me again. But don't worry. Your old man is in the clear. A hundred gallons of propane and burning fuel oil...not a trace of evidence was left of that place. I owed your father that much."

"So he is absolutely still alive then?" *Yes, of course he is,* I thought. "All signs pointed that way, but I could never be one hundred percent sure."

"Well, I thought he might have died for real awhile back," Ruude said. "Or at least left the country. Hell, even a gnat casts a shadow, but not your father. After we killed him off in '02, he dropped out of sight completely."

I could hear the anger coming through my voice, "So now you need me to help you find him because you can't."

"Not for lack of trying over the past five years. There hasn't been a trace of him. I guess he must have done everything right to cover his tracks. Even your mother thought his death was the real deal. At least, until he screwed up and got in touch with her several months later."

"And repaired her furnace and frozen water pipes," I added.

"He should have kept her out of it, but I think she probably already had a target on her head, anyway. Your dad contacted me one more time after that. I was already thinking that his two million bucks would look better stuffed into my own mattress. I told him I wanted to meet with him but he refused. It was the last I ever heard from him. I called Ordway but he didn't have a clue, either. I called your mother and threatened her. She said she was on the run and heading out of state to take care of some business. Then she planned to skip the country. She didn't care about the money. She said she would try to persuade your father to give it to me, if she could ever find him. She just wanted to escape the nightmare."

"That would have been in August of '02," I confirmed, "when she came out to California. I think she wanted to tell me he was still alive but I never gave her the chance. She figured you were the last one who knew where he was hiding. That's why she tried telling me about you. She thought if I could find you, I could find him. But I didn't understand until a few days ago."

"Yup. She knew about the murders and she knew she was on the hit parade. She couldn't tell you any other way, though, without dragging you into it. For forty years, this psychopath has made it a point to follow his victims' every move. Bellows' and Ordway's kids found out the hard way; once you're in, you're in it until you're six feet under. She didn't want that to happen to you but here you are, anyway."

"Yeah, that's why we call the murderer the *Skip*," I said, absent-mindedly. "He's in control of everything. So, why do you think I can help? I'm out here chasing my father around curling clubs all over the state. It seems I'm either one step ahead or one step behind him, though."

"Why curling clubs?" he asked.

Damn, I had let it slip. I hadn't intended to give him any information. I noticed for the first time that he hadn't made any reference to Arv Firpo, champion curler. Evidently, he wasn't yet aware of the connection. But then, why would he know about any of it? The FBI closed the investigation before any of those banners had been hung in the rafters. Dad obviously wanted it kept quiet. I was stuck. I had no choice but to make up a story, but I left Arv Firpo's name out of it. I wrapped up my concocted explanation just as we pulled into a WalMart parking lot.

"So, anyway, when I told the guy at the Heather Curling Club my name, he said there had been a former member in 2003 or '04 named Tommy DuMot. It's a pretty common name but I thought it was worth looking into. There might be a connection. It was the only thing I had to go on. Eventually, my search led me to Dad's message on the answering machine. But until I got your encrypted e-mail, I was never sure what to believe."

"Yeah," he said. "We set up that coded message about a year and a half after he moved out of your house – back in 1998 or '99, I think. We were still on good terms back then. It's an old piece of equipment the FBI once used for staying in touch with undercover contacts in the field. I set it up for him but told him he was making it damned near impossible for you to figure out the security access. He trusted that you would crack it. He knew he could never dare contact you, but he wanted something to give him hope that you might come looking someday. Frankly, I had completely forgotten about it all until he called me to say you left a message a couple of days ago. I'll be damned. After all this time, he never quit calling to check that machine."

"Why didn't he send the e-mail message himself?" I asked. "Why did he have you send it?"

"He doesn't know that I sent it. He didn't remember the date sequence to encrypt the e-mail after all these years. That's why he called me...to get a reminder about how the code works. I was the one who devised that program for Ordway in the first place. The three of us used it to stay in contact during the investigation. Then your father disappeared and Ordway started using it at ProtoCommand. When your dad asked, I lied and told him I didn't remember it anymore, either. I had to go back through some old notes to do the math. He asked whether I thought it was safe for him just to send you a regular message or call or write you a letter after all this time. I talked him out of it. And now, here you are."

"Yeah, and now here I am," I said. "And I suspect the *Skip* is, too. He could be in any one of these cars in this parking lot, you know."

"Yes, I suspect he could be," he said. "But we're safe by sticking together until we find your father. After that, you never know what might happen."

I was discomforted by his lack of certainty and clarity and told him so, "So I lose one safety net in Tina and pick up another with a gun pointed at my ribs. How are you connected to all of this?"

"Your dad knew that I was the only one on the original investigation unit who believed what he and Ordway were telling us. When I informed him in the late '90s that the FBI was ready to fold the case, it was his cue to move out of your house to protect your family. He felt he could do everyone more good by searching for the killer if he was on the outside, looking in. Ordway was the opposite. He felt it was safest to work together right out in the open, stay inside and look out. They argued about it often. For the first few years, your father moved to the Mankato area, where he picked up some plumbing jobs under the table. He learned how to hide in plain sight. He wanted to remain in some kind of invisible contact with you and your mom."

"After a few years of getting nowhere with our own investigation, he decided to move to the woods near a little lumber town in southern Ontario. That would have been about '01. Your mother told him about a wooded lot that had been on the market for several years. The owner lived way out in Calgary and probably hadn't stepped foot on the place in half a lifetime."

"Lake Wasaw," I confirmed. "Why didn't I find a record of ownership when I searched?"

"Because he never purchased the lot. He just parked a small trailer deep off the main road and tapped into a local electrical line. He pumped fresh water from the lake using an old generator. In that neck of the woods, people don't ask too many questions. I stayed in touch as much as I could."

"About that same time, I was assigned to investigate a drug ring that was suspected of bringing cocaine into Canada through the coastal ports, then down through the central provinces into the states. My job was to monitor the activity of some of the suspected ringleaders. After a few weeks, I began noticing that two members of the group were siphoning some of the dirty money for themselves. I traced their private stash to a small storage facility on the outskirts of International Falls. Instead of making the bust right away, I figured I could use it to my advantage to catch the bigger fish. But I couldn't do it alone and the Bureau would never go along with what I had in mind."

"I met with your dad and he agreed to work the sting. He demanded half of whatever money we got away with, but insisted that we destroy the narcotics. Damned shame, too. I figured it was worth another two or three million bucks, easy. The cash in the shed turned out to be just over four million dollars; more than two million unmarked, untraceable dollars for each of us. Your father earned every penny of it, too. He stepped into some real shit when my ass got into a sling. To pull me out, he ended up killing one of the druggies. As far as I know, no one has ever discovered the body."

"He killed a man?" I asked. "How? That doesn't seem like my father."

"It wasn't at all like your father," he continued. "At least not the Tommy DuMot I knew. But it came down to him or the other guy. Your dad had a gun but I suspect he had never used it until that split second. Then, it was like he didn't give a damn about anyone or anything."

"So, how did it all end?"

"We divided the money evenly and emptied the kilos of cocaine and heroin into a swamp. I ditched the surveillance van deep in the woods west of town, but I held onto all the spook equipment. My ass was grass with the FBI but I figured I had my retirement taken care of in unmarked twenties, fifties and Benjamins. Later, I heard that the Bureau suspected an accomplice, but there will never be any proof. They never even opened up an official investigation. They blamed me for the whole thing. We drove in his old Ford Bronco as far as Terry, Montana, where we ditched the car and parted ways. In early 2002, he rounded me up and said he wanted to kill himself off…so to speak. I didn't ask why. I charged him a pile of money and put a stiff into an empty coffin buried at some small churchyard in Hobunk, somewhere. A few months later, he we got together to set up the answering machine message. He said he needed to have some hope that you would come looking."

"And that was out in Montana?" I clarified.

"Yep. He said he was heading out that way on a fishing trip. He broke away from his buddies one day and drove up to see me in Butte, where we met at my place. Montana's a wide open place with one area code. It was just a little precaution in case the FBI ever caught wind of it and tried for a trace."

"So, how do you guys do it?" I asked. "How can you remain so invisible? You still have to live a life."

"Why? Are you interested in joining us?" he laughed. "It's pretty easy, really. In fact, it's getting easier now than it was seven or eight years ago. In this age of credit cards, electronic payments and automatic deposits, everyone is more than happy to see a cold hard a twenty dollar bill now and then. As long as you keep your purchases reasonable, nobody gets suspicious."

"And official things like utilities bills, driver's license, rent, traveling around?" I asked. "How do you handle that?"

"You live in a small town outside of Butte, find work as a farmhand for a visible means of support, register a false name and pay your bills in cash down at the local pay box. You can always find someone who will rent you an apartment or sell you some property under the table. Hell, millions of illegal Mexicans do it every day. As long as you keep your social security number off the record, you're fine. If you need to give your digits, you ask them why. Montana is full of anti-government paramilitary nutcases. Everyone empathizes with someone who doesn't want Big Brother tracking them to their compound or underground bunker. Most of the time, the clerk will agree to write down a bogus number with a nudge and a wink."

"Aren't you giving up control? Putting yourself at the whim of everyone around you, in order to stay under cover?"

"The harder you try to control something, the more it will control you," he philosophized. "Pulling yourself out of the fast lane actually gives you back some sense of control."

I thought about it for a moment and realized he was right. In effect, I had been living the same way my entire adult life.

"I tried to find my father by tracking his car registration but ran into a dead end up in Ontario," I said. "How do you keep your car registered to get around?"

"I haven't owned a registered car or held an active driver's license since I split with the money," he said. "When I need a car, I steal one. Then I find a sucker passing through from out-of-state, parked somewhere at a church or retail mall, and exchange rear plates. Most of the drivers probably get all the way across country before they even notice the difference. I'm smart enough to drive within the speed limit, signal my turns, stop at all stop signs and don't do anything stupid in traffic. I'll bet your father has been getting around the same way all these years."

"So that explains why you left your car parked out on the interstate," I said.

"The police will find it and return it to the rightful owner," he laughed. "I'll be riding with you for a while. Now, tell me more about the girl you were stupid enough to drag into this."

I explained what I could about Tina and the way she helped me put the puzzle pieces together along the way. I thought he might know something about her relationship to Bill Ordway, so I ended up spilling more than I intended. Actually, I found it to be quite therapeutic. He listened carefully until I got to the part about her disappearance at the restaurant. He suddenly jumped in.

"Okay," he said, "You discovered she lied to you about the cop in Grand Forks. So, what causes you to believe anything about her? Did you verify *anything*?"

In truth, I hadn't. People like Ruude, Bill Ordway and my father may have been well-practiced in the dark arts of deceit, but I wasn't. I lived in the world of facts. If the numbers added up, I accepted things. If the numbers didn't add up, then I accepted nothing. It was black and white. It was that simple. For the first time, though, I was realizing that nothing added up about Tina. She just blew in and consumed every corner of my life, then just as quickly blew out again like a dust storm.

He pulled the car keys from the ignition and told me not to try anything stupid. I assured him that I didn't intend to. In the first place, I had no defense against his service revolver. In the second place, we needed each other. He stepped out of the car, searched through his bag and pulled out a device about the size of a deck of cards. He extended a long handle and slowly walked around my car, waving the small green box beneath the undercarriage and bumpers. He stopped for an extended period of time at each tire. After two or three passes, he returned to the passenger seat with a puzzled look on his face. He squirmed around in his seat, waving the device under the seats and throughout the interior. When he opened the glove compartment, the GPS unit fell to the floor, but his little unit didn't blink.

"It doesn't make sense," he said. "There's no tracking device. I would have sworn he would have tracked you here."

"You're so sure he hasn't," I said, equally surprised. "Your little gizmo didn't even beep at the GPS unit. Is it possible that thing is out of date with the latest technology?"

"It's not a metal detector," he said. "This thing is FBI. It's old school, but it's still ten years ahead of anything on the consumer market. The TomTom wouldn't set it off. Your car is clean. I'm damned glad it's clean, but it doesn't make sense that it's clean, that's all. This guy hasn't missed a step in forty years, so why now?"

"Well, not quite," I corrected him. "Apparently, he screwed up on his first attempt to kill Ordway, so maybe you're right, he's starting to slip."

"He didn't screw up on his second attempt, though, did he?" Ruude reminded me.

He suddenly appeared to grow quite upset. That wasn't a good thing for a man who had a handgun tucked into his coat pocket. "But we can't trust that!" he replied angrily. "We don't know if he's been following you or not. Crap, why did I drag myself into this damned thing? It'll be dark in about an hour. That'll be a good time to hit the open road again. What was your planned route before you detoured to the restaurant?"

Without saying anything about ultimately ending up in Hibbing, I worked up an explanation for checking out the four curling clubs on our list. Listening to myself, though, my reasons for running all over the state seemed flimsy and dubious, at best.

"So, eventually, I planned to cover them all." I concluded. "I can't just sit around my house waiting to be murdered."

It appeared that he bought it. I opened the glove compartment and pulled out the sheet of instructions for the GPS unit.

"We were heading to the club in St. Cloud next; then Brainerd. After that, it's anybody's pick."

I handed him the GPS keypad and asked, "Any chance you can make this thing work?"

"Yeah," he said. "Every address in the U.S. has been pre-loaded into the system. The satellite tracks the unit and determines the coordinates of the location you enter."

I started the car and Ruude plugged the unit into the 12v receptor. We followed the operating instructions and the screen blinked to life, lighting the darkening interior of the car with an amber glow. He entered the street address of the curling club as I read it to him and a small map appeared. A woman's gentle voice sprang to life, *"Calculating position."* He handed the keypad component back to me.

"Now, just play with the buttons. You can just hit the settings button to scroll through the different screens."

I toggled through several screens of information until I came to a series of numbers. Ruude reached down and tapped the display.

"Stop," he said. "See, this screen shows you the exact longitude and latitude coordinates."

I continued to fumble for another moment, disturbed by what I was looking at but unclear of exactly why or what.

"Here, give me that thing," he ordered. "You look like a four-year old kid turned loose on an office postage meter."

The lady's voice began issuing driving instructions for exiting the parking lot. I pulled forward slowly but continued to look downward toward the screen, trying to come to terms with the information on the display. *"It's not what you look at that matters, it's what you see"* my mind repeated silently. When Ruude read the coordinates aloud, I understood what was staring me in the face.

"See this?" he said. "We're sitting exactly at 45 degrees, 50 hours, 44 minutes and 71 seconds North latitude and 95 degrees, 22 hours, 3 minutes and 17 seconds West longitude. It displays as N45 50 44.71 and W95 22 03.17. It doesn't mean a damned thing to us, but it's as simple as that."

"Son of a bitch," I let slip from beneath my breath. "It was as simple as that."

I found it nearly impossible to remain calm. I couldn't let him know what I had suddenly come to understand. I needed to figure a way to get him out of the car. We could start toward St. Cloud together, I reasoned, but somewhere along the way, and sometime soon, I would have to break free of him.

"Amazing technology." I said. "I've never used one of these things before. Let's get going. We need to get to the St. Cloud club this evening to see if my dad is playing in the bonspiel matches tonight."

Ruude settled deep into his seat and smirked, no-doubt thinking of my father's money.

"This is going to be one hell of a great date, Jack DuMot" he said.

"Count on it," I promised.

Minnesota Rink - Silver

Lead: Tommy DuMot
Second: Paul Stenner
Third: John Mistovich
Skip: Mickey Bellows

Wisconsin Rink - Gold

Lead: Johnny Milkins
Second: Frank Handler
Third: Steve Metcalf
Skip: Jon Sergott

Championship Match

Because of the unusual circumstances of replaying the semi-final match into the early afternoon, the Minnesota team had only a short time to prepare itself to face Wisconsin for the championship. Immediately following Michigan's forfeit, the crowd watched and buzzed as Freddy Schade was led away by a handful of police officers. With older brother Arv begging hopelessly for an explanation, a policeman and two ACU stewards escorted the young Tommy DuMot through the players tunnel behind the hockey benches, as well.

After realizing what was transpiring, Arv ran down to the edge of the ice and called Mickey Bellows over to the boards.

"Officer Bellows," he cried, "they're arresting Tommy for what happened last night. He didn't do anything. He's getting screwed. He was in the hotel room all night. I need to go with him. I can tell them he didn't do it!"

Bellows looked over the young man's shoulder and caught Willy Ordway's eye.

"I know son," he said. "Everything will be okay. The police will take care of everything. We'll get it all sorted out. I promise."

"What am I going to tell my parents?" Arv said, tears streaming down his cheeks. "They trusted me to keep him out of trouble this trip."

"Your parents will understand," Bellows answered. "Just relax. Hey, I have an idea."

Bellows walked the young man over to a quiet area of the ice and called to his teammates to join them.

"Look," he started, "Schade has been called in for questioning. He won't be able to Skip for the championship game. That means I'll move up to Skip. Tommy was supposed to be our alternate. I don't like the way we got here, but we've come too far to just throw in the towel."

"What are you saying, Mick?" Paul Stenner asked with a sly wink.

"Reducing the team down to just three?"

"No," he continued. "We can't afford to have you two off the brooms. Let's go with Arv as our Lead."

The young man's eyes widened.

"He's not listed on our rink," John Mistovich said.

"Look," Bellows added, "I've been here before. The officials aren't going to know the difference between Tommy DuMot and Arv. All they know is that Tommy is a sixteen-year-old phenom. They're not going to check his ID. It's likely that nobody here knows either one of these boys. They're both young. Same thick dark hair. Same basic facial features."

"I don't know," Mistovich piped in again. "It seems like one more way of screwing- over those boys from North Dakota."

"Look, what have we got to lose?" Bellows said. "We shouldn't be playing for the championship, anyway. Arv, you have to do is toss up some dead weight. Wisconsin will probably take out your shots we'll play six-rock ends instead of eight. As for sweeping, hell Arv you're two years older. You'll be twice the sweeper your younger brother is."

Stenner and Mistovich looked at each other and agreed with a knowing smile. The three men turned their gaze on Arv.

"What do you think, son? If we win it, we'll be in the history books. You'll become bigger than anything that little town of Gluek can ever make you."

The eighteen year old suddenly found the events of his life reduced to a single moment. He stood immersed in a thousand shades of gray; caught in that rarest of times when we can feel ourselves suspended in the murky fog between yea or a nay; between ought or ought not; between shall or shalt not. The young man's faint smile and imperceptible nod signaled a turn in the direction his life would take forever.

Late Saturday afternoon, February 9th, 2008

Ruude ordered me to pull onto the Interstate headed southeast toward the Twin Cities, but the St. Cloud Curling Club was no longer on my travel agenda. In fact, I needed to get the car turned around in the opposite direction. I needed to get rid of him but the only card I held was that I was behind the wheel of a car moving seventy miles per hour. When he wasn't paying attention, I reached down and cranked up the heat then quietly moved the vent to direct the flow of warm air directly onto our faces. After a few minutes, I asked if I could pull over to remove my heavy winter coat.

At the next public rest stop, I pulled into one of the available diagonal parking slots. I left the engine running and my door wide open as I hopped out and slowly folded my coat into the back seat. I stayed outside the car and stretched a moment longer, until Ruude finally stepped out impatiently to remove his long trench coat, as well. When I saw him folding it into neat quarters, I realized I might never get a better chance. I stalled for several more seconds in the cold afternoon air, waiting for another car to pull past our rear. I was in luck when a large vending machine service van pulled off the interstate and slowed down as it crept through the narrow lane behind us. I knew it might be my best and possibly last chance.

As the wide van rolled past, I stumbled toward it, forcing the driver to slam on his brakes and swerve left. As it skidded to a stop, I slapped its rear door panel loudly with my open palm and began hopping on one foot, while letting out a banshee scream of pain. The driver was able to bring the heavy vehicle to a stop about ten feet beyond us and jumped to the ground to make sure I was okay. As I hoped, Ruude also ran around the rear of our car to get a better view of what the commotion was all about. With his bulky coat folded under his arm, locating and unraveling his pistol from the inside pocket would take several seconds. It would have to be enough time.

I quickly jumped behind the steering wheel and threw the shift knob into reverse; simultaneously stepping on the accelerator with every ounce of my one hundred and eighty-five pound body. The Passat jolted backward, sending both men flying for their lives into a snow bank. I continued full-speed in reverse for another fifty yards or more, keeping one eye on Ruude as he struggled to gather his balance while unfolding his coat. I realized that shifting to drive forward would mean having to pass within a few feet of a very desperate man aiming a loaded handgun. No. I would have to continue driving the wrong way down the lane and hope like hell another car didn't try to enter at highway speed coming off the Interstate. But I couldn't maintain control of my speeding car in reverse.

Slamming hard on the breaks while pulling the steering wheel hard to the right, the car spun into a one hundred eighty degree turn. I shoved the shift lever into drive, ready to speed forward. My heart raced as my rear wheels spun impotently on a patch of ice, inching and spinning me forward. Through my driver's side mirror, I could see that Ruude had regained his composure and was running toward me; the barrel of his handgun coming several feet closer every precious second. Suddenly, the contact of rubber tire tread on raw cement jumped the car forward with a jerk, pushing my neck hard against the headrest. The vehicle flew ahead, just as Ruude was taking aim from less than thirty feet behind me. In the rear view mirror, I could see the panic, anger and fear in his dark eyes.

I hit the end of the ramp already moving at forty miles per hour, facing headlong into oncoming traffic heading eastbound down I-94. I pulled far onto the shoulder and inched ahead slowly for a quarter-mile with several drivers honking at me and waving desperately to turn in the other direction. When I felt I was safe, I stopped to catch my breath for several minutes before swinging my car around to pull out into the flow of eastbound traffic. I moved over into the far left lane as I sped past the rest stop, in the event Ruude was standing by the roadside waiting. Five and a half miles later, I exited onto a county road and pulled into the delivery zone behind a truckstop restaurant.

I reached into the backseat and yanked my laptop out of its satchel. When the screen blinked to life, I connected to the restaurant's WiFi and clicked on the Google Earth icon. While the program loaded, I searched frantically through the envelopes on the rear seat until I found the specific notes I needed. I gently moved my fingertip over the keypad to ease the cursor over the satellite image of the United States. I could hardly control my trembling hands as I carefully zoomed in on the precise coordinates my mother had tried so hard to give me from her deathbed. My search was over. I knew exactly where I would find my father. I could only hope he would still be there, alive and waiting for me.

5:00 p.m. Saturday, February 9th, 2008

I plugged my laptop into the cigarette lighter to recharge and drove slowly out of the truck stop parking lot. Before pulling on to the interstate to head west on I-94, I stopped the car and stared down the freeway toward the rest stop. I thought for a minute. No doubt, Ruude would be making his way as quickly as possible to his stolen car, assuming it was still parked harmlessly on the shoulder. If he got to it, he would disappear once again into his rat hole. I realized that ditching him put me in permanent danger. He was resourceful and my father and I would likely be looking over our shoulders the remainder of our lives. I was more concerned, though, about what to do about him in the immediate future?

I drove on the shoulder to within eyesight of the rest area, where I was relieved to see the driver of the delivery van standing near his truck and talking on his cell phone. Satisfied that Ruude wasn't anywhere around, I pulled back into the freeway and drove another half mile or more until I saw a man — it had to be him — walking hurriedly along the shoulder. As each car approached him from his rear, he quickly spun on his heels to try to thumb down a ride.

I quickly pulled into the left lane and ducked behind an 18-wheeler as I sped past him. I needed him thinking I was still on my way to St. Cloud. I had no doubt he would drive there as quickly as possible to finish what he had started. Several miles later, I found the stolen car still parked where we had left it; the windshield marked for towing.

I screeched to a stop, ran to open the driver side door and lowered the sun visor, where I found an insurance card and the vehicle's Montana registration with a name and address of the owner. With the information in hand, I jumped back into my Passat and drove further west to the next exit, where I pulled into a parking lot of a McDonalds and used the payphone to call the local police.

"Hello, this is Mr. James Campanaris, of Butte, Montana," I said, reading the name off the insurance card. "I reported my car stolen three days ago when I was visiting Bozeman. I would like to report that I believe I know where my car is and who stole it."

The woman on the phone sounded as if she didn't know what to do next, so I continued.

"The man is armed and dangerous and is heading to where the car is parked along Interstate 94 near Alexandria, Minnesota."

"How do you know this, Mr. Campanaris?"

"Because the person who stole it picked up a hitchhiker along his route to Minnesota. I just got off the phone with that hitchhiker. The driver showed him a handgun and bragged that they were riding in a stolen car. When they stopped along I-94 near Alexandria to take a pee, the hitcher ran to a nearby truck stop. Later, he found me on the Internet using my license plate number."

The lady could have driven a truck through the large holes in my story, but I was counting on her adrenaline to keep her moving forward.

"He called me a few minutes ago, so I'm calling you. Hurry, please. He said he believes the man is dangerous...like he was wanted for something. I don't want anyone to get hurt. Besides, if he uses my car to commit a crime, I'll never get the damned thing back from the police."

"Oh, God," she exclaimed. "A few minutes ago, I received a call from a delivery truck driver at a rest stop out on I-94, near where you're talking about. He said he just had a run-in with a man who held him at gunpoint for a moment before running toward the highway. I thought the call was a hoax. That must be the man you're talking about. I should have sent a patrol car."

"It must be the same guy," I said, grateful for the unexpected corroboration of my story.

I read the plate number and VIN number into the phone and she put me on hold for a few minutes. When she returned, she was in a frenzy.

"Where did you say the hitcher told you the stolen car was parked?"

She took down the exact location and said she would dispatch a patrol car immediately.

"No, wait," I said. "The hitchhiker said the driver follows a routine to throw off the police. He pulls over and parks the car for fifteen or twenty minutes every hour or so. Then he comes back to it. If the car is still untagged and parked where he left it, he continues down the road."

"Well, sir, we know what to do," she responded, with a hint of buck-up in her voice. "He might still be on foot in the area. We have to check it out."

"Of course you do," I said. "But you might as well kill two birds with one stone. Make sure you have at least two police cars dispatched. Stake out the car from a distance. Just for half-hour or so should be long enough. If the driver returns, you can pull him over as soon as he tries to drive away. Then arrest him for auto theft, illegal possession of a firearm and whatever else the FBI may have on him."

"The FBI?" she asked. "Why do you think the FBI should be involved?"

Oops.

"Well, you know, transporting the car across state lines, maybe," I ventured. "The hitchhiker said the guy seemed crazy, talked about being on the run across the country from a drug bust or something. Also bragged about blowing up a house in Minnesota somewhere, five or six years ago. He bragged that he killed some county official, the coroner or someone. That's like killing a cop, isn't it? Isn't that a federal crime?

"Did you get the hitchhiker's name?" she asked.

"No, he's scared and didn't want to get involved. I didn't blame him. So he told me about my car and figured that would start the ball rolling."

I read the name and contact information off the insurance card again and told her I hoped to have my car back soon. I then drove to a vantage point on the other side of the overpass from the stolen car, where I could wait for the police without being seen from the highway below. About ten minutes later, a black and white police car rolled to a stop immediately next to me. We simultaneously rolled down our windows and I innocently held up an old McDonald's carryout bag, as if I was just enjoying an early dinner.

"I'm afraid I'm going to have to ask you to leave, sir," the policeman said politely.

"But I'm just sitting here finishing my meal," I complained. "It's a great view."

"I'm sure," he said. "But there's been some suspicious activity in the area and we're going to sit for a while and watch over things."

I looked across the highway and saw an unmarked police car pull behind a billboard some seventy-five yards further west. A few seconds later, a yellow TransAm pulled onto the shoulder below us and Sam Ruude stepped out. Evidently, it hadn't taken him long to thumb down the ride he needed. The police would have to move quickly.

"Suspicious activity? You mean like that man down there getting into that parked car?" I asked, pointing.

I didn't wait for the officer to repeat his order to move along. The last thing I needed was for him to take down details about me or my car. He quickly rolled up his window and pulled onto the overpass. I drove away hoping that I hadn't triggered a terrible series of events for the innocent police involved.

Saturday evening, February 9th, 2008

More than two hours later, I was driving west out of Fargo onto the open flat prairies of North Dakota's Red River basin. Against the dim hue cast by suburban lights, I could distinguish the black silhouettes of multiple grain elevators and freight depots that make the Fargo-Moorhead region one of the nation's leading agricultural hubs. With fourteen inches of snow covering the flat flood plain, it was easy to understand why the region faced frequent spring flooding. The Red River is one of the few rivers in the United States that twists and ribbons its way northward toward Manitoba. On years when ice to the north doesn't break up in time and the ground around Fargo remains sufficiently frozen to prevent soakage, the snow melt has no outlet but to refill the prehistoric river basin for miles. Fargo's leaders and the Army Corp of Engineers have done what they can to resolve the problem, but the entire region is at the whim of a severe Upper Midwest winter.

As I headed out of the city into the open country, I lost all light that allowed me to judge distances to the dark horizon ahead. I flipped on the reading light and looked down at my note pad. I read for the thousandth time the cryptic numbers my mother had written in her old address book, as if seeing them for the first time. I bit my lower lip in anger. Why hadn't I recognized the number pattern right away? It was always that simple I repeated to myself.

The series of numbers were the only thing I ever needed to know. Under the letter N: 46-46-25-89 = latitude 46 °46'25.89 north. Under the letter W: 101-04-34-83 = longitude 101 °04'34.83 west. Ruude was wrong when he said my father had made the security code too difficult to figure out. Dad trusted that once I figured out the numbers to break into the answering machine, I should have no trouble recognizing them as positioning coordinates, as well. I was so blinded by LaVon, Bill Ordway, Tina and even George Penski. The random circumstances infesting my world were like a fog before my eyes. But the fog had lifted.

I passed a mileage sign announcing one hundred ninety miles to Bismarck and took a second to read the display on my cell phone screen. Saturday, February 9th, 7:25 p.m. It was later than I wanted it to be and I was still more than three hours from my destination. That was no good, I thought. At my average rate of speed, I would find myself on the western edge of Mandan searching dirt roads in the pitch dark for the exact location. I made up my mind. I would find a motel for the night and then take off driving again before sunrise. I could arrive in the Bismarck area at first light and start my search for the specific location.

I turned on the car radio and tuned it to clear channel 830 WCCO radio out of the Twin Cities. The evening news update led with a report that Douglas County police had shot and killed an unidentified man following a brief high speed car chase on I-94, near Alexandria, Minnesota, just before 5:00 p.m. After law enforcement forced the stolen car to stop, the driver ran from the vehicle with a gun in his hand, apparently seeking safety in a nearby clump of evergreens. After closing the highway and other nearby roads, the police called in backup and surrounded the area. Several minutes of surrender negotiations ended when the man broke from the pine grove and ran toward a nearby farm, possibly in an attempt to reach the house or barn. When he turned to fire two shots in the direction of a pursuing officer, a marksman opened fire from a nearby overpass, killing the man with a single shot. No police or nearby residents were injured in the incident. Authorities withheld details about the man's identity and would only say they were responding to an anonymous phone tip they had received about a stolen car. The police also acknowledged reports that the handgun recovered at the scene had once been registered as the service revolver of a former FBI agent, who had been terminated from the Bureau in 2001.

"Well, at least you won't have to look over your shoulder for Sam Ruude anymore, Dad," I thought. "That one's for you, too, Mom."

I drove another half hour before I found a suitable motel off the interstate in Tower City, where I requested an interior room on the top floor. Although I no longer believed that anyone was following me, I couldn't take a chance. I had lost the advantage of safety-in-numbers. After emptying my belongings into the room, I moved my car down the block to a nearby Volkswagon dealership, where it would blend inconspicuously into fifteen other used Passats on the sales lot. I would be up and driving early enough in the morning before any employee would notice.

Back in the room, I began searching the Internet for a whole new string of evidence. The Vietnam MIA angle Ruude mentioned was so different than anything I had ever heard that I wanted to get to the bottom of it. My quick search brought me to the official Library of Congress Vietnam War database of POW/MIA. I was soon staring at a PDF file listing the name of U.S. Marine Private First Class Thomas J. DuMot, Milwaukee, Wisconsin; reported missing in action from Con Thien Marine firebase, July 22, 1972, Northern Quang Tri Province, Republic of South Vietnam. "Rasterized PDF," I said aloud. "No wonder his name didn't come up on the search engines." One final entry from February of 2002 reported his status officially changed to Killed In Action. It couldn't have been a coincidence that it was the same month and year of my father's reported death.

Although the list showed Milwaukee as the home town, rather than Gluek, I was confident the government listing referred to my Uncle Tommy. Somehow or another, all three of the young men in my father's old 5x7 photo ended up in Vietnam, but I couldn't work out how.

I followed up on the website links that made sense, including Con Thien Marine Firebase and Quang Tri Province. I discovered that the firebase was near the Ben Hai River which formerly served as the border between South and North Vietnam. Because of its location on the edge of the so-called demilitarized zone, just three kilometers inland from the river, it came under frequent mortar and artillery fire from North Vietnamese troops hidden on the opposite shore. Further downriver a few miles, the river emptied directly into the South China Sea, where boats like the Harbough patrolled and ran search and salvage missions. Quang Tri Province was considered one of the worst places for a G.I. of any stripe to serve a tour of duty.

By nine o'clock, I had exhausted my research. I set my room alarm for early morning and rolled onto my back to relax. I turned on my cell phone and discovered a text message waiting for me from Tina.

Jack; I'm OK. I'm sorry. It's too dangerous now. I will do my best to take care of everything.

Take care of everything? Like what, staying alive? I immediately started to reply but thought the better of it. What could I possibly say? Someday, we could talk things through, but I was emotionally drained. I realized that Tina had walked out of my life as quickly as she had walked into it. But I couldn't understand why. What had I done wrong? I remembered that LaVon once told me that to get your heart broken you must first have a heart that works. She said I wasn't alive enough to feel heartache. I lay in that dark space knowing only one thing for certain that night: She was wrong.

Early Sunday morning, February 10th, 2008

I awoke to the blaring sounds of a country music radio station, set by the previous occupant of the room. I turned down the volume and hit the snooze button, then drifted in and out of light sleep. What seemed like three seconds later, a wailing George Jones punched through my dreams and drove me from beneath the warmth of my covers and into the chilly bathroom. I showered, dressed and packed quickly. The office wasn't yet open, so I set the room key card on the bed with a dollar tip lying next to it. The frigid air carried on a light northerly breeze made the two-block walk to the VW dealership to retrieve my car unbearable. I was relieved to find it untouched in its original parking space, but remembered that being followed was still a distinct possibility.

As I threw my bag on the passenger's seat, my eye fell on Ruude's travel backpack, still lying where he had tossed it on the rear seat the previous afternoon. I reached in and pulled out his FBI bug detector. After extending the handle, I circled the car, waving the little box under the car in the official FBI fashion, just the way Ruude had done it the previous afternoon. When the little light didn't blink red after two complete trips around the car, I was satisfied; either nobody had planted a tracking device during the night, or I simply didn't know how to operate the damned thing.

I searched through the remainder of Ruude's belongings. Digging deep into the typical assortment of loosely packed clothing and toiletries, my fingernail suddenly hooked a rubber band surrounding a block of something soft and pliable. "A kilo of cocaine?" I wondered. I worked my hand around the object until I pulled out a two-inch stack of old and crumpled twenty, fifty and hundred dollar bills. I had to count it twice before I was confident the stack totaled twenty thousand dollars. I turned the sack upside down and gave it a shake. In total, thirteen stacks of bills tumbled out across the seat and onto the floor. Either Ruude or the drug lords had taken the time to wrap every stack in a neat bundle of twenty thousand dollars each. After more than a half-hour of counting and recounting, I finally determined that the amount totaled a little more than two hundred and seventy six thousand dollars.

That was a lot of hard cash to be traveling with. I figured it must have been all that remained of his half from the drug bust. It would have been enough to cover his immodest living and gambling expenses for perhaps another six or seven years, at best. He appeared to be in his late forties or early fifties. No wonder he was desperate to get his hands on my father's half of the money. But why would he be carrying so much money with him? I decided that he never intended to return to his little hideout near Butte. Once he could get his hands on the rest of the money, he could live off the cash anywhere he wanted. It was highly doubtful that he had more money stashed and buried in a coffee can somewhere. I shuddered when I realized how desperate he really was and to what lengths he would have gone once he found my father. I slipped a few of the twenties into my wallet and stuffed the stacks back into the bottom of his travel bag. I rolled up the bag into a tight ball and jammed it as tightly under the passenger seat as I possibly could. Sam Ruude would no longer need the money.

Before turning onto I-94 to continue west, I pulled into a nearby *Pankake Haus* restaurant to purchase a travel mug of coffee. The checkout lady pulled a colorful plastic souvenir cup from the shelf behind her and set it on the counter next to the cash register.

"That will be $4.95," she said as she held out her hand for payment.

I paid her with one of Ruude's twenties from my shirt pocket, figuring the small amount couldn't get me in too much trouble in the event the bills were somehow being traced after all these years.

"Okay. So where do I fill it?"

"Oh, you want it filled with coffee? That will be an another $1.50 extra."

As I added creamer, I decided I couldn't let the stupidity go unchallenged.

"I'm curious. Did you really think I pulled in here off the Interstate at four thirty in the morning just to buy an empty souvenir travel mug?"

Out on the freeway, I began to get a nervous feeling again. I wasn't sure what I would find waiting for me when I reached the exact coordinates of my father's location near Mandan. It had been more than five years since he left that code. Perhaps, in fact, he had never been there at all. I was going nearly four hundred miles in the opposite direction from Hibbing, but after all this time and effort it was finally something I could believe in.

As I neared Jamestown, about ninety miles west of Fargo, I began noticing a distinct difference in the silhouette of the landscape in all directions. A poorly-lit DNR sign explained the reason. I was leaving the Red River basin behind me and was entering the Missouri Plateau section of the Great Plains. The elevation gradually rose as the gentle, rolling prairie hills gave way to small, sharp buttes and plateaus that once formed the sedimentary bottom of a gigantic prehistoric ocean bed. As the nighttime blackness melded into a dull pre-dawn pale, I could begin to see that I had clearly entered a different geologic world. To the best of my memory, I had never been to the Dakotas, but the dark moonscape formations felt very familiar at some primal level.

As each half-hour passed toward daylight, I became more overwhelmed by the immeasurable, wide-open space that grew increasingly visible in all directions around me. By 6:00 a.m., the pre-dawn light was beginning to brush a rosy hue onto the bottom edge of the clouds in my rearview mirror. To my right, the waxing quarter moon was beginning to sink itself low into the horizon. I passed a mileage signpost and checked my watch. By my calculations, I would be in Mandan at sunrise.

Somewhat to my surprise, I discovered the snow cover gradually diminishing as I progressed westward. What had been fourteen inches in Fargo had diminished to eight inches in Jamestown. As I entered the eastern edge of Bismarck, however, I figured there couldn't be more than four or five inches covering the ground. In fact, the higher, ridges and rolling hills in the distance appeared windblown and bare. The ditches were brown and only small patches of snow lay in protected hollows or near the scruffy short pines and sage bushes dotting the landscape.

As the freeway carried me past the northern edge of Bismarck, I knew I couldn't be more than a few minutes from my destination. I pulled into a McDonald's for a quick breakfast and made a quick recheck of Google Earth for the exact coordinates. From the satellite image, it appeared that I only needed to cross the Missouri River on the eastern edge of Mandan to begin looking for the turn off to Old Red Trail frontage road, running adjacent to the interstate. From there, I would have to find any small road that would take me south a short way. I could tell by the image that it was not going to be as simple as pulling into a neighborhood driveway and honking my horn. In fact, I had every reason to believe I would likely end up spelunking the depths of some cave dug into any one of the hill or ridges surrounding me in every direction. The first several hundred miles of the journey hadn't been easy. I didn't expect the final one hundred yards to be, either.

7:56 a.m. Sunday, February 10th, 2008

I saved the Google Earth image to a file location and closed down my laptop. As I finished my biscuit, I realized for the first time how truly close I was to catching a cloud in a jar. Either my father would be waiting in his own little world a few miles further down the road or... No, I reminded myself — finding him somehow or somewhere out on that North Dakota prairie would be my only real option.

My hands trembled as I started the car engine and obeyed the GPS lady's stiff mechanical voice instructing me to return to the interstate heading west toward my father. I thought again of Tina and our conversation about what I would say when I finally found him. No matter how hard I tried, I couldn't imagine what script I would follow. I decided that she had been right: I should let him do the talking. After all, he would have more than ten years of pent-up explanations he owed me.

I found the turn-off to Old Red Trail and followed it westward, parallel to the freeway for several miles until the neighborhoods of new construction eventually melted feebly into the prairie. About the time I thought I had certainly driven too far, Ms. TomTom's crisp voice suddenly startled me.

"Turn left in one quarter mile to South Morton County Road 3045."

I quickly re-opened the satellite image file and checked the coordinates. I realized I needed to continue another two miles further south along the single-lane county road before beginning my search on foot. The image indicated that I should be looking along the east side of the road, to my left. The sun's aurora was breaking over the eastern horizon and there was already enough dawn light to search for any possible breaks in the barbed wire fence that delineated the fields. I needed to find any narrow path that might lead up and over the gentle hills and plateaus and into the hidden, undeveloped wilderness beyond.

As I was slowing down to begin a three point U-turn, the GPS lady suddenly announced, "**Your destination is on your left.**" I pulled off the road as far as possible and began walking the fence line. About fifty yards further ahead, I discovered that the barbed wire terminated at a fence post that could be easily lifted out and pushed far enough aside for a man and even a small vehicle to squeeze through. A few dusted-over traces of footprints and a nearby set of vague ATV tracks heading onto the open prairie confirmed that this had recently been used as an entryway.

I gave the pole a playful jiggle, lifted it out and stepped through the opening.

"That's a poor disguise for a secret entry, Dad," I chuckled. "But it's probably good enough."

I followed the old ATV tracks about one hundred yards along flat land until the ground began rising gradually toward the top of a gently sloping hill, cresting three hundred or so yards to the east. Intermittent patches of snow forgotten by the wind allowed me to pick up short lengths of ATV tracks, giving me confidence that I was still on the right trail. I don't need to find every track, I thought, just the next one.

As the hill grew steeper, I gasped at the cold air began taking its toll on my out-of-shape lungs. Just short of the top, my burning legs and pounding heart wouldn't allow me to take another step. I sat on a bare rock, pulled my parka hood back from my head and stretched skyward to catch my breath. From my vantage point, I could see for miles in all directions across the prairie landscape. I sat for a moment, wondering exactly how many miles I had travelled since I walked into that curling club that late-December evening, only to find myself in the frigid pre-dawn hours, sitting on an ice-cold prehistoric rock in the middle of a barren prairie. There was a time I would have known exactly how many miles I had come. In fact, I would have synchronized my watch and set my odometer. Hell, I probably would have recorded the minutes and miles between towns, courthouses, hotels and restaurants, as well.

Somehow, though, none of those calculations seemed to matter anymore. My father might be just over the next hill, or he might be an eternity away. He might be waiting for me with arms stretched wide, or he might run as fast as he could in the opposite direction. Strangely, for all my fervor and search to find him, none of that seemed to make a difference, either. I was learning what Tina meant when she said my search was part of everyone's true story. We are each where we are supposed to be, and we're on time. Perhaps it was never my father I really needed to find, after all.

I looked over the blowing wisps of snow and dust and realized that I was at the highest point in the immediate area. The day would soon dawn bright and blue and I wished I had remembered to grab my sunglasses out of the glove compartment. The clear sky meant that it would be a cold day, with a high of only twenty degrees. At that early sunrise moment of the morning, though, it couldn't have been warmer than ten degrees with a wind chill that felt like absolute zero. If my father was living somewhere over the next hill or the next one after that, I wondered how he could survive the winters. He hated the cold. I recalled my mother rolling her eyes as he flew into his frequent rants every December, *"I'll live my life here. I'll raise my family and watch my grandchildren grow up here. But I will not die in Minnesota."* From where I was sitting on that ragged frozen hilltop, though, I doubted that North Dakota was quite what he had in mind, either.

My foot suddenly brushed against the base of a prairie sage brush, making a soft crunch just loud enough to break my reverie. I looked down to find the toe of my right boot resting against the perfectly-preserved shell of a snake skin, wrapped tightly around the woody stem of the plant. I leaned forward and examined it carefully. From the top of the head to the end of the rattle, the outline of each scale was clearly visible in the lucent-yellow husk. I had never seen a snake moult before and I was impressed that the creature was able to shed the skin in one continuous length. Based on the diameter of the coils and the size of its rattle, I guessed it had been shed by a young adult no more than three or four years old. I reached to unravel the fragile, dry crystallized membrane but immediately sensed that it would probably shatter and flip into the wind like the ashes of LaVon's cigarette. Even a snake somehow deserved more dignity than that. We all do, I thought.

"Just what I needed," I said aloud as I stood to continue my trek, "another message coming to me from under a bush."

As I ascended to the top of the hill, my heart raced when I noticed a faint hint of smoke wafting through the tops of large cottonwood trees several hundred yards in the distance. It must be a campfire, I thought. That surprised me. Had my father who had once been the quintessential suburban homeowner and blue collar working man really reduced his life to primitive hunting and gathering? *Reduced*? Is that the way I was judging it?

8:25 a.m. Sunday, February 10th, 2008

I continued to follow the intermittent ATV tracks toward the cottonwood trees as the smell of smoke grew stronger. The final hundred yards was considerably steeper than it had initially appeared from a distance, forcing me to stop often. I wasn't quite able to decide, though, whether it was because I needed another rest or because I was afraid to confront what lay on the other side of the hill. When I made one final stop, just a few yards from the top, I knew I had run out of excuses.

Reaching for tuffs of grass and scrambling for footholds among the exposed rocks, I scampered up the last bit of escarpment and peered down onto the roof of a shiny aluminum twenty-five foot Airstream travel trailer. Next to it sat an olive green Yamaha ATV. Both were parked on a level area several feet up from the bottom of a deep, dry ravine running along the base of the hill. Beyond the travel trailer, I could see smoke mixed with occasional sparks rising into the trees and dissolving into the lowest branches. I dug my toes behind a sage bush for better footing and slunk out of site behind the steep face of the hill. My heart was pounding in my ears with panic. I looked around and was surprised to find myself feeling so alone, so vulnerable and so naked. Where was Tina? Nowhere. Where was LaVon? I started to retreat toward my car but stopped myself after three or four steps. I had come hundreds of miles, yet didn't know if I could move forward one more inch; but I knew I needed to. The first cuts are the deepest and the last steps are the hardest.

After taking another moment to regain my composure, I pulled myself over the hill, slipped onto my belly and army-crawled about thirty icy yards down the hill as quietly as possible, to within fifteen feet of the trailer. I froze, lying still on the ground, expecting my father to burst from the door with a shotgun to his shoulder. But there was no movement and no sound.

I stood and collected my thoughts before walking toward the rear of the trailer, stopping momentarily at a rear window when I noticed my old curling trophy propped inside on the sill inside. When I reached the ATV, I ducked low and peered through its small windshield. Some thirty feet away, partially obscured by the stump of a dead tree, I could see the back of a stocky, gray-haired man sitting hunched on a log; using a long stick to coax more heat from the center of a small circle of stones.

I quietly walked around to the front of vehicle and stood for a long breathless moment, staring a hole through my father's strong back. For all my creative imaginings about the moment we would finally meet, I discovered myself at a complete loss. Not just a loss for words. That, I would have expected. No. I was at a loss for everything, until some long-forgotten lines from Rudyard Kipling replaced the droning in my head, *"If you can fill the unforgiving minute, with sixty seconds worth of distance run —Yours is the Earth and everything that's in it, and — which is more — you'll be a man, my son."*

I stood frozen in that unforgiving minute. Unable to fill it with even a single second worth of distance run. There was no option for retreat and I had nowhere to advance. I unexpectedly smiled. My world which had once seemed so large and too unwieldy had suddenly been reduced to just a few yards of distance run that lay between us. "Reduced?" I thought. There was that word again.

Despite a lifetime of blending imperceptibly into the middle, there I stood, incredibly visible on the periphery. Despite my father's years of living on the outer fringes of his world, there he sat, incredibly exposed in the middle. For the first time in my life, I said and did the right thing: Nothing.

The silence and cold of the early winter dawn enveloped us and I felt myself shiver. Without turning his face from the fire, he spoke directly into the bright flame tickled to life at his feet, as if expecting an answer from the smoke and cinders.

"Is that you, Jack?" he asked gently. "Did you find me?"

It had been two lifetimes since I heard his mild, confident voice call out my old, familiar and welcome nickname. With my eyes stinging with tears, I ran to his side and fell clumsily beside him on the cold, damp log. Without speaking a word, we each placed an arm around each other's shoulder and held on. There was no running into outstretched arms. No joyous dancing. No looking deeply into each other's eyes. No empty words to fill the unforgiving minute. It was nothing. But it was everything; the only relevance either of us needed at that moment. We just held on. .

At the speed of loneliness, the fire slowly burned itself down to a bed of smoldering embers. With my voice trembling, I finally summoned the strength to say the only few words that either of us ever really needed hear.

"Yeah, Dad, I found us."

Part VII

Reconciliation

Grand Forks Police Station — Sunday evening, March 9th, 1969

Pete and Medora DuMot burst through the doors of the police station, past the security desk and rushed to the police sergeant's office demanding to see Freddy Schade.

"Settle down, Mr. DuMot," the sergeant said. "You can talk to your son in a few minutes."

"I didn't ask to talk to my son," Pete said. "We left our son under the responsibility of Fred Schade. I want to talk to the son of a bitch to find out why he couldn't keep Tommy under control for even one night. One goddamned night!"

It had been less than four hours since the elder DuMots received the phone call from the Grand Forks police, informing them of their son's arrest on charges of underage drinking; felony drunk driving; DUI assault; vehicular manslaughter; leaving the scene of an accident; and evading arrest. Pete and Medora hastily arranged milking and feeding chores with neighbor Jake Highwheeler and sped more than two hundred nonstop miles to Grand Forks, arriving at the police station a few minutes after eight p.m.

"Mr. Schade was released from questioning about an hour ago, after formal charges were placed against your son," came a voice behind them.

Rookie officer Paul Gombrich was standing in the doorway holding a coffee in his right hand and a lit cigarette in his left. He doused the cigarette in the remains of the coffee and tossed the paper cup into the sergeant's waste basket.

"We spent the last several hours questioning Schade and your son. It took a while to get the facts straight — particularly with your kid."

Gombrich took a minute to explain the circumstances of the DUI hit- and-run accident in the small hours of the morning. He ushered them to his desk and allowed Pete to read the formal police report.

"Did Tommy confess?" Medora asked.

"No," Pete said, slamming down the file folder in disgust, "but it sounds like he couldn't keep his lies straight again."

"At first, it sounded like his alibi was convincing," Gombrich said, "but one story led to the next. When we talked to Schade and his son, William, it was pretty clear that Tommy had opportunity and means."

"What about our other son?" Medora asked. "Arvil. Where was he? What did he have to say?"

"He was in the hotel at the time of the incident," Gombrich

replied. "He says he left his brother alone in the room and went down to the lobby, where he met his friend, the Ordway kid. They watched a movie on the lobby television until one o'clock. After the movie, they kept the desk clerk company for another hour. At about two a.m., they both returned to their separate rooms. The accident happened a few minutes before midnight. Their stories check out."

"Where was Freddy Schade all this time?" Pete asked. "He was in charge of those kids."

"Schade was in his room sleeping the entire time," Gombrich said. "The desk clerk said he had no recollection of anybody leaving or entering the building after eleven o'clock. The lobby security camera confirms it."

"Well, then why do you think it was Tommy who snuck out of the building and used Schade's van?" Medora asked.

"I said the security camera in the *lobby* doesn't show anybody," Gombrich replied. "The camera over an unused rear entrance, however, shows a man of about your son's height and build, dressed in jeans and a dark hooded sweatshirt and baseball cap, leaving the building at 11:23. It's dark back there, but the video shows that he kicked a small pebble onto the floor plate, so the door wouldn't completely lock behind him. It's an old trick that only works as well as the security guard. Then, at 12:52 a.m., the video shows the same man sneaking back into the building through that same door."

Gombrich offered to show the DuMots the black hooded sweatshirt and hat confiscated as evidence, but Pete waved him off.

"Yeah, don't bother. We know the sweatshirt you're talking about," he said. "**Montevideo Curling** is stitched across the back. He's been arrested in it three or four times, already."

"He's been wearing it night and day for more than a year," Medora added.

Freddy Schade suddenly appeared at their side and offered to shake hands with the DuMots. Neither accepted.

"I got here as soon as I got the call at the hotel," he said. "God, I'm sorry about all of this, Pete."

The DuMots ignored him and returned their attention to Gombrich.

"So, what happens now?" Pete asked.

"Well, the District Attorney is considering charges as an adult, Mr. DuMot. "You're son is in some very deep hot water this time, I'm afraid. He needs a good lawyer. We can provide a public defender if you can't afford to hire one. His arraignment is scheduled for first thing tomorrow morning. The bail may be set pretty high. Or, he can plead guilty and throw himself at the mercy of the court for sentencing."

"We want to talk to our older son, Arv" Medora said. "Freddy, are the boys hanging out together?"

"Yes, I suspect so. The rink played for the national championship this afternoon."

He handed her a large key tag.

"You can use my rental car. It's in the third row. It's a maroon Chevy Nova with a large Hertz rental sticker on the front bumper. The police have impounded my van as evidence. I was hoping you could give Willy and me a ride back to Gluek...when you leave, I mean...not that we're in any hurry."

Medora ripped the key tag from Schade's fingers and bolted through the door. Pete requested a private space where he and Freddy could discuss matters alone. Gombrich registered some concern, but finally ushered the two men to a small conference room. As he pulled the door closed, he warned Pete that he would be watching through the window, in event the discussion turned violent. Once inside, the two men sat hunched over the table with their backs turned to the mirrored window.

"How did it go down, Freddy?" Pete whispered. "Anything we need to worry about?"

"Slick as snot, Petey" Schade replied. "It was a little touch and go when they took him out of the arena. The ACU officials didn't want to make a scene so the cops agreed not to handcuff him until they had him outside in the parking lot. Apparently, he broke for it and ran quite a ways before they corralled him."

"And what about covering your tracks, Freddy? Are you clean?"

"There were a few problems, but Bellows is helping us take care of them. The head detective's name is Hank Stenner. He's the uncle of Paul Stenner, the guy who threw Lead for my rink. It turns out he's looking for a job somewhere down in western Minnesota, to get closer to his daughter's family. Bellows promised to pull some strings at the Montecello courthouse to help him get in at Chippewa County — if he agrees to look the other way when certain details don't add up."

"Christ, Freddy," Pete said, "It sounds like you've got your whole rink involved."

"Nope," he replied. "My guys will come out clean. Mistovich

doesn't know anything."

"But why did you get Bellows involved? It makes things real sticky. Why would Mickey agree to be part of this?"

"It turned out we needed him and he needs us. The local cop investigating the accident isn't a dumb chump. So I came clean to Mickey. He wants Tommy out of his life as badly as you do. That kid is ruining any chance he has for moving to a big city police force. He wants to do more with his career than picking up drunken farm kids in Gluek or Maynard on Saturday nights. He has some good connections and agreed to work with the local authorities up here."

"So how does this go down the rest of the way?"

"In exchange for a guilty plea at the arraignment on Tuesday, Tommy will be released to your custody under house arrest, pending final court decisions about his sentencing here in Grand Forks. That will take several months, during which time Tommy will probably screw up again and make things worse for himself. By the time this is all over, Pete, you'll finally have that bastard out of your hair forever."

"Will his attorney go along with it?" Pete asked.

"Don't hire a lawyer. You aren't required to," Schade answered. "Just waive the right. The kid is under eighteen, you can represent him. Order him to cop a plea. Tell him to keep his mouth shut or risk going to prison for life. This whole set up can look like premeditated murder with just the turn of a few details."

Pete stood up and paced the floor, watching carefully until he caught Gombrich's eye through the door window. For show, he scowled and turned angrily toward Freddy again.

"And Arv?" he asked. "You left him out of this, right? I don't want Arv involved in any way. Freddy, promise me that you kept him out of this."

"He is completely in the dark about any of this. I talked with him this evening. He doesn't understand how this could have happened, but he's also just as certain that Tommy did it. Willy made sure Arv had an airtight alibi."

Pete sat down again and sunk his face into his hands, "Oh, Jeeze, Freddy, Willy, too? I didn't want that to happen."

Schade stood and rested his hands on the trembling shoulders of his lifelong friend and neighbor, "Don't worry. My son will stick by me through everything. Relax, Petey. It's the last end and we have the hammer. Tommy will be irrelevant and out of your life forever."

Sunday Morning, February 10th, 2008

After several minutes of silence, my father stood up, shivered his arms and asked me to help him rebuild the fire. I added some small sticks from the nearby wood stack and stirred the embers until a flame popped into life. As I poked at the coals, he made several trips to and from the Airstream, returning with a metal coffee kettle, a large frying pan and what he quaintly referred to as his breakfast fixin'.

"You strike me as someone who discovered coffee somewhere along the line, Jack. Can you brew us a pot over the fire while I get breakfast going?"

"Well, I guess we have that much in common after all these years," I laughed. "I've been on a caffeine high for the past six years, Dad. You don't want to be around me if I ever start coming down."

"Frankly, I don't trust people who don't drink coffee," he laughed. "It's a cold morning, but if you don't mind, I'd like to cook out here over the fire with you. We can carry our plates inside to eat so the food won't get cold. I'll show you around afterward. Not that there's very much you can't see from right here."

We sat for more than an hour over a breakfast of the best bacon and eggs I had ever eaten. It turned out that he did very little talking while I explained everything I had learned about his rise to the tops of the curling world. Although I made the coffee my customary two-scoops-too-strong, my father was kind enough to ask for three refills from the pot left steaming on the fire.

"There's no such thing as coffee that's too strong," he quipped. "Just too old."

I looked out the large kitchenette window and asked how on earth he managed to get such a large travel trailer settled into such a cramped space halfway up the side of a gulch. He described the three days of help he received from the property owner after swinging a cash deal to rent the narrow twenty-acre site in the Autumn of 2002.

"After Mom died?" I asked.

He paused as if to compose himself before continuing.

"Yes," he said in a subdued tone. "Until then, I had been drifting from place to place, two or three months at a time. The longest I ever stayed in one spot was up in Canada. But damn it got cold up there. The owner of this patch of land lives in Devils Lake. He once used it for deer hunting but lost the use of his right hip somewhere along the line. He didn't want to give it up completely so he was trying to sell it off in parcels. I ended up paying cash under the table to lease all three parcels — on condition he pull the land off the market."

I thought back to the list of real estate properties I had discovered in the filing cabinet in my mother's bedroom. I recalled only two or three properties listed in North Dakota but none as far west as Mandan. He filled me in on other details. By handshake arrangement, the property owner promised to keep the transaction a secret. In exchange for absolute confidentiality, my father agreed to pay the annual property tax bill on the owner's entire two hundred acre spread, for as long as he was allowed to keep his trailer set up.

"It's expensive," he said, "but I can trust that the landowner won't divulge anything about the transaction. It would be like butchering his cash cow."

After clean up, we began a brief tour. It struck me that the trailer was generally tidy and uncluttered; a far cry from our house in New Brighton. While our home was never dirty, I couldn't recall a time when our countertops, tables and any other flat surfaces weren't muddled with piles of my mother's business dealings or a few of my school books. I decided that the ship-shape appearance of the trailer — inside and out —reflected the way my father wished things had been.

To keep the conversation flowing, I asked technical questions about heat and electricity, as well as sewer, running water and maintenance. The Airstream proved to be a comfortable self-contained unit. Prior to moving it into place, he paid the property owner to dig a well and determine the best place for a cesspool. It required about two weeks of hard work and more than thirty thousand dollars to convert the rough plot into a livable home base; one he could rely on as far as he needed to into the future.

As we entered the eight-by-eleven bedroom at the rear of the unit, I immediately lifted my small junior bonspiel trophy from the narrow window sill. "I've always wondered what happened to this thing."

He took it from my hand and placed it gently on the nearby chest of drawers, "No you haven't," he said, more to himself than to me.

He was right. In truth, I hadn't given it a second thought in years.

Tucked deep into a corner behind a clothes rack, I saw my old bright green nylon curling bag with ***Steve's Curling Supplies, Madison, Wisconsin***, printed in large white letters running the length of one side. It was the bag he had purchased for me at the conclusion of my one curling season, expecting and hoping that I would continue with the program the following year and many years thereafter. I didn't.

"From what I understand, you're one of the best curlers in the world," I said, pointing at the bag. "But you still use that old thing?"

"It's not the bag that carries the game that matters," he said. "It's the game that carries the bag. Besides, that old thing holds equipment just as well as the fancy leather kits a lot of the younger guys show up with these days. In my position as Skip, I don't get to do a lot of sweeping, so I still use your old ***8-Ender*** broom and your old curling gloves, too. I get a lot of playful snickers from the other players at major events. I did get my own shoes, though."

"Big spender," I said.

Outside the trailer, we walked further down the dry creek bed for several hundred feet. As we rounded a curve, my father scrambled several yards up the bank and invited me to follow. When I reached his level, we worked our way down another short path, where I could detect the quiet purr of a gasoline engine. A few yards further around the next bend, he pulled back a heavy canvas to reveal a hand-dug cave, just large enough to contain a Honda generator and approximately ten metal gasoline cans. An electrical heater was plugged into one of the generator outlets, filling the small space with warm air. The cans were rigged with a single line to feed the engine with a continuous supply of fuel.

"How do you keep these cans refilled?" I asked.

"The land owner drives out here with a small tanker truck he used when he ran a cattle operation on this property. To make it worth his while, I pay him twice the town rate for the gas."

To vent the room from exhaust, he had attached a long flex-tube to the generator's muffler. He explained that he had buried the fifty-amp power cables many years before and eventually figured out how to install an electronic remote starter inside the trailer. With sensible use, he typically needed to refill the gas cans about once a month over the winter months; far less frequently in summer. He re-covered the opening with the canvas and we descended the slope to the bottom of the gully, where the engine noise melted into little more than a low hum. By the time we walked the length of the creek bed back to the trailer site, the hum had evaporated altogether.

"Okay," I said. "I can see how livable you've made this place, but what about the times you need to enter the real world. You can't eat tree bark and drink melted snow."

"Well, yes you can, actually," he said. "But I don't. That's what the ATV is for. I use it to get out to the main road. When the snow isn't too deep, I typically walk so I can keep the tracks to a minimum."

"And how do you get around to curling practice? You know, bonspiels and playdowns?" I asked. "Certainly not on an ATV."

"I drive an old unregistered 1989 green Ford Escort wagon," he responded. "There's a billion of them on the road. Same deal. I bought it cash-on-the-barrelhead and paid extra to watch the previous owner burn the title. I keep it parked in a shed tucked behind a small rock outcropping down the road about a quarter mile. You wouldn't have seen it on your way in. It's on my landlord's property, so I don't have to worry about the police poking around without probable cause. And I make damned sure I never give them probable cause. I drive the ATV as far as the shed and swap it out for the car. It sometimes takes me several trips to get the groceries and supplies brought in, but I've got nothing but time."

"And you don't worry about somebody in town asking questions?"

"I've figured out how to mix things up. Sometimes, I get a little lazy and head into Mandan or Bismarck. Usually, though, I drive to other small towns or poke my nose into a small store wherever I happen to be curling that week. I keep an old set of permanent North Dakota plates on the car, but I attach updated annual registration stickers each year, which I peel off someone's car every June. I always leave a hundred bucks cash in an envelope tucked under the windshield wiper — to pay the owner for the inconvenience of getting the tabs replaced."

"But where's your Ford Bronco you owned up in Canada," I asked.

He paused for a moment, as if uncertain of how much he wanted me to know.

"I don't want to drag you into any of that whole scene, Jack. But, since you asked, I had a chop shop strip it of all identification, then dissemble it and send the various parts to the four corners of the world. That was way back in '01, after living in Montana with a friend for a few weeks. There may still be a warrant out for my arrest. The less you know, the better off you are."

"No," I said, anticipating the next discussion. "You're not wanted. An old FBI agent-turned-bounty hunter assured me that you're in the clear."

"Ah, you talked to Doug Chimny," he said. "Well, that's one less worry, anyway. That leaves only the *Skip* and Sam Ruude."

"Sam Ruude was the friend you stayed with for a short while in Montana," I said, matter-of-factly.

He looked at me for a long pause before speaking again.

"You learned more about me than I expected," he said. "What else do you know?"

"I know that Sam Ruude is dead," I answered, hoping I wouldn't have to divulge too much.

The news brought a slight smile.

"So that was Sam Ruude killed in that highway shootout yesterday afternoon?" he confirmed. "I wondered if it might be. I heard about it on the 'CCO radio evening news yesterday evening. When the reporter said the man's handgun was once registered as an FBI service revolver, I wondered if I could be so lucky. When I contacted Ruude last week after receiving your phone message, I worried that I might trigger one of his jackass episodes."

I felt a strange sense of comfort settle over me for a second. Although separated by half-a-lifetime of years, tear, miles and smiles, it was reassuring to know that we had unwittingly shared a solitary moment listening to the same radio news broadcast skipped off the same clouds all the way from downtown Minneapolis.

"Yeah," I said, "I was listening to that same news report. It's funny. Until now, I always thought the moon was the one, single observable thing that all humanity could share and contemplate together, across all hemispheres, across all generations, across all time. Now I come to find out it's actually WCCO radio."

My father roared out his old familiar laugh. God, I had forgotten the amount of empty space his periodic bursts of joy once filled in my life.

I decided I might as well tell him everything. When I wrapped up the story, he said, "I figured Ruude wasn't telling the truth when he said he could no longer remember the code system for sending you an encrypted message."

"So Ruude contacted you?" he summarized. "He was the only one on that FBI unit who believed us about the murders, but we couldn't trust him as far as we could throw him."

"He was after the rest of your money from the drug sting," I answered. "In the end, I ended up with what remained of his stash. Is the money clean? I spent thirty-five bucks for gas and breakfast this morning. Nothing to worry about the bills being tracked?"

"It's from the same pot of money I've been living off of all these years," he said. "Enjoy it in good health. I've never dared to deposit it into a bank or invest it, though. A large sum like that, well, somebody's likely to start asking questions. It might be on the FBI radar somewhere. Apparently, Ruude had the same worries. It'll be better if you treat it like a nice handy stash of cash to help you make ends meet during tough times. You'll still have to work at life."

I relayed everything that had transpired since we had last seen or spoken with each other in 1996, up to the beginning of my search to find him. It was embarrassing to realize that I could condense the previous twelve years of my life into less than half an hour — leaving out nary a detail. In fact, were it not for the ballroom fire that introduced my mother's death and LaVon into the narrative, I would have been hard-pressed to expend more than ten minutes.

My marriage came as a surprise to him and he feigned disappointment that he wasn't an unwitting grandfather. He admitted that he had privately stayed in touch with my mother for several years, so he was aware of my college years and the Bay Area venture. But in '02, the year my mom was to turn fifty-six, things got kind of crazy, going so far as declaring himself dead. It still wasn't enough to save her, though.

"Maybe if I had been living out here then," he said sadly, "she could have moved here with me until things blew over after a year or two. She might still be alive."

"No, Dad," I said. "You know that Mom couldn't have lived like Wilma Flintstone. She would have made some mistake in some town or with some cop along the way. You would both be dead by now."

"Come on, Jack," he said, wishing to change the subject. "Let's go for a little ride. There so much of my world I want to show you. I'm sure you have a thousand questions, too."

"No," I answered. "Not a thousand. Just one: Why did you choose to do things this way, Dad? There must have been better way than to just walk away from us and everything else in your life. Bill Ordway didn't cut and run."

"We had our difference of opinions about that, Jack. Let's drop it."

I was surprised and disappointed that he truly had spent the past five years completely ignoring me and everything about my life. How could he have separated himself so far from my world but continue to be so sure that I would someday try to reach out to find him?

"Bill Ordway is dead, Dad. The *Skip* got to him in late December."

He became sullen for a moment and his eyes filled with tears as he thought about his best friend from his youth.

"Yeah, I guess that would figure," he said. "He was nearly a full year younger than me. It would have been his fifty-sixth birthday, wouldn't it have?"

I took the somber moment to explain how my mother apparently pulled strings with Bill to get me a job at ProtoCommand.

"Mom was a big part of my life," I said. "Even when I moved eighteen hundred miles away."

"I'd like to be part of your life again, too, Jack," he said.

"Well, that's what this has been all about, isn't it? But I hardly know what to say. I'm afraid I don't know you anymore."

He chuckled sarcastically.

"You say you don't know me anymore, Jack? When did you ever really know me? From what you're telling me, you've learned more about me over the past six weeks than you ever knew when we lived together as a family under the same roof for seventeen years."

I knew he was right. As a kid growing up, I knew *of* him but I didn't know anything *about* him. In fact, for the first two-thirds of my life, I treated him as if he was completely irrelevant. Perhaps I had been irrelevant to him, as well. We both wanted and needed that to change. Well, at least I did.

Sunday afternoon, February 10th, 2008

"I need a few minutes to pack," my father called out from the rear of the trailer. "I don't think I'll be coming back here anytime soon. Do you mind if we drive in your car? Or should we take mine?"

"Well, I've spent the past hour trying to talk you out of this suicide trip but nothing will change your mind. So I'm in it up to my neck with you now, anyway," I yelled back. "If nothing else, I'll be there to call the police or the ambulance...or the city morgue. So, yeah, we can take my car."

He loaded his U.S. Navy duffle bag onto the rear luggage rack of the ATV and we climbed on. We took a circuitous route around the hills to get back to the main road, where I had left the Passat parked. I let my car engine warm for a moment before following him about a half mile further south, where he motioned for me to turn my car around, pointing it back north toward the interstate, while he hid the

ATV. He rolled back another section of fence, drove the small four-wheeler around a steep hill and re-emerged a minute later with his duffle bag slung over one shoulder. I realized that walking in and among the hills, buttes and gullies that surrounded the area must have kept him in remarkably good physical condition.

He tossed his bag into the back seat and hopped into the passenger seat.

"There's a small shed back behind that hill," he explained. "Some rocks and overhanging shrubs make it nearly invisible from the air. I keep my Ford Escort parked there when I'm not out on the road. Getting to and from the place is a tight fit but it's out of sight. I appreciate your willingness to drive. As you can imagine, whenever I'm behind the wheel it's pretty tense, particularly when I get caught up in fast traffic."

A minute later, we were nearing the I-94 overpass where I flipped on my directional signal for a right turn to hit the entrance ramp heading east toward Minnesota.

"No, not east," he said. "Let's go west on 94. Drive over the overpass and take a left."

"If I go west we'll be heading in the wrong direction. To get to Hibbing we'll need to head east on 94 for quite a while."

"You don't need to tell me where the Hibbing Curling Club is," he chuckled. "Out here there is no wrong direction, Jack. Nobody is standing one hundred twenty feet down the road holding a broom as your target and telling you to curl your life to the left or right. It's your choice. Every day is a new end with a blank scoreboard and no rocks cluttering the path."

I didn't know how to respond. To put things into his terms, my entire life had been predicated on cold-drawing every shot to the center button. I calculated the correct curl, angle and delivery weight before every decision. Now he was telling me that none of that ever really mattered.

After another twenty minutes of uncomfortable small talk, he fell asleep as I continued to drive further west across the rising plateau. The contoured gently rolling buttes of central North Dakota gradually increased in height with each passing mile. In places, entire sections of the terrain became scarred with steep ridges, escarpments and slumps. We had entered the North Dakota Badlands; surrounded by the most beautiful panorama I could ever remember, including Northern California.

I looked over at Dad's graying, thinning hair sitting atop his weathered face. He looked tired. The fatigue from a dozen years of watching his back and looking over his shoulder was beginning to show through his tough outer veneer. Sometime later, as we neared Dickinson, he finally roused himself from sleep with a stretch, a yawn and an apology.

"How far are we going?" I asked.

He scanned the horizon to get his bearings amid the snowy hilltops, planes and wide open space surrounding us. "Pull over at this rest stop up ahead. I think we've come far enough."

"A rest stop? That's it?" I asked. We drove three hours to sit at a rest stop?

He stared out the window for a long moment ignoring me.

"Well, no, but even if we did, isn't it one of the most beautiful rest stops you've ever seen?"

"Yeah, it's beautiful," I said. "So wide open. So big. It's such a distant world from what I'm used to."

"Only about five hundred miles distant," he responded. "That's not so very far. But I know what you mean. When I first came out here, it scared me. I didn't know if I could handle the expansiveness. Everything seemed so far away and so unreachable. Not at all like the little dairy farm that I remember as a child or even the suburban life your mother and I carved out for ourselves. It took a while for me to realize that this plateau is really no bigger than anywhere else on earth, though. It's only different because it's not as crowded with sights and sounds and movement. Out here, you can see beyond your own little world. I've traveled about a million miles over the past several years, Jack, but out here I feel like I'm home."

"It's so vacant," I said. "I think it would be easy to lose your way in these hills and buttes, if you lose sight of the highway or town, I mean. Have you ever gotten lost?"

"I think it would be impossible to get lost out here," he replied. "You only feel lost when you no longer feel comfortable in your surroundings. Trust me, it doesn't take a wilderness to start feeling lost. You can get lost in a phone booth."

His words recalled something Tina once said, "Wilderness comes in all sizes and shapes." I realized my father wasn't talking about losing our physical bearings. He was referring to losing our way in life and not knowing how to find it again. I also understood that he wasn't just talking about himself. The shoe fit the predictable, comfortable little world I had stitched for myself, and he knew it. I was beginning to feel attacked, so I changed the subject.

We sat for about an hour telling each other stories of where we had been, what we had done and where we were heading with our lives. I told him everything about meeting LaVon, marrying LaVon and misplacing LaVon somewhere along the way. He listened intently but didn't have much to say. I suspected that my world was dull and alien to him so I decided to join him in his.

"People say you're one of the best curlers in the world, Dad. Old George Penski said you have a unique philosophy. Where did you learn it?"

"Most of it came from my old curling coach," he said. "Forget the rocks that are lying in your way. It's a twelve-foot circle. There's plenty enough room to put your best shot somewhere in the house and still make a difference. It's not the shot you make that matters; it's the shot you leave your opponent. That's what I've discovered out here, Jack. Life is really nothing more than a twelve-foot circle. Sometimes you shoot for the center button. Sometimes just biting into the outside ring is the best you need to do. But it's still enough. Freddy Schade never let a rock stand in his way."

"***Freddy Schade***?" I asked, astonished. "Bill Ordway's step-father. He was your coach?"

"Whoa," he said with a nostalgic smile. "So you know about Freddy Schade, too? You really have come a long way to find me."

I continued to tell him everything, starting with the Heather Curling Club in Mapleton and ending with Tina. He was disappointed that I had dragged her into it but he agreed there wasn't much I could have done to avoid it. I searched through the manila envelopes in the back seat and handed him one of the little slips from Bill Ordway's large envelope: *Willy — December 21 — 18.*

"We figured these were warnings sent to you and Bill every year," I said. "Were we right?"

He rubbed it between his fingers for a few seconds before responding. "I haven't seen one of these in years. Yeah, you were right. For some reason Bill kept his. I never did. I dreaded receiving that damned thing every year."

"I still have the one you sent me," I said. "Well, the one you tried to send me, anyway. It blew out of the mailbox."

I pulled the slip from my wallet and he examined it carefully.

"Arv – February 23 – Ø," he read aloud.

'It's in rough shape," I added. "Back in late December, I found it in an old envelope under a neighbor's bush, almost a year after you mailed it."

"What do you mean after I mailed it?" he asked, incredulously. "I never mailed you anything. Other than my little gimmick of setting up the answering machine with Ruude, I haven't done anything to drag you deeper into any of this."

"Well, if you didn't mail it to me, then who did?"

"That's what I've been trying to discover for nearly forty years, Jack," he answered. "Now that we're together, maybe we can work together to finally find out."

Late Afternoon Sunday, February 10th, 2008

We hadn't stopped to eat along the way and I commented that I was getting hungry. We drove onto Dickinson's Main Street and my father asked me to park in front of the ***Dakota, Wild and Free Sporting Goods***. Inside, the shelves were stocked with enough hunting, camping and fishing gear to supply the entire population of the Dakotas and eastern Montana.

"Do they serve food in here?" I asked.

"I wouldn't be surprised," he answered. "Beef jerky maybe. It's the best little outdoor shop I've ever found."

Inside, Dad knocked on the counter in a friendly way, as I tested the whip action of a six-hundred dollar fly rod, hoping I looked as if I knew what I was doing. From out of the back room, a middle-age man with a snow-white head of hair and shaggy beard gave a long, gravelly "Heeeeeeyyy" as he rushed to the counter with his hand outstretched. He quickly stuck his head into the back room again and hollered, "Hey, Bill, come on out and see who's here."

A somewhat older man with longish curly hair, sparkling blue eyes and the friendliest smile I had ever seen shuffled out with a big hello and a hug for my father.

I was suddenly pulled over to the counter. "Jack, I'd like you to meet Gary Lien and Bill Wood. These young gentlemen have been running this little shop since the earth cooled."

"We're not young gentlemen anymore" Gary said. "I've been married for more than thirty years and have two grown kids. Bill has three great grandchildren. What brings you to town?"

My father condensed several years into a plausible thirty-five second explanation.

"...so, I haven't stopped by since our fly fishing trip a few years ago. And since we were just out on the Interstate, I thought I'd introduce you to my son."

"We're all lucky you found us open," Gary said. "We typically don't start our Sunday hours until March, but this year has been one of those unusual weather years. We figure the fly streams west of here will be open early and the spring turkey count should be at an all-time high after the mild winter in these parts."

Bill jumped in and explained their relationship. In the early summer of 2001, my dad was on his way to a solo fly fishing trip to Red Lodge, Montana, and stopped at the store for supplies. The three developed an immediate friendship and Gary and Bill decided to leave the store in the hands of their very capable wives for a few days to accompany him as personal tour guides. The three reminisced for a moment about the highlights and lowlights of the expedition. Altogether, the trip sounded wonderful and I jealously added that I would look forward to going on a vacation like that.

"That trip was one of the most important things I ever did for myself, Jack," my father said. "When you're ready, these are the two guys to talk to."

After a few more minutes of friendly conversation, we bid farewell with assurances to stop by again whenever passing through the area. I took a business card from a thin stack on the counter and promised to contact them to arrange an outdoor adventure in the near future. I didn't admit that I had never been fishing in my life.

"We can head back east toward Minnesota now, Jack," my father said. "I just wanted you to meet a few of the people who have been part of my life along the way. It hasn't all been about curling. Damned near — but not completely."

"That fly fishing trip you took was deep into the isolated mountains, Dad. Nobody would have located you out there. Couldn't you have found a way to invite me along? I would have loved to join you."

"No you wouldn't have," he said bluntly. "You would have hated every minute."

It hurt, but I knew he was right. I recalled the handful of times in my junior high and high school years when he asked about taking me fishing or camping. With Mom fighting firmly on my side, it was easy to turn down cold, rainy, mosquito-infested weekends in favor of my favorite Saturday morning television shows.

I stewed quietly for a minute before speaking again, "What do you do over the summer months, when the curling clubs are closed?"

"That's why God gave us Canada," he answered. "I don't curl nearly as much as during the winter, but some of the clubs up in northern Manitoba and Ontario are open year-round for summer leagues. I head up to northern Minnesota to the *Lost River Wildlife Refuge* near Warroad. From there, a Canadian friend swings down into the U.S. for a day trip and picks me up. The last few years, though, the border guards have been getting pretty ugly. There seems to be a lot more distrust than there used to be. It's a bit more of a smuggling operation now. After a few days practicing, I slip back into the U.S. again."

We ate an early supper at a small diner near the abbey in Richardton, then continued further east with the setting sun at our back. I was surprised that my father didn't have many questions about my search to find him. I was equally surprised that I didn't have more questions about his life in exile. Unexpectedly, it was somehow enough to just sit quietly in each other's company after so many years. When I finally commented on our long periods of silence, he reverted to his old form with a story.

"One day a man returned home from work and told his wife that he had experienced a terrible day out in the fields. His wife sat him down at the table and said, 'There, there dear. Have a nice warm supper and tell me all about it?' The man gave her a puzzled look and said, 'What do you mean tell you all about it? I just did.'"

"I don't get the point," I said.

"All I'm saying is that there are different ways to communicate, Jack. Silence isn't only golden. It can also speak volumes."

I recalled that whenever I approached him with a question or problem as a child, his answer to everything was to respond with an old quote or proverb. I never thought too much of it until the few times when I really counted on his advice and experience. His stale, half-relevant anecdote from his self-styled world of wisdom literature never seemed to help.

I wasn't likely to change him after all these years so I succumbed to his viewpoint.

"Yeah, I guess silence really is the best comfort sometimes."

"Among men, anyway," he chuckled. "Your mother always hated that story."

We drove east until we crossed the river into Bismarck, where he directed me to drive to a large civic building placed on one end of a municipal golf course. The sign above the main door of the building read ***Capital Curling Club***.

"We won't be here long," he said as we stepped out of the car. "I want to talk to another old friend."

Inside, the Sunday evening league play was getting underway and my father searched the faces in the lobby until he recognized who he was looking for. The two men shook hands warmly and carried on a quiet conversation out of my earshot. After a few minutes, they walked toward me and I was introduced.

"Dave, this is my son, Jack. I'll be riding with him to Hibbing this week."

Dave Nielsen served as the coordinator for the club's youth curling program and the person responsible for running an annual youth curling camp called **No Boundaries**. I shook his hand and recalled having attended one year as a young boy. The weekend instructional sessions gave kids from all over the country an opportunity to receive coaching from American and Canadian curling champions. Apparently, my father had worked with Dave frequently over the previous few years.

"Nice to meet you, Jack. Your dad tells me that Hibbing will be his last, hurrah. Curling will miss him."

I didn't know how to respond, so my father kept up the conversation, "Dave, curling needs someone like you more than they need a washed up old recluse like me. I just wanted to stop by and tell you to keep up the good work. It means a lot to so many people. If you don't make it up to Hibbing, I don't know when I might see you again."

"Heck, Arv," he replied, "Even if I do get up to Hibbing you know we likely won't see each other, except through the plexiglass."

With a nod and an awkward smile, my dad acknowledged the truth behind Dave's statement, "I'm sorry things had to be this way, Dave."

"Nobody pretends to understand you, Arv, but good luck up there."

They hugged again and wished each other well. I shook hands one more time and we were back in the car a minute later.

"So that's what this is going to be between now and Thursday?" I asked. "The Arv Firpo farewell tour?"

We continued east from Bismarck with a goal of spending our first night in Jamestown. Along the way, I opened up with more information about LaVon's affair. One thing led to the next and I found myself explaining how Tina entered my life through the front door, only to head out the back when things started getting hot. He listened and nodded in all the right places but offered no real words of hope or encouragement.

"It's not like me to let the whole thing get out of control the way it did" I said. "I should have known it was too good to be true with Tina. It all happened too easy and too fast."

"What makes you think good things only happen with a great amount of time and effort?" he asked. "The universe was created by a single explosion in a fraction of a second."

"Yeah, the Big Bang. That's my life with women, all right."

"I don't have much worthwhile advice to pass on about relationships, Jack. Somerset Maugham said, *'The love that lasts the longest is the love that is never returned.'* Does that help?"

"Yeah, thanks," I said.

I continued relaying the details of my search and reasons why I eventually decided to look for him on the bonspiel circuit after talking to Mary Coventry at the USCA.

"Mary meant well," he said, "but she had it all backward. A week or more before a regional or national championship, I deliberately plan a route that will take me to six or seven different clubs, none of which will be hosting a bonspiel. That way, I have an opportunity to play in one or more of the competitive league matches. Generally, one or two teams will need a sub on any given day or night. When the league players go home, I stick around an extra hour or more for practice. Typically, it takes that long for the manager to close down the bar and clean up the place, anyway. I'm familiar with most of the club managers on a first-name basis. They're all happy to keep the club open until I'm finished, or they trust me to pull the door closed behind me when I leave. Hell, I even have the keys to a few of the smaller clubs around the region."

"So, by the time you get to the playdown location, you will have played on about a dozen different ice surfaces that week," I said. "Makes good sense. When you lived at home, I never knew you curled, Dad. Why didn't you say anything when I played juniors that year? I might have stuck to it."

"No, you wouldn't have," he said pointblank.

Ouch, again. "Yeah, I guess you're right," I admitted.

"You never thought too highly of sports, did you Jack?" he continued.

"No," I replied. "I never understood why sports become so important for some people. Guys at work used to talk a lot about going to Twins and Vikings games. It always seemed like such a fantasy world to me. I mean, playing might be fun, but what does anybody really get out of watching a pitcher walk a batter and then talking about it ad nauseum the next day? It's all just a temporary distraction."

"Distraction from what?" he asked sarcastically. "Your so-called real world? Watching a ballgame isn't just a balm or an ointment that you apply skin-deep to relieve a minor skin irritation, Jack. It's understanding what is happening at a level beneath the surface, deep in the pores and down in the bones. Pitch after pitch, inning after inning, game after game and, yes, season after season. Hell, Jack, a good bar room discussion about sports — has been the cure for more sin-sick souls than all the cathedrals in Christendom."

"Straight from the Arvil DuMot School of Theology 101," I said, "but it still doesn't explain why you never told me you were into curling."

"I had my reasons for keeping my past out of your present."

I was fed up with mystery and shadows. I wanted answers and told him so.

"I get that, Dad, but to go from zero-to- sixty in the curling world must have required a hellacious amount of time and work. That was all time and work we could have used together to try to figure out this mess we're in."

"And have you killed like Jason Ordway and Jenny Bellows? Is that the way you mean work it out together?"

"Yeah, okay," I acknowledged. "There wasn't much I could have done as an 18-year old kid."

"Besides," he continued, "it wasn't exactly zero-to-sixty. I knew how to win at the sport. I played alongside some of the best curlers in the country when I was growing up at the old Montevideo club. But, yes, it took a lot to get my skills to where I am now. I joined a curling league at about six different clubs throughout Minnesota. That meant traveling for league games five days a week. On top of the games, I made time to throw an additional hundred practice rocks every day, too...either early mornings or late nights. I entered every bonspiel I could find throughout the Midwest, including Manitoba and Ontario. I had a single-minded routine for the first four years. Then, when I thought I was good enough and started winning regularly, I started putting teams together for various championship playdowns."

I was disappointed and looked for a way to tell him so. Curling, I had hoped, was a mere diversion until we would fall into each other's arms again. Instead, there he sat telling me about his hopes to move on with his life and dreams to become the best at something — other than fatherhood.

"And all the while you were moving around in your so-called real world, you were finding ways to become more and more invisible to mine," I confirmed.

"That was the idea, but everything I did — everything — was an effort at some kind of reconciliation."

"So after four or five years, you decided to resurrect as Arv Firpo, hoping that I would someday notice and come find you. What changed?"

"I don't know," he said. "Why does a caterpillar crawl across a thousand blades o grass before stopping to eat one? I thought everything was fine. You were safe. I was safe. Then..."

"Then what?"

"Then...unimaginable loneliness, Jack."

"Loneliness?" I asked sarcastically. "From everything I've learned, you're about the most popular guy in the climate zone. Players would kill to get a chance to curl with you, against you or on the sheet next to you. You walk into a club and people swoon. You mysteriously appear at a bonspiel and the newspapers write about it the next day. And you say you're lonely?"

"I didn't say I was just lonely, Jack," he replied. "I said unimaginable loneliness. You're right. I could call any one of a hundred people on an hour's notice and throw a few rocks. But I needed relevant relationships in my life. I wish I had an answer that would help you make sense of that, but I don't."

"Relevance?" I practically shouted. "Mom wasn't relevant enough for you? I wasn't relevant enough for you? Why couldn't you have found a way to reach out to me, other than hanging your name in some dusty rafters with some impossible expectation that I would walk into that rundown fleck of a building to find you some day? There were times I needed you, Dad. And I mean at my side, not just a memory hidden in some dry gully somewhere. It would have been good to know for certain that you were at least out there watching me fail if nothing else, rather than expecting me to play some warped game of hide and seek. Is that how you treat members of your curling rinks, too? Unless people come to you on bended knee they haven't earned the right to count on you? You know that crap about knock and the door shall be opened? Well, would it kill you to just open the door when you see someone coming up the sidewalk? Sometimes Dad, people don't even have the strength to stand up and knock. I didn't."

"But one day, you did come knocking on the door of that little curling club," he said. "Where is it written that when a man has a child, the family becomes all the meaning and life-support he needs? Look, Jack, I'm sorry. But if you'll think back to when I was still living at home, I wasn't exactly number one on your priority list. I tried to get involved in your life but I didn't have a pause button you could push. You didn't want anything to do with me. Maybe we should have been enough for each other, but we weren't. We apparently needed and deserved more from each other. I had to leave home for your sake and your mother's. But after I left home, I still had the right to make the best life I could for myself."

"Deserved more?" I asked. "So, where is it written that a kid is bound by some cosmic law to honor his parents?"

"Actually," he answered, "that one actually is written somewhere, but I get your point. I've been in your shoes."

"God damn it," I thought. He was right again.

"People are like water, Jack. We all seek our own level."

"Your own level?" I said. "More like your own center."

"Look," he said, "I know you came out here searching for the father you hoped to find. Instead, you found the father I am."

"But did you have to make it such a mystery, Dad? Couldn't you have just picked up the phone some quiet Sunday afternoon to call me?"

"Do you think all this was about you, Jack?" he spat back. "I spent seventeen years of your lifetime waiting and hoping you might possibly become what I wanted you to be; what I knew you could be."

"So you finally just walked away without helping me understand anything?" I finished. "Nothing about my future. Nothing about life. You could have been there for me. Maybe not in the same house. Maybe not even in the same city, but we could have stayed in touch somehow. Somewhere. That would have meant a lot to me."

"No, it wouldn't have," he sighed. "What did you think was supposed to happen, Jack? That I would just invite you to some remote cabin for the weekend, where we could sit down together over a griddle of pancakes and work out your troubles? It doesn't work that way. We never get to meet the people who have all the answers. Nothing is that simple. Believe me, I wish it were, but it's not!"

I couldn't disagree with him. We both grew quiet for several minutes, trying to calm down. When he finally spoke again, I rolled my eyes as he slipped back into the comfortable vernacular of the little world he had created for himself.

"Everyone needs to read the ice in their own way," he continued. "Some shots are easier to make than others but we all have to make the shot that's called for. You don't get to just walk down the sheet and place your rocks where you want them to stop. Even when the answers seem easy, you still have to make your shots. From what I could tell at home, you never wanted to go through the effort of making the shot. And that was hard to watch."

"Well, I'm sorry, Dad. You expected me to be the son you wanted. Instead, you got the son I am."

We drove another twenty minutes in silence before he spoke again.

"I needed reconciliation with myself," he said cryptically.

"Reconciliation? With yourself? Explain that one," I demanded.

"I needed to forgive myself for what I had done and for what I had become, and for the pain I brought to so many people. I needed to find some relevance in my own life, beyond you and your mother. But I couldn't do that if I was always looking over my shoulder and trying to protect you and Mom. I needed a fresh start. Yes I was scared. After nearly forty years, there wasn't a damned thing we could do about being on that son-of-a-bitch's death list. I figured the best I could do was to try to keep your name from being added to it. I was a marked man. I was part of the Curse of Cane and I'm not some superhero. I loved you and your mother very much, Jack. That may not be what you expected to hear after all this time, but there you have it."

"I guess we're just more different than I ever expected," I said.

"Different in what way?" he replied. "You've spent your life hiding from your future. I've spent mine hiding from my past."

We drove in silence the remainder of the way to Jamestown, where we checked into separate hotel rooms for the night. As I dropped my tired body onto the bed, I admitted to myself that the events of the day hadn't gone quite the way I had scripted. In fact, I realized that I might not even find him in his room the next morning. Worse, I wasn't sure I even cared.

Early Morning Monday, February 11th, 2008

My father's voice penetrated the hotel room door, accompanied by a few sharp knocks, "Jack, it's time to wake up and get moving. Hey, Jack, are you awake? It's five-thirty, Jack."

I jumped up and stumbled through the darkness to unlock the door, tripping over my travel bag along the way.

"Why so early?" I asked as he stepped into the room. "I thought we had until Thursday evening."

"I need to get to the club in Moorhead by seven o'clock for an early hour of open ice. Afterward, their morning senior mens' league starts at ten. Hopefully, I can get in a game as a sub. Then I have lunch scheduled with the club manager at noon."

"Then we head toward Hibbing?" I asked.

"Considering what might be waiting for us, I don't know why you're in such a damned-fire hurry to get to Hibbing," he said. "No, then we head to Detroit Lakes. We'll go to two clubs each day until late Thursday evening, when we're scheduled to meet my guys."

"Christ," I said, "this is going to be worse than those cold-ass weekends on the junior bonspiel circuit, isn't it?"

After watching me yawn and stretch half a dozen times over my coffee and fruit plate at a nearby truck stop, he offered to drive and I readily agreed. I dozed for the first half-hour before slowly rousing to the sound of classic rock on the radio.

"Tell me more about your life since we lost touch," were his first words.

Lost touch? Is that how he described deserting our family?

"Not much to tell," I answered. "I came. I saw. I got conquered."

"Well, start with your wife. Tell me more about how you two met?"

I recapped my mother's visit to California. He asked several questions along the way, which surprised me. He was clearly more interested than I thought he would be, so I took the next several miles to expand on the entire evening leading up to the banquet hall fire.

He broke in to bring the story to a merciful close, "So you kind of figured out that your mother was involved in something over her head?"

"Well, not until we — Tina and I — discovered some things along the way."

I reached behind me and pulled the writing board onto my lap.

"We found this in Bill's desk. We figured this is the list the killer uses. Are you really certain the murders are real, Dad? I mean, they're spread out over such a long period of time. How could one person do all those murders over nearly forty years? Is the list real?"

He reached over and tapped the board with his pointer finger, "It's real enough for anyone who's ever been on it," he answered.

I pointed to his name, followed by (*Tommy*) in parenthesis, "Explain this."

"First," he said, "tell me how much you think you know."

I took several minutes to tell him what I had learned from George Penski. I also explained Sam Ruude's confusing one-liner about Tommy turning up missing or KIA in Vietnam.

My father looked uncomfortable and was silent for several seconds before beginning.

"Okay, since you're in as deep as I am now, I owe you an explanation."

He started as far back as he could remember; when he was approximately five-years old. As George Penski said, Pete and Medora apparently couldn't have any more children and decided that bringing young Arv a little brother would be a good idea for the family. Pete reasoned that the two boys would also prove to be a great help around the farm. For many years, his parents let the two young children believe they were biological siblings.

During a heated discussion about Tommy's repeated misbehavior in first grade one evening, he overheard his father say something about sending Tommy back. Medora was forthcoming and explained that Tommy was a foster child and adopted. That was the first he ever heard or knew of it.

"So, what happened to him, Dad?" I pressed. "Was he the teenager arrested for the DUI accident during the curling championships in '69?"

"Yes," he said. "He was arrested and the prosecutor charged him as an adult. My dad served as his legal representative and made him enter a guilty plea. It was supposed to help reduce the sentence. I'm not sure whether it helped, but it did allow Tommy to come home under parental supervision, as a form of house arrest pending the sentencing hearing. We all returned to the farm in Gluek and life continued as best it could under the circumstances. After that, the story gets ugly."

"We've got all day," I said. "I'd like to hear it."

He summarized Tommy's legal problems as an adolescent but also talked fondly of sibling loyalty and love. It seemed there was nothing they wouldn't do to protect each other and their close friend Willy Ordway.

"And the kid could curl," Dad interjected nostalgically at one point in the story. "At sixteen or seventeen years old he was already considered one of the best curlers in the country. He was good enough to be named the alternate for the national championship playdowns that year."

"Yeah, I saw his name listed on the roster for the championship game," I said, "but I didn't see Freddy Schade's name. I heard that Freddy was the Skip of that team."

"Freddy was," he replied. "Up until the final match, anyway. But he never got the chance to curl in the championship game. Immediately after Freddy and the Minnesota rink won the semi-final replay game, the police arrested Tommy for the DUI homicide accident. Freddy was technically responsible for us on the trip, so he was taken away for questioning at the same time."

"Then who took Tommy's place as alternate for the game?" I asked.

He looked at me and seemed unable to wrap his tongue around what to say next.

"I did."

"So...you curled as Tommy DuMot, not Arv DuMot?" I clarified. "And your rink won the national championship."

"Well, it was a hollow victory. We would never have beaten those guys from North Dakota. We shouldn't have even played the match."

He tapped Mickey Bellows' name on the list.

"Actually, Mickey stepped into Freddy's spot as Skip. Everyone moved up one and I took over as Lead. So I played as my brother, Tommy DuMot, that afternoon. Not that I made a very good showing of it. But, no one in the arena ever discovered the switch."

"But Tommy must have known," I said.

After a long pause, "Yes, he knew."

"How did he end up in Vietnam if he was in prison?"

"He never went to prison. In April, about a month before Willy — I mean Bill Ordway — and I were ready to graduate from high school I overheard some conversation at the seed store in town. Freddy Schade and Mickey Bellows were bragging about something or another and they mentioned Tommy's name. I heard Freddy say that he had seen to it that Tommy wouldn't be a pain in anyone's ass anymore. That afternoon, I asked Bill to explain what his stepdad was talking about. Bill broke down and admitted everything. He knew from the very beginning what was going to happen that night. That's why he made sure Tommy was passed out in bed from an early drunk, while I was kept occupied watching a movie in the lobby all night."

"How did Freddy get away with it?" I asked.

"Freddy and Bill shared one hotel room. Tommy and I shared another. Both rooms were registered under Schade's name, so he had an extra key to our room. While Bill and I were down in the lobby, Freddy snuck into our room and found Tommy passed out drunk. He stripped him of his hooded sweatshirt, grabbed his ball cap and snuck out the rear door of the hotel. He didn't know what stunt he intended to pull, but he knew it had to be something serious enough to screw my brother forever. When he saw the group of North Dakota players come out of the restaurant about midnight, it was his perfect opportunity."

"He got away with it cleanly?"

"There were suspicions. To this day, I don't believe that the arresting cop in Grand Forks ever believed my brother really did it."

"You mean Gombrich," I interrupted.

"Yup, Paul Gombrich. He was a young cop. Having an arrest and conviction on his official career record looked better than letting a high profile case get away, so he never stepped forward and said anything about his doubts."

"And Bill knew about all of this?"

"Of course. Everyone suspected Tommy. Only a handful of people knew that Tommy didn't really do it. Mickey Bellows, Hank Stenner and..."

"And who?" I demanded.

"And my parents — well, my father for sure, anyway. He hated Tommy like he was the devil's spawn. Tommy knew it, too. I've never been quite sure whether my mother knew, though. I like to believe she didn't. After facing years of shame and trouble in that small town, my dad was willing to do anything to get rid of him."

"And what was Bill's role?" I asked. "He never stepped forward?"

"What, and nail his dear stepfather the great Freddy Schade to the wall? No way. All he knew was that Freddy needed an alibi, so he stuck by him. He was too scared to do otherwise."

"And you didn't go back to Gombrich or the police to push for the truth or report what you overheard?" I asked.

"There was never time or need to go back," he said. "Until I overheard Freddy's conversation in town that day, I had every reason to believe that Tommy was guilty. Hell, back then, the kid swore oaths denying everything. It wasn't the first time he had been arrested for hot-wiring a car and taking off on a drunken joy-ride. He had opportunity and means that night. Everyone would have just told me I was wrong about what I'd overheard."

"So he had no alibi?"

"Hell, the kid could never keep two thoughts strung together, Jack. During the questioning, he told the police five or six different versions of his side of the story. Nobody knew what to believe. You have to remember, Tommy DuMot had been nothing but trouble from day-one and had a county rap sheet a mile long. When the police questioned Bill later that day, he corroborated the whole story. Whatever he told them, it was close enough for their version of the truth.

"Convicted as an adult?" I asked, incredulously. "Even though he was still technically a minor?"

"That was part of the plea deal," he replied.

"He didn't even have a chance at a trial?" I asked.

"Trial? Hell, he wasn't even given a public defender. You have to understand what those years were like for my family, Jack. We all needed him out of our lives. His arrest was just as convenient for me as it was for my parents and everyone else in the county."

"So what finally happened?" I asked. "Did he do some time in jail?

I've talked to people who claim there was early speculation that he murdered your dad and mom — I mean Grandpa and Grandma."

"No, Tommy never went to prison," he answered. "But he couldn't have murdered my parents. I know first-hand that he can't possibly be the *Skip*.

"What makes you so certain?"

"I went back to the farm and told Tommy what I had overheard in town — that he had been set up by Schade. I expected him to go on one of his violent streaks. To my surprise, though, he didn't. He grew quiet for several minutes and then said he wanted me to take him away somewhere. He wanted to go to New York, where he could get lost in a crowd and feel safe. I argued that he was too young to make it on the streets, but he said he had a better chance in New York than he did in prison. When I refused, he threatened to tell the curling people about the stunt I pulled to take his place for the championship game. They would have disqualified the rink and awarded the championship to Wisconsin. Everyone in western Minnesota was so damned proud of that national championship trophy. Looking back on it today, it doesn't sound like much. But back then, to a young high school kid like me, Tommy might as well have been threatening to cut off my penis. And I knew he would, too. When I told Bill about the threat, he agreed that we couldn't let anything happen to ruin Freddy's championship. Bill agreed that he was through lying for his stepfather, though. We all decided to make a run for it early the next morning."

I reached into another envelope and pulled out the photograph of the three young men standing in front of the old car at Miller Brewing Company.

"And this is a photo of you three on the lam?" I asked. "That's you, the tall one in the middle? Bill on your right? Tommy on your left?"

"That's us," he answered.

He turned the picture over and read the back: April, 1969. He chuckled at the ridiculous memory.

"Has it been that many years already? We only got as far as Milwaukee in that old beater car of mine. Then I sold it for fifty bucks to the first person stupid enough to buy it for parts. The three of us went down to the nearest Navy recruiter. We wanted to sign up under the old buddy plan so we could stay together throughout our entire enlistment. But Tommy was rejected when he couldn't prove he was of legal age. He bolted from the room in an angry tirade and ran into a Marine recruiter's office down the hall. When he came back about an hour later, he told us the Marine sergeant said he could find a way to get him enlisted; he knew how to sneak the paperwork through the system. The Marines would take him and they promised to send him to Vietnam right out of basic training. We took our battery of aptitude tests early the next morning and reported to the local induction centers the next day. Tommy and I went our separate ways."

"And he went missing in Vietnam?"

"After basic training, Bill and I did our initial three-year enlistment on Diego Garcia, a little naval resupply island in the middle of the Indian Ocean. Tommy was sent off to Parris Island for boot camp and then straight to Vietnam. In April the following year, I received official word that my father died in an awful tractor accident. He had been a farmer all his life, so it was hard to believe. But accidents happened all the time on farms back then. I didn't bother flying home for the funeral. He would already be cold in the ground by the time I made the thirty-six hours of military flight connections."

"It wasn't too long afterward when Bill was notified that his stepfather Freddy died. It took some digging around to learn that it was from alcohol poisoning. That was equally suspicious. Everyone knew that Schade loved searching for the bottom of a bottle of bourbon, but he was never known as a commode-hugging drunk. Bill's mom had moved out of the house sometime earlier, so he flew home to attend to funeral arrangements. He returned to our base about two weeks later."

"About a year and a half later, the Navy informed me that my mother — grandma Medora — died in an accident at her house in town. I tried to get home but was on special assignment at the time. There was no immediate family to be found, so the little local church took care of the arrangements."

"Were you suspicious of her death, too?" I asked.

"Well," he continued, "I had to ask myself why the hell she would be sweeping the porch roof all by herself on her birthday? Neither Bill nor I ever believed any of the deaths were accidents. We knew instinctively that they each had something to do with the 1969 curling tragedy in Grand Forks. Like everyone, our first thought was that Tommy was somehow behind it all, but when I followed up, I realized it was impossible. Tommy wasn't even in the country."

"You were sure of that?" I asked.

"Positive," he said quietly.

"And how were you so positive?" I pressed further.

He paused a minute and I realized he may have been telling the story for the first time.

"Right after Bill and I got to Diego Garcia, I received a letter from

Tommy telling me about his orders to Vietnam. Over the next couple of years, he sent me a few short letters assuring me he was fine and doing well as a Marine, although each time he was promoted, he somehow managed to get himself busted back down to buck private."

I pulled out the Navy photo and held it in front of him. "When was this picture taken?" I asked.

"That was on the The Harbough," he said with a smile, turning it over to read the old message he had written across the back, so long ago.

"Bill had it hanging in his office," I said. "But I suspect you knew that."

"No, I didn't know that," he said. "I haven't had any contact with Bill in a long time. Anyway, in mid-1972, as the war was winding down, he and I re-upped for another three-year hitch. We were shipped to Vietnam and assigned to the Harbough together. Our job was to patrol the river inlets along the South China Sea. I learned through unofficial military scuttlebutt that Tommy was stationed at Con Thien firebase, not too far from our patrol area."

"Did you ever manage to see him and talk to him?" I asked.

He drew silent for a moment, as if to compose himself before continuing, "Yes, I saw him briefly. But no, we never talked. In late July, our boat was on a recovery mission on the Ben Hai River, in the so-called demilitarized zone along the North-South border. We were salvaging the remains of a downed helicopter gunship. I got a note through to Tommy that my crew would be working in his area for a few days. I received a message back informing me that he was already thinking of signing on for another tour of duty."

"Three tours in-country as a combat Marine?" I asked. "How did he survive that?"

"Vietnam was perfect for someone like him," he answered. "As long as you were willing to take a bullet for the cause, people left you alone. Anyway, in the message he said he missed me and hoped he would have a chance to catch up with us."

"And did you get the chance to catch up?"

"On the third day of the recovery operation, we came under heavy mortar fire from both banks of the river. We scooted to the southern bank and were ordered to dig in to defend ourselves and protect our boat. Within a few minutes, all hell broke loose around us. Small arms. Mortar shells. Grenades. Men were screaming. You couldn't think through all the fear."

"You came out of it alive."

"Not as alive as it might appear," he said.

"You never said a word about this to anybody, Dad."

"And in a minute, you'll understand why," he continued. "I was ordered to hold a position at the far end of the line. It was near the edge of the jungle brush and the worst possible place to be. I was cut off from everyone in my unit and I was terrified. When a buddy of mine suddenly took a direct mortar hit on his shallow hole about forty feet to my left, I jumped up and bolted into the underbrush. I didn't give a damn about the boat or any of the men on the river bank. I ran about a hundred yards, not knowing or caring where I was going. It was suicide to run into the jungle like that. Hell, I was probably running right through the thickest part of the shooting. I knew I was lucky to be alive with every step I took. I just needed out."

"So you kept running all the way to Saigon?"

"No. When I reached the edge of the trees near a clearing, I dug myself a hole under a large root and waited it out. Within a few minutes, some Hueys landed and off-loaded about three dozen Marine grunts from the nearby Con Thien firebase. The Marines began running toward the river but stopped about seventy five yards in front of me to get their bearings. When mortar shells started coming into their group, two of the men were ordered in my direction to secure their flank. As the two men drew to within fifteen feet of me, I saw that the man carrying the grenade launcher was Tommy."

"I yelled out to him. Both men froze in their tracks, unable to see me and not knowing if I was friend or enemy. I was lucky as hell they didn't unload everything they had on the sound of my voice. I'll never forget it. As they squatted down searching the brush line, Tommy calmly lit up a cigarette as if he had just stepped up to a bar to order a beer. He had been a heavy smoker since he was about fourteen years old. It was that cool-headed approach to trouble that I remember most about him, even when he was in the thickest possible crap."

"I was about to holler out again when a mortar round exploded directly between us. The young Marine nearest me disintegrated into a cloud of red mist. Nothing was left of him, Jack, and I mean *nothing*. God, I've lived with that image every day of my life. I caught shrapnel through my shoulder and side. When the dust cleared, Tommy laid writhing on the ground with the lower part of his face nearly blown off. His arms and hands were chewed like hamburger and he had a gaping hole ripping his chest open. He could hardly breathe."

I interrupted his narrative, "Oh, God, I'm so sorry, Dad. You don't need to tell me anymore."

"Yes, Jack, I do," he said. "Because it's the next part of the story that will start to make sense. I pulled his body under the tree root with me but there was nothing I could say or do. I held him there, looking into his eyes until there was no life left to look into."

"How did you come out of it?"

"The Marines began skirmishing their way toward my boat crew. Within ten or fifteen minutes, the shooting and mortar fire stopped. Through the dense brush, I could hear the muffled shouts and screams of the wounded coming from the riverbank. I rested my brother's body in the root-hole and covered it with dead brush scattered throughout the area. As I looked down on my brother for the last time, it struck me that his face was completely unrecognizable. It was then that I had the idea that would change my life forever."

"You didn't report his death?"

"Before putting the last large palm branch over him, I pulled his dog tags from around his neck and rummaged through his combat pack until I found his military ID card. With our heads shaved for duty, most of us young white GIs all looked pretty much alike on our small ID photos. I knew I could pass for him in the coming years, if I ever needed to. I didn't know how, but I figured that taking over Tommy's identity just might help me escape whatever injustice the *Skip* had waiting for me back in the states. From that moment on, I unofficially became Tommy J. Dumot from Milwaukee, Wisconsin, whenever the need arose."

"But, officially, you also remained Arv DuMot?"

"Yes, for official things like driver's license, marriage certificate, car tabs, taxes, or anything else that might require paperwork that would end up buried in the bottom of some bureaucrats filing cabinet somewhere. Those were the days before every little town had their records on computers. But to the rest of the world, I was Tommy DuMot. I needed the murderer to think that Arv DuMot was nowhere to be found.

"So you left his body hidden there in that mud hole and let his Marine unit report him MIA?"

"Most of the rivers in Vietnam flooded every year with the rains. I figured the body would wash away and decompose or his remains would be eaten by a wild pig. His lower jaw was blown apart so his dental records wouldn't be able to identify him. I didn't take any chances, though. I used my bush knife to cut off his name tag from his uniform shirt and field pack. I covered his body as best I could and quickly pulled my way through the jungle to get back to my fox hole, where I passed out until a medic finally came around to treat my wounds. Nobody from my unit ever knew what happened. We lost six of our crew that day and two more Marines. Tommy was officially listed as MIA, along with that other young Marine. I still carry a small piece of shrapnel pressed up against one of my lower vertebrae. The military surgeons could never completely pull it out."

"Bill Ordway came through the battle all right?" I asked. "You never told him what you did."

"He was holed-up on the far side of the line, where there was less shooting and mortar fire. He survived unscratched."

"So how did you two keep tabs on the *Skip* all those years?" I asked. "I mean, you weren't even completely sure he was real, were you?"

"Well, the string of deaths came to a stop for many years after that," he continued. "It was Bill's mother, Cynthia, who first put two-and-two together; that the victims were all dying on or near their fifty-sixth birthday. By the time we mustered out of the Navy after our second hitch, she was also dead."

"Murdered?"

"Well, we're not so sure," he answered. "She had been sick with cancer for quite a while. She died about a month short of her fifty-sixth birthday. Bill was never fully convinced that the *Skip* had anything to do with her death. It didn't matter. We learned enough to know he was real and he would be gunning for us. But we were still very young and we felt we had time. Bill and I did everything we could to convince the FBI to get involved, though. We even gave them the list of possible victims, including our own names. But the murders had stopped because nobody else on the list was near the right age yet. Most of the FBI investigators lost interest. All but one, anyway. But I guess you learned all about Sam Ruude for yourself."

"Did you think you beat the *Skip* somehow?"

"Well, we were cautiously hopeful. We still got together frequently over the next several years to try to figure things out, though. Then people on our list began turning up dead again periodically. They fit the pattern. We pleaded with the FBI to get more involved but they didn't lift a finger. Somewhere along the line, I finally admitted to Bill what I did to Tommy down under that tree root in Vietnam that day. He said he would have done the same thing. We both thought we could use it to our advantage somehow, if we could keep it quiet between ourselves."

I took a moment to think things through. There were some inconsistencies that bothered me.

"But I discovered that the government database now officially lists Tommy's status as killed in action rather than MIA" I said. "How did the record finally get set straight? Did they find his body?"

"In early 2002, when I decided to kill off Arvil DuMot and start this invisible man act, I knew I had to finally kill off the real Tommy DuMot, too. I did some research and discovered that the name of the other MIA Marine blown up that day was a young man named Lance Corporal Maxwell F. Borwin, of Kalamazoo, Michigan. I contacted the U.S. government office of POW/MIA Affairs and reported that I was former Lance Corporal Maxwell F. Borwin, a deserter from the battlefield that day. After all these years, I told them I felt guilty about deserting and wanted to come clean. I should be removed from the MIA list. I also wanted to report that I knew for a fact that Private First Class Thomas J. DuMot should not be listed as MIA. He should be listed officially as killed in action. When they asked questions to verify the facts, I was able to give them a second-by-second account of what had taken place, just fifteen feet in front of me that afternoon, including where they could find the remains of Tommy's body."

"And they took your word for it."

"No, they said I would need a lawyer. So, I hired Sam Ruude again to play the part. He was a very valuable asset in that way. He submitted the required reports and paperwork. They apparently checked the official after-action reports from the battle and must have decided that my story was close enough to the truth. Within a few months, the brave, dead Lance Corporal Maxwell F. Borwin was no longer listed among the honorable MIAs. Tommy's status was officially changed to KIA — killed in action."

"But doesn't that mean that the brave, dead Lance Corporal Maxwell F. Borwin of Kalamazoo is now officially listed as a deserter?" I asked.

"Yeah, that part bothered me a little at first," he answered. "So I checked the records for his surviving family members. I'm not sure what I would have done if his parents or any siblings were still alive. But after more than thirty-five years, I have never been able to find any relative who would still be ashamed of that little injustice to his name."

"So now you have no actual living physical identity other than Arv Firpo," I said.

"Yeah, how'd you like to get stuck with that handle for the rest of your life?" he laughed.

"And that would explain why you never enter world championships or Olympic qualifiers," I concluded. "You can't get a passport. What do you do if someone asks for official ID?"

He pulled out his wallet and showed me a legitimate birth certificate for Arvil Dwayne Firpo, born February 23, 1951.

"It's a copy of my original with my last name professionally doctored, that's all."

"And a driver's license? In case you ever get pulled over by the police?" I asked.

"I've been driving since I was a fourteen year old kid on the farm, Jack. I've never had a ticket or been in a fender-bender in my life. I make sure I don't get pulled over. Whenever possible, I have someone else drive. This is America, after all. Nobody ever asks to see a photo ID. But, in case someone ever does, I show them this."

He lifted a flap in his wallet and slid out a perfect replica of a North Dakota driver's license.

"Nobody ever checks beneath the surface. It was all part of Sam Ruude's comprehensive makeover services."

"You've got it all set up," I said. "Congratulations. You really are Arv Firpo."

"And congratulations to you, too, Jack," he said. "You are the sole survivor of the Peter and Medora blood line and heir to the DuMot legacy."

"Not that it's anything to be too proud of," I thought silently.

7:00 a.m. Monday, February 11th, 2008

We arrived at the Moorhead Curling Club a few minutes after seven o'clock, where we were greeted in the front lobby by club manager Mike Erickson. I was relieved to feel that the ceiling heaters were already beginning to remove the morning chill from the building. My father introduced us politely while carrying his curling bag onto the ice.

I watched Dad as he stretched and took several practice slides out of the hack. *"It's the choices we make that make us who we are,"* I recalled hearing him say once. For whatever past faults he may have had, people throughout his world clearly admired him. He returned the adoration by working hard to be an ambassador for the game he loved.

I knew I had several hours to myself as I watched shot-after-shot stick to the button or within four-foot circle. He moved quickly across all eight sheets of ice and then changed ends and repeated the routine. After forty minutes, he began placing rocks in strategic locations in front of the house to practice drawing around and between guards. Each set up became increasingly more difficult. After about an hour and a half, Mike stepped onto the ice and took up a spot on one end. I watched as he set up several shot configurations and then held the broom as a target. Again and again, every rock curled exactly on cue. It was true what everyone said: Arv Firpo never missed. From my perspective behind the plexiglass, he often appeared to squeeze his eleven inch rock through a ten inch opening.

After working on his draw weights, he began to practice raises, rolls and freezes. He clicked his shots off target rocks at such razor-thin angles that his stone rolled only an inch or two left or right. He moved on to double-takeouts and bump-and-rolls then twenty-foot run-ups. I recalled something Dan Graber at the USCA once said about him, "He can pick a snow flea off the edge of a guard rock." Amazingly, he could.

Mike came off the ice and stood near me as we continued to watch.

"Do club managers all over the country bend over backward for him like this?" I asked.

"We're all proud to do it," he answered.

I wondered if so many people would feel that way if they knew everything I had learned about him over the previous few days. I watched his determination on the ice and remembered what he had said about reconciliation. So many years ago, he had robbed the world of his brother's God-given curling talent and skill. Perhaps such a singular obsession to be the best was now Dad's only means of atonement and restitution.

I realized that I would be facing several long days on the road ahead as we followed the intended practice route from club-to-club while inching our way toward Hibbing. I decided to bide my time by seeking answers to some unresolved questions about Tina. It was nearly ten o'clock. The ProtoCommand receptionist would be at her desk and most employees would be in their departments. I punched the speed dial button on my cell phone and the receptionist answered immediately.

"Hi, I'd like to talk to a man named Gary in the purchasing department, please."

"Do you have his last name or a direct extension number?"

"Well, no I don't. All I know is the man's first name is Gary and he works in purchasing."

"We only have one man named Gary down in purchasing."

"Well then do you think it's just *possible* that he's the Gary I want to talk to?"

Without another word from her, I was put on hold. As I listened to the soft jazz, I began to worry for the first time about what I would say when Married Gary answered the phone. I didn't have long to think about it.

A click interrupted a Whitney Houston song and a very young-sounding Gary Schmidt introduced himself as a purchasing assistant.

"Hi, Gary," I said. "I'm Jack DuMot. I used to work upstairs for Bill Ordway in the contract programming department. We both know Tina Bucholz. I won't ask too many questions. I just want to know that she's all right."

"Who is this," he asked. "What are you talking about?"

I realized that I had caught him off guard so I backed up and gave him as much back story as I thought he needed.

"...so, anyway, it's none of my business but I understand that you're in a relationship with her."

"I don't know a Tina Bucherwald or Buchholz, or whatever you said her name is," he answered. "I've only worked here for about a month."

I started again.

"Okay, I know this must be strange, but do you mind if I ask you some questions?"

"Knock yourself out," he said sarcastically. I instantly started to dislike the young jerk.

I asked him about the few details I could remember from Tina's description of their relationship.

No, he had never been married. No, he didn't have a child. No, he never lived in Illinois. He graduated from Concordia College last May and he still lives with his parents in Apple Valley.

The more he talked, the more I realized he was probably telling the truth. The timbre of his voice was significantly less mature than a man who was supposed to be a good friend of Bill Ordway. The man I expected would have been an experienced professional manager, probably in his early to mid-forties.

"I'm sorry," I said. "I think I'm following up on some wrong information. Can you transfer me back to the receptionist, please?"

He said he'd be happy to but, of course, our call was disconnected as soon as he punched the wrong button.

I redialed and talked to the receptionist to confirm what the young man had told me. Sure enough, the Gary Schmidt I had just spoken to was not the purchasing department manager. In fact, there was no other person named Gary working at the company. Neither did anyone else fit the description of a department manager who had moved to Twin Cities from Decatur. Coupled with Tina's lie about talking to Paul Gombrich in Grand Forks, I decided I had heard enough.

Married Gary didn't exist — at least not at ProtoCommand.

I tried to remember every other detail Tina had shared with me about herself or her family. I recalled that she said her family lived in Pipestone and her father had once been mayor of the city. Her sister Sophie was a senior at Pipestone High. I searched the official city website and started with the city administrator's office. I learned that no one named Bucholz had ever been elected mayor. Per policy, the high school refused to confirm or deny that a girl named Sophia Bucholz was registered as a student.

I had already caught her in three lies, so I figured I might as well try for a complete boxed set. I turned my attention to the man from Nebraska whom Tina claimed was working on Bill Ordway's probate administration. From directory assistance, I was connected to two men named Joseph Nehmer listed in the Omaha metro area telephone directory. One was a young construction worker who had recently lost his job. The other was a retired postal worker living at the St. Agnes Center for Independent Living. Neither had ever heard of anyone named Ordway and neither knew a jot or tittle about probate litigation. I had heard enough. Nothing about Tina checked out. Sam Ruude's words echoed back to me: 'What part of **trust no one** was so difficult to understand, damn it?'

When my father came off the ice about thirty minutes later, I relayed what I had learned.

"That just means we have to watch our backs a little more," he said. "I'll call the rest of the curling club managers that I've scheduled practice sessions with. We'll mix up the route. We'll arrive at each club unexpected after the doors are already open for league play. If I can get a few minutes of open ice time, I'll need you to help me set up the practice shots. If we can't get open ice, I'll do what I can to get into a league match. That way, if anyone calls and asks, none of the clubs can say they're expecting me."

My father and I sat with Mike for several enjoyable minutes until players began stretching for their games. Mike excused himself and talked to several Skips privately before returning to inform us that a rink on sheet four needed a substitute player. My father quickly grabbed his broom and returned to the ice to introduce himself to the men milling about. I could see by the smiles and handshakes that many of the players knew of his name and fame.

An hour and a half later, we enjoyed an early lunch with several club members before saying goodbye and rolling out of the parking lot.

"Where to now?" I asked. "Detroit Lakes?"

"No, I called the club manager over lunch. Billy's no longer expecting us. I had a good practice session this morning. Let's take a good long drive down to Mapleton. I never have seen those banners you told me about. They must have hung them after I left the area. It'll give us a chance to just hang out together for awhile."

Tuesday through Thursday, February 12th - 14th, 2008

The remainder of the week was a repeat of Monday. Each morning, we arrived at our chosen club in time for stretching and a little open-ice practice, in preparation for league games to begin. Without fail, my father would find a spot as an alternate or someone would gladly give up his position for the day. After two or three hours of practice and game play, we would be back on the road toward the next club. One day, we even managed to hit three separate clubs. The towns and restaurants, the curling clubs and the names and faces all began running into one another. It dawned on me that he had been maintaining that schedule for more than five years.

"This isn't a life I would want to live for one week," I commented after driving for another two hours toward another obscure club in another obscure town. "How have you done it for so many years?"

"I don't do it for me," he replied cryptically, but didn't bother to say more.

Along the route, we said little unless it was to share some anecdote about our next destination. Often, long stretches of quiet passed between us. Not painful silence as if wishing for something to fill an imagined disconnect. The trip was like Steinbeck's travels through a man's soul with his dog, Charley.

I had spent my young teenage years communicating very little with my father; followed by my young adult years living with the shriek of my mother's world and the shrillness of my marriage to LaVon. Neither he nor I felt the need to fill the time and space with further arguments and nitpicking at each other's life-choices. Everything that needed to be said had been said. I wasn't ready to call it the love. After all, what had we done for each other lately? Nonetheless, the comforting stillness of simply being in each other's presence was worth more to each of us than a lifetime of idle chatter. I could feel a tranquil white noise binding us together; drowning out the red cacophony of disappointment that once resonated.

We zigged and zagged our way across Minnesota. From Mapleton, we headed east to Owatonna then north again to St. Cloud and Duluth. Altogether, we crisscrossed more than six hundred miles to eight curling clubs in three days. At every stop, my father was welcomed and got the ice time he needed. But it was also clear that he had come to expect club managers and players to meet him on his terms. When he walked into a club, he would find hands extended in friendship, followed just as quickly by players moving over one sheet to make room for his practice sessions. I never saw him have to ask.

We spent Wednesday night at the Bemidji AmericInn, directly across the street from the Bemidji Curling Club.

"Remember this place?" he asked as he directed me to drive down the main drag into the hotel parking lot. "You and your friends almost got us thrown out in the snow one Friday night when I brought you here for a bonspiel."

"I remember getting yelled at by the hotel manager one night," I said, "but I didn't remember it was at this place. I sure remember the curling club, though. Why are we stopping here? You have to be in Hibbing tomorrow evening. Shouldn't we just head straight there?"

"Late tomorrow evening," he replied. "Two of the members on my rink play out of this club. We're going to meet tomorrow morning to go over some things. We might be in there awhile. I hope you find it interesting."

Over a light snack at the club's upstairs bar the following morning, I was introduced to John Paulheim, who would be throwing Third. Paul opened a briefcase and tossed a notepad and some papers on the table. We each pulled a copy of the playdown drawsheet toward ourselves and sat silently for a moment to review players' names.

1. **Birr rink**: Todd Birr, Bill Todhunter, Greg Johnson, Kevin Birr, Paul Pustovar
2. **Brown rink**: Craig Brown, Rich Ruohonen, John Dunlop, Pete Annis
3. **Disher rink**: Craig Disher, Kevin Kakela, Zach Jacobson, Carey Kakela, Kurt Disher
4. **Fenson rink**: Pete Fenson, Shawn Rojeski, Joe Polo, Tom O'Connor
5. **Firpo rink**: Arv Firpo, Kent Marquis, John Paulheim, Gusty Steinham
6. **George rink**: Tyler George, Kris Perkovich, Phill Drobnick, Kevin Johnson
7. **Larway rink**: Jason Larway, Colin Hufman, Greg Persinger, Joel Larway, Steven Demlow
8. **Roe rink**: Jeremy Roe, Pat Roe, Richard Maskel, Mark Hartman, Matt Hamilton
9. **Romaniuk rink**: Greg Romaniuk, Leon Romaniuk, Doug Pottinger,

Mike Calcagno, Cory Yalowicki

10. Shuster rink: John Shuster, Jeff Isaacson, Chris Plys, Shane McKinlay, Jason Smith

11. Wilberg rink: William Wilberg, Charles Taggart, Alex Leichter, Andrew Quigley, Andy Campbell

"There are eleven rinks on this draw list," I remarked. "Why the odd number?"

"They're experimenting with adding an alternate rink this year," Paulheim answered. "Two of the rinks will play each other to advance to the final ten. The loser will stick around as an alternate, in case one rink can't compete. That way, the tenth is already on site."

My father returned his attention to the list of rinks and game times.

"I don't like having to take on Pete so early," he said.

"Are you referring to the 2006 U.S. Olympic Skip Pete Fenson?" I asked. He plays out of Bemidji, too, if I remember right."

The two men nodded.

"I hope we can get past Disher," Paulheim said. "His boys are all from North Dakota. Whenever these national playdowns are in Minnesota, they show up wearing their game faces. But they won't know the ice. I ran up against Craig in the regional semifinals a couple of years ago. He played aggressively. The man can hit cold draws like nobody I've ever seen before — even you on some nights, Arv."

My father picked up the conversation.

"Hmm. When we don't have last rock, we need to clog the front of the zone and make him hit his long run-ups and side rolls. Then we might have a chance of stealing a point or two when he's not looking."

One by one over the next two hours, the two men meticulously picked through the list.

"Has Gusty down in Mankato seen this?" my dad asked, referring to Gusty Steinham of the Mankato club.

"I've run through the draws with him," Paulheim said. "Steinham came up here last weekend to work with Marquis and me. It's tough to get in a good practice without you involved, though, Arv."

"I know, John, and I'm sorry. But that's why we're meeting late tonight in Hibbing. I want to have a meeting to get the lay of the land. The USCA won't allow us on the ice until our practice time but I've arranged a few hours of open ice time early Friday morning in Chisholm. The clubs are only about fifteen minutes apart. It's the best I can do, John. I'm sorry."

"Well, as long as you don't wear us out for the games," came a voice abruptly behind us.

It was Kent Marquis, the other player from the Bemidji club. Kent was scheduled to open the first game as Lead but would probably be shifted to Second if the rink advanced through the rounds. We shook hands and Marquis took a seat at the table. The three men quickly returned to the business at hand.

"I promise that you boys will never have to deal with this again. As I said, this will be the end of the line for me, win, lose or…"

"Or die," I mumbled under my breath.

I sat listening quietly, sensing I was in the presence of greatness all around the table. It was fascinating to hear them work their way through the strengths and idiosyncrasies of every Skip, every individual player and every rink.

"To hear you guys talk," I interrupted, "not a player on this list has a weakness. Everyone misses a shot sometime, don't they?"

"We're talking about the best curlers in the world, son," Marquis admonished. "We all miss a handful of shots, but you never plan a strategy based on your opponent playing poorly. We're going to make most of our shots. We have to figure they'll make theirs. Forcing the other player into throwing the rock he doesn't want to throw is what will make the difference on each end."

"We won't know what the ice will be like until we get there," my father said. "Last week, I called Paul Vendetti, president of the Hibbing club. Originally, the plan was to hold the draws at the community hockey arena. But, we're talking about the Minnesota Iron Range. Not even a national curling championship takes priority over youth hockey games up there. Vendetti said the USCA brought in five top pros to get the ice right at their club. Each sheet should play fair."

"It's going to be crowded on the runways between the sheets" Kent Marquis said. "There could be lots of people standing between all those rows of roof support columns that old building is famous for. That ice can frost up pretty quickly if humidity becomes a problem. Of course, it could go into a meltdown, too."

"It depends upon the seating arrangements," Paulheim said. "If they keep everyone behind the glass, we'll be okay. If they set up seating in the sheet area it could be tricky."

At one o'clock, the club manager approached our table and informed us that two rinks for the mixed seniors' league would need substitutes for their two o'clock matches. Marquis and Paulheim respectfully declined with an apology to my father. Dad checked his watch as if seriously considering the opportunity for a moment, but then declined, as well. That came as a surprise but I was relieved.

"Gentlemen," he said, shaking hands sharply, "thanks for coming along with me on this last great ride. It means more to me than you'll ever know. We'll see everyone tonight in Hibbing. Meet in the club parking lot at eleven o'clock."

Thursday Afternoon, February 14th, 2008

There is no direct driving route to shorten the two-hour drive between Bemidji and Hibbing. Since my father had made the trip dozens of times over the years, I asked him to drive and he cheerfully agreed. The quiet time gave me an opportunity to tell him a little more about my confusion over LaVon and Tina. The previous evening, I had received a reply message from LaVon, informing me that she decided not to immediately return to our house in Minneapolis. She correctly recognized that there wasn't anything there for her to return to. She and Bussy had re-read the local newspaper article about my father's rink and assumed that I would be heading to Hibbing to meet up with him at the championships. Since Tony intended to return to his wife and family in Grand Rapids, he offered to drive the extra miles to drop her off at a convenient location where she and I could get together to talk. The final line of her message caused my heart to dig into my throat: **We can discuss ways to make our marriage work.**

How could we make our marriage work with Tina still banging around inside my heart? But how could I quit on my wife with my wedding ring still banging around inside my pocket? I knew I couldn't.

I began a brief reply without saying more than I thought she needed to know.

> **Dad and I are on our way to Hibbing right now. We'll get there by late afternoon. We can find some time between his curling matches to mull things over.**

My father suggested that I should ask LaVon to meet us at the Sportsman's Restaurant and Taverna on East Howard Street in downtown Hibbing, where he would like an opportunity to meet her. He would then use my car to drive over to the Chisholm club for some additional practice by himself for the evening then return to pick us up in time to get to the Hibbing club at eleven p.m.

I typed the name of the restaurant, some basic driving directions and recommended we try to meet about seven o'clock. Before clicking the send button, I added a closing line.

> **Tina is no longer along for the ride. LaVon – I suspect that neither you nor I are the same people we were just six weeks ago. Sincerely, I look forward to seeing you this evening.**

I closed down my laptop and asked whether it was really necessary for him to squeeze in more hours of practice, this close to the start of the playdowns.

"This one isn't about needing more practice," he explained. "These Iron Range clubs — Hibbing, Chisholm, Virginia, Eveleth, Grand Rapids — are typically all under the same weather patterns. The crystal structure of the ice changes with the temperature. I won't know exactly what the ice is like until the matches start on Friday. But it helps to get some idea ahead of time. How you handle the ice during your practice sessions can make a big impact on how the other rinks play you during the games."

I suspected that he was really concocting a reason to give me some private time with LaVon.

"Really?" I responded. "You guys really pay that close attention to the science?"

"Well, I don't," he admitted with a chuckle. "But still, it's a great theory and it never hurts to know how the ice is behaving."

I was nervous about meeting LaVon later that evening and I was relieved when we pulled into a hotel and checked into a room, where we showered, changed and took a brief nap before heading to the restaurant.

As we settled into a booth near the front window, I tried continuing the conversation about LaVon and Tina, but received very little feedback or advice.

"I'm afraid I'm hardly the one to talk about rebuilding a broken relationship, Jack."

"I don't need answers, Dad," I said. "I guess I'm just looking for direction."

"OK," he replied, "Then follow the direction of your heart."

"Yeah," I said, "that's exactly what Tina warned me NOT to do when I started searching for you. There's a place for calculated reasoning in this world, too, Dad."

"It's like curling," he said predictably. "I play against guys all the time who would love to make precisely the right shot but at precisely the wrong time. Every end in a curling match has to be engineered, not just..."

I held my palm up to his face to stop him, "No, Dad, not everything is like curling."

A late model SUV screeched to a stop along the curb immediately outside the window. The glow spilling out from the restaurant was just enough to illuminate the face of Tony Perkovich, leaning forward and staring straight ahead from behind the steering wheel. The vehicle had hardly come to a stop when a young woman jumped out, yanked open the rear passenger door and snatched out a large plaid suitcase. She had barely stepped safely onto the sidewalk when the SUV sped away with a sudden jerk; allowing speed and momentum to slam shut the heavy door with a thud.

"Oh, that's LaVon getting dropped off now," I said.

"She didn't even kiss him goodbye," my dad observed. "And on Valentines' Day, no less."

6:00 p.m. Thursday, February 14th, 2008

LaVon stepped into the restaurant, removed her gloves and pulled a small knit cap from the back of her head. She pretended to act nonchalant about the poignancy of the moment but I knew it must have been as wrenching for her as it was for me. My father came to the rescue by waving his hand and calling out her name just loudly enough to be heard over the low buzz of conversation throughout the room. She smiled to acknowledge us and walked toward our booth, where my father met her with a warm handshake.

"You must be LaVon. You're as pretty as Jack described."

"I'm sure," she replied. "And you must be the long-lost Arv DuMot, back from the great beyond."

"Not so long and not so lost," he responded in like tone. "I'm only about five foot ten inches and I've always known exactly where I stand, even if nobody else does."

LaVon must have realized she was in the presence of her own form of greatness. Small talk between us continued for several minutes as we ordered a light dinner. I could tell my father enjoyed the opportunity to talk so freely about shared interests, without concern about me dredging up remorse and angst. Without noticing, more than an hour and a half passed. He suddenly checked his watch.

"Oops, it's nearly a quarter to nine. The Chisholm club is only about fifteen minutes from here. Jack, if I can borrow the car keys, I can make my way over there and get in some licks before we meet up tonight. That will give you two a chance to catch up. I'll be back."

He bid us goodbye with a promise that he would return to pick us up sometime before 10:45 p.m. I shuddered internally at the thought of being stuck for another hour and a half trying to sift through the critical issues of where our marriage had been and where it might be heading in the future.

Sitting alone in a mostly-empty restaurant, we stared down at the special Valentine's Day placemats and decorations overcrowding our table. After a few awkward seconds, I flagged down a passing waitress and ordered another Coke for each of us. I also asked whether it would be OK to continue killing time sitting in the booth, just talking. The waitress looked at us intently and seemed to size up the situation accurately.

"We don't kick our customers out into the cold. I'll keep the drinks coming. At ten o'clock, I'll bring you each a piece of pie, will that be enough time?"

Again I was faced with Kipling's unforgiving minute, as LaVon and I struggled with the awkward silence between us.

"Well," she finally said. "We have a long evening ahead of us until your father gets back. Since we really didn't know where to start talking about us. Maybe we can start talking about the other people in our marriage."

"Sure," I said sarcastically. "We can start with Tony."

"No," she answered. "You learned everything you needed to know down in our basement. There are no more secrets about my past with him. So let's start with Tina. Then I'll explain what's left of Tony."

"Okay, I'll start by explaining what's left of Tina," I nodded.

I smiled at her, grateful for finding a shorthand method of summing up the real issues we were facing. I started by explaining everything about the search for my father. I reminded her of my mother's final moments as we stood at her bedside so long ago.

"Oh, God, yeah," LaVon said. "I remember what she said that afternoon in her hospital room. It was haunting."

She gnarled her fists and twisted her face to mimic the dying look.

"I...I...find...you...rude," she growled.

"Hey, not a bad imitation," I commented.

"So she was trying to tell us something?"

"Yeah," I said. "It turned out she was talking about a man named Sam Ruude. He's dead now, too."

Slowly, I got around to telling her about the various scenes, actors and scripts, including the coded message, my discussion with former

FBI agent Doug Chimny and my afternoon with Sam Ruude. I finally brought the explanation around to my father's connection to championship curling. At the outset, I tried to keep Tina stitched loosely onto the hem of the story, as if only adding a button or bead for embellishment. But increasingly, she became the essential element, inextricably woven into the fabric of the entire chronicle.

"Isn't it funny," LaVon interrupted, "you had everything you needed to find your father all along. You just weren't able to see things clearly enough until you were able to wipe Tina from in front of your eyes."

I hadn't thought of it that way, but she was right.

I continued retelling the story to the end but was careful to leave out the part about finding the travel bag stuffed with more than a quarter of a million dollars, still tucked tightly under the passenger seat of my locked car.

"So, LaVon, it all ends here," I wrapped up. "At this particular table, at this particular restaurant, on this particular night in Hibbing. My father and I have no idea what lies in store for us tonight or over this weekend. Unfortunately, you may have stepped into this thing as deep as any of us now. That's what Tina ran away from."

"She has a story, too," LaVon said, echoing Tina's words.

She grew quiet and I could tell she was putting her sharp mind into gear.

"That young woman dropped everything and followed you out here on this crazy trek," she said after a moment. "I suspect there's a great deal more you either don't know or aren't telling me. I mean, for a woman to put her life on the line like that, it tells me there is more history between you two than just two or three days of running around the cold Minnesota countryside in the dead of winter."

What was LaVon accusing me of? Having a long-running affair with Tina?

"Well, there's a case of the fire hydrant peeing on the dog!" I complained. "First of all, I don't owe you any excuses or explanation. Nothing happened between Tina and me...either before or after you left me for Tony. Not that we damned sure didn't want things too. But stupid as I am, I made sure we didn't do the wrong thing."

"Did we do things so wrong, Jack?" she asked.

"Don't sound so smug, LaVon. You were cheating on me from the very start. On our honeymoon, for God's sake. Why the hell did you ever agree to marry me?"

LaVon sighed.

"No, Jack. That's what you assumed after reading all those letters and cards," she said. "I knew you would, so I let you. Those pictures and cards in that old metal box were all from before our marriage. None of them were from our honeymoon week. But I owe you an explanation. I met T — I mean Tony — during my junior year of college in Mankato, long before I met you. He was Jeb's best friend from Grand Rapids High School. Jeb moved to Mankato for college and ended up driving a cab."

"Unlicensed," I threw in.

"Yes, Jack, illegally. That's how Bussy and I met him. Tony stayed in Grand Rapids and got hired by a logging company where he met his wife, Paula. She got pregnant a few months later and they married. They had a little girl. A year and a half later, she got pregnant again, this time with a little boy born with severe autism. The kid's problems led to some tough times between them. He eventually lost his job and took whatever odd work he could find in the area. On and off, he would leave Paula to sort things out. At times, he moved to Mankato for a few weeks or a couple of months where he would make ends meet by driving a cab illegally for Jeb's employer. I met him during one of those cab rides home from a bar late one night."

"And he put up his off duty sign and the rest is history?" I asked.

"You make it sound so dirty, Jack," she replied. "It wasn't like that. He really loved Paula and his kids but he just couldn't figure out a way to make things work. He kept going back to her. He kept coming back to Mankato. He needed me, Jack. For the first time, a man really needed me for more than cleaning up his vomit. And I was such a damned good caregiver by then that it felt wonderful to be needed."

"But you still ended up marrying me," I noted.

"He was ready to leave Paula for good. We were even discussing getting married right after his divorce was final. We were going to move up here to the Range. I was in my last year of college. The school districts around here were hiring teachers and he could be close to his kids. God, how he loved those damned kids. Then he called me to say that his wife was begging him to work things out. He couldn't leave her. I told him if he went back to her, I was finished with him forever. By then I was in my final semester before graduation so I jumped all over the opportunity to travel out to San Francisco with a friend. That's when I met you. You were good material to work with, Jack. Funny. Young. Educated and good looking enough. You had a spark that brought me back to life. You may not have seen it in yourself but you were salvageable."

"But Tony never really went back to his wife, did he?"

"No, not really," she continued. "About a month after your

mother's funeral, right after we got settled together in the house in Minneapolis, he called me. I pushed and pushed and pushed him away. He begged and begged and begged me back into his life. I said he needed some serious help. He said he couldn't do it without me. But he never really moved out from Paula and the kids. Not emotionally, anyway. So, he just kind of followed me around and we got together when we could. That's why I could never say yes to marrying you for the first six months after I moved in. You were convenient for me, Jack, but I was never certain that he was completely out of my life. But as time passed, you became more than just a matter of convenience. I actually fell in love with you, God help me."

"But you kept every card and letter he ever sent you." I reminded her. "I burned all those cards in the furnace that night, you know."

"Well, I didn't think you would frame them," she said. "But I want you to know that I never sent him anything in return or initiated anything with him. Not until the very end, anyway."

"The very end?"

"Well, I finally I agreed to marry you...expecting that it was finally over with him. I swear, Jack, after we were married I never saw him again until a couple of months ago, before we went to visit Bussy and Jeb for the holiday party over New Years."

"And that time you said you were pregnant?" I asked. "Was he the father? Is that why you ended the pregnancy?"

"No, Jack," she answered quietly. "You were the father. I lost that child to a natural miscarriage. I didn't have an abortion. I knew you didn't want a kid so I just let you think whatever you wanted to think."

"So what finally changed with him?" I continued. "Why did you decide to leave me and move in with him?"

"It wasn't anything that changed with him. It was something that changed between you and me. It began about mid-summer. The thought of returning to teach another school year in the fall was unbearable. You could see that I was starting to drink more. Between that and your constant weekend work and bitching about your job every morning, noon and night, I couldn't even recognize us. When you were fired after Labor Day, things hit a low point. Then, he suddenly showed up at our door one day in late October, when you were out. By then, Jack, I had given up on trying to salvage whatever it was that you and I were trying to save. He seemed like my only hope. But I was wrong — again."

The waitress interrupted us with our drinks and lingered for a few seconds too long before LaVon gave her a sharp, "Thank you" accompanied by an exaggerated nod.

"He and I had built up so much history," she continued. "I never felt that you and I built up anything. I just needed someone I could turn to. He took it as one more opportunity to try to break away from his wife and kids. Bussy and my other friends all said I should jump on the chance to leave you and move in with him. I...I mean we...you and I were just so miserable, Jack. I didn't know what to do or where to turn."

"Yeah, I guess my shoulders never were strong enough to cry on, were they?" I interjected seriously.

"I wouldn't know if that was the case" she said. "It was really the first time in my life that I ever thought I needed a shoulder to cry on. I never gave yours a chance."

She smiled and wiped away a tear.

"He told me he was leaving Paula and the kids for good this time. He had already made arrangements to move in with Bussy and Jeb down in Mankato. Jeb would let him drive cab illegally again until he got his license. So we made our plans. I didn't want to make a big scene about it with you. You were miserable enough being out of work and I was miserable enough teaching and with life in general. I arranged to take a family medical leave of absence from the school, beginning right after the Christmas break. I told them it was to take care of an elderly parent. Only my closest friends knew the truth and nobody at the school district ever checks the facts. Then, all through December, I slowly moved my clothes and other personal belongings into small boxes in the garage. From there, I secretly sent them by FedEx down to Bussy."

"Right under my nose," I sighed. "It served me right for crawling into my own little shell."

"No," she responded, "not right under your nose. You never held your head high enough to do anything right under your nose. Let's just say it was all done right behind your back, though, which you always seemed to have turned toward me, anyway."

"But now you have come back" I said. "What happened this time?"

"Same old-same old," she said. "After a few weeks, he started making noises again about missing his kids. His wife would call almost every day to complain about raising a disabled child on her own. Shame and guilt are very effective weapons."

I thought of my father's own guilt and lifelong shame over his younger brother.

Yeah, I've heard that," I added quietly. "And now it's over

between you two?"

"Yes, It has fully run its course," she answered. "Jeb and Bussy were drinking one night and admitted to me that Tony was seeing some little barmaid on the side. Christ, Bussy knew about it, too. That's what really hurt."

I thought back to that night Jeb drove me to Mapleton and remembered the waitress who had asked about Tony.

"Yeah, I met her at the Haymaker Bar in Mapleton, the night of the reunion party. If it means anything, LaVon, you're prettier."

She started to say something caustic but stopped herself.

"Thank you, Jack. Yes, it does mean something to me."

I had heard enough personal confessions for one evening.

"Jeesh, I'm so sorry for what I became, LaVon."

"Well, after all, it's what we've done that makes us who we are," she said, quoting a line from a favorite old Jim Croce song. "Don't blame yourself for becoming anything, Jack. We weren't wrong. We weren't right. We just were. And that's what needs to change."

"That's what is so confusing about being here with you," I said.

"Confusing?" she chuckled sarcastically through her tears. "What is it about this entire mess you could possibly find confusing?"

"Well, to use my father's curling vernacular, it's a crowded house. There are you and Tony. There's me. There's Tina. Is there enough room in this twelve-foot circle for just you and me?"

"My God, you aren't at all the same Jack DuMot you were just a month ago, are you?" she said. "There are only four players in the game. OK, five with your dead father come back to life, and suddenly you can't do the math. Regarding Tina, you need to settle some unresolved issues, Jack. Tony and I have dealt with ours. There may still be a chance for you and me, depending upon how you deal with her. The question is pretty simple: Are there more feelings remaining between you and Tina than there are between you and me? From what you have told me, she would need a damned good reason to risk her life the way she did. Are you enough of a damned good reason for her?"

Good question. I wasn't even enough of a damned good reason for her to stay with me all the way to meeting Sam Ruude.

We talked for the remainder of the evening but avoided the tough issues that we knew we would eventually need to face. But all of that could wait. Shortly after 10:30, my father stepped through the restaurant door and motioned to us silently.

"We need to get going," I said. "It's Valentine's evening. Should we consider this our first start at a second chance?"

She smiled sincerely; something I hadn't seen her do for far too long.

"We'll see if it goes better than the last time we got a fresh start," she said. "But Jack, let's try not to burn the place down this time, okay?"

"Let's go," my father said, dropping a twenty on the table to cover our twelve dollar tab. "I've got people waiting for me."

11:00 p.m. Thursday, February 14th, 2008

The Hibbing Curling Club was originally formed in 1942 and has produced several champion curlers. To the average league curler, however, it is best known for hosting the Last Chance Bonspiel in March of every year, during which nearly one hundred thirty rinks from throughout the United States descend on the heart of the Iron Range. For all of its history, today's club is housed in an old cinder block building with unique rows of columns supporting a low ceiling above eight curling sheets.

We circled the parking lot once and then once again before backing into a vacant spot at the outermost edge, some forty yards from the door. I noticed that my father left the engine running for heat but extinguished the headlights. The last remaining stragglers from the league games were exiting the building and heading to their cars for the cold drive home. Within a few minutes, we found ourselves alone in the vacant lot with no other cars anywhere in sight within the complex. When LaVon commented on the rather non-descript appearance of the building, my dad warned us not to judge a book by its cover.

"Don't kid yourself," he started, "When I was a younger man, a rink from this town won Worlds. That would have been back in '76, I guess. I remember watching them play that year. Some great curling names. Bruce and Joe Roberts, Gary Kleffman, Jerry Scott. Hell, Bruce Roberts was Skip on a number of Minnesota state champion rinks in the late '70s. Kleffman is still considered one of the best curlers to ever throw a rock in this state."

"Do they have a rink in the championships this weekend?" I asked.

"None of the Skips but some individual players will be on the teams. Their members haven't fared too well over the past several years, but the top-level players from this club are among the best I've ever played against. I don't like coming up against any Iron Rangers. The players step onto the ice with fire in their belly."

"And that's a good thing?" LaVon asked, continuing to warm to my father.

"It's a remarkable thing," he said with a smile. "Against the right kind of competition, assertive play can be a good thing. But an experienced opponent knows that it can also cause the Skip to make some questionable decisions."

"And you, Mr. DuMot?" she piped in again in a tone that sounded suspiciously like flirting. "How do you play when you come up against guys from the Iron Range?"

My father smiled. I could tell that he genuinely liked her but I couldn't fathom why that mattered to me. The two had struck up an immediate conversation as soon as we left the restaurant, with particular delight at learning that each shared some experiences living in the Mankato area. I wondered what he would have thought of Tina, her polar opposite.

"Please, LaVon. I would really like it if you called me Dad," he said. But I noticed that he didn't answer her question.

We scanned the parking lot, apparently trying to determine whether any of his team members had arrived early and stepped into the club for a late beer.

"It's five minutes to eleven o'clock," he said. "I know I said to meet at 11:00 sharp, but something's not right. One or two of my boys should be here by now."

He explained that he had left a voice mail message with each of his players, informing them to meet at my VW Passat at the outer most edge of the lot. From there, the men would move to the privacy and warmth of a locker room inside the adjoining hockey arena.

Less than minute later, a car turned through the gates, stopped briefly near the building entrance then turned slowly toward us. Through the glare of the headlights it was impossible to see who was sitting behind the wheel or even make out the model of the vehicle. It pulled to a stop about fifteen feet directly in front of us, with headlights blazing into our eyes.

"Is that one of your players?" I asked. "What kind of a joker is this guy? Seven hundred empty parking spaces and the jerk pulls right up front to blind us..."

"Quiet, Jack," my father demanded. "That's not one of my men. It could turn out to be anyone stepping out of that car."

Sitting exposed in that abandoned parking lot, my body reacted to our immediate danger. My heart pounded with fear as I felt for the first time what it meant to live in my father's shoes. In every town, at every curling club, in every abandoned parking lot, *it could turn out to be anyone stepping out of that car.*

The car door opened and out slid a short, round man pulling the brim of a large hat low over his face. He walked to the front of the car and stood directly in front of his headlights, causing his features to blacken and diffuse into the aurora. He pulled something from his coat pocket and pointed it at us. It was impossible to determine exactly what it was, but there could be only one possible assumption: a gun.

"Turn off your car engine," he yelled. "Step out of the car, DuMot. Come out of the car slowly with your hands where I can see them. I've waited years for this, so please don't try anything stupid."

I looked down at the license plates. Iowa.

"My god," I said, that must be Doug Chimny."

"Which one of you is he talking to?" LaVon asked from the general direction of the floor behind my seat.

"He's talking to me," my father whispered. "Stay down back there, honey. Chimny fancies himself a modern-day bounty hunter. But he's after Sam Ruude, not us. When you telephoned him, Jack, he must have realized that I might make the connection to Ruude that he's been trying to make all these years. He must think there's still a reward."

"But I don't think I said anything that would lead him to you," I protested quietly, through gritted teeth.

"You probably didn't. He's old-school FBI. It was enough that he had a hunch. It's the only clue he's been able to follow in years. He tracked me down somehow. Probably by talking to one of my players."

"Who's that in the car with you?" Chimny demanded. "Tell them to step out, too."

My father did not turn off the car engine as ordered, but instead rolled down his driver's side window and leaned his head partially out to make himself heard above the loud hum of the competing car engines. A cold blast of frosty wind blindsided me and I pulled my parka hood forward to protect my face.

"Ruude's dead," my father yelled. "You don't want me, Chimny. And you sure don't want to hurt my son. My whole curling team of witnesses will be here any minute."

"No, I'm afraid they won't be coming tonight after all," he laughed. "I got hold of each of them and told them not to show up until tomorrow morning. I used your own modus operandi against you, old bean. I added just enough secrecy and subterfuge to the message. Your men had no reason to doubt it wasn't you. You live by the sword and you die by the sword, eh?"

"Sam Ruude is dead," my father repeated. "You can look it up. Last weekend. He was the guy who died in that highway shootout over in Alexandria."

I whispered some additional information about the incident. Something that would give Chimny just enough to chew on.

"It happened about five in the afternoon," he relayed loudly. "It all started at a highway rest stop south of Alex. He was trying to make a run for it when the cops surrounded him along I-94. The police received an anonymous tip and were waiting for him on the overpass. They recovered his old FBI service revolver at the scene."

As always, the devil proved to be in the details. Chimny was caught off guard. He paused for a second and paced a few feet back and forth, clearly distressed that the revelation probably wasn't a bluff. I pulled my hood back in time to see a car suddenly pull out of a dark alley behind the club, creeping toward us with its lights off. Facing the opposite direction and standing between two running engines, Chimny could neither see, nor hear it approaching. As it drew to within thirty yards, it suddenly revved its engine and bolted forward with a violent roar. The driver yanked the steering wheel hard right and swung the car at ramming speed directly toward us. I tried pulling at my door latch to jump onto the pavement but my shaking hand came up with only a fistful of hopelessness. I leaned across the center console and buried my head into my father's shoulder and waited for the inevitable impact.

LaVon screamed and tucked herself low behind the driver's seat. But nothing hit. At the last fraction of a second, the driver swerved several feet further right and threaded a needle between our two cars. With a loud thud, the speeding vehicle struck Chimny squarely in the side, folding him like a jackknife. His large, limp body was thrown several feet into the air up and over the car, where he landed head-first on the pavement. I couldn't be sure whether I actually heard the sickening thud of impact or just added the soundtrack inside my head. Either way, I instantly became nauseous. Peering down at him through the window, I could tell by the contorted neck and unnaturally-twisted back, legs and arms that Doug Chimny had hit the ground dead on arrival.

The mystery car came to a screeching halt and the driver cut the engine. A tall, thin, haggard-looking man stepped out and walked slowly over to take a disgusted glance down at the rumpled heap on the pavement. After a soft kick in the ribs, he reached down to pick up Chimny's hand gun lying a few feet away.

My dad killed our car's ignition, as well. He slipped out from behind the wheel and walked several feet forward as if resigned to whatever was destined to happen next. I crawled cautiously out from my passenger seat and stepped toward Chimny's car. The thought of being so near to his gnarled, twisted bulk suddenly caused me to vomit the remains of my evening meal onto the pavement. A few seconds later, I felt LaVon take me by the hand. We walked slowly forward together to switch off the engine and headlights. We watched from the side as the men stranger stared silently at each other for a long moment across the space and time between them.

"I didn't mean for it to happen this way," the man yelled. "Like everything in my life, he left me no choice."

He pointed down angrily.

"Why did you leave me no choice you son-of-a-bitch? Why did you make me do it to you?"

Very slowly and as if in shock, my father suddenly said something I hadn't heard in years.

"Because it always comes down to needing the hammer."

It was clearly something he knew the man would understand.

"Is it really you, Tommy?"

The man turned and stared into my dad's face for a moment.

"Yes, Arv, it's me," he replied in a quivering voice.

Dad sank to his knees and fell into a heap with his face buried in his hands. The man rushed forward a few steps and stood over him. Then he also swayed once or twice, as if unsure of what to do next. He finally steadied himself before retreating ten or more feet. My father was able to raise himself as far as one knee but didn't seem able to stand. I started toward him to take his arm but LaVon held me back with a silent shake of her head.

"I've been waiting almost forty years for this minute, brother," the man finally said. "I just wanted to...and now..."

He looked again toward the dead body.

"But, it's impossible that you're still alive," my father said, still down on one knee, trembling. "You died in my arms that day."

Could it really be Tommy, I thought? I recalled what my father had told me about mutilating his dead brother's fingers and teeth to prevent any identification. I looked down at the man's bare hands. Under the pale light of the overhead street lamp, I could see that two of his fingers on his left hand had been amputated. In his right hand, he held the revolver awkwardly as if it was difficult to grip. I looked at his scarred face. It was thin evidence but, as impossible as it seemed, the man certainly could have been the real Tommy DuMot. I could see that my father believed it, as well.

"You mean you *left me for dead* in your arms that day," he said. "No, Arv. I didn't die in that mud-hole. A young woman from the local village walked by to pick through the battle scene, I suppose. She heard me rasping with my last dying breaths. She came back with some villagers and they took care of me until the U.S. pulled out and the war ended. It was the one single act of kindness anyone has ever shown me, Arv, and to think I only had to travel half a world away and get myself blown all to hell to find it."

"Afterward, I became a poster-child for the North Vietnamese. Their doctors nursed me back to life and I lived in Hanoi. I had nowhere else to turn. I couldn't stay there. I only knew I needed to find any way possible to come back here and finish what I started. There were still so many people I had to pay back. Eventually, I made it to Singapore and talked my way onto a freighter to New Orleans. It was only then that I learned that my half my hands and face weren't the only things I lost that day."

I looked into his face more closely. I could see the contours of a pronounced, unnatural twist to his lower jaw. No doubt the repair was the best effort by some untrained dentists and plastic surgeons at some medieval Hanoi hospital all those years ago.

"What do you mean finish what you started?" my father asked, shaking uncontrollably, still unable to rise. "How could you have killed those people? Four people on that list died while you weren't even in the country."

"I let you believe I was in the Marines all that time," he explained. "The whole town schemed to screw me. So I screwed them right back. I talked you and Willy into running away with me to New York, but you'll remember it was my idea to pull up short in Milwaukee, where we could all join the Navy together. But I knew they wouldn't let me in; not at seventeen years old and running from a manslaughter conviction. The recruiter told me to come back when I looked a little older. He said the military had ways to get people like me through the system. So when we said goodbye at the induction center that day, you thought I was heading into the Marines. It took more than a week to thumb rides back to Gluek, but I finally made it back to to start waiting for my opportunity. I set it all up so carefully. Letters home from a bogus military address. Some realistic details about Nam."

"Mom never discovered the truth?"

"Mom? Oh, God no!" Tommy shot back. "That's where your phone call to her helped me out, explaining I had joined the Marines. She was happy as hell that I wouldn't be going to prison. Funny isn't it? She would rather have me blown to hell than live with the shame of raising a convict in the family."

"No one in that small town ever found you out?"

"I almost starved living by my wits, but I survived for a year while waiting for the right time. Remember, it was the following spring. You were stationed god-knows-where in the world with Willy. I camped out at the far wooded corner of our farm for several weeks, about a mile from anybody who might see me. From there, I started to plan how to kill that bastard father of ours. It gave people quite a scare when he turned up dead."

"But he died in a tractor accident."

"You never really believed that, Arv. In fact, a whole lot of people never really believed that. Not until word got around that it couldn't have been me, anyway."

"So you did kill him. There is a piece of me that always knew it was you, Tommy."

"My opportunity came one night when he was out tilling a section of the field about fifty yards from my little makeshift lean-to. The wind was blowing dust across the fields. I watched and I waited until nearly dark. When he jumped to the ground to adjust something under the tractor hood, I broke from the woods. I cold cocked him with a field stone. The son of a bitch never knew what hit him. Then I laid out his body and drove over it with the tractor. I set up the scene to look like a pure accident and then drove the plow around the field to cover any tracks. I don't know why I bothered, though. The truth is Arv, I didn't really give a damn whether they caught me or not. What did I have to lose? Come morning, I discovered that the wind and rain had taken care of any evidence I may have missed; I knew I was actually going to get away with it."

"And then you hid out where...in silos, barns and chicken coops?"

"Oh, I had to leave town for a few months, while the police tried to prove I did it. I knew I had one ace in the hole, though; the local cop, Mickey Bellows. He really didn't want me found and sent back to Grand Forks. He knew that as long as the facts and circumstances of the case stayed as far away as North Dakota, nobody at the Chippewa County sheriff's department would care. Not their problem. I suspect there were a few other people in town who tried to keep the police out of it for that same reason."

"And Mom?"

"Mom? Oh, don't get ahead of the story, brother."

He stopped to light a cigarette but the wind extinguished his lighter several times before he finally threw the pack to the ground angrily.

"Screw it," he coughed out. "The damned things killed me."

He re-leveled the gun at my father and continued.

"Before Mom, there was Freddy Schade, the real prick behind the wheel. I spent about a year following Freddy and learning everything I could about him. Stalking him taught me every trick I would use over the next forty years. Did you know that he never threw another curling rock after that match in Grand Forks that Sunday afternoon? In fact, he never stepped into a curling club again in the short time that remained of his miserable life."

"You poisoned him?"

"I watched every move he made. You know yourself, Arv, how easy it can be to stay hidden in plain sight. Over time, Freddy started drinking more and more. At first, he would go to bars and cry into everyone else's beer about how much he missed Willy. When he wore out his welcome in town, he stayed home to drink. His wife finally had enough and left him. Finding him passed out drunk at his kitchen table one night was all the opportunity I needed. I revived him long enough to pour some poison into him and spiked his homemade brew with the same stuff."

"By then, the detective Hank Stenner, the same dick who looked the other way up in Grand Forks during the hit-and-run investigation against me. He was damned relieved to find Freddy dead and quickly passed it off as alcohol poisoning. Either way, nobody was going to run the tests because everyone felt the same way about the son-of-a-bitch. Nobody really gave a damn. You know it took somebody a week and a half to finally find the poor lonely bastard's body lying there stinking."

"But why at fifty-six years old?" I blurted out.

LaVon tugged hard at my arm to let me know she wanted us left out of it.

"Just a happy coincidence, nephew," he said.

Until that moment, I hadn't realized that I was looking at my only uncle for the first time. He continued to explain everything as if he had waited a lifetime to tell his story.

"As I left Schade's house that night, I noticed a birthday card lying open on the kitchen counter. On one corner of the dining room table was a half-eaten piece of birthday cake. When I realized I had killed the man on his birthday, I started thinking about our father and remembered that, by happy coincidence, it had also been on his birthday. It wasn't until I did some digging that I learned that it just happened to be their fifty-sixth birthday for both of them. That started me thinking: If I was going to carry this out to the end, I would need a distinctive calling card. I thought, 'What was it about the number fifty-six that would fit the coincidence?' In a way, I suppose we all look for justification for our actions, don't we. So, I rationalized that my own life had effectively ended in 1956, when I was officially made a member of the Peter and Medora DuMot family. Hmm. 1956. Fifty-six. That seemed as good a connection as any."

"Mom didn't deserve to die," my dad interrupted. "She didn't know anything about Freddy's plan that night."

"Oh, she knew, Arv. She would never admit to it, but she knew. And she did nothing to get me off the hook. So I waited until her fifty-sixth birthday, like the others. It turned out to be the one little piece of genius in my whole plan. I had nothing but time."

"Christ, when I stripped you of your identity under that tree root that day, I helped make you invisible."

"It all worked in my favor, Arv. By deliberately waiting until each one of you reached that ripe-enough age, the murders would be spread out across years and decades. The local flatfoots in small towns across the country wouldn't know what to make of the deaths. It also forced me to be patient for the first time in my life, so I could do things right for a change. After all, wasn't that what it was all about for the DuMot family, Arv? Doing things right? And didn't you do everything so right by everyone?"

"But you did get into the Marines."

"After I killed Mom, I headed back to Milwaukee. I was nineteen by then. The original recruiter had moved on but they're all the same and they were still looking for enough chumps to go to Nam. They all knew how to tweak the paperwork so nobody would discover I was on the run. I held up a few liquor stores around town so I could slip the sergeant a couple hundred bucks under the table. A few days later, I was on my way. Money talks. It all worked out."

"And the notes with dates on them?" I heard myself say loudly, ignoring LaVon's painful squeeze of my hand.

"You mean my idea to send a little reminder note to each victim every year on their birthdays? Well, that added an element of drama and drawn-out horror to your lives, don't you think, Arv? At least, that's what I hoped for. Everyone on that list tried cheating me into living a life of no consequence. No relevance. Hand-to-mouth. One-day-at-a-time. Those notes gave me power. I may have been invisible but I wasn't insignificant. I made them count their days, the way you left me counting my minutes, Arv. And there was nothing you could do about it. Until ..."

"Until you finally caught up with the last one of us," my father concluded.

Tommy began coughing violently and half-collapsed before checking himself suddenly and re-aiming the gun in the general direction of my dad's stomach. After several more retches and wheezes, he swung the barrel toward me and barked an order to step closer where he could keep me covered. I shook my hand free from LaVon's tight grasp and told her to slip back into our warm car.

"We'll be all right," I whispered as convincingly as I could. She retreated carefully between Chimny's crumpled body and my chunks of half-digested burger frozen to the pavement. Initially, it seemed as if Tommy intended to stop her but he either thought the better of it or simply couldn't summon the energy for another angry outburst.

"Go ahead and call the local police, sweetheart," he yelled to LaVon as she hunkered down below the back seat. "By the time they get here, this will all be over."

I walked cautiously toward my father and helped him to his feet. At closer range, I was able to see just how sickly and weak Tommy looked. Though I knew him to be less than two years younger than my father, his slumping stature added twenty years to his appearance. I wouldn't have bet he had strength enough to survive another five minutes if he didn't get to an emergency room.

I took a chance.

"You look weak," I dared. "We need to get you to a hospital."

"No," he answered, spitting something dark and thick onto the ground at his feet. "No hospital. It wouldn't do me any..."

He was suddenly interrupted by bright headlights and a car racing diagonally across the open parking lot in our direction. It couldn't possibly be the police already, I thought. They would have come with lights blazing and sirens blaring. Perhaps it would be one of my dad's teammates, after all? It was our only hope until the police arrived.

As the vehicle slammed to a sudden stop about thirty feet away, the back trunk flew open and I recognized that it was Bill Ordway's gold Chrysler Sebring. I was surprised when Tina emerged from the passenger side front seat. But then who was driving, I thought?

"Tina!" I yelled. "Get back in the car!"

"No, Jack," she said calmly, "You don't understand."

A second later, my mouth dropped open as Bill Ordway emerged from the driver's seat. He stepped toward us with palm pushed out toward Tommy, as if to tell him not to do anything too hasty.

"Hello, Tommy," he said, nearly without emotion.

"W-Willy? You're dead!"

"No, I'm very much alive, Tommy," Bill said. "Your daughter and I just did everything we could to make you think you were successful. We've been looking for you for a long time."

"***Your daughter?***" my father and I repeated in shocked unison.

"Daddy, don't," Tina yelled toward Tommy.

"Daddy?" I thought; stunned.

"This is nearly over between all of us," Tommy said. "I didn't intend to hurt anyone here tonight but I've got to finish it my way, sweetheart. I've got to have one single, god-damned thing in my life go my way."

"No, Daddy," Tina said. "Things have changed now. I can't let you kill him. Because if you kill him, Daddy, you will have to kill Bill, too. And you will have to kill Jack, too. And he may be the only one mixed up in any of this who doesn't deserve to die. And if you do that, you might as well kill me."

"You don't understand, Tina," he replied. "I came here tonight because I need to end this. I need to finally end this."

Tommy reached into his pocket and pulled out his own short handgun he had brought with him. He looked down at the guns in each hand then motioned for me to stand next to him. He aimed the other gun vaguely at Bill and ordered him to stand at my father's side. From the corner of my eye, I saw LaVon jump out of the rear seat of my car and run toward Tina.

"Make him stop, bitch!" she screamed. "He's your father, make him stop!"

Tina ignored the outburst and stepped coolly over Chimny's crumpled body as she walked forward, stopping only three or four yards from Tommy.

"I'm sorry it had to end up like this, Jack," she said, "but there was no other way."

"You owe me a hell of a lot more than just an apology, Tina," I said.

"Yes, Jack, I do. And I'll give you more. My father and I had been drifting for so many years. He was becoming sick from poor diet, cigarettes, drinking and just plain running scared. He's had a price on his head since he was seventeen, Jack. Since he was seventeen! It was getting harder and harder to find places that would give a man with no money or identity any kind of medical care. Neither of us could keep it up any longer. Then several years ago, we drifted through Thief River Falls. Like so many other towns along the way, I didn't understand what had brought us so far from civilization. A few days after we arrived, the local newspaper ran a story that an elderly indigent man

— Mike Bellows — had died of an apparent poisoning at a nearby drug treatment center. The story said the authorities were searching for the man's daughter named Jenny. I remembered seeing the names Mickey and Jenny Bellows in a notebook among my father's few belongings. Some things started to add up. So, I went through the pages and traced our travels backward over time. I did some basic records searches and discovered that each time we arrived in an unknown town, someone in the notebook would turn up dead a few days later."

"Don't tell him anymore, sweetheart," Tommy said. "You don't need to be part of this."

"But I am part of it, Daddy," Tina whispered, choking back tears. "I've been part of this ever since I started writing out those slips and mailing them for you when you became too sick to remember. If the people on your list stopped receiving them, I was afraid they might think everything was finally safe. I couldn't stop you but I needed to warn these people that they were still in danger. Maybe then they could look out for themselves."

I recalled the evening she and I stretched the slips out in a snake-like trail across my living room floor, where I noticed a change in handwriting.

"I wanted to tell the police, but I couldn't do that to you," she continued. "Not after all the betrayal you had already faced in your life. Then you disappeared. I searched everywhere but I knew it was impossible. So I worked hard to find the last few remaining people. I learned that Arv was dead. But when I found Bill, I lied and pulled some strings to get hired at ProtoCommand."

Tina turned her face toward me and added quietly, "I'm sure you discovered that it wasn't the only false front I put up along the way, Jack."

Suddenly, Tommy dropped to one knee. Tina jumped forward, squatted and held his arm to steady him while helping him to his feet again.

"Thanks, Baby," Tommy said quietly, barely able to breathe. Gently, he pushed her back a few feet.

"It's time to let everyone know what really happened, Daddy."

"Sure, honey. Why not? Go ahead and tell them everything. What do you say, boys? Should we all come clean with each other tonight? Last chance."

"Yes, we all need that tonight," Tina replied.

Once again, she turned her face toward me as if I was the only one who really needed to hear the details. Perhaps for her, I was.

"I'm sure you can fill in some of the blanks yourself, Jack. It didn't take long before I was working as Bill's secretary. It was the only way I could secretly protect him while searching for my father after he disappeared. Bill was the first man who ever showed me what it was like to have a roof over my head and a name I could be proud of. I was able to rent a small apartment, hoping that if I found my father, he could move in with me and I could stop this insanity. About a year ago, I discovered Bill's anguished cry for help scrawled across the inside of his office closet wall. When I asked him about it, I learned that he knew he was on the list and was going mad searching for a way to save himself. I finally admitted who I was and everything else he wanted to know. I wanted us to finally go to the police about the whole mess but Bill said it would be no use. He said that our only hope was to find Arvil, so we could all work together to put an end to this thing."

She turned again to look at Tommy.

"I was afraid you might be dead, Daddy. It's been so long since I've seen you and you've been so sick."

"I was always keeping an eye on you, honey," he coughed out. "It killed me to let you go but I needed to finish this."

He looked down toward Chimny.

"But I'm so sorry it turned into this tonight."

"I know," Tina said, choking on her tears. "I know you are always sorry."

Bill's voice broke in.

"Arv, if we could have found you, we would have told you that you didn't leave Tommy dead in Vietnam. We tried everything we could think of to find you or at least let you know somehow. But we had to make sure he didn't know we were searching. We didn't want anybody else dragged into it, especially not Jack. Have you been back to the church in Maynard where your grave stone is? Where your parents are buried? We donated a commemorative stained glass window. It was meant as a silent clue for you. We figured it might be the one place you would go once in a while when you felt overwhelmed."

I interrupted by reciting aloud the inscription I recalled reading on the plaque at the base of the Lazarus window, "Thy Brother Shall Rise Again." I felt foolish as I suddenly realized that it was in front of those very church windows that I first knew that I was developing real feelings for Tina. It was no wonder she had acted so light and airy that day. She must have been laughing at me as she danced in the colorful light sprinkling the sanctuary space, with Bill probably parked only a quarter of a mile down the road. Suddenly, I realized that the two of them may have visited the church often together. Old Knoblechner must certainly have known her.

Bill made a sideways glance at me as if to silently acknowledge what I was thinking.

"Yes, that's right," he confirmed. "It's installed next to the Betrayal window I donated to commemorate Freddy and my mom back in '73. Fitting, wasn't it."

Tina jumped in again.

"We hoped that if we could root you out, Arv, maybe you could put things straight with the authorities. We still had time to stop my father from killing again."

"You had your chance, Bill. Why didn't you try to set things straight after you discovered Tommy was still alive?" my father asked.

"Tina begged me to," Bill replied. "But I'm no hero, either, Arv. Remember, I was in on everything from the very beginning, too. I was only eighteen at the time but old enough to be tried as an adult. There's no statute of limitations on conspiracy to commit murder. You may have gotten off for aiding a fugitive but I knew everything about what was going down that night and lied to cover it up. I was looking at some serious trouble if I went to the police. A town like Grand Forks will never forget that kind of tragedy. The people would have been out for blood even after all this time. I was scared. I had already lost my son and I still had too much more to lose. My career. Tina. I couldn't live like you did for the rest of my life."

"When I checked the facts about your car accident, things just didn't seem right to me but I couldn't be sure. You set up everything so carefully at the courthouse and the church. Then, just before your wife ran out to California, she contacted me to say that she needed to find you. She admitted that you had recently talked to her and that your death had all been staged."

Suddenly, everything came into clear view for me.

"And that's when I got sucked in," I surmised in a matter-of-fact-tone, more to myself than anyone else. Suddenly, so much of it made sense. The sudden, inexplicable job offer. The hasty phone interview. Getting hired sight-unseen. The jimmied trunk latch on Bill's car. Tina's lie about calling Gombrich. In fact, every phone call I listened to her make had been staged for my benefit. Bill certainly would have told her about Sam Ruude. I looked at LaVon and wondered if she had also been part of the ruse. She shook her head no, as if she understood what I was thinking.

"Yes," Bill said, "Those bonehead owners upstairs at ProtoCommand didn't have a clue. I could have hired half of NASA and they wouldn't have said anything."

Tina picked up the story.

"When Bill and I decided we needed to work together, I talked to the guys on your programming team. I told them I wanted to learn more about you. I learned that you occasionally talked about your father. They said that, other than your wife, you really had no one else to talk over your problems with. I did some digging and discovered everything I needed to know about Arv's disappearance and your mother's death."

I glared at Tina.

"So you mailed the little warning slip I found under that bush that day?" I asked.

"Bill showed me the large envelope full of warning slips he had been saving over the years. He remembered that Arv said you had intercepted one or two of them when you were a kid, Jack, but you didn't know what to make of them. That slip I sent you was intended to get you thinking...even if it did take you several months to finally find it. I didn't count on a random wind blowing it out of your mailbox."

"And I fell for it like a blind roofer," I said, almost embarrassed.

"No one here is laughing at you, Jack. You have to understand that you were our last chance. So when I called you down to the office that Sunday morning to look through Bill's belongings, that's when we knew you would get the chain of events rolling. We just let your own heartfelt need and loss take over from there. I came along for the ride to make sure you stayed on track."

For some reason, it still mattered to me, so I asked her, "So like everything else, your affair with Bill's kid wasn't real, either?"

"My only mistake was dragging Jason into it," Bill interrupted. He turned on Tommy. "You didn't have to kill him, you son-of-a-bitch. Damn you. My son was innocent."

"He was just like Bellow's daughter," Tommy answered. "They were both getting close to putting it all together. I couldn't let that happen, Willy. Not until after I got to you and Arv. I didn't want to add them to the list, but they left me no choice."

He again looked down toward Chimny's crumpled body.

"Nobody ever left me a choice."

I pressed forward.

"So, when things got too dangerous with Sam Ruude in the picture..."

"He was about the only other thing I hadn't counted on," Tina quickly added. "Well, that's not entirely true, Jack. I also hadn't counted on starting to develop real feelings for you. When that happened, I knew I had to call it off."

She swung around to face LaVon.

"In case you don't know it, honey, you have someone worth going back to and something worth holding on to, even if he doesn't always know it himself. He was just missing a part of life that he didn't even know he lost, that's all. If it helps you rebuild things, you deserve to know that Jack could never get you off his mind, not that I didn't give it my best shot."

LaVon started to say something but apparently thought better of it. I added it to the long mental list of things we would have to clear up later.

Tina continued, "When you received the encrypted message from Ruude, I thought we had sucked you in too far. So I made arrangements for Bill to pick me up at the restaurant in Alexandria. With me out of the picture, we thought you would figure things would be too dangerous to be out here by yourself. We hoped you would give up and go back home and nobody would be any the wiser. But somewhere along the way, Jack, you discovered that it's always about the search."

I shrugged.

"I should have known you would never give it up, though," she added. "We never intended to put you into any kind of danger. I swear we didn't."

I glanced at my car and thought of the two hundred and seventy six thousand dollars jammed tightly under the seat.

"No blood, no foul."

My father made a three-quarter turn to look into Bill's eyes.

"You knew about Tommy for a long time, Willy. I've been in and out of the national spotlight for the past several years. Jack found me, why couldn't you?"

"Because you wanted Jack to find you," he replied bluntly, but offered no further excuses.

"Oh, it took me some time to figure out who the hell Arv Firpo is," Tommy interjected. "And that you weren't really dead. I was right on your tail a few times this past year but I always seemed to end up one or two steps behind you. I almost had you during the qualifying playdowns in Duluth back in December, but you disappeared into a snow cloud. Take it from another shadow, big brother, you're damned good at this whole secret wilderness thing we have going on. No matter. I knew you would show up here. You couldn't resist one last chance at reclaiming the championship that belonged to me all those years ago."

He was suddenly gripped with a violent cough and grabbed me by the hood of my parka, half to hold onto something for support and half to pull me toward him. From six inches away, I could smell a stench coming from deep within his lungs. A second later, I felt the cold barrel of a gun pressed against the back of my skull, then ease off as if it required too much energy to hold it there.

"No, Daddy," Tina yelled. "Bill will get you the doctors you need now. Nobody will turn you in. There's still no proof. Nobody can prove who you are. The police and FBI dropped their investigations years ago. Arv and Bill won't turn you in. They promise. It's over. Please. It's over now. You don't have to die and you don't have to kill any more people. You can live the rest of your life with me. No more betrayal. You can finally live in peace. You deserve that. We can all take care of you."

For a brief second, Tommy lowered both guns and looked into Tina's streaming eyes. Both father and daughter were shaken to the depths of a common despair.

"No, I'm not going to kill any more people here tonight, Tina," he said. "Like I said, I didn't come here for that. For me this is all over. But it isn't over for Arv and Willy. Not quite yet."

He ushered me forward several feet and thrust one of the guns into my father's left hand and then pulled me back seven or eight feet again, nearly stumbling. He pushed me to one side and held his gun in the direction of my left temple. I pulled my parka hood over my head in a feeble attempt to block my periphery view of the barrel.

"Finish this, Arv," he said gruffly. "I'm dying anyway. Finish killing me. Right here. Right now."

"Daddy, no!" Tina yelled.

"Stay back, Tina," he said. "He's either going to kill me or we're going to see how much his son means to him. Go ahead, Arv. Now is your time to finally stop running. It'll be justifiable homicide. Self defense, even. You've been killing me a little at a time every day since that Sunday afternoon in Grand Forks nearly forty years ago, so let's get it over with once and for all. Pull the trigger. Finish what you started."

My father looked at the gun and then lowered the barrel.

Tommy saw the look on his face and continued.

"You can't do it, can you?" he said. "No, I knew you couldn't. Is it because you thought you killed me once already in that mud hole? Believe me, brother, I started dying long before that battlefield in Vietnam. It started when you took my place on the ice that day but it was much more than my name on a trophy. As you know best, a name is just a name, but you stole the only thing of mine I could ever truly call my own. Those butchers were able to patch my face and body back together but they could never give me back my soul. What you took from me...there's no way to replace that kind of loss. I was inconsequential. I had no relevance. I had no past and I had no future. God, what I had to put Tina through. What you took from me cost me everything. And it cost you nothing. Sure, it's all easy to bury me from half-a-world away, isn't it? But when you have to look me in the eye before pulling the trigger, that puts a human face on it, doesn't it? Even when that face looks like a monster."

A tense look spread across my father's face.

"Did you say *Nothing*, Tommy?" He replied with a tone of indignation. "You think it cost me *nothing*? It cost me half my soul when I took your place in the arena that day. And it cost me the other half when I kept quiet about Freddy betraying you. When I watched you die in my arms that day, little brother, I was already more dead than you will ever know. Yes, I took your worthless name, damn it, but don't you dare say that it cost me nothing. I have spent my life fighting to turn Tommy DuMot into something to be proud of — something you would never have become yourself. Everything good and decent in my life has been done in your name as reconciliation for a mistake I made when I was that eighteen year old farm kid. It was me, Arv DuMot, who died that long slow death, damn you. So, you tell me, brother, which one of us is really the faceless one here?"

Tommy pushed his gun barrel up to my head.

"Dad!" I yelled. "Help me."

LaVon jumped out and ran toward Tina.

"Say something, damn you!" she yelled. "Make that freak end this before someone is killed."

Tommy ushered me forward again and yanked the gun out of my father's hand. He grabbed Bill by the coat sleeve and pulled him to the front, pushing the revolver into his left hand. We retreated once again.

"Here, Willy, you do it if he won't," he rasped. "It was Freddy Schade who put the first bullet in the gun but it was you who cocked the hammer by lying for him. All that's left now is to finally pull the trigger. You finish what Arv can't, Willy. God, let me finally go in peace."

I pulled the hood off my head once again and got a good look at his face. His eyes were drifting in and out of focus. He was fading fast. Where were the damned police, I thought.

My father turned toward Bill.

"Willy," he said softly, "put the gun down. Nobody is going to pull any triggers here tonight."

Bill immediately tossed the gun down at Tommy's feet.

My father slowly motioned with his fingertips toward me.

"Jack, walk away slowly," he said. "Tommy is not going to hurt you."

I hesitated to steady my quivering legs and slowly took a step forward. Tommy tried raising the gun a few inches higher in my direction but let it drop impotently to his side. I inched several feet further forward until I felt safe enough to make a sudden lunge toward LaVon. I took her trembling hand in my own and pulled her quickly to safety behind our car. I called to Tina but she wouldn't budge. Clearly, we had already become an afterthought. Ducking low, I whispered to LaVon to call the police again. She flipped open her cell phone but then quickly pointed to flashing squad car lights rushing in our direction.

"Look," she said. "I don't need to."

Suddenly, Tommy began buckling but Tina rushed forward to catch his arm. Together, they slid slowly to the ground, his frail body coming to rest across her lap.

"Oh, Daddy," she cried, taking the pistol from his hand and slipping it into her coat pocket. My father and Bill were soon kneeling at their sides.

Tommy's eyes blurred over as he tried to focus on the faces surrounding him.

"I've put everyone through so much for so long. Especially you, Tina. I'm so sorry. I never had anything that was my own. I stole your life from you all because I could never let go of what had been stolen from me."

"No," Tina cried, "You have always been everything in my life."

"We're the ones who should be asking forgiveness from you, Tommy," my dad said.

"We betrayed you, Tommy," Bill chimed in softly. "Nobody should have done what we allowed to happen. I should have come clean about Freddy right away. None of this had to happen."

"It's all right now, Bill. Right here, right now, it's the last end and I have the hammer. Funny, isn't it? Ending up the way we all began in the first place, in the cold parking lot of an old curling club. Remember, Willy? Arv and I met you for the first time when we were young kids, waiting for a ride home from the old club in Montevideo. We were all huddled together after they locked up, just like this. Freddy never did pull himself away from the local bar to give us a ride home that night. Remember, Arv, mom finally got worried and had to drive all the way from..."

The sound of a loud siren wailing into the park entrance overpowered our thoughts.

"The police are here now, Tommy" Bill said. "We're going to get you help."

Tommy shook his head.

"No, Willy. No help."

He looked up toward Tina's face.

"I'm exactly where I am supposed to be and I'm on time. Take care of my girl for me, will you boys?"

His eyes closed but we could still see his chest rising in shallow bursts.

"Sure, little brother," my father said. "You and Tina will always be part of each other. And now she will always be part of us. Count on it."

With his final breaths, Tommy told Tina to reach into his coat pocket to take his car keys.

"Drive away, honey. Get out of here before the police come. Stay one step ahead of them like I taught you; like we always have."

She found the keys but remained still, holding tightly to her dying father. His body gave one final convulsive heave and slumped limply in her arms. As she held his head to her breasts, she could find no words. Only the darkness and depth of her own lonely abyss showed in her glistening eyes.

LaVon and I stepped out from behind the car and drew close to the group. Just as a police car pulled to a stop with one final whoop of a siren burst. As one officer jumped out and headed toward Chimny's frozen body, the other walked hesitantly toward us.

"Take it easy," I said, holding up my hand to assure them that everything was under control. "Nobody is in any danger."

Within a few seconds, a second squad car wailed to a stop alongside the first, followed immediately by a screaming ambulance. Twenty minutes later, the medical examiner was on the scene and the area was roped off from on-lookers gathering from the nearby neighborhood. While the police talked to Bill and my father, two burley emergency medical technicians loaded the two dead bodies onto gurneys and slid them into the rear of the ambulance. Tina jumped in immediately, insisting that she ride with her father wherever they were taking him. After conferring for a moment, the police and EMTs nodded their approval.

I thought of LaVon's comment at the restaurant an hour earlier, "Tina has a story, too." This beautiful, articulate and sensitive young woman had spent nearly her entire life living by her wits and surviving on the run. No matter where Tommy's troubled wanderings led them, getting things right with his daughter had given both of their lives some tangible meaning. I envied her for it. She had once told me that the search to find my father was part of some universally true story told at some innate level that we all share. But as the ambulance driver pushed the doors closed behind her, I couldn't help but wonder about Tina Bucholz's own true story of a life lived in the shadows.

LaVon and I slipped quietly back into our car to wait things out. We would have a long night ahead of us at the police station, giving our separate reports and sorting out the details of the evening.

As we pulled out of the parking lot behind a squad car leading us with lights flashing, LaVon gave me a hard, playful punch on my upper arm.

"I've told you before — You are one hell of a great date, Jack DuMot."

Part VIII

Restoration

Saturday, many summers later

I came down stairs at eight o'clock on Saturday morning and was surprised to find LaVon already hunched over the newspaper enjoying her morning Coca Cola. When she moved back into the house following our return from Hibbing that cold night in 2008, I insisted she refrain from smoking indoors. The first few months, she moved her morning smoke out onto the front porch but eventually decided to quit altogether. For my part, I agreed to switch to decaffeinated coffee.

"How many years since my last cigarette?" she asked proudly, holding up her Coke as if to offer a toast.

"Five, at least," I replied, as I clinked my coffee cup to her glass, spilling a mixture of our drinks onto the table. She wiped up the small puddle with the sleeve of her terry cloth robe and squeezed my hand.

Chaos theorist Margaret Wheatley once said, "When we seek for connection, we restore the world to wholeness. Our separate lives become meaningful when we discover how necessary we are to each other." I looked at LaVon as she spread the comics section of the St. Paul Pioneer Press across our large oak dining room table. So much had happened in our lives, yet so little had actually changed.

Upon arriving at the Hibbing police station just after 12:30 a.m. that night, my father explained that he was Skip of a rink scheduled to play in the national championship playdowns and showed the match schedule as proof. As part of his official report to detectives, he and Bill Ordway explained what relationship they had with the dead men at the scene. Police followed up on every avenue of the story, which eventually led them to the FBI and back to the DUI accident in Grand Forks, including the outstanding 1969 warrant for Tommy's arrest as a fugitive. After nearly eighteen hours of investigation and internal squabbles about jurisdiction, we were finally ushered out to the front desk, where a short, graying plain-clothes officer handcuffed my dad and Bill, explaining that he would escort them back to Grand Forks. Only then did he flash his official badge toward me and identified himself as Paul Gombrich.

"I would invite you two kids to ride along in the squad car but I don't have room. But please, I hope you can follow in your own vehicle."

I looked at LaVon for approval and she nodded with a smile.

"Sure, thanks," I said, "I think we can do that."

We followed the police car out of town about six miles west, until Gombrich suddenly flipped on his directional signals and pulled into the parking lot of an isolated abandoned roadside motel. He hopped out and ordered the two men to step out of the back seat. I futilely ordered LaVon to stay in our car as I jumped out to ask for an explanation for the unexpected stop. Gombrich pulled the handcuff keys from his belt and uncuffed my father first, then Bill.

"You two have been through enough," he said. "And the last thing the good people of Grand Forks need is to pick at that old scab."

"I really don't want to run anymore," my father said. "I want this to be over."

"It is over," Gombrich said. "The FBI closed down their investigation years ago. Tommy DuMot, Freddy Schade and everyone else involved in this mess are all dead. Before driving over here, I purged any records that were still on our local files. Neither of you face charges for anything here in Hibbing and nobody in North Dakota knows you two even exist. It's your call, Arv, whether you want to bring yourself back to life and face the possible legal trouble that may come along with it. Frankly, I wouldn't. I envy the hell out of you."

"You won't be in any trouble for letting this drop?" Bill asked.

"When Tommy disappeared from your parents' custody back then, I said good for him. I never did believe he was guilty. I kept on top of the case, even though I was certain that the only person guilty that night was Schade. But there was no way to prove it against the circumstantial evidence and all the versions of the story we had on file. When the Hibbing cops called us to straighten things out last night, it was my chance to finally end this case. I figured I saved the North Dakota tax payers a few hundred thousand dollars. Now, we can all let it all go and I can retire to Fort Myers in peace. But I've got to tell you two, back in the '80s and '90s when you had the FBI breathing down everyone's necks, you almost did yourself in."

He may have saved North Dakota taxpayers a lot of money, I thought, but how much personal misery could have been prevented if he had just done his job in the first place all those years ago?

The two old friends rode in the back seat of our Passat back to the Twin Cities, laughing and catching up on the years since they had last seen each other. I had my mind on Tina and wondered whether LaVon and I would try to save any semblance of marriage that remained between us. Periodically, though, Dad would tap my shoulder and call me into a story about raising hell on some local farm or some long-forgotten curling matches played at the old Montevideo club. After a four-hour drive back to the Twin Cities, we dropped off Bill at his apartment and returned to our house in South Minneapolis.

As we stepped through our rear kitchen door, however, I knew that something wasn't right. How was it possible that everything had stayed the same, yet I felt as if nothing fit. It was like my feet were too big for my shoes, my pants too tight to buckle or my sweatshirt too small to slip over my head. I no longer felt part of the small space that had once consumed me. I thought of all the lost evenings and weekends I had once spread out across our tiny dinette table. Its three-by-five foot avocado green surface no longer seemed capable of holding what my new expanded world was destined to become.

I stood a moment longer and looked around the room before setting my travel pack on the kitchen counter. Nothing had changed. Not really. A few boxes of my mother's old belongings remained scattered about the room. Dirty dishes remained in the sink. The tattered blanket was still folded on the arm of the sofa, just as neatly as Tina had left it. Had it really been just eight short days since she and I walked out of the house together that morning? I looked at the answering machine. We weren't even gone long enough for someone to call and leave a message. It was impossible to see any physical evidence of the change I felt inside me, yet I felt the uncomfortable urge to brush away the remains of my old life like cobwebs.

LaVon and my father stepped through the rear kitchen door a few minutes behind me.

"If it's okay with you, Jack," she said, "I've asked your dad to stay with us for awhile. I think it might be exactly what we need."

"Well, anyway," he chirped in, "I'd like to at least stay long enough to see how the curling championships finish up. Then I need to leave to take care of business."

He gazed around the living room to take in the general state of neglect and disrepair.

"And you two could probably use an extra pair of hands around here for a short while."

I reached to open our kitchen junk drawer and tossed him the old local union #539 pipe cutter tool I had discovered in the basement.

"Maybe you can use this again," I said with a laugh. "Funny, isn't it? When I tossed it into that drawer six weeks ago I was crying uncontrollably.

During the following few days, we followed the curling championships closely, with my father placing several phone calls every day to old friends in Hibbing or using my car to drive over to the St. Paul Curling Club in the evening. He once commented that it was the first time in years he was able to enjoy a beer while looking into the faces of his old friends. In the end, Skip Craig Brown of Madison led a rink of players from various clubs in Wisconsin and Minnesota to win the championship.

"He put together a hell of a team," Dad said. "I've played with all of those guys over the past few years."

From memory, he listed off the names as if reading it off a blackboard.

"Skip *Craig Brown*. *Rich Ruohonen* from right near here in Brooklyn Park. He curls out of St. Paul. *John Dunlop* out of Milwaukee. Back in '05, that guy made one of the greatest curling shots I've ever seen. *Pete Annis* from Owatonna. I was hoping to introduce him to you last week when we swung down that way for some ice time, Jack. But we missed him."

"Any chance your team could have beaten them?" LaVon asked, warming to the discussion.

My father gave a hearty laugh. "No way. Not with Ruohonen, Dunlop and Annis throwing in front of Brownie. Not a snowball's chance in hell. With everything I had on my mind the past year, we were lucky to make it through the regionals."

He unfolded the list of match-draws from his shirt pocket and mumbled over it quietly for a moment.

"Frankly, I don't think we would have beaten any of these rinks," he finally said. "Great field this year. My players should be happy I gave them an excuse to keep the egg off our faces."

Dad remained living with us for a brief while, helping me clear out my mother's belongings and once again turning the first floor storage room into a spare bedroom. During that short few weeks, the friendship that developed between him and LaVon proved to be a wonderful distraction for what we knew lay ahead in our marriage. Predictably, though, he came home from dinner with Bill Ordway one evening and announced that he would be leaving the next day. Bill had agreed to accompany him out to Mandan where he would make arrangements with the land owner to vacate his rented lot. I made him assure me he would stay in touch.

"If not with you, Jack," he joked, "then with LaVon."

Although he said I wouldn't be able to reach him for a while. I made sure he had our phone number. I noticed how he haphazardly stuffed it into his wallet; already filled with dozens of other loose slips of phone numbers, names and addresses.

"Here Dad," I said, pulling the *Arv — February 23 — Ø* warning slip from my wallet. "Carry this in your wallet with you as a final souvenir of everything you've been through."

He walked over to our gas stove, turned the knob and touched the slip to the flame.

At first light the following morning, Bill pulled his Sebring in front of our house and honked until we all appeared on the porch together to say our goodbyes.

"It's been great being with you again, Dad," I said.

"I'll always be around for you, Jack."

"You mean out there. Somewhere?" I made a broad sweeping motion with my left arm.

He mimicked the motion.

"Yeah, out there. Somewhere," he said and then tapped my chest with his index finger, "And in here somewhere, I hope."

But it will always be up to me to find him, I thought silently to myself.

As we expected, the empty house left us searching for ways to salvage whatever we could of our relationship. At times during that first year, the silence became almost deafening. LaVon quit her teaching job at the middle school and took a job teaching English three evenings each week at local tutoring center. I no longer felt in a great hurry to find a job but I knew I needed to press forward. My unemployment had come to an end and I was facing the added pressure of explaining where my visible means of support was coming from. Initially, I had elected not to say anything about Ruude's sack full of money, which I secretly moved into the broken dryer in our basement before selling the Passat. I just didn't trust ourselves enough.

As I figured, it was less than a year before LaVon admitted that Tony Perkovich had come calling again. He wanted to get together some evening with her to, "*You know, just catch up*." She finally agreed but invited me along for the evening. After ten minutes, he slammed his napkin into his plate of spaghetti and stormed out of the restaurant. To the best of my knowledge, it was the last time LaVon ever heard from him. But then again, I don't go down into our basement very often.

As for Tina, I haven't seen her since they pushed closed the ambulance doors and drove away with Tommy's body. While restricted to the police station, I asked several people about her whereabouts. Over the course of the following day, I started getting trickles of sketchy information. Apparently, neither she nor Tommy's body ever made it to the city morgue. A few minutes after the ambulance pulled away from the parking lot, she pulled the pistol from her pocket and ordered the driver to backtrack toward the curling club. She then forced the driver at gun point to call into the station to report engine trouble and explain they would be late arriving with the bodies.

While parked in a dark alley behind a nearby building, she held the gun on the EMTs until the police cleared the scene two hours later. She then ordered the drivers to cut the lights and move the ambulance alongside Tommy's car. Pulling the keys from her pocket, she unlocked the doors and ordered the two men to quickly transfer her father's body to the rear seat. Less than a minute later, one of the terrified drivers called in to report that Tina Bucholz was last seen driving an old Toyota Camry with Indiana license plates, heading toward State Highway 37, south of town. The story was in the news for several days following the incident, but I knew the police had no idea about the caliber of fugitive they would be hunting.

I tried to stay in touch with Bill Ordway, phoning periodically to see whether he had heard from either my father or Tina. The answer was always a polite no, followed by a pleasant conversation about general goings-on in each other's lives. The day inevitably came, though, when my call switched over to an automated message informing me that the line had been disconnected. My heart sank, as I realized that I had possibly lost my final connection.

As time moved along, communication began to improve slowly between LaVon and me. After several smooth interviews, I found a job as a steady freelance programmer for a banking technology firm based in Caspar, Wyoming. I was wary, at first, until they promised to keep the project durations short and to write the programming objectives in stone. Most weeks, I manage to finish the code requirements by Thursday and take a long weekend to get the house ready to sell. Our proudest accomplishment has been turning our large, single upstairs bedroom space into a proper master bedroom suite, complete with a built-in closet and full bathroom. LaVon joked that if we could make it through six months of home restoration, there was hope for reconstructing our marriage, too. Gradually, the spark that I had once found so attractive about her began leaping into a full flame again. I could only hope that she had rediscovered the same energy source in me.

To stay on a steady course, we have been attending a weekly marriage therapy group for the past several years. The session is comprised of couples our own age, most of whom face many of our same problems. Now years into it, we know we are probably long-past getting any benefits from the counseling, but we continue to attend. The search for who we want to be as a married couple has become the fabric of who we are as individuals. Through everything, I have discovered what my father must have learned in his own hard way:

Nobody can ever really occupy space alone. No matter how small or large the wilderness we try to carve out for ourselves, it is our relationship with others that defines us and gives us relevance.

Trust is building up between us, as well. For the first year, I continued to sleep upstairs while LaVon slept in the guest bedroom on the first floor. After sharing a glass or two of wine late one evening, however, she found herself absent-mindedly following me up the stairs. Without further discussion, she gradually moved all of her clothes and personal belongings up to the master suite again. I fully realized that we were stealthily moving back into each other's lives the same way we had once slipped out.

Nearly three years passed before I was finally able to tell her about the money. I was afraid that if I waited any longer, she would resent me for hiding the secret. But when I explained everything over an argument about bills one night, she greeted the news with a smile that soon broke into a hearty laugh. She admitted that she had known about the stash since that night in Hibbing when she hid trembling in the back seat of our car. While nervously trying to call for help, she dropped her cell phone onto the floor. As she reached for it in the blackness under the seat, her fingers hooked onto a strap and she yanked the travel bag toward her. She pulled out one stack of money, then another and another. At that particular moment, with guns pointing in all directions just a few yards outside the car, she didn't take the time to count it. She re-hid the money and decided to say nothing more about it until I was ready to explain.

"No wonder it took so long for the police to arrive," I joked.

"I figured it was only about twenty thousand dollars," she said. "If I had known it was ten times that amount, I would have said something right away."

"Which is why I never said anything until now," I replied, ending the discussion abruptly.

All these years later, not everything is always smooth between us. There are times when we find ourselves reverting to form and tossing biting darts across the room toward each other without thinking of what we are saying or why. *"Manchmal schneit es tiefer als man denkt,"* we warn each other in her beloved German. "Sometimes it cuts deeper than we think."

We have discussed trying to start a family and it's fair to say that we aren't trying *not* to have one. She has decided to see a specialist if she doesn't become pregnant within the next eighteen months. I figure that bringing a baby into our world is probably the best possible use of Sam Ruude's money, considering that my father had to kill a man to come by it in the first place.

Several months ago, I received a message notification on my iPhone screen and scrolled through dozens of apps to open my e-mail. It was a message from Tina.

Jack;

I am fine and I hope things are going well for you and LaVon. I think of you often.

I regret the way things hit so suddenly that night so long ago. What I didn't get a chance to explain is that Tommy was not my biological father, but he was the only parent I have ever known. Despite the awful things he did, he was a wonderful 'Daddy' to me and I loved him and miss him very much.

He always told me that I was adopted but my mother died when I was too young to remember. Of course, the more I learned as I grew older, the more I wondered about the truth. In his dying words that night, he said he never had anything that was truly his own. So where did that leave me, I wondered.

When sorting through the few possessions in his car, I discovered an old scrapbook hidden in the trunk. On a page labeled March, 1985, he had taped a news article from the Winnepeg Free Press, about the unsolved murder of a Quebec man named Lawrence Thibault. The article said the police had been unable to locate the victim's wife, Susanne, after she disappeared with her young daughter during a national curling tournament. I can only assume the man and woman in the story were my parents. The young child, of course, was me. Funny, isn't it? You and I may still have that one thing in common — curling.

If my mother is still alive somewhere, I need to search for her. Everyone involved in Tommy DuMot's life deserves to finally put an end to the pain he caused. And now, Jack, that includes me.

I don't know what I will discover in Canada or anywhere else my search may lead. But like you, I will certainly find what is left of myself.

Best regards and with much fondness, Tina

I recalled Tina's short stature, dark hair and flashing, deep brown eyes. French-Canadian, I thought. It made sense. That might explain some of the French she remembered from when she was a very young girl, too. I checked the return e-mail address but realized immediately that she had used a public computer somewhere. I tried to reply but immediately received a non-deliverable message.

Her e-mail stabbed at a wound in my heart, which I thought had long-since scarred over. It started me thinking about some loose ends that I had never bothered to tie up. I pulled an old scrap of paper from my wallet, scrolled to open my smartphone Navigator app and punched in an address near Gluek, Minnesota. I stared at the screen for a minute and smiled when I thought of how far technology had come since dash-mounted GPS units and WiFi hotspots along the highway.

I called upstairs and asked LaVon if she would be willing to take a long afternoon drive with me. In short order, she bounded down the stairs and said she would love to take a break from repainting the upstairs rooms. We quickly packed some snacks and sodas into the back seat of our Toyota Tercel and we were on the road. Along the way, I filled her in on some details which I had never shared with her. She knew the large framework of the story, of course, but there were some leftover feelings I could never bring myself to explain.

Two hours later, we pulled off Highway 7 at Maynard and drove slowly through town. We pulled the car to a stop on the new asphalt parking lot of Holy Savior Lutheran Church. How very different the churchyard looked when it was surrounded by the unmatchable beauty of a Minnesota summer. I explained that the church building had also received a new coat of paint since I had been there last in early '08. I took her by the hand and we picked our way down through the gravestones, just as I had done during my first visit. At the bottom of the hill, I showed her my grandparents' grave markers and pointed to what I had first believed to be my father's headstone. It took me a moment to realize that the surface of the stone was no longer blank. A metal plate had been screwed into place: **Tommy DuMot, 1954 – February 14, 2008. Rest in peace, Daddy.**

"I guess I should have realized that she would have him buried here," I said.

LaVon bent over and picked up a dried bouquet that had been placed at the foot of the marker. I didn't say it out loud, but it felt nice to know that Tina had been standing on that very spot, perhaps just months before.

We retreated up the hill to the church building, where I tested the side door to the sanctuary and found it locked. A middle-aged man heard the rattle and opened the door to let us in. I inquired about old Knoblechner.

"Old Ed passed away back in 2012," the man said. "I'm John Gleason. Council of Elders. It's my turn to spruce up the place this weekend. We can't afford a regular caretaker these days. Never could, really, but nobody wanted to let go of Ed."

I looked around the sanctuary and recalled Tina's dance of a thousand colored lights. I showed LaVon the two stained glass windows that Bill had referred to that night in Hibbing. Suddenly, I realized something felt and looked different about the room. It was the colorful light filling the corner, streaming through the Lazarus window. Sunlight was highlighting every shard of glass and dancing over the pews at the once-dark rear of the church. The face of Lazarus no longer appeared ugly and dead. I poked my head out of the door and looked along the outside of the building. Indeed, the tall, dark pine which had once blocked the corner of the building had been removed, leaving only a rough stump.

"You pulled that tree down," I said as I re-entered the sanctuary, pointing to the corner through the window.

"Nope," Gleason responded. "Several years back, two old jackasses were arrested and charged with criminal trespass after they were caught one evening hacking it down with an axe. Old Knoblechner tried to stop them but by the time the police arrived, the damage was already done. If you ask me, the place looks a lot brighter now. Now we refer to it as our Resurrection window, at least until someone donates a real Resurrection window for the other side of the room. We're planning a restoration project for next spring. It would be a perfect time."

I looked at LaVon.

"I can't think of a better use of some of that money," she said.

I smiled at the thought of my father and Bill being arrested for the same kind of prank that Tommy might have pulled forty years earlier, perhaps even on these same church grounds. I stared at the window for several minutes and tried to imagine a life lived on the run; always seeking the next valley of shadows and without a name to call your own. I noticed that the brass plate on the window sill had been removed and a new one attached in roughly the same place, with only one line of inscription: **He is risen. He is risen indeed.**

"It's too bad that a man has to die before anybody acknowledges that he ever lived," I said.

We left Maynard and headed a few miles north into Gluek. I explained that I had missed the opportunity to see the old DuMot family farm on two previous occasions and I wasn't going to blow it off again. I also joked that it was even possible that I could be the owner, pending a legal fight at the county courthouse, of course.

I rebooted my Navigator app and the woman's reassuring voice informed us, "**Recalculating based on traffic.**"

"What traffic?" LaVon snorted.

A few seconds later, we were directed down dusty roads through head-high fields of corn. A dozen left and right turns later and it was obvious the dear GPS lady meant well, but had no idea where we were. I closed down the application and pulled my old dog-eared atlas out of the glove compartment. After another quarter hour of covering the same ground several times, I pulled over out of frustration. LaVon suddenly pointed to a mailbox lying on the ground next to a broken fence post. Only the letters P. Du remained barely visible beneath a veneer of rust. I got out of the car to retrieve it but was quickly forced to retreat from a stream of angry hornets pouring out of a bolt hole.

"I guess it won't look very good in our garden, after all," I joked as I dove back into the car and quickly rolled up the window.

Ahead a few yards, I discovered a faint pair of narrow tire tracks leading toward a small spread of buildings about one hundred yards further off the road. I followed them a few yards down a small incline before stopping and turning off the car engine.

"Aren't you going to drive all the way down to the house?" Lavon asked.

"I've come far enough."

The driveway ahead cut through a narrow strip of hayfield which seemed to have been seeded with no regard for vehicle traffic. Then I recalled that a farm neighbor named Highwheeler had usurped some of the land for grazing and crops after he heard my father was reported dead in '02. But it didn't appear as if the field had been used at all during the past several growing seasons.

"Maybe after you talked to him back then," LaVon said, "it scared him off."

"Yeah, maybe," I answered, "but I told him I didn't care. More than likely, the old guy died or got out of farming."

We sat for a moment looking at the tidy layout of structures that served as the focal point amid green, gently-rolling hills in all directions. We both noticed that the buildings seemed remarkably kept up, although the fields had gone to weed. What would once have been fenced pastureland for cows had grown into a thick mass of underbrush. Clearly, the land hadn't been farmed in decades.

The traditional, two-story shingled farmhouse was nestled among tall mature pine trees, making it difficult to see all sides. The house had a very small foot print of no more than twenty-five feet square. From where we were sitting, it appeared to have only one entrance at the front. A single-car garage that probably doubled as a work shed was attached to one side.

The narrow drive path ran through the yard and parallel to the front of the house, just a few yards away from what may have once been front porch steps.

"If this is supposed to be the front yard," I said, "it hasn't been mowed in years."

The tracks continued past the house a few yards, where a short spur jutted off to the right and served as an entry into a large shed that included an oversized sliding garage door on one half. The roof of the building slanted downward at a shallow angle, to just three feet above the ground running along the right-hand side.

"I've got to believe the three boys spent some time up there on warm summer days," I commented.

"The left side of the building probably served as a granary," LaVon said. "It has a higher roof."

Immediately adjacent, stood a dilapidated corn crib with slatted boards for airflow. It appeared that a small tree had pushed its way through the floorboards and was trying to burst through one side. Clearly, it hadn't been maintained since my grandfather's death.

The main path twisted back around on itself to form a tight loop. Anybody using it as a driveway could circle the car or tractor around and point the nose back toward the direction of the main road.

"That old water tank in the middle of the driveway loop means there might have been a windmill standing there once," LaVon said. "Our family farm had a driveway loop exactly like that, with a windmill and water tank in the center island. It may also have been where a large fuel tank once stood."

Down the hill another twenty yards from the corn crib sat an old, low red building with a flat roof. I pointed out that it seemed too small to be of much use on a farm. In addition, the structure had only one narrow door and two or three small windows, all trimmed in white.

"A garden shed?" I asked.

"Chicken coop," LaVon replied, matter-of-factly. "Over the summer, your grandmother would have kept a few dozen hens and a rooster."

The large red barn at the bottom of the hill running away from the house was far and away the most imposing edifice in the entire complex. I could imagine my grandmother standing at the kitchen sink watching for Pete and her two boys to return to the house for breakfast after early morning chores. On the left side of the barn, in clear view from our car, there stood a topless cinderblock silo, including the traditional checkered pattern of faded white bricks circling the top.

Altogether, the entire diameter of useable buildings in the barnyard circle encompassed only about fifty yards. That made sense, I reasoned. On an eighty-acre dairy farm, every square yard of pasture or soil for feeder crops would have been precious. From the front door of the farmhouse, my father and Tommy would have walked no more than forty yards across the driveway, past the windmill and down a gentle slope to the front entrance of the milk house attached to the front of the barn. Handy layout, I thought, until I remembered that it would have been every morning at five a.m. — even through the coldest winter months — to start their day.

An old dirt tractor road led away from the barnyard and out into the pasture and fields beyond the buildings, ending at a thicket of woods in the far distance. It must certainly have been the same woods Tommy had camped in for three weeks as he looked for an opportunity to kill his father.

We sat for a long while taking in the view. I suddenly realized that it couldn't have been easy for LaVon to recall her own unhappy childhood memories stretching out before us.

"Do you think your father came here after he left our house back in March of '08, after Hibbing?" she finally asked.

"Well, somebody painted those doors and fixed up the barn," I said. "And look, there's a small pile of construction scraps and lumber behind those pines. It looks as if the old place is being restored."

Just then, we noticed a low cloud of dust kicking up behind a small all-terrain vehicle rolling across a hilltop more than a quarter of a mile in the distance. We could clearly see the silhouettes of two riders sitting tandem atop the machine.

"That's them," I said. "He probably left his old Airstream trailer back in that North Dakota canyon but kept the ATV."

I interrupted myself.

"Well, I'll be damned..."

"Yeah, I have no doubt you will be damned," LaVon joked, "but exactly what will you be damned about this time?"

"Oh, twenty-five years ago, my father wrote a letter to Bill on the back of an old Navy picture. In it, he said, 'We'll weather this storm and then we'll be together forever.' And here they are together."

LaVon completed my thought, "Forever."

"We should go home," I said.

"Go home? Don't you want to drive down and see him?"

"No," I answered. "He knows where I am. Besides, part of me always suspected I would find him here. He paid those taxes all those years to keep it in the family. This is their little kingdom now. Let's leave them alone to it. They seem to want it that way."

"After everything you went through and after all these years, don't you think you need him in your life?" she asked. "If you don't try to build a relationship with him, you know, he won't build one with you, either."

"Yeah, I know, LaVon, but even if I try to keep the relationship going strong, he will just leave me again, anyway. And that's the part I don't understand about him. He drifts through the world taking everything on his terms. I guess I'm just not hard-wired to give him a free pass on that."

What was it I once heard so many years ago? We are each where we are supposed to be, and we're on time. And it would have to be that way between my father and me. I would have to place my own value on whatever relationship developed; if, in fact, any ever did. I thought about the randomness and unforeseen consequences that had affected so many peoples' lives for so many years. It had all led me to that particular moment sitting next to my wife, looking down onto that old farm on that summer day. I had come to realize that there is no way to control or calculate any part of it. Perhaps my father's analogies were right: Life, in fact, may be very much like curling. We often throw our shots with the wrong turn of the handle; perhaps with too much rotation or too little weight. But every shot makes a difference and accounts for something, even if it is only within our own little twelve-foot circles.

I watched the ATV dash around the hillside for another minute before starting the car engine and backing onto the main road. I reached across the console and took LaVon by the hand.

"If I ever need him, I'll know where to look. I'm sure we'll drift in and out of each others' lives. Searching for him restored and enriched my life in ways I never thought possible. What happens now that I've found him, we'll just have to wait and see."

The End

Made in the USA
Columbia, SC
20 January 2021